SCENT

SCENT

A DARK SECRET HIDDEN
IN PETALS OF PINK

C. L. KELLY

THORNDIKE PRESS

An imprint of Thomson Gale, a part of The Thomson Corporation

Detroit • New York • San Francisco • New Haven, Conn. • Waterville, Maine • London

THOMSON

™

GALE

LIBRARY OF CONGRESS CATALOGING-IN-PUBLICATION DATA

Kelly, Clint.
  Scent : a dark secret hidden in petals of pink / by C.L. Kelly.
    p. cm. — (Sensations series ; #1) (Thorndike Press large print Christian fiction)
  ISBN-13: 978-0-7862-9504-3 (alk. paper)
  ISBN-10: 0-7862-9504-X (alk. paper)
  1. Perfumes — Fiction. 2. Perfumes industry — Fiction. 3. Large type books. I. Title. II. Series.
PS3561.E3929S28 2007
813'.54—dc22
                           2007002216

Published in 2007 by arrangement with The Zondervan Corporation LLC.

Printed in the United States of America on permanent paper
10 9 8 7 6 5 4 3 2 1

To Cheryll, my sensation.
We dreamed us a good one.

ACKNOWLEDGMENTS

Thanks to the Creator for the human senses by which we can know him.

Thanks to Karen Ball for telling, cherishing, and recognizing good stories.

Thanks to Diane Noble for making good stories shine.

Thanks to Steve Laube for not letting good stories go.

Thanks to all who march for a heavenly cause along the road called Adventure.

CHAPTER 1

For the twelfth time that day, Nick Dixon cursed his stupidity. Cursing was for the uneducated, but if conditions warranted, he could blister the circumstances in Turkish, Polish, or Russian. Give him three months, and he'd be able to question a moron's ancestry in Mandarin.

He pushed through the dense rain forest, shirt open, body awash in perspiration from the withering heat. The thick damp clogged his lungs and made breathing difficult. The air stank of rotting vegetation. The ground scuttled with creeping things. Nick struggled to find a vantage point, a clear lookout from which he could find his bearings.

He prayed to God he didn't come nose-to-nose with a Komodo dragon.

Overhead a disgruntled Malaysian giant squirrel, dressed in creamy brown, leapt the impossible gap between two trees and fell four stories before thudding onto a branch that held. An orchestra of oddly harmonious twitters, chirps, whistles, and screeches erupted from the forest canopy.

Nick felt the patter of lightly falling objects on his battered Aussie hat. Insects. Dropping from the leafy heights in a rain of life as ancient as earth itself. More than half the known life forms on the planet crept and crawled, bloomed and died, within the humid boundaries of the world's rain forests.

And thirty million of them were insect species. Too many of these insects, for Nick's liking, were predators. Fist-sized spiders. Beetles and bugs and grotesque horned things. Poisonous, bloodsucking . . .

But these were not what drove him to flail at the air, to harbor the heart-thumping, stomach-churning suspicion that he and Cassie and everything they had built together hung by a slender thread. No, it was the feverish heat, the cloth-rotting humidity, the aching loneliness, the yawning distance between Nick and — and what? His daily jogs through the streets of San Francisco? Lombardi's chicken alfredo? The soft curve of Cassie's beautiful neck?

He sat on a log and held his head, the swamp-green army surplus pack shifting under its load. He twisted the hastily scribbled map in shaking fingers. It might help him find his way back, but sure as flies in a barnyard, it had little to say about what lay forward.

He removed the hat, swiped at his brow with a grimy forearm, and scanned the forest lid for answers. No doubt this time.

He was lost.

Not little-boy lost like temporary separation from his mother in Golden Gate Park. Not lost like in-over-his-head lost in the ruthless, take-no-prisoners world of perfume and cosmetics.

Lost like Hansel and Gretel standing at the door to the witch's oven. Flames ahead. Witch behind.

Lost.

A wave of flycatchers and cuckoo-shrikes spread through the branches overhead. Insects camouflaged like bird dung remained rock-still to avoid detection. A flying tree snake launched into space, flattened its ribs up and outward, and with a rapid lateral writhing, hooked a safe landing on a branch twenty feet away.

Nick laughed — a high, reedy sound — and patted a damp pocket. Sure he was rattled. Here he sat astride a fallen tree somewhere in the steamy jungles of Papua New Guinea, incubator of the world's rarest disease, Kuru syndrome. Those afflicted with Kuru slowly go mad, then die in a burst of convulsions. The madness was contracted by eating the brains of another human being.

And here was one of the two executive officers of Azure World stuck on a log with a smudged paper covered with hasty ballpoint pen scratchings.

Nick bent over, elbows on knees, and ran his fingers through a sweaty thatch of hair. He wiped a clammy palm over three days' stubble, increasingly difficult to tell from a thick caterpillar of a mustache. Oh, he was a piece of work, all right. Lost among cannibals, with thick, pasty tuna military rations, a dozen granola bars, and — he patted his pocket again — one Gold Card good at more than six thousand locations worldwide.

He'd had to come alone. The jungle people no longer trusted expeditions of outsiders. A lone explorer would appear less likely to represent exploitive, corporate foreign interests. No elaborate encampments, no loud noxious equipment, no mass slaughter of the local food supply. One man, one trust.

Nor could Nick risk attracting undue attention from governments or the astoundingly acute ears of the perfume barons. For this to work, he needed secrecy, privacy, the fewest and mutest of confidants.

Nick had taken precautions. Only one man knew of his location. The closest secure emergency contact point for Cassie was the mission hospital at Wewak, a hundred air miles from where he'd been dropped off. The same bush plane would pick him up again in five days.

He couldn't tell her more. The competition came after that kind of truth. Word had already leaked out about his expedition. Probably someone at Azure World working both sides of the fence. But that alone wasn't enough for the competitors to act on. Everyone had senior researchers out looking for a bonanza. His past hunts had taken him to Puerto Armuelles, Costa Rica; Monte Alegre, Brazil; and Kinshasha in the Congo. He had returned from each with fresh fragrances, but every one only a variation on something already in mass production.

He needed a scent that would take the cosmetics world by storm, and his bones told him he was close to finding it.

Gerald Ruggers had paid a debt he felt he owed from the days they were roommates at Cal Tech. They'd spent summers mountain climbing, extreme kayaking, spelunking, and rappelling into and out of otherwise inaccessible canyons. Nick was still that way. He loved tight spots and difficult terrain, whether the raw wilderness or the uncharted regions of the business world.

Nick spent an extra semester after graduation coaching Ruggers in rain forest taxonomy and human anatomy until he passed the courses with sterling grades and eventually became a medical assistant certified in tropical diseases.

Fifteen years later Ruggers repaid his college tutor. When he was sent to Wewak and fifty thousand square miles of human suffering along the Sepik River, he kept his eyes and ears open. One day, among the Waronai tree people, he heard of a sacred plant of great mystical powers, so beautiful in appearance that the world was worthy to see it only twelve days each year. But by far the most distinctive feature of the great flower was its potent and beguiling fragrance.

"It has to be the *celerides*," Nick breathed, remembering the barely coherent transcontinental conversation. Rugs had been a babbling mess. *Jasmine, lavender, cinnamon, powdered babies! The scent of a woman! A whole grove of lemons!* That had been the beginning of a ten-minute tirade of aromatic imagery.

A week had vanished while Nick verified that the orchid was in its annual flowering cycle and then made travel arrangements. And now five days remained of the cycle.

Without the new scent, Azure World wouldn't last another year.

The shadows lengthened, closing down the jungle domain beneath an unseen hand. The sun was fading fast in the twilight world of vegetation. He was about to spend another sleepless night, but this time with the curdling certainty he was unable to find his way — or to be found.

He shook off the descending doubts. Tough this one out. Be right. And Giorgio and Karl Lagerfeld would lose shelf space to Cream Base #6 by Azure World. The dark horse wins.

Gone overnight would be the condescending gossip, the snide comments about soda pop fragrances and variety store positioning that too long had undermined Azure World.

With a hideous scream, a cockatoo flew at a monkey. Nick's heart jumped. When he could breathe again, he lay back against the fallen tree . . . and smelled water. Just like that. And heard it. Running water.

What direction was the sound coming

15

from? He had climbed a couple thousand feet as the map indicated, but fresh water was abundant here, and only major rivers were marked on the makeshift map.

Nick cocked his head and closed his eyes, concentrating on the rush of the distant stream.

He turned, squinting into the dark jungle. No good. Everything ahead looked identical to everything behind. No change in light to indicate a nearby riverbank. Tall, buttressed trunks festooned with vines diffused light and sound. Noise bounced off the trees so that the monkeys he thought were ahead were really the monkeys at his back.

Cassie would leave a trail. That quickly it came to him. She would park the backpack right there with a piece of yellow surveyor's ribbon tied to the top, then walk in whatever direction she elected, playing out the ribbon as she went. If it proved the wrong way, she would simply follow the tape back to the pack before striking out again.

Nick's first two attempts ended in futility, the sound of the water rapidly disappearing. On the third try the sound intensified, and instead of coming at him from all directions, settled into one. With each new step the volume grew.

It was a pretty little chasm of orangey-pink rock, and a gash was rimmed in a profusion of brilliant heliconia flowers, long chains of blood red blooms with yellow-green tips. Startlingly blue hummingbirds flitted about them in iridescent majesty, injecting each blossom with a delicately curved beak perfectly suited for extracting nectar. A drowsy buzz caught Nick's ear, and he saw that bees had made a home in an abandoned termite nest at the chasm's edge. The dark-brown structure was wide at the top, narrower at the bottom, and only waist-high off the ground. Nick had heard that jungle bees could be aggressive and that the jaws of some species were powerfully designed for mining resin from tree bark or chewing through the tough material at the base of a flower to rob it of its nectar.

Honeybees with an attitude. He would give them a wide berth.

Nick felt easier. The chasm opened a slit through the forest canopy, admitting a bright stream of sunlight. The sound of cascading water brought welcome images of icy cold mountain streams. He went back and fetched the pack and prepared a small repast of tuna and noodles topped off by a chocolate-coated granola bar. The map made little more sense under the sun, but tomorrow looked as if it might come after all.

Thirsty, Nick thought of the canteen with its depleted contents, warm and brackish after riding about in the afternoon heat. Perhaps he could find a way down to the stream.

The ground was steep and slick with undergrowth. He didn't have a clear view of the creek bed and looked around for a handhold. A sturdy vine hung from a branch of the bee tree. It seemed free of the main supports holding the termite nest, so Nick gave it a vigorous tug. It held nicely, and best of all, the fuzzy flying neighbors seemed not to notice. He grabbed on with both hands and leaned out over the chasm.

The soft dirt bank gave way and sheered off into the racing stream fifteen feet below. With a cry of alarm, Nick kicked the air and swung back for land. He made a lunging grab for the tree. Too late he realized his mistake.

He slammed into the termite nest. A white-hot pain seared his bare chest. He hugged the nest to keep from falling, his upper body blocking the bees' exit. Their rage was immediate. Deadly.

Within seconds a swarm of angry black bees wanting back into the nest enveloped his face like a living hood. They bit his skin, crawled into his ears and hair, and tried to get at his eyes. Blinded by insect fury, he shoved back from the tree, hung suspended for a split second above the roaring chasm, and let go of the vine.

He hit the cool waters feetfirst and felt instant relief, even as he fought for air. Hurled downstream, free of his tormentors, he fought to keep his face above water to see, to stop before plunging off a waterfall or getting sucked under a log. He slammed into a boulder, arm pinned at his side, before swinging into the calm on the other side of the rock. His arm tingled and would not rise above his shoulder. His face ached and tightened with swelling. He looked down at his chest, red-raw with stinging welts, and was surprised it was still closed, considering how hard the bees had attacked.

He lay for a long time in the soothing shallows, allowing the water to reduce the swelling in his battered extremities. The light turned a gauzy gray, and Nick felt cold and alone.

The darkening forest grew eerily quiet, and had the water been a little warmer, he might have tried to sleep right there in the stream. The bank at that point was steeply sloped, but not the sheer drop it had been at the bee tree. He was about to rise and claw his way back to the pack and search for a safer place to make camp, when something deep in his nasal cavities began sending messages to the brain.

His nostrils twitched. Faintly . . . faintly . . . enticing, unlike anything else . . . the aroma intensified on the evening air. The fine hairs stiffened at the nape of his neck. He got to his feet, slowly, more from fear of losing the scent than from soreness, and sniffed the gases in the atmosphere. Expertly, automatically, his trained nose sorted and differentiated the smorgasbord of jungle smells. Strained at the one scent above all others. Strained to seek the direction of its source.

Downstream.

Intoxicating . . . here . . . at this distance . . . Dear God, what will it be at the source? Oh, Cass, if we can get this in a bottle, your fame is assured!

He lunged, slid, found traction, and crab-crawled up the slope toward the last of the light, ignoring insects and chameleons and sticky substances of unknown origin that shared the rain forest floor.

Near the top, a strange puff of cool air caught up with him and chilled him in his wet clothes. He stopped, turned, and

watched the parted leaves of a monstrous
fern close on the last of the fading light.

CHAPTER 2

Cassandra Dixon could think of thirteen ways to kill Brenda Gelasse. That was the short list.

If you eliminated guns (too noisy), knives (too messy), and poison (too gothic), there still remained a wide range of possibilities, from suffocation to vehicular "accident." For days Cassie had been partial to a well-timed shove from the roof of the Gateway Tower, San Francisco's elite high-rise housing the Gelasse woman's corporate headquarters, but today Cassie favored a nasty ocean drowning involving barbiturates and a great white shark.

Fr. B will revoke my baptismal certificate. The impish priest at St. John's faulted her ungrace-filled thoughts. Called them borderline heresy. There was nothing borderline about it. She could live quite peaceably in a world free of Brenda Gelasse.

Early dinner at the Hilton's Black Swan

was not crowded. Good thing. Cassie hated crowds almost as much as she hated sales pitches — and pitchwomen named Brenda. But today the pitch would be all hers. She had just enough credibility left to lure Brenda to sit for one final spiel. She could imagine the headlines in the trades. *"Dixon Makes Last-Ditch Pitch: Gelasse Dies Laughing."* Cassie smiled despite her tossing stomach. She added death by laughter to her list but considered it too generous.

Cassie sipped an iced lemon tea and waited, scanning the room. She smoothed the trim brown suit jacket, purposely chosen to compliment her eyes. Smart necklace, an unusual twist of copper and bronze that accentuated her light summer tan and cascading amber hair. She knew she looked good — and felt lousy.

She spotted Brenda at the elbow of the maitre d', advancing toward her table. Short ebony hair, pale skin. Slender and fluid in a black sleeve of a dress, with mood to match. Their eyes met, and by her sickly smirk of recognition, Cassie could guess the other woman's thoughts. *What does Nick Dixon see in you? You're all wrong for perfume. Commercial real estate, maybe, or travel agent, but never the high-stakes arena of bottled allure.*

Cassie fought the nausea. If only so much weren't riding on her performance. If only they had not agreed to meet in so public a place. She made a mental note to put poison back on the list.

She rose and greeted Brenda with extended hand. "Ms. Gelasse, how kind of you to come."

Brenda had agreed to this meeting with good reason. Azure World, the Dixon perfume company, had two things she wanted.

After today there might be a third.

The women shook hands warily and were seated. A gin and tonic materialized in front of Brenda. Another iced lemon tea appeared in front of Cassie at the same time but went untouched. She glanced nervously about, took a deep breath, and began.

"Ms. Gelasse, I know you're busy, and I won't waste your time." She hoped the woman would interrupt and urge the use of her first name. She didn't. "We're about to release a new line that — and you've probably heard this before, but trust me, this time it's no hype — a new line with more promise than Gucci, Opium, and Obsession combined. We have isolated the natural flora oil of a blossom so rare and of a fragrance so enticing that it will be the most socially compelling aroma this millennium. And here's the best part." She leaned forward, betraying her excitement, as if to impart directions to the Fountain of Youth. She looked around once more before saying in a low voice, "Never has its scent been inhaled before!"

Brenda's nostrils quivered ever so slightly in an otherwise unyielding mask of professional detachment. *Is she cataloging me?* It was well established in the trade that Brenda analyzed the scent of an adversary before pinning the hapless creature to a display card and adding it to her collection. *What does she think of our Cosmos? Probably that the rose and vanilla are vastly understated, as forgettable as yesterday's poached egg. And God help me if she catches a whiff of the Strawberry Soda I bathed in. She'll have me committed to the Jelly Belly factory for life.*

"Never?" Brenda wet her wide coral pink lips with the gin and tonic. Cassie felt as vulnerable as a kitten on the interstate. Everyone, most especially Brenda, knew the buzz in the industry. Azure World was about to slip in red ink and fall on its corporate backside.

Brenda sat back in the chair and crossed long smooth legs. She placed both hands on her knee and gave Cassie a penetrating look. "Mrs. Dixon —"

"Cassandra, please."

"Cassandra . . ." Brenda drew the name out as if it were a blended scent and she were separating each essence. "I don't need to tell you that Mother Earth's olfactory repertoire is all but exhausted. We must cease these fantasies of finding a pristine aroma. The future of perfume lies in the combining of food, spice, and forest scents. I know you've heard that the Costa Rican rain forest contains an insect that when crushed emits the aroma of ambergris, but those prospects are mere oddities. We have a crew down there now burning up a thousand dollars a day, but the fickle little bugs aren't cooperating. No, dear, I have better things to do than to sit here when all you offer is another garden bouquet. Candy and flowers are for blue collar schmoes with the imaginations of dust mites."

Cassie fought an extreme dislike for the woman, focusing on Brenda's long pink nails rapping an impatient tattoo on the tablecloth. The woman's head tipped forward on its slender, pale pedestal, and heavy-lidded eyes considered Cassie with studied indifference. "Mrs. Dixon, I don't mean to be curt, but we both know that I am no trend chaser. When Elizabeth Taylor's Black Pearls backfired, you could have smelled the stink a thousand miles at sea. Print ads featuring Ms. Taylor immersed in a lagoon couldn't draw fleas. Twelve million precious advertising dollars in the toilet. Enough surplus scent strips to paper Manhattan. The rocket scientists at Elizabeth Arden couldn't find a hole to crawl into. No, I've smelled your line and frankly, it lacks the heart to make it in the universe where I operate."

Cassie stiffened and narrowed her eyes. "Look, Ms. Gelasse, I'm not talking about a nostalgia wave here, or some fleeting infatuation. *Without* advertising, celebrity endorsement, or additives of any kind, we have created the most stimulating fragrance since Adam first sniffed the rose. Teenage girls, women over forty, and everyone in between will snap this up by the gallon. We'll market it on television during commercial breaks in *Insomniac Theatre* if we have to, but we are going to introduce this aroma. What we want is for deBrieze to have exclusive instore rights. California test market, then coast-to-coast and international distribution. How about it?"

How about it? Is that the best closing line I can find?

Cassie held her breath, then let it out slowly as Brenda glared at the accursed ceiling speakers and ordered a second gin and tonic. "Ugh, this sugar music is so bourgeois. What I wouldn't give for some virile Rachmaninoff."

She fixed Cassie with a look only slightly more nuanced than the one she'd launched at the ceiling. "I didn't become head buyer for five hundred high-fashion emporiums nationwide by allowing just anything into the deBrieze aromalariums. We've spent an obscene amount constructing those biospheres of glitz and glass and manning them with bare-chested bodybuilders named Max or Stefan. Every one of their fragrance belts is equipped with atomizers that propel only the finest — and most expensive — scents on earth. Surely you are aware that The Boys of deBrieze created a heat wave from Sunset Boulevard to Madison Avenue. You're asking me to jeopardize my boys and my reputation on a whim."

Cassie wasn't about to react. A second gin and tonic meant at least a faint ripple of interest. She waited.

Brenda's expression turned sour. "You lost me back there when you said *everyone* will clamor for your virgin fragrance. Surely you've read *Perfume for Dummies*. No scent ever made appeals to everyone. Besides, I thought marketing was your husband's domain. You are still married to the hand-some Nicky Dixon?" The tongue wet the lips.

Cassie ignored the question, but not without difficulty. "My statement of this scent's mass appeal should clue you to how convinced I am we've found what we all — you, me, Ms. Taylor, and Calvin Klein's masseuse — have been after for decades!"

The last was said too loud, catching the embarrassed attention of two nearby diners. Cassie drained her tea and forced herself to calm down. "Shall we order?"

The suggestion went unanswered, as if beneath comment. *Bad sign.* Although her researchers had found no one who had ever seen Brenda — slender as a spiked heel — consume so much as a Triscuit.

Brenda arched finely etched eyebrows and fixed Cassie with a wicked, penetrating stare. "Nick?"

The name from her lips sounded raw, perverted. Would Nick's one moment of weakness stalk them forever? The look in Brenda's eyes was nothing short of trium-phant. Cassie wanted to hurl the iced tea in the woman's face.

"News flash, Brenda. As much as you'd like Nick in your stable, he's not available." If a knife fight was what Brenda wanted,

Cassie could stab with the best of them. She watched the woman's face for any hint that the direct approach unsettled her in the least. None showed.

Brenda held her drink close as a microphone and spoke over the edge of the glass. "I plan to attend the launch of Nick's new shower soap for men Saturday next. It was generous of you to include me, though the invitation seems to have gotten lost in the mail." She set her glass down and smiled with all the warmth of a python. "If you don't mind a little advice from a war veteran, dear, your puritanical approach to marketing has cost you millions. In my hands, the launch of Block & Tackle would invite the vice squad. I'd suspend a shower stall right over the main floor and let the soap fly. And when the police arrived, we'd have a lively discussion over freedom of expression."

Cassie bit her tongue. She would not be drawn in. There was nothing to be gained by filling the trades with the gory details of a catfight.

Another sip and Brenda shot her a self-satisfied smirk. "Without something sensational very soon, word on the street is that Azure World is just one case of aftershave shy of Chapter Eleven."

"You need to pay your informants more, Brenda." Even as she said it, Cassie knew with sinking heart that her adversary's intelligence was sound. "Swirl for women and Jamaican Bark for men were a solid double-release that earned us a sizeable piece of the Neiman-Marcus perfume real estate, going on six seasons."

"Bravo!" Brenda feigned applause, the fingers of her right hand fluttering the air just above the palm of her left. "You are to be credited with building a quiet, if small, business model." She made it sound no more significant than a couple of sidewalk carts. "And for bringing a handful of perfectly serviceable little fashion fragrances to the forefront, not to mention conducting yourselves with saintly diligence."

"Cut to the end, Brenda."

The woman jerked forward, planted elegant elbows inelegantly on the table, and trapped Cassie's gaze in a scathing stare. "Very well. I am personally authorized to buy your controlling interest out at seventeen million. Furthermore —"

"You're joking. Plus you're about eighty million shy of a serious offer. I didn't come here to play charades."

"And why did you come? Surely not to dangle some preposterous fiction in my face in the hope of delaying the inevitable? Frankly, I could let them foreclose on you and pick up the remains at auction, but Nicky deserves better than that." Then, as if suddenly finding her appetite, she said, "The alder-smoked salmon is superb here. Shall we?"

Nicky deserved better? Cassie fought the urge to scream. The woman was a vulture in a French-cut dress. "I came here to tell you that not since earth, wind, and fire has there been something so elemental, so captivating, as this natural scent. You know full well your Night Tremors line ran its cycle long ago and has been treading water for five years. Word on the street is you're desperate for something new, something to give the public a good hard shake. I say that something is within grasp. I'm talking of an unlimited future, and all you can think of is making a corporate kill?"

"I prefer to think of it as a mutually beneficial acquisition. You could finally have time for your circus lessons, plan for retirement to a sun-drenched villa in Martinique, and pay off the Miata. Very, very tidy."

Cassie rose with a jerk, tipping the vase of fresh flowers. The maitre d' turned to glare. "How dare you?" Cassie hissed. "What do you know of our personal affairs, and what business is it of yours?"

Brenda gathered her handbag and stood, looking down on Cassie. The maitre d' hovered nearby, looking as distressed as if he had a table fire and no extinguisher. Behind him, other diners had stopped their conversations to watch. "I almost regret having offended you," Brenda said. "But you are foolish to turn down my offer and to chase after phantom fragrances when all you have produced thus far is little more than mediocre toilet water. And you are quite clumsy on the attack. Don't you have someone on payroll who can do that for you?"

Cassie wondered how many years she would get for forking someone to death.

"The offer remains for seventy-two hours. My card." Brenda held out the business card between two long fingers. Cassie refused to take it. Brenda set it next to her glass and walked away. She called back, loud enough for the other diners to hear, "I apologize for dinner, but neither of us have the stomach for it," and was gone.

Cassie felt weak in the knees and sat. Had she oversold their situation? Said too much? What if Nick couldn't find the flower? What if he failed to . . . ?

She squeezed her eyes closed and forced

away dark thoughts and rising panic. *He has to succeed. Has to, dear God!* She'd stayed away from St. John's too long. Fr. B would have some light for her. He knew God's mind, God's will. She hadn't been to see him in ages, had skipped the last two appointments without calling. There simply weren't enough hours in the day. And Beth . . . She hadn't even had a good heart-to-heart with her daughter since . . . when?

Cassie shook her head and steeled herself. *Pay attention to business.* Even a no-deal meeting with Brenda was good for two inches in Brandon Kirk's "Eye on the Bay" in the *Chronicle.* That buzz, plus tomorrow's interview on *Midday by the Bay,* was sure to set the stage for the bombshell about to detonate upon Nick's return with Cream Base #6 — code for The Mother of All Fragrances.

She looked around the restaurant for Brandon's paid eyes, but no one seemed to fit the description. Around Cassie the murmur of conversation resumed. She caught the eye of the maitre d' and fumbled in her purse for money to cover the drinks.

"It is not necessary, madam," he said with a cautious smile. "Your, um . . . friend . . . already paid."

■ ■ ■ ■

At the San Francisco School of Circus Arts in the Haight, Cassie Dixon pulled on leotard and T-shirt. Shivering, she strode into the cavernous gym, cold as an abandoned warehouse, and rolled onto a trampoline to warm up.

All around her, stockbrokers, cable car operators, airline pilots, interior decorators, and work-at-home moms bounced, bent, and flew to overcome phobias, bad marriages, assorted addictions, and predictable lives.

Cassie soared higher with each bounce to keep from taking a cab downtown and strangling Brenda Gelasse.

Her mind too intent on the frustrating conversation, Cassie gained too much altitude too fast. Dizziness came in a wave and she felt herself tipping backward. Arms pinwheeling forward to compensate, she landed awkwardly and pitched headlong over the metal springs and frame into the muscled arms of an experienced spotter.

"Whoa, Mrs. Dixon, easy does it!"

She felt foolish, as much the amateur as the day six weeks previous when she'd chosen flying with the greatest of ease over a class in oriental wok cooking. She had to do something or have an aneurysm worrying about Nick trekking through the New Guinea jungles on his quest for the orchid *celerides.* Their ticket to the stars!

She sat on a bench, head between her knees, and felt a strong hand knead the muscles of her back and neck. "You're tighter than a Scottish banker." Gentle as the familiar voice was, years of cigarettes gave it a husky rasp. Nick labeled it "maple sugar and gravel."

"Mags!" Cassie didn't look up. Her neck started to feel loose and rubbery. "I thought you were in Shanghai at the world congress of the ICCACS." Margaret O'Connor had treated herself to the International Conference of Chinese Aesthetics and Cosmetic Science for her sixty-fourth birthday. The Asian market was set for a hydrogen explosion in Western perfume and cosmetics. Mags, grande dame of modern fragrance and the genius behind the rocket ride at Regina-Floria, let it be known she was entitled to light the fuse.

"Was," Mags said. "But when you get Tommy Hilfiger, Calvin Klein, and Yves Saint Laurent in the same room, those honey boys are too smooth for me. You forget I grew up with Ralph Lauren and

Christian Dior, who are at least capable of growing beards if it came to it. Nor do they mask the body's natural musk as if it were somehow too nasty to admit. No, you give me the real men of fragrance, doll, and let the kids tinker with their toys."

"Maggie May O'Connor!" scolded Cassie, coming up for air. "That tart talk'll get you blackballed." They hugged affectionately.

"Listen, cutie, if I haven't been harpooned for wearing this leotard in public, no amount of trash talk's gonna do it. Now what's got you committing hari-kari off the tramp today, may I ask?"

Cassie hesitated. Mags had aged in the aroma wars despite a still-trim body and loads of energy. Once considered the celestial rose of New York perfumers, she had been midwife to some of the world's most revered scents, including White Shoulders, Obsession, and Oscar de la Renta.

Mags, just over five compact feet and still pretty despite the gathering lines of battle, eyed Cassie suspiciously. "Tell me what's up," she said. "You've got something going on that's tying you in knots." She pulled her silvery brunette hair into a purple scrunchie and slid her feet into a pair of scuffed dance slippers. When Cassie said nothing, Mags stood, threw a towel about her neck, and made no effort to disguise the hurt in her voice. "Don't worry. Waggy Maggie's tongue is in the upright and locked position." She turned and walked off in the direction of the twenty-six-foot ladder that would take her to the top of the trapeze rig.

Cassie sighed. If the orchid did not exist, if she proved inadequate to run Azure World in Nick's absence, if Brenda decided on a more devious course of action, Mags O'Connor might be her last friend on earth. Besides, if they were going to catch each other today, they needed to be emotionally connected.

"Maggie, wait. Let me help you tape up!"

Cassie bent over the older woman's graceful hands, took them in her own, and ran her fingers over the newly formed calluses. "Those were hard-won," she said, bringing the tape around to begin wrapping.

She received an answering squeeze but no reply. Cassie glanced up. Maggie's lips were pressed so tightly together, they were nearly drained of blood. A merry twinkle shone in pale green eyes.

Cassie laughed. "Okay, Sherlock, I know my secrets are safe with you. Let's finish taping and get our fannies up there. I always spill my guts easier when I'm terrified!"

CHAPTER 3

"Who are they to call us yawningly unoriginal?" Skip Lyons, Azure's comptroller, sat across from Cassie in the tastefully appointed company boardroom. The rest of her staff was seated on either side of the dark oak conference table.

"I know, Skip," said Cassie, feeling the fatigue. "The biggest in the business are guilty of mass mediocrity. They pump new product onto the market and think they can fool the public with a curvy new bottle and a new name, but it's the same old content."

"It's those outside formulators." Forrest Cunningham, from sales, leaned back in his chair and steepled his fingers. "Almost all the Liz Claibornes and Paul Sebastians in the business use them. We're one of the few remaining who blend their own fragrances." Phlegmatic, head small and round like a bulldog's, Forrest was affectionately known as Poochie on the loading docks.

"So how come we've not produced a home run?" Lyons looked as if he battled chronic heartburn. He was a gangly man, a person of as much pattern and reliability as the numbers he crunched. "Silent Breeze, Crystal Sea, and Bermuda Gale have all been solid producers for the Sears crowd, don't get me wrong, but none of them have rocked anyone back on their heels."

"It's a fickle market, Skipper," Forrest said, addressing the man by his office moniker. "Everyone's in panic mode; it's just that some have deeper pockets. Overall, sales are sluggish, and the perfume hunters have exploited the same resources year in and year out. They've run dry. Take that His and Hers 'Stand-up,' rumored to be in this year's Christmas catalog for the online fashion boutiques in the UK. They call it a funny little aroma for the comic in all of us! Did you ever hear such garbage?"

Lyons scowled. "The only funny smell in the business right now is the scent of fear in the pores of perfume execs reaching for something, anything, with perceived bang."

Cassie flinched. *Is that what they think I'm doing — reaching? Where's the trust? Somebody in management is playing both sides. There are too many leaks. Files have gone*

missing. Rumors are flying. But it's all circum-
stantial.

She hated these thoughts. She peered around the table at the fourteen senior administrators of Azure World and swallowed hard. The team was solid by anyone's standards. They'd had little turnover in twenty years, and their loyalty quotient was the envy of the industry. Her VPs, production line managers, sales directors, fragrance chemists, package designers, copywriters, and front office support staff weren't perfect by any stretch, but they were solid citizens with families and mortgages and dreams — and the odd skeleton-in-a-closet, she supposed — as in any corporate entity in America. And like any CEO close to her troops, Cassie laughed at their fortieth birthday parties, celebrated the arrivals of their babies, wept at their funerals, supplied silver cake servers for their marriages and remarriages, loaned money to newlyweds, sympathized with the recently divorced, consoled the suddenly widowed, and tried to reward their faithfulness with a decent wage, stock options, employee discounts, and free samples.

That at least one of her staff should be working for the competition came as little surprise. The bitter pill was that until the

Benedict Arnold — or Mata Hari — was discovered, all were suspect. Though the air in the boardroom at 8:19 a.m. was redolent with the white lotus succulence of Day Break, a high-end scent at forty-two dollars for a sixth of a fluid ounce, Cassie could smell the stink of betrayal. It was the nature of the business.

Skip coughed and studied a computer printout with grim determination. "Fourth quarter earnings last year are off pace with the year before by twenty-two percent. On this news, Azure's stock should drop a full four, maybe six, bucks a share —"

"That's today's gas pains." Forrest, an ever-present white plastic insulated coffee mug glued to his grip, liked his talk unadorned. He understood nothing of stocks and bonds and considered them voodoo. "What's going to sink us good is the piece that's coming out in *D&C*. It says we're using the musk of endangered animals and quotes more 'anonymous, well-placed sources close to the company' than the Pope's got lapsed Catholics." He glared about the table pointedly, but few took it to heart. Poochie would give both his kidneys to any one of them, and they knew it. He just felt the walls closing in same as the rest.

But why won't he make eye contact? Cassie

took a couple of deep breaths. *He's in a prime position to scuttle us, and he's acting as shifty as a rat in a rain barrel. Probably just the java jitters. The man sucks down caffeine by the gallon.*

"Something's rotten in Danzig, all right." Bridgette Sigafoos, vice president of product development, was as determined to misstate her adages as to formulate the most enticing aroma since baked bread. "It's all over town that Gelasse is engineering a buyout. And Nicky's trip to Ghana —"

"New Guinea," corrected Cassie.

"— to New Guinea," continued Bridgette without a skip, "is about as secret as the formula for Kool-Aid. Do you think it's smart to pour all we've got into Cream Base #6 when the wolves are on the phone?"

"At the *door,* Siggy, the wolves are at the *door!* For crying out loud, if we're going to sit here and discuss the coming apocalypse, let's at least be on the same planet, shall we?" Forrest's color approached magenta, and Cassie knew it was time for a little stress reduction all around.

She stood and smiled confidently, no small feat considering the knots in her stomach — *I need word, Nicky; please send word!* — and circled the table, hands on hips, red-lacquered nails tapping sequence

43

against the intense cherry hue of her Donna Karan dress. She paused to stare from the third-floor window at the Canada geese gliding across the man-made lake framing three sides of Azure's corporate offices. Remembering the scene at the Black Swan, she took a deep breath and turned to face the team, lips dry.

"The best thing to repel wolves," she said in careful, measured tones, "is a loud noise like an explosion. Mark?" Mark Butterfield was her VP for marketing and media relations. He was also a jazz trumpeter for a local blues band. He twirled a silver pen and visibly squirmed in the warmth of her smile.

Bridgette and Forrest exchanged knowing looks.

Mark jabbed the silver pen behind one ear in his thicket of blond hair and leaned forward. "Tabloid tactics! Cockamamie supermarket crud! The *D&C* ignored most of the insiders I recommended and talked instead with a freak show of faceless, nameless cowards who wouldn't know perfume from skunk spray!"

Cassie doubted that Mark Butterfield had been this upset since the day he'd shipped to Vietnam. The *Drug and Cosmetic Weekly* was the industry's Little Red Book. "Forget it, Mark!" Cassie said. "This time they've got it flat wrong. This time, Mark, no more code, no more Cream Base #6. I am confident that what we've got is Perfume #1, so why hide it any longer? I want you to take all calls resulting from the *Weekly* article. *All* of them. And here's what you tell them: this fall Azure World will launch the greatest fragrance the market has ever known!"

Her enthusiasm caught their attention.

But Forrest looked skeptical. "What's the formulation?"

Cassie stood behind his chair and put a hand on both beefy shoulders. "I'll tell you what it isn't. No more modest claims of precious little florals. No more oleander, orange blossoms, and lilies of the valley. No more geranium oil, bourbon, and sandalwood extract. No more essence of saffron or handpicked blends from the mountains of Greenland. No, Azure World — you, me, Nick, the entire team — will debut an exquisitely rare and captivating fragrance that will stun man, woman, and child with so rich and exotic a scent, it nearly defies description."

Forrest turned in his chair and gave her a dubious expression. "You sound like a female P. T. Barnum!"

Cassie gave a small nod. "Thank you. It will be up to Safi" — here the beautiful face of Safi Voronin, a Ukranian Muslim and director of product packaging, turned and fixed Cassie with a regal smile — "and her team to control the language that expresses the inexpressible and take it out of the realm of empty hype. I know you've already fashioned a good deal of the message, and from what I've seen, it is spun of pure gold. Fine work!"

Safi's refined countenance scarcely changed, but her opaline eyes flashed pleasure at the compliment.

"Mark, the press must never know what hit them! I want them hand-fed everything on this one, no secondary sources, no plants, no additional rumor. They get what they get through only two sources, people. Mark or me. That's it. Anyone else gets quoted, it's automatic termination."

Mark waved the silver pen.

"Yes, Mr. Butterfield?" Cassie said in the exaggerated tone of an elementary school teacher. "What is your question?" A few of the others laughed.

Mark grinned. "As much as I would like not to hide this wonder scent from the public any longer, it would be easier to let it out of the bag if I knew what 'it' is. No more code, you said, so . . . ?"

The moment had arrived. She took a deep

breath. "Well, Mark, you tell them it's called
. . ."

Face flushed, Cassie paused more from emotion than from any sense of the dramatic. So many hopes were riding on the hunch in her gut. Her coworkers, her Azure World family, seated about the table where they had cut cake, wrung hands, and shouted at each other over two decades, leaned forward, eager to hear at last the name of the scent.

"What!?" Forrest's curiosity had obviously overcome his misgivings.

"You're killing us here!" Skip said.

Lyle Mortenson, accounts receivable, placed his index fingers on his temples and pretended to read Cassie's mind. "Singapore Stinkweed," he guessed. The others laughed and shouted him down.

Still, Cassie waited. The Naming, as the moment was known in the trade, was always fraught with tension and expectancy. So much at the cosmetics counter was sizzle and fantasy, often bordering on the preposterous. Mascara that "envelops and nourishes each lash." Moisturizing cream "synchronized to your skin's natural rhythm." Custom-blended, environmentally sensitive, vitamin-enhanced beauty preparations to "coax the inner being into full flower." A great deal to expect from a dab of essence diluted with chemical solvents.

But expect it they did, and Cassie knew that the exhilaration the staff at Azure World felt now was a hopeful indicator of the public buzz about to be uncorked.

The Name, and the mystique that went with it, was a crucial part of the package.

Cassie laughed at the interest such an announcement always sparked, especially this time. "My, aren't we the impatient ones?" They laughed again, and some of the worry washed away in magical anticipation.

A dreamy seriousness came over Cassie. The drumroll had gone on long enough. "Nick and I, after more than a little lost sleep and against my protestations, I assure you, have chosen to name our greatest discovery . . . *Cassandra.*"

She scarcely dared breathe.

The executives of Azure World sat motionless. Cassie knew they were swishing the name around their minds, much as a wine taster sloshes a fine Bordeaux over his tongue and palate to capture the true flavor in all its nuances.

After nearly half a minute, the room exploded in noisy applause and whistles, everyone rising to congratulate Cassie. She had waited twenty years to find a fragrance worthy of her personal signature, one that could embody all the hopes and dreams inherent in so risky and subjective a venture as perfume, and it was only then that all of them could appreciate how truly exquisite the new scent must be.

Poochie pulled an actual bottle of Bordeaux from beneath the table. Wineglasses materialized with a magician's flourish, and before long the room was rife with toasts and countertoasts.

"Where's the caviar?" grumbled the sales manager. A collective cheer went up. "I've nothing to spread over my corporate relief!"

"To Cassandra, the woman and her scent!" Mark shouted, glass raised high in Cassie's direction. Thirteen more glasses joined his, the sunlight turning the wine in them a rich blood red.

Despite a pounding heart, Cassie bowed slightly, her smile radiant.

When all the other glasses had lowered, she raised hers in a wide arc. "To the makers of Azure World, without whom we could not have survived two decades to make such an announcement!" Clinking glasses and shouts of "Hear! Hear!" rang in the air.

Cassie stood apart, her glass untouched after the first bitter taste. *Where is Nick?*

Where is our precious gift to the world? She stared down from the window at the geese preening themselves on the corporate pond, fighting over crumbs tossed on the water by someone just finishing a morning croissant. *Who is the snake among us? Who wants us to fail?* She couldn't bear to think it was one of the happy, joking bunch in the room with her, being loud and brave for each other but worried about their futures.

She brushed the smooth surface of the credenza with trembling fingertips. As important a launch as this was, did it warrant so much of the company's resources? The team had already gotten the word that to make way for the signature perfume, production was cutting back on much of the Azure line, and that three scents were being discontinued altogether. Spray, cream, cologne, or perfume, every Azure item was a child they'd helped birth and raise. To see so much of their hard work shoved out by royal decree was a shock of Richter proportions. They had no choice but to trust her.

And that fact alone terrified Cassie.

With increasing nervousness she glanced occasionally at the boardroom door, willing it to open. Admit one short, balding Royce Blankenship, artist, scientist, sorcerer, nose without equal, face pinched in a perpetual sniff, the only one on senior staff besides Nick who was not there. The Nose had created more than one hundred thirty singular scents by alchemy of memory, patience, repetition, and association. His beak, now red, wrinkled, and hairy with age, could differentiate a thousand various fragrances. He could tell synthetic from natural, and where the natural scents geographically originated. Within six hours of a competitor's debut product hitting the stores, Royce Blankenship had it broken down into its several parts and could tell you if that was Greek labdanum or Corsican, Madagascar ylang-ylang or Manilan.

"Why so glum?" Mark asked, following her gaze to the geese. "This is your big moment."

She checked her Seiko with its slender diamond wristband and saw that it was five minutes slower than the fine timepiece on the credenza. "I was just thinking how blessed we've been with good people. Yet nothing is assured, is it?"

He smiled. "Unless you want to hear about death and taxes, my guess is the answer is no. Don't worry. He'll be here. He may be guilty of cantankerousness, but never treachery. Not Royce."

Cassie hoped so. People like Royce were

the Beethovens of fragrance. But for all his greatness, Royce had his eccentricities. For one, he was a purist, roaming the halls at Azure holding a blotter of scent first to one nostril, muttering self-absorbedly, then to the other, emitting another burst of coded comment only he understood. The process often repeated itself for hours and was not to be interrupted, even if one could penetrate the perfumer's dreamy state.

And he was obsessively punctual. He arrived for work each morning precisely at 8:45 by his Swiss chronometer, to which the company clocks were now synchronized. He was poured a quick morning cup of hot filtered springwater — no aromatic beverages or chlorinated waters to interfere with his olfactory equipment. He left the cup of steaming water to cool while he visited the restroom, then returned to drink the water at exactly 8:59 and thirty seconds. It took him twenty-five seconds to walk from his desk down the hall to the central lab. He began his work precisely at 9:00 a.m. The extra five seconds were to allow for unforeseen interruptions such as a visitor to the building or the ringing of his phone. As he ignored both visitors and phone, the extra five seconds were moot.

"I just wish he were more of a company

man," Cassie said.

Mark nodded. "Isn't he good because he's such an individualist?"

Mark had a point, but individualism had its own set of annoyances. When she had delicately informed the perfumer the previous day that she had a noon interview on *Midday by the Bay* and needed to meet with the staff first thing, he had sniffed disdainfully. She and Nick had had a series of dreadful rows with the Nose over the means of capturing the molecular fundamentals and base character of Cream Base #6. Gerald Ruggers had warned that the only way to avoid New Guinean tribal resistance was to artificially record the *celerides* fragrance, then copy it in the lab. Blankenship, however, considered synthetic scents on a par with velvet paintings. "Bring me the blossom," he insisted, "for only then are the natural connectors preserved for the proper formulation. No good can come of approximating nature. I will not guess at what the Creator intended!"

Cassie felt fairly certain Royce would detour from the lab to the boardroom in deference to her, but that it would be on his timetable. Who, after all, would fire Royce for anything short of embezzlement — and probably not then?

8:43 a.m.

She desperately needed him to come through the boardroom door in his fastidious little shuffle — now, before they dismissed. That might help quell the rumors that he was King Rat and suspect number one. It was no secret he was at the top of Brenda Gelasse's acquisitions list. She'd do anything to hire him away.

Cassie's stomach soured.

Still the door did not open.

At exactly 8:45 a.m. the Nose made the customary beeline toward his office in a neat, precise, gliding two-step that never made noise. At the center hall credenza he nodded crisply to Mavis, the green-uniformed plant lady from Planted Earth busily giving the miniature palms their biweekly feeding and spritzing. He would attend the senior staff meeting but planned to be late — all that cork-popping and spilled grape would not be good for the nose. He also planned to insist upon another meeting with Cassandra the moment hers concluded.

She had asked him to compromise his personal code of professional conduct. If Nicholas returned with the flower by which all others were mere reflections, then Royce wanted to bottle all its glory, not a portion of it. The soul of a rose was the sum total of all its components. Reducing the number of particulars no more resulted in a real rose than reducing a person to only water, calcium, and salt resulted in a fully human being.

"Good morning, Mr. Blankenship." Joy Spretnak, the plump, middle-aged receptionist, stood as he passed. "Mrs. Dixon says she hopes if you have a moment, you would please stop by the boardroom to hear an important announcement. Nice tie."

It was the same dark-blue-striped tie he always wore on Fridays, but he seemed to have become Joy's personal project, though he couldn't begin to imagine why.

He smiled and said nothing. The cup and its steaming contents was in its proper place just to the right of center on his spotless desk, so he proceeded to the men's room.

About to push the restroom door open, he glanced down the hall to Cassandra Dixon's dark-walnut office. Behind the floor-to-ceiling windows facing the hall, a second Planted Earth employee was inside, presumably to care for Cassandra's rampant philodendrons, thick and tough with age.

Instead, the man was hunched over Cassandra's desk, rifling through her papers.

Royce squared neat, narrow shoulders and two-stepped soundlessly to the door of the office. He stared at a broad back, now bent over the open drawer of a filing cabinet, then glided closer.

Eyeing the stand of philodendron vines to the right of the thief, Royce slowly closed his hands on a double set of sinewy growth. Quickly he whipped the noose around the man's neck and yanked.

The thief let out a strangled yell, which brought Joy screaming into the room.

"Security! Security!" Royce shouted. "Miss Spretnak! Throw boiling water in his face!"

The intruder whirled, ripped the philodendron out of its pot, and pawed at Royce, who now clung to his back. Dirt clods sprayed the room. Royce poked his fingers in the man's eyes, which produced a bellow of rage.

Royce held on for dear life. "The water! The water!" he shrieked. Out of the corner of his eye he saw Joy dash for his office.

Glued to the miscreant's burly back like a cowboy on a bull, Royce was determined to ride him to the finish.

Joy ran into the room and watched them whirl. She bobbed back and forth, dodging revolving legs and flying clods of root ball.

Afraid of getting burned, Royce yelled, "Wait until I give the signal! Steady, Miss Spretnak, steady. *Now!*"

She flung the contents of the cup and caught the thief square in the ear. The man bellowed again, slipped, and fell to the floor, Royce clinging to him tight as cellophane wrap.

"Somebody arrest this man!" Royce hollered.

The intruder cursed. When he tried to rise, Joy kicked him in the shin. She grabbed the paper spike off Cassandra's desk and thrust it at his cheek. "One more move out of you and I'll poke your eye out!"

Two building security officers and the senior management team ran into the office. Royce, who had lost a shoe, maintained a chokehold of vines while Joy, her normally neat coif now a tangle of dirt clumps and leaves, held the imposter at spike point. Between them the red-faced man in green uniform dug at the vines around his neck and struggled to retreat from the metal prong near his eye.

"Who are you? Who sent you? Call the authorities!" Royce barked. "The man's a thief and I will press charges! Get me the police! Get them now!"

By the time the police arrived, Skip, Forrest, and Mark had broken up the melee. Cassie seethed as she watched Joy serve the disheveled Royce a fresh cup of hot water, and housekeeping clean up the dirt and other office debris.

"This is a new low, even for Brenda and her lackeys," she said to Mark, who was standing near her.

Mark shook his head. "You'd think the titans of glamour would at least show some sophistication when it comes to dirty tricks."

Cassie's foot tapped the parquet floor. "So much for Azure being dismissed as a failed venture. They want to know what we've got, and they're willing to stoop to get it. They wouldn't do that unless they were convinced we're on the verge of something big."

"That's why today's TV appearance is so critical. It puts the competition on notice that Azure is not about to roll over and play dead. You ready? Your cab should be here in a few minutes."

Cassie could be transparent with her VP. "I thought I was ready, Mark, but first Royce doesn't show for the strategy meeting, then a thief helps himself to proprietary information, and a brawl breaks out in my office. I don't know if I can do this."

"Are you kidding? You've given birth!" When she didn't react, Mark took her hand and gave it a friendly pat. "That was a joke, m' dear. Stop worrying about Royce. Nobody fights like a badger for the corporate honor unless he's foursquare behind you. He may be eccentric but he's no turncoat. As for thievery, whoever's responsible has paid you a compliment. You're right. They wouldn't risk detection unless they were afraid."

The muscles of Cassie's jaw were rigid. "You're the right guy for head cheerleader. So you think I should go on air and put the world on notice?"

Mark grinned. "My money's on Nick and you to unleash Cassandra on an unsuspecting world. Get 'em talking now, anticipating, salivating, so that when it does release, people will throw their pocketbooks at your feet."

Cassie hoped Mark was right. Her nerves were taut with the morning's events, but she would give it her best and send whoever was responsible a clear message. "Okay, Mark. It'll be great for morale, especially mine."

"That's the spirit. I'll brief the police,

press charges against the bogus plant guy, calm the Nose — although the receptionist appears to be handling that nicely — and keep a tight lid on things while you're out. Now go break a leg!"

Cassie brightened. "Nothing says good times like a televised jab to Brenda's smug chin!"

CHAPTER 4

Night came suddenly to the jungle, inky and achingly remote.

A snuffle here, a rustle there, a last guttural protestation before the cacophonous world fell silent. The night forest steamed, the air it exhaled thick and wet and secretive.

The light had gone out, and with it all trace of the intoxicant that had set Nick's heart racing. Grabbing the pack, he scrambled back down to the water's edge, frantic to plunge after the aroma of the gods — only to find it had vanished. Ephemeral as the genie in Aladdin's lamp. Nothing but the thousand-year-old pungency of rotted leaves and fecund earth.

With its going he panicked. *What if Ruggers miscalculated? What if the twelve days are up and the orchid is clamped closed for another year? What if Ruggers got it right and the* celerides *just took it in its herbaceous little heart to end its efflorescence prematurely and call it a year? It wouldn't be the first time nature did what nature wanted.*

Nick's sensitive nostrils still retained the residual quiver of that beguiling fragrance. He could picture thousands of brush-shaped receptors at the top of his nasal passages waving in futility, the memory of that enticement haunting the nerve "hallways" leading to the scent interpreters at the brain's center. Nick slumped by the stream, its bubbling chatter strangely muted by the night, and felt sick with loss. He had not even the strength to hold his throbbing face and neck, and instead let them dangle between trembling knees, low to the water, where it was perceptibly cooler. Occasionally he splashed water on the bee welts that riddled his chest and face.

Gradually a more likely truth seeped in. Plants, like all other living things, experienced a "downtime," when the rapacious growth of the rain forest ebbed as if gathering strength. Little wonder. Many tropical species were known to grow feet a day. The *celerides* merely rested.

Nick set his jaw and hoped to heaven he was right. What else could he do? He was in an exotic land where orcas ate sharks and kangaroos climbed trees. Here men fished with nets made of spiderwebs and yams were sacred. At Wewak he had listened with amusement to bushmen speak pidgin, a musical mixture of Melanesian dialects and English. Like good citizens everywhere, they complained that the government was broken, or *gone bagarap.* He made a mental note to kid Ruggers that thanks to the missionaries, a helicopter would forever be a *mixmaster bilong Jesus Christ.*

A heady amalgam and altogether unsettling. But for all his amusement, he had listened carefully. There were only 1,300 words in pidgin, and with his language skills, a couple days of linguistic immersion and he had acquired enough to get by. Still, he maybe should have listened to temptation and gone south to Daru, where trade in pearls and crocodile skins was said to be brisk. He could make a stake, a new life, then send for Cassie. Together they would bury themselves in a paradise where no one could find them, and Charles Revson of Revlon and the other *dimdims* (white foreigners) could just fight over the bones of Azure World to their hearts' content.

The snap of a branch high overhead jerked him back to the present. A heavy object fell out of bed and in a rapid succession of heavy cracks, ended on the ground in a crashing thud. There was a split-second pause before whatever it was — monkey, lemur, or one of the tree kangaroos, most likely — scampered away through the undergrowth in search of a more secure perch for slumber.

Nick sighed. What about Beth? What would his headstrong daughter do while they were prospecting for pearls? Probably run off with that hairdresser and never speak to them again. And Cass. She'd be in a fragrant fury at his defeatism. There was no way on earth she would simply walk away from Azure without one hellacious fight. Ever since his fool dalliance with Brenda Gellase, he'd regretted it. Cass was convinced that Brenda, to get back at him for breaking off the affair, was behind Azure's present troubles. Maybe not so far-fetched.

The memory of that first, virgin whiff of the *celerides* gripped him with desire. He had to have that flower. The world had to have that flower. The loss of it was unthinkable, but if defeated, he would roast over hot coals before revealing the plant's location to either creditor or competitor.

Nick had bet the farm on this gamble, all their chips on one roll of the dice. They were so far in debt, it would take a freighter full of miracles to bring them back. Or lucky sevens.

He frowned at the analogy. In Las Vegas, casinos injected into the air certain aromas that increased a customer's willingness to gamble by as much as fifty-three percent. Of course, it wasn't the first time false optimism had flowed from a bottle, as any alcoholic could attest. But it irked Nick that he was as prone to risk as a cocky, Bermuda-shorted New Yorker out to take the house in Sin City.

How did he keep getting into these tight places?

His father's favorite Fijian saying came to mind. *I like it. If not to like it, must to like it. If not must to like it, then forced to like it.*

It didn't help. He didn't like it. He couldn't accept defeat. *Please God, bring it back. Please don't snatch it away. If you do . . . if you do . . . I'm* gone bagarap.

At dawn, and the sudden chatter of life around him, Nick stirred.

Sometime past midnight, unable to sleep, he had bathed his head and upper torso in the stream, toweled off, and by the light of a hands-free miner's lamp applied a home-remedy paste that Ruggers said would combat any insect damage, "and the bite of a werewolf, come to that." Should a pack of the hairy creatures decide to attack, the foul smell of the stuff was sufficient to send them yelping. Ruggers had been evasive when it came to ingredients. Nick had recoiled when his nose detected a faint whiff of dung, and thanked God it was fast-drying.

Nick glanced under the mosquito netting at the thin brown smear on his chest and was relieved to see that the swelling had receded. The burning had diminished as well.

He turned to check for the map in a pocket of the pack. His hand froze in midair.

His nostrils quivered.

Yes . . . yes . . . unmistakable . . . overpowering the smell of the paste . . . stronger now . . . sweeter now . . . there . . . it is . . . it is!

He sprang to his feet, jammed a granola bar in his mouth, yanked on a T-shirt, danced into his pants, checked that the headspace analyzer was still secure in the pack, and threw everything else inside the pack on top of it before securing the flap. Boots half-laced, backpack slung by one arm, heart and head throbbing, Nick bolted downstream.

At first the going was slow and awkward. Thwarted by branches, snarls of roots, and shin-cracking boulders, he pushed away from the stream bank twenty yards and found a wild-pig path wide enough to follow. He did not speculate on the size of creatures that could clear a trail that size.

A quarter of a mile, and dizzying aroma strengthened all about him. He imagined the forest air hazy with it, much like the drifting smoke from a campfire. He broke into a lope, heedless of the trailing vines and buzzing insects that whapped his sweaty body. A loose bootlace caught in a stony crevice, and only half continued with him on the pell-mell descent.

He plunged into a small, sunlit glade at a leveling of the trail. The giant root balls of two fallen trees formed two sides of a neat triangular bowl, the third fashioned by the stream, which had cut into the forest close to the pig path.

The enchanting aroma filled the glade with mixed messages, at one moment soft and demure, innocent and babylike, at the next provocative and sensual, enticing and fertile with longing.

Nick slowed and stared. Of the nine thousand plant species in Papua New Guinea, two thousand were ferns and fern-like, and three thousand were orchids. The glade contained half a dozen different ferns and a riot of orchids. Several pale to light-purple flowers, looking for all the world as if carved from wax, grew on a host tree-fern, six feet off the ground. Vivid yellow orchids with blue-streaked "tongues," litho-phytes, laced a stair of small boulders dredged up from the forest floor and en-tangled in the roots of the fallen trees. Cascades of blood red orchids, epiphytes, were suspended from the soil trapped in the top of the root balls, floating in air like tiny parachutes.

What had Nick riveted, however, was the magnificent lone orchid at the center of the glade, a terrestrial. It borrowed no support from tree, fern, or stone, derived no suste-nance from any host but the rich soil beneath it. With one dominant dorsal sepal and four smaller laterals, and bloom the color of pink champagne, the plant grew a regal two feet tall. Sturdy of base yet slender of bloom, its single flower resembled the delicate lady slipper in form. The resem-blance ended beneath the flower's classic bottom "lip" pouch, or labellum, where a shimmering iridescence gave the illusion of a preening exotic ornamental bird.

The *celerides.*

Unaware that he had been holding his breath, Nick let it out in a gust of exhilara-tion. He had not a speck of doubt that the fragrant haze enwrapping his head in God's own scent was emanating from the little temptress at the glade's center stage. Heart pounding, he rushed to the flower's side and knelt.

This close, the concentrated scent was almost anesthetic. Nick fought to keep his wits. He knew not to touch the orchid, for fear of inciting the Waronai tribesmen who populated the territory. He was surprised they hadn't appeared to protect their sacred interests. Ruggers had had the devil's own time convincing a Waronai chieftain that no harm would befall the sacred plant.

Nick had no intention of jeopardizing his friend's delicate relationship with the people of the forest. Ruggers couldn't be here now without appearing to be in league with outside interests. The trust of the Waronai was a long time in coming and fragile as bone china.

Equally important to Nick was his own skin. One false move — some species of orchid bruised extraordinarily easily — and he had it on good authority from the bush-men at Wewak that he would be as good as *pepek,* or human waste, to the tree people. In any way molest their sacred orchid, and he would be killed. End of story. He remembered the bushmen's faces flush with menace as they pronounced his fate should he slip up: *kilim i dais pinis.* Kill him he die finish.

As if reading his mind, the champagne orchid dipped in a sudden waft of air from somewhere beneath the vegetation lining the streambed. Not usually of a fanciful bent, Nick likened it to a curtsy and almost nodded back. He was smitten. The orchid appeared to gleam and dip coquettishly in the rising heat of day. An entrancing droplet of morning dew glinted sunlight from the swollen pink papilla and slid along the underside of the snowy plume and down the central stem.

A warning signal sounded in the back of his mind, faint at first, then more insistent. He had been cautioned by the veterans of the perfume wars not to neglect the other senses. Human sense was an orchestra, not a solitary instrument, and the perfumer who forgot that was doomed to fail. Nick, dizzy in the spell of discovery, had for a few moments blanked to the fact that something was strangely wrong.

Usually a banquet of sound at morning light, the forest surrounding the glade was eerily quiet. The muted buzz and clack of insects, yes, but no sound of monkeys or rooting boars or the magnificent birds of paradise. He tried to remember the last time he had heard an animal. It was back at camp. He had been awakened by a flock of sulpher-crested cockatiels and a pair of parrots, cleaning their beaks on the branches overhead. When he moved, the parrots squawked in protest and flew off in an explosion of sherbet-colored wings. The cockatiels had hesitated politely before also taking flight.

But as he rushed down the trail, the forest on either side had faded to quiet. Here in the glade it was now silent.

Nick looked around. Nothing else moved.

He shook his head. It wouldn't clear. His limbs felt leaden. *Am I awake or dreaming?*

No sound. Not even the thudding of his heart. *Is it still beating? Why can't I feel my pulse? What . . . what's happening?*

A wave of dizziness. Nausea.

Nick fought to arrange his thoughts but could not remember how.

A moment of clarity. *I've come to take the fragrance home.*

Waves of confusion. *What is this forsaken place?*

"Stop!" he shouted, just to hear a sound. The word was no sooner from his lips than it fell hard to the ground. The unnatural

71

silence formed a wall that sound could not penetrate.

Nick dropped to all fours, fighting for breath in the oppressive heat. For one horrifying moment, he feared air had gone the way of sound. Then, one small sip at a time, he extracted from the smoldering jungle a little oxygen, and a little more.

When he could again connect his thoughts, he stood and faced the enigma of the flower.

The enchantment was gone. Bells, sirens, and car alarms aplenty sounded in his head now. Arms crawling with goose bumps, palms slick with sweat, Nick removed the pack and flipped open the top. Hastily jettisoning socks, insect ointment, miner's lamp, a damp paperback, a dozen foil-wrapped granola bars, a waterproof box of matches, another of Band-Aids, the mosquito netting, a change of walking shorts and underwear, he came to that which occupied the bottom half of his pack. The headspace analyzer.

From the pack and out of its protective sleeve came a small, rectangular metal box, a length of clear plastic tubing, and a domed glass container. In the essentials, it was a vapor analyzer or electronic nose. By extracting the odorous, volatile molecules exuded by the flower and trapping them in a series of filters, he could leave the orchid in the field unharmed. Back in San Francisco, the Azure lab staff would flush the molecules out of the filters and inject them into a gas chromatograph for analysis and duplication of the floral essence. As rain forests evaporated under human assault, it was the only responsible way to conduct business.

Royce Blankenship, the purest, would have a sharp commentary on real versus synthetic, but it was a sermon he'd given before. One whiff of the *celerides* and Royce would come around.

Carefully, hands trembling, Nick slipped the glass dome over the orchid bloom. This close to the source, he fought a woozy sensation and at least twice feared he might black out from the flower's potency. He could see the marketing department having a field day with "a fragrance so captivating, he'll melt in your arms." Azure's chemists would seek the proper intensity, of course, before ever bottling and shipping to market. If they didn't mind their beakers, melting man would be stone unconscious.

"Where is the wildlife? This doesn't feel right." The words came out like a whisper in church. While keeping a reasonable distance, the arboreal residents had been his constant companion until a short time ago. It didn't make sense for them to disappear.

Uneasily he activated the pump, which pulled the air from around the bloom through a tube and a chemical collection trap connected at opposite ends to glass dome and metal box. Another filter on the side of the dome removed contaminants so no alien chemicals entered the equation.

The process completed, Nick carefully removed the glass dome and marveled again at the *celerides* that emerged splendid and unscathed from its trip to the chamber. "Little vixen," he scolded, "thank you for sharing your secrets so willingly and saving the farm in such brilliant style. You have my undying gratitude." He did bow this time.

Nick packed away the equipment with its precious knowledge now captured and stored inside, before permitting himself a solitary celebration. He pumped a fist in victory. "That," he said aloud, "was a multimillion-dollar extraction!" He could not wait to see Cassie's face when he told her they were on top. Or Beth's when he told her to up her hair appointments to two a week. Or perfume hunter Grayson Kent's when he informed him he could stop muck-ing about in northern Madagascar in search of moss or resins or whatever the devil he thought contained something sufficiently pungent to pique the interest of a Faberge or an Elizabeth Arden. Nothing else would ever compare with what Nick had just captured. Grover Magnin would need an entire floor of his department store devoted to the perfect perfume by Azure World.

And Brenda would be begging for a distribution contract but would find them painfully difficult — and expensive — to come by.

He hated to leave the flower that was clearly queen of the glade. He removed a small disposable camera from a side pocket of the pack and photographed the prize from several angles and distances. Satisfied that his work here was done, Nick turned to make the triumphant journey home.

His heart jumped.

Twelve tall and deadly looking warriors blocked his way. Their long, razor-sharp spears glinted in the sunlight, tips stained dark with blood.

CHAPTER 5

Studio Nine at KSF-TV bustled with organized chaos. Technicians, gofers, camera operators, and the frizzy-haired producer of the region's top-rated show *Midday by the Bay* moved in a last dance of lighting, sound, and set prep before showtime. A boisterous studio audience laughed at the warm-up announcer while on-air personality Barbara Silverman settled into one of the uncomfortable maroon-and-gray wingbacked chairs designed to force host and guests to sit up straight, lean forward, and look earnest.

Behind her, a stunning photo mural of San Francisco Harbor and the Golden Gate Bridge filled the entire back wall of the set.

Cassie watched all this on the TV monitor from the greenroom, where she received a final fluff and brush. The woman attending her wore a headset with a short stick of a mouthpiece, into which she barked updates between swift brush strokes of Cassie's hair and powder puffs to the face.

A disembodied voice emerged from speakers in the wall. "Three minutes and we go live, people. Three minutes!" Everyone's pace quickened.

Cassie's daughter Beth stormed to her mind. The row that morning had once again been over the hairdresser. *Andrew — no, some more foreign name. Andre, that was it. French, dear heaven, French!* Worse, five years older than Beth's tender sixteen and, Cassie suspected, full of R-rated moves. Whatever happened to mother and daughter arguing over finishing a helping of peas?

"Two minutes to air!" The woman with the headset had a thin, pinched mouth that looked predisposed to bite, perhaps explaining why the mouthpiece was so short.

"Greenroom ready!" headset woman barked into the stick. She gave Cassie a sharp, appraising review and did not seem pleased.

"Red provokes," she said with a sniff, shading furtive eyes with a black clipboard. "The perfume you're wearing —" She waggled long, slender fingers, indicating that a large, invisible mist of fragrance had followed them into the room like a cloud of doom.

"Free Spirit." Cassie's stomach butterflies crowded the sesame bagel she had wolfed down on the cab ride over.

Headset woman nodded vigorously. "You could stand to cut back. It's not a bad fragrance in small doses. Too many women, too much perfume."

"They can see that on TV?" Cassie said with as much innocence as she could muster.

The irony was lost on the makeup person. Ignoring the question, she turned to give a short, stocky redheaded woman a quick, calculating inspection while consulting the clipboard. "You the gal who balances a poodle on her forehead while twirling plastic rings on each wrist?" The stout-shouldered poodle juggler gave a cool nod and patted a tiny black dog that peeked out from her sweater pocket. The dog shivered and bared its teeth at Cassie.

"Which would make you the —"

"Perfumer," finished Cassie, taking inordinate pleasure as the woman suddenly began shuffling papers on her clipboard.

She held out a perfectly manicured hand. "Cassandra Dixon," she said. "CEO of Azure World. Always glad to receive customer feedback. That's Flamingo you're wearing, one of our most popular from last fall's line. Subtle citrus with a tease of thyme. Good choice for the hectic world you're in."

The makeup person, still busying herself with the clipboard, gave Cassie's hand one downward shake.

"Thirty seconds, people, thirty seconds!" warned the control room.

Cassie smoothed her dress and smiled wanly at the woman with the dog. Never mind. Controversy, breaking scandal, and the occasional carnival act were mainstays of *Midday.* Corporate CEOs across the city were known to end international trade meetings early so as not to miss the spectacle or a single sentence of Silverman's sassy commentary. For that matter, the big-screen TV in Cassie's office was almost always tuned to KSF Channel 7 because the one-hour midday show was about the only program she ever watched. KSF had a regional viewership in the hundreds of thousands who, from cafe to auto body shop, from San Jose to Sausalito, had to have its daily fix of MDBTB-TV.

"Three . . . two . . . one . . ." The screen in the greenroom filled with a swooping over-head camera shot that panned 180 degrees from Silverman's right, swung out over the audience, and sped dizzyingly toward the ending mark at Silverman's left.

"And now, live from Studio Nine, high atop the Hotel Oceana in the heart of downtown San Francisco, it's your modicum of mayhem, your nitro at noon, the one, the only *Midday by the Bay,* with your host, Bar-bar-a *Sil*-ver-man!" The studio audience gave another convulsion of adoration before they whistled and hooted themselves quiet.

The face known to half the West Coast turned to look into the camera. "You can have your Cirque du Soleil," Silverman said with her trademarked pout and dramatic pause, "just give me my Cirque by the Bay!"

"Olé!" screamed the studio audience, aided by three giant cue cards. The scene instantly switched to a camera with a head-on view, zooming in for close-up. Silverman locked eyes with her viewers. "You may find it hard to believe, as do I, that my first guest has never before appeared on *Midday.* She is Cassandra Dixon, one-half of the leadership team of Dixon and Dixon. Together, Cassandra and her husband, Nick, direct Azure World, a scrappy little perfume manufacturer that the industry says is on the eve of destruction!"

The studio band broke into ten seconds of the rock classic of the same name before

Silverman laughed it to a halt.

Cassie's stomach did a crazy gyration. *Was it a mistake to come here? Why welcome public ridicule?* The greenroom felt suddenly as inviting as a mausoleum.

"But ever the mavericks of fashion fragrance, the Dixons have defied their critics, first by thumbing their noses at the New York fashion world twenty years ago when they set up operations in San Francisco, then by deliberately snubbing the high-class perfume market to target instead our middle class, Wal-Mart sensibilities. That is, until now."

Silverman paused momentarily, wet her Botoxed lips, and pushed them forward ever so slightly in what every man at every bar stool, lube rack, and television sales department in umpteen counties took to be a kiss.

"For her, the smell of success comes in a bottle, and she tells me she has an exclusive announcement to make on this show that will sock us right in the senses. Welcome, please, mom, wife, determined businesswoman, and gutsy boardroom broad, Cassandra Dixon!"

The band played "Eye of the Tiger" to match the pugnacious flavor of the announcement, and for a fleeting moment Cassie toyed with the idea of shadowboxing out to her seat at Silverman's right. Instead she walked her "First Lady walk," as Nick called it, graceful but not stuffy. Assured. Safe. Unlikely to make her trip and end up facedown in the artificial shrubbery.

Applause and unintelligible shouts followed her. It seemed to take forever, and by the time she reached the chair, she had barely resisted breaking into a run.

Everyone sat and Barbara lost no time. "Where's Nick? With Azure on the ropes, it hardly seems the time for him to go AWOL."

Cassie almost blanked. She prayed for strength. She had decided in the cab that she was not going to allow Silverman — who had to be from the same pit bull litter as Brenda Gelasse — to steal the show.

She struck a hesitant pose, as if wrestling with private thoughts, then leaned conspiratorially forward. "Can we talk?"

Barbara flashed the camera an amused smirk. "Why, dawling, of course we can talk. Tell Barbie everything."

Cassie laced her beautifully manicured fingers together, positioning them so her scarlet nails and hammered brass bracelet reflected the bright overhead lights. "Then before I answer your question, Barbie, let me speak to the person who wants to shut down Azure World."

Before the startled host could react, Cassie, heart thudding, looked into the camera and said, "At about nine o'clock this morning, a paid industry stooge invaded my office with one thing in mind — to steal our secret for a competitor's gain. The thief failed. In fact, he came close to losing his life for that inglorious cause. Someone's playing nasty and someone almost died. Well, hear this. Nothing can stop us and nothing will!"

She unclipped a small vial from the inside cuff of her dress and sprayed the inside of Barbara's right wrist. She fanned the dampness dry, then held it close to the host's nose. "Sweet Amber Waves," she said, "with strong, exotic, spicy bass notes of cloves and nutmeg, floral middle notes predominantly tuberose and iris butter, and top notes largely patchouli and jasmine. Verdict?"

Barbara nodded agreement. "Lovely. Sensual. Hardly the little blue-collar bouquets you're known for," she said in tones both wicked and smooth.

"Does Sweet Amber Waves smell like the funeral fragrance of a dying company?"

"Not at all," said Barbara, ignoring a signal to go to commercial. "Nor does it smell like a truly great perfume in the French tradition. If this is your grand announcement, I'd say we've been duped. Nor have you answered my first question. Where is Nicholas Dixon?"

The shrew. Cassie recrossed her legs, rested her elbows on the arms of the chair, clasped her hands, and pointed both index fingers at the host. She took a deep breath, banished all second thoughts, and said, "My husband is out of the country, harvesting the most sensual and evocative scent since Cleopatra seduced her paramours with exotic pomades and powders paid for from the pharaoh's treasury."

The audience members buzzed. Some laughed cautiously, unsure how to take the brazen announcement. Silverman pursed her lips and laid a light hand on her guest's arm, girlfriend to girlfriend. "Come now, Cassandra. Did someone stay five minutes too long under the heat lamp?" A big laugh from the audience. Barbara's sarcasm was familiar ground.

The host rushed on with blood-in-the-water urgency. "Cass-sss," she hissed, "you're saying he's found a fragrance that surpasses anything created by the house of Guerlain, *more* than Molinard, *more* than Lancome, *more* than Chanel?" On each exaggerated and signature *more,* she was joined in unison by gleeful audience mem-

84

bers familiar with the Silverman style.

"More," Cassie said quietly, locking eyes with her.

The floor technician, signaling commercial break to no avail, was by now apoplectic, arms waving frantically.

Silverman looked annoyed. She turned to the camera. "When we come back, the boss lady of Azure World reveals the name of her sensational knockout scent, and we learn just how stinky the perfume business can really be. Then we go to your questions. Stick around!"

An advertisement for the newest Gucci fragrance filled the monitors, causing Cass a grim smile. No opportunity was ever lost to grab the advantage in her business. Azure did not have the three hundred thousand dollars the station charged per sixty-second *Midday* spot.

While the makeup woman — who, Cassie detected with satisfaction, had freshened her Flamingo — fiddled and fussed, Silverman eyed her guest appraisingly. "You've crawled out on a mighty tiny limb," she said. "Should I hand you a saw?"

Startled to see a sympathetic smile accompany the question, Cassie said, "None required, thanks." Inside she fought nausea. Without a single word from Nick, she'd told the world she had Cleopatra beat in the perfume department. She'd stuck a thumb in the eye of the dirty competitor who had ordered the thief into her office. And, judging from the knowing glint that had suddenly replaced any trace of sympathy in Barbara's piercing eyes, she was about to be forced to apply a few distasteful tactics of her own.

Silverman was handed some papers. She looked them over, and as the countdown to air was repeated, she straightened and stared into the camera. "Is she heir to the throne of the six-billion-dollar perfume dynasty, as she claims, or the manufacturer of one last desperate attempt to save the farm? My guest is Cassandra Dixon, CEO of San Francisco's own Azure World, who says she and Azure cofounder, husband Nicholas Dixon, are about to unleash the most irresistible aroma since theater popcorn. She will now reveal the name of this amazing aroma, exclusively here on *Midday*. Drumroll, Mickey!"

The band conductor pointed to his drummer, who responded with the appropriate cadence. At the same time, Silverman pointed to Cassie, as prearranged.

Cassie felt suddenly overheated and dizzy. She fought the urge to faint. Why in the world had she thought this was a good idea?

She paused dramatically and humbly lowered her shoulders. And just as Mark Butterfield had coached, she smiled directly into the camera, a smile that made every man at every bar stool, lube rack, and television sales department in all surrounding counties pledge in his heart to wear Azure products for men.

Ten seconds. Twelve seconds. Thirteen. Drumroll. "We present Azure's gift to every woman who ever dreamed of being the focus of someone special, the very breath of beauty, *Cassandra*!"

To loud applause, the curtains at stage left parted, and out glided a giant gilded box of pale rosy pink iridescence, the name Cassandra in flowing gold script, framed by twin pink pillars of marble shot through with veins of gold. Two statuesque blondes, dressed in tight, sleeveless black gowns, black opera-length gloves, and thousand-watt smiles, turned the eight-foot box left, then right, to catch the studio lights. The shimmering graphics shifted and glowed like sunset-tinted clouds. Though the one-off box had cost her a fortune, just the towering, gorgeous sight of it settled Cassie's stomach.

The audience was standing, their whistles

and shouts all Cassie's.

Even Barbara clapped for the artistry on display. Cassie wished she had enough left in the Azure account to give the design department a raise. But no, every last cent was there on stage, and then some.

Nicky, please come home with the contents of that box!

When calm finally returned to Studio Nine, Barbara deadpanned, "It's the story of my life when a container gets a better hand than I do." Cassie knew they were laughing in the Laundromats, the barber-shops, and the arrival and departure gates of San Francisco International Airport. That Silverman, what a crack-up.

"Impressive," Barbara said. But there was something in her tone that said it would take more — far more — than a fancy box to save Azure World.

As long as she was in this deep, Cassie said, "We ask everyone in the studio audi-ence to please leave your name and address on the way out. Two ounces of Cassandra will be delivered to each of you as soon as we ship to stores." At the pronouncement, Cassie saw someone in the dark recesses of the studio rifle around for paper, she as-sumed to record names and addresses. She forced another smile and imagined Mark

Butterfield's look of shock.

More applause. If it was buzz she wanted, the studio was swarming in it. Cassie prayed against any hidden stingers.

Without warning, Barbara rounded on her. "You have a lot of cheek, giving this mystery fragrance your name and declaring before God and country that it's — what did you call it — 'the very breath of beauty'! Explain yourself!"

Cassie willed herself to remain calm. "Christening the perfume in this way really harkens back to the high and elegant position, and mystique, of the Russian czarina in the early twentieth century, for whom I was named. Once you've smelled the fragrance, then you can better judge whether we have been too generous with the trademarked 'definition of essence.' As to how we can deliver, I'm confident of our sources. Honestly, there is an element of timing that makes every difference, but Nicky has two decades of experience harvesting nature's best. Believe me, he can squeeze milk from a coconut without cutting it open."

"Can he squeeze musk from an endangered whale?" Barbara said with exaggerated innocence.

"If you are referring to the *Drug and Cosmetic Weekly* article, those charges are anonymous, ludicrous, and false. The formulation process has advanced a great deal in the last fifty years, and fixatives from animals such as beaver, civet cat, and, yes, the whale, are no longer required. Besides, have you ever tried to milk the scent glands of an agitated wildcat?" The humorous image worked with the audience, but not on Silverman.

"How do you respond to the statement in today's *New York Times* from your friend and mentor, Margaret O'Connor? O'Connor, formerly vice president of marketing at Regina-Floria, said, and I quote, 'Cassie Dixon always could make something bouncy out of a squirt of this and a dash of that. But really, Azure World has run its course. Most Americans can afford better.' "

Cassie was stunned and failed to hide it. Mags was famous for shooting off her mouth, but she was always supportive of the Dixons. Why would she give the press the verbal equivalent of an obituary for Azure World, especially now?

Silverman, known to be a graduate of the school of brawler journalism, saw the stricken look on her guest's face and decided to pile on. "The facts would seem to support Ms. O'Connor's assessment. You've cut overall production by a fourth and discontinued three of your once-popular fragrances. Azure stock as of noon is down eight dollars a share on news your earnings last quarter were off twenty-two percent over the same quarter a year ago. One well-placed player in the fashion world tells me she recently offered what seems, in light of everything, a generous offer to buy the company. But, according to this player, you declined the offer in order to take a high-risk gamble on what we have all seen" — she motioned toward the stage and the leggy models in their perfect smiles — "is, for all its shine, still a very empty box. What are you thinking?"

Studio Nine went eerily quiet as everyone waited for her answer. The camera people and Miss Flamingo herself appeared to strain forward in anticipation. Even the technician who had been frantically gesticulating that it was past time to bring on the poodle juggler ceased his gyrations.

Taken aback by Silverman's assault, Cassie was pleased to find that ire won over nausea. "You want to know what I'm thinking, Barbara? I'm thinking that as often as people say they want peace on earth, they are more fascinated with someone else's battle. This is especially true in fashion, where the competition can turn pretty ugly. The picture you've painted is one of pending disaster. Admittedly, we've suffered some business struggles of late, but as soon as we fill that pretty box, I challenge you to have me back. On that day I will expect an apology from you for doubting that the good people of Azure — and there are many — could pull this off. And I promise to bring with me another round of Cassandra for everyone in that day's studio audience."

Judging by the stir, the audience wanted to applaud but was not cued by any of the sign holders to do so.

Barely hiding the Silverman smirk, Barbara turned to the camera and spoke in the instantly serious voice of a news anchor. "I was informed during the commercial interlude of breaking news at the downtown de-Brieze shopping emporium. My apologies to my guest, who is also learning of this for the first time. According to police reports, earlier today a local shopper purchased a bottle of Swirl parfum manufactured by Azure World. Upon opening the package, she discovered what authorities say was a large leech *inside* the bottle."

Cassie was astounded. If the report was true, her day was about to end even worse than it began.

Barbara continued. "Apparently, the

woman was so traumatized upon discovering the bloodsucking creature, she suffered a heart attack in the deBrieze parking garage and had to be airlifted to Mercy General."

Can this get any worse? Cassie bit her lip and locked her hands together to keep them steady.

"Doctors will not comment at this time on the woman's condition, but the family told reporters they will sue for the physical and emotional trauma caused by this shocking incident. KSF News will of course update you as further reports become available."

When Barbara at last turned to her for comment, Cassie gave a shaky response. "I will personally look into these allegations, of course. Should the facts be as stated, we will certainly do all that we can to help this family. Please keep this woman and her loved ones in your prayers. I ask too that people reserve judgment until all the facts are known." Even as she spoke, one name flashed through her thoughts. One hateful, ruinous name.

Barbara kept things moving. "Amazing developments, proving once again there's never a dull moment on *Midday by the Bay*. Caller, you're on with Barbara Silverman and today's guest, Cassandra Dixon of

Azure World. Your comment."

"Yes, I just wanted to ask Mrs. Dixon what she thinks of teenage girls wearing provocative perfume. If it's as sensual as she says, will there be an age restriction on Cassandra?"

With the little giggle at the end, Cassie knew for certain the young voice belonged to Beth. It was some kind of teacher in-service day. No school. She'd bet her birthright the call was coming from Andre's hair salon.

Silverman mugged her approval of so astute a young person. "Excellent point, caller. What about it, Mrs. Dixon?"

Keep it even, nice and even. Plenty of time later to ground Beth for life. "Well, caller, that has to be left up to the individual. Teenagers will need to consult their parents. Not only is Cassandra a beguiling scent, it will also be an expensive one."

With thanks and another giggle, the caller hung up — but not before Cassie heard Andre tell Beth he'd help her buy a bottle. Not if she moved her daughter to an unnamed island in the Azores, he wouldn't. *French wolf.*

She did not stay to watch the poodle juggling. When Barbara cut to commercial after two more phone-ins, Cassie excused herself to check on the hospitalized woman and the leech in the bottle of Swirl.

There was little doubt in her mind that a leech named Brenda Gelasse was, even now, wriggling with satisfaction.

CHAPTER 6

Faces painted jet-black — eyes, noses, and mouths stark white — they wore breast-plates of dark-brown tortoise shell and sported giant headdresses of white and purple bird feathers. Cloth-and-grass woven belts accented with shells and bone covered most loins. Two Waronai were naked except for bead necklaces hung with curled tusks of boar ivory. Brown, lean bodies rippled with muscle and glistened with oil.

They hefted their spears as deftly as Nick would knife and fork. He harbored no doubts as to just how far he would get should he follow his gut and bolt.

One warrior held a spear in one hand and what looked to be a small wooden flute in the other. His headdress was bigger than the others, and his bearing more chiefly.

Slowly Nick lowered the pack to the ground and raised both hands in surrender. Waronai muscles tightened and fingers gripped more firmly, twenty-four eyes the color of molasses following every move.

The rain forest animals kept silent, their senses more keen than any human's. He'd been in the forest three days, and it had been louder than an elephant stampede everywhere but here. *Here where the orchid grows.*

The sudden scream of a nearby cockatoo broke the silence, each note a mockery. Then no sound but the rush of the creek. Nick shrank inside, painfully aware of every mile between him and home.

Jungle humidity wrapped him in breath-sucking damp. Sweat ran from his pores. The bouquet of the orchid billowed about the glade. He felt lightheaded, overcome with nausea.

Still the Waronai did not move, nor did they invite him to do so.

Just when Nick thought he might be sick, the warrior with the flute and kingly head-dress thrust his spear at him. It stopped mere inches from his belly. Nick jumped but kept on his feet. With the flute, the chieftain indicated the disposable camera still clutched in his hand. *Toss it over,* the move seemed to say, *or I'll carve my initials in your gut.*

It was the only existing photographic

evidence of the *celerides.* Nick was still deciding how he might hang on to it when a spear blade slapped the back of his hand. The camera fell to the ground. The chieftain strode forward and stomped it into the earth with his bare heel. He shifted the flute to the spear hand, scooped up the crushed camera, and tossed it into the stream.

Helplessly Nick watched flattened plastic float a moment before disappearing in a swirl of foam.

"Steal stink!" said the chieftain in loud pidgin. The accusatory tone with which he said it was plain in any language. He jabbed the spear in the direction of the *celerides* and glowered at Dixon.

Nick fought rising anger but opted for what he hoped was a conciliatory tone. "No sir. No steal." He edged a little closer to the orchid but halted when twelve spears began to shake. "Flower here. No steal!" With an exaggerated sweep of both arms, he indicated the sumptuous orchid at the center of the clearing.

The chief snorted, clearly unconvinced. His eleven counselors snorted in agreement with their boss and added a unified scowl of pure skepticism.

"Yes, steal!" shouted Chief Waronai. "Steal spirit!"

"No, no," Nick said. "Borrow smell." He sniffed the air with exaggerated pleasure. "Leave flower." He pointed to the orchid and backed away, arms extended, palms out. For good measure, he threw in the warmest smile he could muster.

The chief laughed derisively, white mouth gaping in a maniacal grin. A chorus of hoots burst from the others. Nick's annoyance grew. The eleven grunts knew who cut their paychecks, that was obvious.

"Steal flower face." Chief Waronai waggled his fingers, then mimed picture taking with the other. "Steal flower stink." He brandished the spear at the contents of Nick's pack, as if about to run it through. Clearly, Nick had been under surveillance. He edged between the warrior and the pack, the headspace machine tucked inside with its priceless chemical sample.

The carnival smiles vanished from the tribesmen's faces. Chief Waronai lunged toward Nick, hooked two fingers in his nostrils, and yanked his head downward. He clubbed him across the shoulders with the shaft of the spear, and Nick sprawled on the forest floor.

He turned his head so as not to inhale the insect and forest matter clogging the sweaty junction of nostrils and upper lip. From the corner of one eye he watched the chief kneel on the ground, facing the lone orchid. The others sank to their knees and dropped their heads as if in prayer. A stream of strange, high-pitched language spilled from the chief's lips, earnestly beseeching the orchid. This continued for ten minutes, then another ten while the chorus joined in.

The pain in his nose spread to his neck.

The vision in his right eye came and went.

All he could see and hear was a disturbing pagan ritual. *"Uhhh . . . gip . . . gip . . . haaa-a . . . gu-go-greel . . . ya-had!"* intoned the chieftain.

"Hun . . . hun . . . barrum-mmm . . . ya-had!" his warriors responded.

Nick's lungs felt like wet sacks of cement, and a leg that had fallen asleep began to spasm.

But no amount of discomfort could trump the beguiling aroma filling the glade with suggestive redolence. Had it intensified under all the attention?

Incredibly, ever so gradually, the flower seemed to suck the resolve from the Waronai, who were now swaying on their knees as if following the unseen oscillations of the orchid. Their supplications slowed, becoming disjointed and slurred under the hypnotic influence of the orchid's undiluted fragrance.

Flat on the ground, Nick did not receive the full effect of the *celerides*. Still, he wanted nothing so much as to plunge his face into its sweet petals, drink its nectar, lose himself in its intoxicating chemistry. He was not so far gone, however, that he could totally ignore one incessant reminder that hammered the anvil at the back of his mind.

It was faint at first, but insistent. *Get out. Get out now. Go or die.*

He ignored the anvil initially. Let it clang. Just lie there and let Madame *Celerides* find you. Lean into her embrace. Surrender to her wiles. Let go, fall back, trust the senses . . .

Clanging. Louder. Warning. *Get out, get out. Escape or never see Cassie or Beth again. Now! Now!*

He tried pushing against the ground with arms gone rubber. He rolled onto his back and sat up. The naked backs of the Waronai swam before his eyes, their headdresses like exotic birds perched on the ground.

Standing, he shook his head. Wobbled unsteadily to the pack. Managed to raise it halfway before bending over and grasping both knees in the hope his head would de-

101

fog. Almost of their own weak accord, his arms slid through the straps, and the pack settled into place against his body.

Nick staggered off in the direction he had come. A hundred feet away he regained equilibrium. He broke into a clumsy jog which quickly became more purposeful. At the base of the ridge, he did not hesitate to fight back up the incline to the place where the bees had so noisily asserted themselves.

He skirted what remained of the termite nest with the bees busily rearranging their affairs. One thought crowded all others. *The weight of Cassandra in all its glory rides with me!*

His mind sharpening by the minute, Nick found his earlier trail and picked up speed. He had no way of knowing when, or if, the Waronai would come to their senses — an odd expression, given the circumstances. But now, away from that enchanted glade, he knew that everything depended on a clean escape.

"God, don't fail me now," he murmured. "Give me winged feet." He hadn't thought of that phrase since childhood, when Kid Dixon — the ring name he gave himself when pretending to be a professional wrestler — used to pick fights with the wrong people and had to rely on fleet feet to escape a pummeling. He fantasized he was Mercury for that burst of speed that more than once had saved his neck.

The clear, pure note of a flute penetrated the forest from behind.

A war flute.

A bloodcurdling cry made the neck hairs stiffen and Nick's heart skip a beat. A chorus repeated the cry, and he knew with dread certainty that the superstitious Waronai had awakened from their fragrant stupor and were after the scent stealer.

He ran, ran like Mercury, but another warrior cry sounded closer behind, and by the third he was convinced his pursuers floated above the forest, immune to the roots and vines and uneven ground that kept him from going full out.

They were used to the terrain, acclimated to the oppressive humidity. They were gaining on their prey and, from the sounds of it, enjoying the hunt.

The blood roared in his ears, and pain stabbed at tortured lungs with all the subtlety of shattered bone. Every labored breath was a gulp of hot steam that rather than refresh seemed to coat his throat and lungs with a thick, heavy paste. He was desperate for a draft of cool mountain air instead of this awful choking wetness.

A piercing squeal rent the forest ahead. He stumbled, stopped, ears straining to sift through the jungle's horrors to determine which one would kill him soonest.

Behind, the clear note of the flute, the lusty battle cries of intoxicated orchid worshippers, closed with deadly speed.

Ahead, the approaching grunts of fast-moving *sus scrofa,* bad-tempered forest boars, a pack of savage pigs with canine teeth ending in grotesque tusks of death, each set driven forward by as much as two hundred pounds of ham.

He tried to think. Tried to pray. Tried to breathe. Tried to still the banging of his heart. On the plane ride over, he had heard a report of wild boars derailing two Japanese bullet trains, injuring seventy-five people. The first train braked after running over a pig; the second train slammed into the first from behind.

He had also heard that indigenous tribes survived by their wits and the accuracy of their weapons. The fertile Waronai, among all the forest dwellers, were said to thrive.

Nick would take his chances with the pigs.

He slid the pack from quaking shoulders and turned to face them. He hadn't long to wait.

With a ghoulish gabble of squeals, the pigs

burst from the vegetation like devils on holiday. Thin legs churning, long snouts siphoning air, rat eyes glinting with ancient intelligence, they charged the creature in their path.

And with eyes wide, teeth bared, roaring raw defiance, the creature charged the pigs.

CHAPTER 7

As the cab took her back to Azure World, Cassie closed her eyes and forced herself to think rationally.

The leech episode was sabotage. Brenda Gelasse would stop at nothing. If she could not own Azure, she would sink Azure.

Cassie grimaced. Would Nick get absorbed as well? He had his limits, and if Cassie proved incapable of preventing a Gelasse victory, might Nick become a casualty of war?

Where are you, Nicky? Call me, darling. Tell me we've won the battle and thus the war. I love you. I . . . I don't want any of it without you . . .

He liked — needed — his women strong. That's where Beth came by her strong will. Daddy rewarded independent thinking. Lavished praise on her earning a brown belt in the martial arts. Rewarded her "cleverness" with a gold credit card. Should Cassie let Azure slip through her fingers while Nick was in New Guinea, his disappointment would be more than she could bear.

And yet he would be justified. She should not have entered such a competitive field if she couldn't hold her own. But who knew that behind the beguiling fragrances and shapely bottled seductions lay a cynical and cutthroat subculture that shot its wounded and played to win whatever the cost? It all looked so elegant and glamorous on the surface. Like church.

You'll see. It'll be different once we break through the clouds. It's our turn to soar. Hear that, God? Our turn!

She'd done Beth no favors raising her amid the suspicions and the high-octane race to succeed. Still, true success meant that Beth could attend the best schools, marry the pick of any litter, and raise her children without the struggle Cassie remembered all too well. Alf and Elise had labored dawn to dusk at common jobs, and for what? Ketchup and mustard sandwiches. Fried baloney and onions. Tuna everything. And attached to every one of those memories, a strong aroma that Cassie had spent all her adult life trying to cover over.

No, no one was going to ruin her beautiful, promising, headstrong daughter's future. No one, that is, who valued her own life.

She frowned and tried to quell the churning in her stomach.

The cab lurched to a halt to keep from hitting a bicycle messenger. The horn blared. The driver leaned out the window and screamed, "You are the discharge of a diseased camel!"

He and the cyclist exchanged hand gestures. Life resumed.

A persistent thought scraped at the back of Cassie's mind. Collusion. How else could Barbara Silverman have known that Cassie was not aware of the leech incident until the dramatic announcement on *Midday*? The timing was too perfect. Had Barbara and Brenda somehow orchestrated the whole thing?

Cassie punched up a number on her cell phone's speed dial. While she waited impatiently, San Franciscans drifted past the cab windows, oblivious to her turmoil. She desperately needed six terrifying minutes on the trapeze to restore her self-confidence.

Even more desperately, she needed Nicky to make contact. She removed an earring and placed the phone to her ear.

"Butterfield." Mark's bark instantly reassured her. His tone was steel tempered with acute irritation. Whoever had leaked the leech nonsense to the media without first verifying all the facts would feel the full wrath of Azure's VP for marketing and media relations.

"Tell me that you've squelched all rumors of carnivorous bloodsucking worms in the perfume, that there is no woman in the hospital, that Brenda Gelasse has gone deep-sea fishing with the Mafia."

Mark's laugh was short and bitter. "I think I saw that movie. No, actually, it only gets worse. The woman at Mercy General will, thank God, recover from the leech trauma. Amazing what a hundred-thousand-dollar settlement will do for pain and suffering. Unfortunately, the same woman and five other plaintiffs just filed a class action lawsuit in the Ninth District Court, alleging loss of the sense of smell from prolonged use of Azure's Swirl parfum."

Cassie slumped against the cab window. Trust Mark to give her the unadorned truth. Partway into an intersection, the light changed to red. The cabbie cursed, stomped the accelerator, and was berated by six pedestrians in the crosswalk and a dozen passengers on a turning transit bus before jolting to a stop behind a woman and a ferret on a moped. "The traffic, she's heavy," the driver said to no one in particular. "Heavy and stupid like cow."

"Loss of smell?" whispered Cassie. *"Loss of smell?"* Her shoulders sagged. They didn't have tens of thousands of dollars to spend on payroll, let alone frivolous lawsuits. Suddenly, instead of being the color of proud roses, the Donna Karan dress she wore reminded her of garish stoplight red.

Mark sighed wearily. "Yes, Cass. Some of the damages are unspecified, but essentially they demand compensation for medical costs as well as past and *future* emotional distress, and of course the aforementioned pain and suffering."

"But . . . but how? How could Swirl cause the loss of anything?" She felt weak, almost sick, but spoke with sufficient anger to cause the cabbie to glance anxiously in his rearview mirror.

"Well, that's the kicker. The suit alleges that the perfume they purchased contains zinc gluconate."

"Zinc gluconate? Are they out of their minds? Zinc gluconate is an astringent. Why would anyone put it in perfume?" Her sharp words earned another apprehensive look from the front seat.

"Good question. The suit cites clinical studies dating all the way back to '37 that show zinc gluconate is toxic to the olfactory epithelium." They both knew that the epithelium membrane, essential for the sense of smell, was located about seven centimeters up and into the human nose. Only a few centimeters wide, the olfactory epithelium contained more than a hundred million receptor cells. Despite the fact that most smells hovered about ten inches off the ground, the human nose overcame its height disadvantage by being equipped to distinguish between as many as ten thousand odor-causing chemicals. It was the king of human anatomy as far as she was concerned. She had built a life playing to it, enticing it, teasing it with a panoply of scents.

"Of course it's toxic!" She sat forward now, elbows punching dents in the vinyl of the driver's seat, phone gripped in a stranglehold. The cabbie leaned away from her and nervously fingered the radio handset.

"Mark, they can't do this!" She fought for calm. "Any boy with a chemistry set knows we'd never put zinc gluconate in our fragrances. It's pungent and produces mild discomfort. Why in heaven put something caustic in our products? That's insane!"

"Which is exactly what makes their case.

If it's true what they claim, and if they can prove prolonged exposure to this substance from the use of Swirl, with no attempt by Azure to justify its use or list it as an ingredient, we're in dire straits. Potentially hundreds more could pile on, bogus claims or not."

"Thank you, Dr. Hope!" She wanted to lash out at someone, and though she adored him and his loyal service, her VP was handiest. "You listen to me. We both know that even if someone has been exposed to zinc gluconate, it could have come from a thousand different sources. Household cleaners, cold medication. Didn't I read about a case against the maker of a nasal spray that caused some kind of smelling loss?"

"Allegedly —"

She moaned. "How I hate that word. I hear 'sledge' in it, as in sledgehammer, as in sledgehammer attack, which I'm feeling under right now." Another thought, as yet unformed, niggled at the back of her mind. She suppressed it. All she wanted was to crawl into bed, pull the covers over her head, and not have to think.

Mark's tone soothed. "Take a deep breath and let's talk damage control. The suit yanks the heartstrings with all that the so-called victims stand to lose. I quote: 'The plaintiffs can no longer enjoy the smell of fresh air, or newly cut grass, or a bouquet of flowers, or the taste of a meal,' et cetera. Now, you must be seen to be sympathetic, but not cowed. I wouldn't go see the woman at Mercy, and flowers obviously are out of the question, but do pay her your respects and warmest regards, and we'll tip the press. Why not get that Episcopalian priest friend of yours, Father Wills, to pay her a visit?

"Then you get on the media as forcefully as you did just now on *Midday* and say that you are pulling out all the stops to get to the bottom of these incidents. That's what Tylenol did with the poisoning incident, and they're stronger than ever. Tell them you will not sleep until the perpetrators are brought to justice. No stone will be left un-turned. Et cetera, et cetera. Puts you on the side of the little guy. We're already tracing the leech bottle back to the day, time, and batch, what chemists formulated the batch, which employees manned that bottling and packaging shift. Same with the bottles said to contain zinc. We can easily stall the legal proceedings until Nick returns with the prize and the whole world forgets all about these shenanigans."

He paused after placing so insignificant a label on the day's disturbing events. The edge was gone from his voice. "That's all it is, Cass. Really. Jealous competitors reduced to petty pranks. We'll outlast them. We will."

He could not entirely hide the doubt in his voice, but Cassie appreciated the effort. The fact that he had not used the name Brenda Gelasse only accentuated the omission. "And these pranks, Mark. How do we *afford* them?"

His mellow reply, despite all her instincts to the contrary, did provide comfort. "Azure's credit, though battered and bruised, still carries a modicum of weight. Enough of our creditors, while spooked to be sure, are nonetheless staying the course to see what Nick's got. It all rests on the treasure in that box of gold and pink. The one you used to dazzle the entire country on network television."

She swallowed hard and settled back in the seat once more. She had gambled on an empty box. The cabbie flashed her a reassuring if crooked smile. He slowed the taxi and stayed well clear of the next intersection.

"The entire country?" she said. "I thought *Midday* was regional."

"It is. But you know that all the smart reporters and news chiefs in every newsroom across America are going to put this all together, and by nightfall your appearance on KSF will go national. We couldn't buy this kind of exposure for Cassandra. Despite the negative press, there's a huge payoff in this."

Cassie hesitated. "How, Mark? How was it possible for the leech, the lawsuit, and Barb Silverman's news flash to come together so fast, so perfectly synchronized?"

Another sigh. Mark was less convinced than she that the planets were aligned against Azure. "The zinc deal took me by surprise, I admit, but not Silverman's breaking news. Her fans are always looking to pick up a few bucks by feeding her sensational bits. She advertises a bounty for that stuff. Do I think the timing was coincidence? No, but that's ratings wars for you. I honestly think the buzz created by you and that box — not to mention the gorgeous models — will far exceed anything generated by any scurrilous scuttlebutt. You let me worry about the loonies. You just concentrate on filling that box with the very breath of beauty."

Tears stung the corners of Cassie's eyes. The question that had been hiding, that she did not want revealing itself, rushed to her lips. "Did Maggie really say those things to the *New York Times?* Oh, Mark, how could she?"

She was making him earn his salary this day. To his credit, Mark came right back with, "Yes, the quote is in the *Times,* but I'll bet my bottom dollar it's either out of context or a muddled summation of a much longer conversation."

"Even under the influence of spirits supplied by an enterprising reporter?"

"Old Mags has had her share of indiscreet interviews, I'll grant you," Mark said. "But I think she is past this level of criticism. Trust her friendship and her enormous love for you and your family. Do you want me to call her?"

Cassie thought about it. "No, thank you, Mark. This is one call I need to make. And do you think you can keep spitting on fires awhile longer? I think I'll have that chat with the Reverend Wills before coming in. That should give him something for the next General Synod."

Mark laughed nervously. She knew her tepid attempts at spirituality smacked to him of occasionally buying fire insurance and every time allowing the policy to lapse. Or worse: opportunism. His center of peace was found at the altar of jazz. Toot a little horn and feel the absolution come down.

Cassie hated the cynicism these thoughts always stirred.

"Hang on, Mark." She told the cabbie of her change in plans. "Drop me at St. John's," she said. The cabbie didn't have to ask the address. It was the beautiful marbled Episcopal cathedral that was a city landmark.

"Before I go," she said to Mark, "do you have any good news for me?"

They both knew this was code for, "Heard anything from Nick?" Both knew too he would have begun the conversation with that news had it been good.

"Nothing new there," he said lightly, "but I do have two pieces of information that ought to cheer you. One, Beth will be eighteen in another two years, and I predict you'll be a grandma in five. By the way, I wouldn't deny her phone privileges if I were you. The phone-in was nothing more than a schoolgirl dare. And two, Letterman's producer called and wants you on the show tomorrow. You're booked first class nonstop to New York on Continental."

"We'll discuss that." Cassie rubbed a stiffness that had settled into her neck. "Tell me, do you do everything around there?"

"No, but I do work with some awfully good people."

"Me too," said Cassie with feeling, "me too."

Cassie skirted the main structure at St. John's. The great dome and the sanctuary beneath always put her in mind of the courtyard where she imagined Jesus was judged and beaten. But the stone, the space, the urge to cower beneath the great ceiling and the vacant gaze of scowling apostles in sculpture always made her feel an excess of humiliation. While Christ had not come to condemn, she was certain the architect of St. John's had.

It was in the modest stone rectory around back of the cathedral that she experienced acceptance. Perhaps it was because this was Fr. Byron Wills' turf, where his apartment and office were found. Though she did not know how many priests ministered at St. John's, she knew that Fr. Byron, as he insisted on being called, was priest enough. One of the small number of African American priests in the mainline Episcopal Church, he seemed to know just a little more about being on the edges of faith.

"Welcome, Cass," he greeted her with genuine warmth. "How many choir directors does it take to change a lightbulb?" That was how he began most of their infrequent meetings. With a joke.

He pulled a straight-backed wooden chair away from a small writing desk and motioned for her to sit. "I don't know, Father," she said, playing along. "How many choir directors does it take?"

Compact in tailored blue vest made in church brocade of ancient crosses and other Christian symbology, the short, goateed priest grinned his brightest, most inviting "come to the table of the Lord" grin and said, "Nobody knows. Nobody ever watches the choir director!"

Cassie laughed and thought how good it was to see this man. Why had she stayed away this long?

She leaned forward on the chair, gave a slight cough, and meant to come to the point of her visit, but he held up a restraining hand that his gospel choir knew only too well. "Do you know what you just did?" He beheld her with penetrating eyes the color of burnished copper. "You folded your mother's hands, wrinkled your father's nose, and cleared your own throat."

She smiled, not surprised the strain of the day showed. "So they left their mark, did they? Has it been that long since I was last here?" The previous fall, Fr. Byron, her childhood priest, had laid her elderly mother and father to rest just two months apart, and here it was autumn again. Her parents had their only child late in life and had insisted on regular church attendance. And though Alf Seton eked out a living wage as a bridge maintenance worker, Cassie knew their modest lifestyle had been more a result of generous tithing to the church, a habit she had not adopted.

"Blessed are the flexible, for they shall not be bent out of shape," he said, gracing her with a wink. "If priests lived by the dependability of their parishioners to get to church, they would all take to drink."

Three years of sobriety gave Fr. Byron more than a single pulpit. As treasurer of the four-hundred-member Recovered Alcoholic Clergy Association for Episcopal bishops, priests, and deacons, he knew more than a little about temptation, relapse, and the little celebrations of victory that came one precious day at a time.

"How are you, Father?" she began again. "What keeps you going?"

"Well, Holy Eucharist at seven thirty every morning, for one," he said, the words brisk and lively. "Rush hour people are not at their best, let me tell you. But they want to start their day right." His voice softened. "Just this morning, a gentleman knelt at the rail, the back of his neck still slathered in shave cream. A mother with rowdy triplets drags them in here every Wednesday on their way to school. I'm not supposed to, but I give them sweets with the wafers. I don't want them to think the grace of God is tasteless, now do I?"

Another wink. Another grin. Cassie felt a longing for his reassurance. She shrugged dispiritedly. You could be real with Fr. Byron.

"Tart?" he said, offering her a small box of pastries with what looked to be raspberry centers. "Jewish parishioner, caught between works and grace. Brings me fresh baked tarts on Thursdays." Cassie declined. "She believes *homo mensura,* man is the measure of all things. I ask her why she comes to Holy Eucharist, why a Christian church? She has never expressed faith or come forward to participate. She has no answer for me, but the strange longing inside that awakens her at five a.m. every Thursday and compels her to come. She says it's almost as bad as a husband poking her in the ribs and demanding breakfast. I tell her that is the Spirit prompting her, and she says maybe he should learn some manners. She starts catechism next Thursday right after Communion. 'No promises, I'm telling you,' she says, 'but we'll see what this Spirit has to say.' " He eyed Cassie closely. "If you think about it, pray for Lydia."

He waited. She fidgeted, not really knowing why she had come. "How are all the changes in the church affecting you?" she blurted.

"Ah, you are concerned for my welfare, a busy executive like yourself? To be frank, I am appalled at the placaters and the accommodators. We have priests we must call Mother. We have recognized same-gender unions and consecrated gay clergy. The Scriptures have gone out the window. The conflict is crippling. Fortunately, we have conservative clergy worldwide offering to forge relationships with disaffected Episcopal congregations. The US church is afloat in a sea of compromise. And I have this lower back pain that just won't quit."

"What of St. John's? Are you a lone voice or do you have consensus?"

Fr. Byron sprang to his feet and began to pace the room. "Very astute of you. We are not all in agreement, but I am pleased to say that we have strong support for our position despite a philosophical liberality that strides in step with this city and its leadership." He gave her an appraising, ecclesiastical once-over. "Now that we have heard the report of the state of the church in America, let us discuss Cassandra Dixon's moment of crisis. I saw you on *Midday.* Don't look so surprised. We priests are allowed a TV along with our bread and water. It would appear that you, my dear, are under attack."

She was so grateful that he had acknowledged her situation, she almost wept. "The opposing forces have gathered," she said. "Have you a couple thousand candles I could light?"

"That's the Catholics," he said, not unkindly. "We go in more for *Christi crux est mea lux,* the cross of Christ is my light."

"I thought Latin was the Catholics too, Father," she said innocently.

"My little affectation," he said, giving her a droll look. "Wouldn't want two years of Latin studies to go to waste. Walk with me."

They went out into the pretty courtyard in the center of the residences and walked among the shrubbery. The air was balmy for autumn.

"Why have you come, Cass?" said the priest, hands clasped behind his back. "Why now?"

She was taken aback by his bluntness. Who needed to justify going to church, albeit sporadically? "For comfort, I guess. It's been a rough morning. Truth be known, it's been a rough twelve years. I'm tired of fighting and only moving by inches. I need to know I'm okay and that God still likes me. I need you to give me some of that sweet daily comfort you get from above."

Cassie felt foolish at the weak little catch in her voice. At the vulnerability. What she needed was for the phone to ring and for Nick to say, "Sweet cheeks, meet me at the airport and bring an escort. Cassandra's coming home!" Of course, she wasn't about to say that to Fr. Byron.

"I see." He stopped at a holly tree loaded with berries, picked a vivid green branch heavy with red jewels, and handed it to his guest. "Our daily comfort is not the kind that dries my tears, wipes my nose, and pats me on the bottom. It is *cum forte,* with strength — that is the sense in which the Holy Spirit comforts me. The strength to get out of bed. The strength to get on my knees. The strength to minister to Lydia and shave cream man before the captains of industry have finished their poppy seed bagels and kissed their two-point-five children good-bye for the day."

She picked a bright berry and flicked it into the grass with a red-lacquered thumbnail. "Is that what you think I'm after, God's sympathy?"

He looked up into the tree, as if searching for a bird's nest. "I don't know. Where are your priorities these days? Do you rise saying, *'Gloria in excelsis Deo,'* or wondering how many units you can move with your latest ad buy?"

"Is that what you see when you look at me, Father? Greed?" She had to ask, yet dreaded the answer.

"You tell me. It is one of the Seven Deadlies. But God is the only parent you have left, so tell me how your heavenly Father has been treating you."

All she heard was, "Tell me." A sudden anger welled up in Cassie and spilled over. Easy for this cleric to point fingers. If he wanted to know how it was, she'd oblige. Out tumbled the hurt at being marginalized by the fashion critics, the name perfume companies, and the media; the suspicions over Brenda Gelasse and her designs on Azure, and worse, on Nick; the financial struggle to keep it all afloat when everything seemed to conspire against the company she had built on a dream and maxed-out credit cards; the walls that were closing in and the way "the game" had lately escalated, taking a weird and dangerous turn; the fears she had for Beth, and the strain the business placed on their relationship at a most fragile time in a teenager's development; the hurt caused by the comments of her best friend, Mags; and the marriage to Nicholas that, Brenda or no Brenda, she didn't want to see mortgaged to a shaky bottom line.

"And now, Father, it's make or break with Cassandra, the scent that will either save us or turn out the lights for good." She felt drained and sat on a carved stone bench supported by four innocent-faced cherubs.

Fr. Byron plucked another sprig of holly, then methodically pinched and tossed one berry after another into the shrubs.

It was a full minute before he spoke, the words measured and tinged with sadness. "You are an educated and capable woman. I could never do what you do. I favor frankincense, but would a two-hundred-pound steelworker want to spread it under his arms? I have a nose that can detect bad tuna or a cat box that needs changing. But to parse an emulsion for its zesty this and its sumptuous that, or to perfect the ability to tell what in combination with what results in ooh-la-la, is quite beyond me. You have a gift.

"However, a gift implies a Giver of that gift. And the gifts are many." He threw his arms wide. "What of the oxygen we breathe? The flowers he makes to come up in our gardens and surrender their essence? The child that bears your likeness and kisses you good night? The heart that beats within you, and the beauty that you radiate when you're not chasing the next great scent? That incessant chase drains you, lessens you. The perfume should be in service to the God who gave it. *God first* makes sense of the rest. When those priorities are flipped, you will live a life of anxiety and confusion. *Kyrie eleison.* Lord have mercy."

She could not help but laugh despite the rebuke. "Homily by Byron Wills," she said, taking his hand. She kissed it and made no effort to hide the tears. "You are a good man with a simple message, and I am privileged to hear it. It is not, I'm afraid, a message that plays well in my field, where cunning is prized and the most successful are self-made. But I pledge to you that once Nick is back and things have settled down a bit, I'll come back to church and try to bring the rest of the heathens with me. Deal?"

Fr. Byron sucked air through his teeth and said, "I wouldn't make light of this, Cass. You were seen at the Black Swan having a discussion with Brenda Gelasse that did not end well. I'm guessing she made an offer for Azure and you turned it down flat. I'm also guessing that you met with her in the hope of striking a deal with your new scent and that she likewise turned you down."

Cassie was surprised and annoyed by his "intuitive" abilities. "What, Father, do priests now have listening devices to aid them in doing God's work?"

He held up a hand and rushed on. "I wouldn't normally say this, but there are those who believe Brenda is not a woman you want to cross, Cass, believe me. She's deliberate. Calculating. She might even be dangerous. You have a marriage and a daughter to consider. No perfume, however sublime, is worth that much risk."

Cassie felt weary and drained. It bothered her to see the priest upset, but also to have him so well informed of her personal business. This talk was not helping either of them.

"Your spies got it mostly right," she said, "though it's unlikely I'll be having anything more to do with Brenda." She stood. "Thank you for your concern, Father." She forced a lighter tone. "I think at this point what I need most is another of your choir jokes."

The priest said nothing but took her arm and walked her back to the cab.

Cassie considered bringing up the woman in the hospital. No, she would not drag this good man into the fray. Instead she opened her purse and withdrew a small bottle of Hunter lotion, "for the adventurer in all of us."

"Here's some ooh-la-la for you that might just turn Lydia's head on Thursdays," she said, handing him the bottle. "Who knows? The woman may convert in half the time." She settled into the cab, whose driver looked relieved that she had consulted a priest.

Fr. Byron shook his head in mock disapproval and gave a little wave. Cassie rolled her window down. "You've been trying to marry me off for years," he scolded, looking only a little flustered. "Not to change the subject, my dear Mrs. Dixon, but do you know the difference between a choir director and a terrorist?"

Cassie was pretty sure she did, but shook her head. "No, Father, what is the difference?"

"You can negotiate with a terrorist."

She smiled obligingly. "I thought it was a lawyer and a terrorist, Father."

"Same difference. *Pax vobiscum.* Pray for Lydia."

Cassie observed the perceptive little priest in church brocade and tidy goatee and wished he wasn't so well informed or so troubled. "I will, Father, and peace be with you too," she called. The taxi accelerated out of the parking lot.

She gave a final wave and said under her breath, "Peace be with us all."

CHAPTER 8

Nick swung the backpack like an Olympic hammer thrower. The sturdy headspace machine inside gave it heft and momentum. The wild pigs scrambled aside in squealing disarray.

Because he met with no resistance, Nick barely avoided sprawling face-first into a thicket of wicked-looking spines growing like a hairy wart from the decaying bark of a fallen tree.

The boars regrouped behind him in a hail of screeching and returned to the path, streaming away from him, hooves pounding.

Nick, dazed, listened to the piercing notes of the war flute and excited cries of men as their prey abruptly changed.

No Waronai tribal provider worth his manhood could pass on fresh meat dropped in his lap. Crashing and grunting turned into terrified squeals, then finally the strangled bleats of dying game.

He was but fifty yards from death's door. He yanked the backpack on again and bolted from the killing ground. The Waronai would be on him again like ants on carrion. Move he must.

With each loping stride he gained precious distance, and soon the sounds of pigs and men faded away. He stopped for a quick gulp from a narrow rivulet. Elation returned. He had escaped without injury. The prize was literally in the bag.

The jungle, the heat, the fear, the years of struggle fell away. Within forty-eight hours he would meet Ruggers at the appointed rendezvous. He ran faster, oblivious to everything but the box thumping against his back — the precious, glorious box full of the aroma of the gods.

I'm coming, Cassie my love. Buy the diamonds and the pearls both. You are about to become Queen of the Universe!

Nicholas Dixon's unbridled laughter rent the forest.

High above in the forest canopy, an unruly collection of parrots and monkeys joined in the racket.

The Waronai chieftain raised the yearling boar by the hind legs and allowed the warm life stream to splash onto his chest and belly. He relished the hot gush of fresh blood that made the hunt so rewarding.

The distant screams of the tree creatures made him pause. All about him, blood-streaked warriors straddled dead boar. They too heard the far animals and, murmuring among themselves, waited for a signal from their leader to resume the hunt for the white one.

"He must not live," the chieftain told them in their ancient language. "He is one of the *Kukukuku* (mountain thieves). They pick a village clean faster than a man can dance a single *singsing*. And this one is an albino, from the farthest of the far, not a good omen."

Because he knew his men shared his thoughts, the chieftain consulted the pig's entrails. The steamy contents offered up no twisted intestines or tumorous growths, the usual confirmation of required action.

He relaxed, flashed a gory smile of teeth stained red-black from the betel nut. "You could easily overtake the albino, despite this mess of pigs the ancestors have provided. But the inside of the yearling boar says no need. All is normal, all is well. The ancestors themselves will take their revenge on the thief who has stolen the sacred stink."

The warriors murmured; a few shook their heads.

"Even now the albino flees back to the hole he has crawled from, taking with him the very thing that will be his — and his village's — undoing."

The warriors gave shrill cries of pleasure.

"Many are sure to die, including the filthy white one. Such is just punishment for stealing the power of the sacred flower!"

A roar erupted from his men.

The chieftain signaled for their silence. Instantly they obeyed. "Worthy hunters" — he addressed them in their language mixed with pidgin, a mockery when an English speaker was not present — "*mi no klia gut* (I don't understand why), but the ancestors have spoken. We tell albino, '*Lusim* (Don't touch)!' But he takes what I say is *tambu* (forbidden). You know, I know, he cannot escape the curse no matter how far he goes. Soon he will hate the flower. *Hia* (Here) it is beautiful. *Hap* (There) it makes everything ugly. *Yu save or nogat* (You understand or not)?"

The men grinned and slapped each other's backs. The albino would soon regret his thievery. From *pastaim* (the very beginning of time), the sacred flower was to be honored and left alone. Even the animals knew that. Long ago, out of respect and the need to survive, they had abandoned the glades and clearings inhabited by the flower. But in the *taim bip* (the time before their leaving), something awful had happened. Though the details were never spoken, it was forever known as "the mad time."

The chieftain smiled, rare contentment easing the ache deep in his bones. Though the albino had meant them evil, the trouble with albinos was their grievous lack of judgment.

He spit betel juice and repeated the curse aloud. "Run, white one. Soon the flower will be your undoing, and you will run never again."

As the sun beat down and the humidity intensified, Nick's elation quickly turned to anguish. *It hurts to breathe. My legs are heavy as logs. My head is going to explode. I feel sick.* He hated the jungle for all its misery and mystery.

He had felt the same kind of despair and hopelessness after the Brenda affair. Why he had strayed was the real mystery. Cassie and he had gotten married in a beautiful little chapel in Sonoma. Thanks to the generosity of family and friends, they honeymooned in Tuscany to recapture many of the golden memories of the year they met in Italy. He loved their first years of marriage. They were magic and filled with the excitement of building something together, a legacy in fragrance fashion. By scrimping and saving and receiving a small inheritance from Nick's uncle, who ran a successful deli franchise in Chicago and San Francisco, they purchased production equipment and set up shop in a leaky warehouse near Fisherman's Wharf.

"We can do this!" was their battle cry. By sleeping little and spending less, they experienced modest success, enough to grow the business and stay in the game.

Nick met Brenda at a regional trade show. "Hello, Nicholas. Let's be friends." *I was flattered. What an idiot!* She was everything the transparent Cassie was not — secretive, dangerous, beguiling, tough, and without child. She reminded him of Catwoman, a human jungle of emotions and motivations that invited exploration. He should have run hard in the opposite direction but had accepted her invitation to the Gateway Tower before entertaining anything remotely related to flight.

What he thought could be kept low-key and hidden swept through the fashion world with gale force. The phone rang at home.

He watched Cassie, stomach round with life, pick up. He watched her face crumple. She dropped the receiver. "Is it true?" was all she said.

His silence was her answer.

It was as if he had been physically blind and was suddenly given back his sight by a searing bolt of lightning. He begged forgiveness and received it. He pledged himself to her anew. Rebuilding trust took time but it came. Eventually she listened to his desire to raise the company's visibility, to never grow content with midlevel fragrances but always to have their ears to the ground for a knockout scent.

The one thing he never could repair was Cassie's fear that if she wasn't innovative enough, driven enough, adventurous enough, Nick would walk.

"I wouldn't, Cass. You've been true to me, to us, when what I deserved was your wrath. You could have walked, and who would have blamed you? You're an angel of faithfulness, and I won't make that mistake again."

The monkeys grew louder. His heart had a double knock in it now — fear he would keel over any minute to heat prostration, and fear he might not see his wife and child again.

An unexplained strength gripped him.

With a cry of longing he ran faster.

Brenda Gelasse sipped the wine without tasting it and dredged the evening edition of the *Chronicle.* She was surprised the story of the Azure perfume scandal merited only page three. She would have thought the loss, from a single source, of twenty percent of the human sensory perception in six people quite worthy of page one. Especially as it was a scandal certain to spread.

Despite the stone wall that had been erected at the Black Swan meeting, Brenda surmised that in another day or two she could have Azure — and Royce "the Nose" Blankenship — for a mere $15 million. To get out from under growing scandal and mounting debt, Cass Dixon would fold. And Brenda would have the prize that had so long eluded her.

One thing more. Leech or no leech, she would sue the *National Weekly* into the ground if it so much as hinted that shopping at deBrieze was anything less than the ultimate retail experience.

Molinard, her silver-black Abyssinian, stretched along a sunny swath of carpet and squinted brilliant-green, almond-shaped eyes. Named for the French perfume house where Brenda purchased scented furniture polish and the toilet water highly prized by Queen Victoria, the feline listened to her mistress vent when her usual confidant was unavailable. Brenda checked her watch and wondered where her two o'clock was. *Not like him to be late. Not like him at all.*

She walked to the window and stared out at the San Francisco skyline. Most did not know that she maintained a beautiful penthouse apartment directly above her office. An elegant but hidden spiral staircase passed between them. A palatial fifty-foot veranda allowed her to entertain captains of industry beneath the twinkling stars. Anymore, the estate in the Santa Cruz mountains was too remote, too empty without . . . well, certainly without Nicholas. But too much house, really, even for two persons, unless those two persons happened to be engaged in combat. Then it was much too confining. Her joke of a marriage had proven that.

Lately Sea Cliffs was quiet as a tomb, and as inviting.

Today of all days, I do not need him to be late. She counted on his observations. Banked on his counsel. If he told her to bet the mortgage on Lame Louis in the fifth, she would do so without question.

She needed his advice on Azure World.

She needed to know how best to leverage these latest developments. She needed to know what to do with Cassandra Dixon. The woman was insufferable. Anyone with half a wit could see the *Midday* bluff coming a mile off. A box was a box was a box, no matter how lovely, or how svelte the models framing it.

The deBrieze marketing team was already at work on a sleek advertising campaign to underscore the industry dominance of Night Tremors, the fragrance that had put Brenda on the map. "The message plays off the empty promises of Azure and is pure genius," she told Molinard. "At the top of the ads for TV and print, just two words: 'Once seductive . . .' In the middle, scantily clad lovers embrace. Below them, just two words: '. . . always seductive.' Next to that declaration, my capricious kitty, is the shapely bottle known far and wide: a quarter moon the color of sapphire, resting on a pedestal of silver. Some might wear Azure's economy scents by day, but I own the night!"

She felt the chill of loneliness. *How many one-sided conversations can one have with a cat?*

And how long had it been since she'd painted anything? It relaxed her, and in her early teens she had shown promise. Mother had a real eye for detail and form and knew exactly how to mix the paints to capture nuance of color. The long summer afternoons in the sand dunes, their easels side by side, had been some of the best.

"Now, child, hold your brush firmly but freely and let it become an extension of your arm. That's it, that's my Brenda. Don't be afraid of earth, water, or sky. And no timid sandpipers, please. Watch them go about their business and see how definite their movements. Not at all like the unruly gulls, who lord it over one another. No, the pipers are in agreement — see how they turn as one and each minds its own business? Good, good, that's the way!"

Those days, precious and few, had flitted away like a flock of startled shorebirds. Who could regain them?

Daddy was always working, selling excellent handmade shoes to fit feet, as supple as second skin. But she had lost respect for her cobbler father about the time Mother had. With Mother it had to be high-fashion this, high-fashion that, but her father's passion never rose above the pavement. "What are you, Colin, that you should stoop at the feet of others? Raise your sights, man, get off your knees. Drape a woman's figure, accentuate her fragrance, design her handbag. The real money, my poor man, is found above the ankles."

He died of pneumonia, according to the medical report. Brenda came to the conclusion it was death by discouragement. Mother thought he lacked ambition; Brenda believed he was born a generation too soon. Today, with her connections, he would be designing thousand-dollar shoes for Ferragamo on New York's Fifth Avenue. But a young daughter's peeves were his Old World sensibilities and embarrassing polish-stained hands, whereas Mother's world was all sensual satin and scent. Too bad she hadn't taken Brenda with her.

"You're too reckless, Brenda, too brash. You could do with a bit more finishing before society is ready for you." That was a laugh, coming from a woman who browbeat her way into fashion circles and publicly scolded anyone who disagreed. Brenda had been forced to do it her way and to invent all that nonsense about an ancestral shipping dynasty. The press ate it up.

Why did we ever stop painting the birds?

She might as well pick at old sores. "Nicky, Nicky." Brenda spoke the name into the silent room, remembering vividly the torrid affair that had flared out as quickly as it

142

began. Other men had desired her in the same way, with little thought to the long-term but every thought to the passionate, unattainable present. In her world, the high-powered Brenda was the Everest of conquests. But after Nicholas, other men found her more the black widow than ever. Now she devoured without the intimacy.

Another empty chill rendered her leaden inside. Ambition, achievement, a name feared throughout corporate America. A penthouse apartment atop the highest-priced real estate west of the Mississippi. All the material gain to satisfy a hundred upwardly mobile males in her trade, let alone the rare female. "Why can't I be happy? Why did the one man who ever made me feel real vanish from my life in the time it takes to wave a magician's wand?"

Molinard peered at her through narrow slits.

" 'You can't help it. You kill the incompetent and poison the rest.' That was Laughton's diagnosis. Can you believe it? Our chairman of deBrieze can be brutally blunt." In a puff of Cuban cigar smoke, he'd added, "But I'll be horsewhipped and left for dead if you're not the most driven person with the best instincts I've ever seen. To take another man's name would ruin you."

At times, though, she wondered if success wasn't one of ruin's many fathers.

I can't seem to get it right. I need help. But I'll boil in oil before I admit anything in public. That's why I need him to be here on time. That's why I keep a .38 special behind a sliding door at the head of my bed. My ex thinks I'm a fool. And though they've never met, jealous John Lexington hates Nick Dixon just for being in my past. If he only knew how often I still think of Nick, he would go ballistic.

She was glad she had neither kept his name nor lived long with him at Sea Cliffs. He had connections in low places. Dangerous he was, lethal he could be. So lethal he smelled of gunmetal.

Two fifteen. She had a photo shoot for *Vanity Fair* at three. Anxiety clawed her insides. Her fuse was lit. She did not tolerate lateness in business; why should she ever excuse it in her two o'clock?

Because he is different, she decided. *He is discreet. He is the only trustworthy male, other than Laughton, the only male who matches my intelligence. Truth be told, and I'm not about to tell it, his intellect comes dangerously close to exceeding mine.*

She would remind him, however, that he should not test her patience.

She went to the island counter and poured

herself another drink. *That Mags O'Connor is one piece of work.* Of all that troubled her, Mags was most troubling of all. Anymore, one could wave a bottle of cough syrup in the woman's general direction and she would utter the most indelicate comments . . .

Horribly, a tear formed and threatened to fall. She yanked a tissue from a box on the counter and angrily daubed at the errant moisture.

The bell sounded. "At last."

He would know what to do about Cassie Dixon. About how to pay her off and once and for all get her out of the sacred and ancient business of perfume, where she had no business being.

Brenda waited — just to make her visitor wonder — then set down her wineglass and steadied the slight shaking in her hands.

She crossed to the door, drew in a deep breath, and opened it.

"Fr. Byron," she said, offering a formal hand, "how good of you to come."

CHAPTER 9

The cab lurched to a halt in the driveway. Cassie snapped her cell phone shut, relieved to be home and glad she had skipped a return to the office. In another call to Mark Butterfield, she had vetoed the appearance on Letterman too, and her VP had advised her to observe a press blackout for the remainder of the day.

"What do I owe you?" she asked the driver.

He turned with a wary expression, as if upon hearing the damages, she might shoot out his tires. "Lady, this not a good day for you. What you think fair?"

She only half-listened.

Mark would handle further inquiries himself. Members of the media, and a jam of news cameras and vans, were already tying up traffic in front of Azure World headquarters. Better to see how the day's events played out on the eleven o'clock news, then get a solid night's sleep before facing whatever tomorrow would hold.

She glanced at the meter and paid the fat bill plus a twenty-dollar tip. It was a splurge she could ill afford, but if it was the last bit of pleasure she purchased, it was worth it.

"You like moon in June — big and generous!" gushed the cabbie before screeching away.

"Big and generous is better than small and petty, no matter the bank balance." Her mother's credo. Cassie winced.

She napped on a couch for an hour and a half and awoke rested. A quick change and she was in the garden, tying back her hair with a neon green elastic. The best therapy in the world was a little soil and a water hose. Armed with garden snips, she gathered an armload of impossibly yellow dahlias. The scarlet ones she left alone, too reminiscent were they of all the negative ink Azure generated these days.

Equally unacknowledged was the desire to be at home in their private world when Nicky phoned to say, "Eureka! I've found it!" And she needed reassurance that he was all right. She should never have agreed to his one-man assault on New Guinea. But God bless Ruggers, he would not agree to reveal the location unless his friend came alone.

Call, Nicky, call!

The phone remained silent. Cassie wondered how long it would be before a zealous reporter laid hold of their unlisted number.

Night fell and the automatic yard lights came on. A car slid into the driveway, the pleasant purr of its engine testimony to Nick's obsession with mechanical maintenance. The black Miata Cassie regretted buying lurched to a stop. Out popped Beth in white tennis shorts and blue knit shirt, a swirl of blonde curls freshly created in the latest "revolutionary cut." She clutched three bags and a box from Nutley's on the Ave.

Annoyed, Cassie leaned out of the bushes for a better look at the results of the panic run to J. Primo's. *So that's what eighty dollars buys, a fashionable tumble of barely controlled anarchy. And phone access to harass one's mother on television. What a bargain.*

A stunning sixteen-year-old, Beth was a sleek product of daily swims, low-cal shakes, and good breeding. Cassie peered down the garden path past the Chilean flame trees to where her daughter, bathed in the yard lights, stood grinning for no other good

148

reason than she was young and in love.

"We're a little late, aren't we?"

"Hey, Mom, I'd know you anywhere. What's green and goes slam, slam, slam, slam?"

Cassie wiped sweat from her cheek and wondered at the good fortune of having both a priest and a daughter who cracked wise. "I don't know," she called, "a moldy basketball?"

Beth made the unpleasant sound of a penalty buzzer. "Nice try, though."

"What then?"

"A four-door pickle."

Cassie obliged with a derisive hoot. "That's it, young lady, no more Saturday morning cartoons for you!"

Beth made a face and headed for the side entrance to the Tudor brick trilevel that overlooked San Francisco Bay.

She had loved growing up there, her mother knew. Family room and huge game room on the lower level; living room, dining room, kitchen, and spare bedroom on the main floor; and her bedroom, her parents' master bedroom, plus a study on the upper level. It was light, airy, and smelled of citrus.

Gretchen, the Great Dane, began woofing an excited bass welcome from her dog run adjacent to the driveway. Beth set her purchases on the stoop.

"Cartoons, nothin' — that's an Andre original. He can rinse *and* tell a joke at the same time." She said it dreamily.

"But can he cut hair?" Cassie mumbled under her breath, distractedly snipping one massive mane of yellow dahlia too close to the blossom. Louder she said, "If your comedian hairdresser is as in demand as you say he is, how does he find the time to help his clients place prank phone calls to shows like *Midday?*"

"Gretchen, hush! What say, Mom?" Beth unsnapped Gretchen's leash and brought her bounding out of the run.

Cassie sighed. "I said nice style, dear. Did Andre think of that all by himself?" This relationship was no match made in heaven. Beth had a teenage crush, and Cassie could have predicted her defensive response.

"He's a genius, Mom, practically a protégé. He's only twenty-one and owns his own salon. He says this is tomorrow's look. We found it in a book by Ormange. Can you believe he didn't charge anything extra?"

"Amazing."

"Yes, and he's invited me to Sangrio's for the Wednesday poetry reading. Can I go?"

"If I'm invited." Cassie made for the

house, arms profuse with blooms.

"Mom!" Beth wailed. "Gretchen, will you pipe down? Mom, I'm sixteen and five months. I do not need a chaperone to brush my teeth. Give me credit for having some sense!"

Cassie groped for the side doorknob, and Beth ran to open the door. "Did you show good sense buying out the store when you know things are tight right now? Did you show good sense placing a call while I'm on the air, knowing it would upset me? Besides, you I know about. Him I don't know from the Jolly Green Giant. Have him over for lasagna. I promise I'll putter in the petunias. Now, what did you buy that couldn't have waited a couple more weeks?"

Beth buried an unpleasant response in the nape of Gretchen's enormous neck and avoided the question. She permitted two pounds of canine tongue to make one wet swipe across her cheek before making the dog sit and mind her manners. Then she extracted a biscuit from her shorts pocket and watched it disappear down a cavernous pink maw.

"Any news of Daddy?" She followed her mother into the house, Gretchen at her side.

Cassie flinched, though she'd known the question would come. It always came when the topic was males. Nick was more lenient, and Cassie always came out the bad guy. Maybe she should bargain with God. *"Make Beth fall for the math nerd in second period, bring my husband home alive, give us the mother lode of all scents, and I'll pad the pews, robe the choir, and buy Fr. Byron a lifetime supply of raspberry tarts. Promise!"*

Instead she plopped the load of flowers onto the dining room table. She saw the worry in Beth's eyes. An unexpected wave of cold dread broke against Cassie's spine. "I expect a call from him by this weekend," she said with forced calm. "Don't stop praying and he'll be home in no time."

Beth ruffled the dog's ears and permitted Gretchen to place both front paws on her shoulders. "Hear that, Gretch?" she asked the powerful creature. "Daddy needs our prayers." Obediently the Great Dane bowed her head. Beth giggled. "Good girl, good Gretchy. Mom?"

"What, honey?" Cassie said, poking her head inside the cupboard in the adjoining kitchen where the vases were kept. She extracted two suitable ones and felt suddenly sick and apprehensive.

"Do you know the Spanish word for pickle?"

"Can't say as I do."

"It's *zanahoria.*"

"Nice to hear you're putting fifth-period language to good use."

"Not really." Beth pointed to a rug in the corner of the kitchen and Gretchen obeyed. "Andre was quizzing me and that's one he knew."

"Amazing. Does he know 'back off' in Spanish?"

"Funny, Mom. You want me to invite him to lasagna so you can strike fear in his heart?"

The ruby-colored cut glass vase showed the yellow dahlias to best advantage. Cassie stepped back and leaned against the island counter to gauge the visual impact. In resignation she said, "I swear I'll pretend to be the maid, and no matter what he says, the answer is always *'No comprende, señor.'* How's that?" She went to the sink and tossed the flower trimmings into the wastebasket.

Beth folded her arms, a favorite defensive stance. "And I swear I'll pierce my lip with a fishhook if you so much as attempt Spanish with Andre. He's very cosmopolitan, you know."

"I'm sure." She caught her daughter's glare and hastened to add, "I'll hang out with the toaster. You won't even know I'm here —"

"Listening to every word, looking for ammunition you can use against him."

"A mother's prerogative." Cassie smiled. "That's my girl. Foot rub?"

It had been ages since Beth had rubbed her mother's tired feet. Cassie kicked off her sandals and watched her beautiful daughter wash her hands at the kitchen sink, muttering only a little. She marveled at the girl's clear skin, shining hair by Andre, and rich, allover glow, kept golden by San Francisco tanning beds. Strong cheekbones, full lips, and warm, healthy smile. Vibrant goat girl of the Alps. Heidi with an attitude.

"What?" Beth laughed, drying her hands on a towel beside the sink. "You look like you might want to snip me off at the knees and stick me in a vase."

Her mother nodded. "You're about two years too wise, Miss Bethany. Let's debrief each other's day; then I'm going to take a quick soak and get to bed." They sat facing one another on the dining room chairs. While Beth rubbed the ache out of Cassie's arches, Cassie gave the abridged version of the day's events, minus any talk of attempted robbery, bogus lawsuits, or impending bankruptcy.

■ ■ ■ ■

Beth tried to read between the lines. It was obvious she was receiving the censored version of all that happened. Several times her mother steered down one direction of thought only to abruptly change her mind and head off on a very different tack.

Perversely, it made Beth wonder what scent would make tonight's bath. Most of the fragrances blended at her parents' perfume plant were too much or too little of something. They'd slaved for years hoping, dreaming, putting in the long hours in search of the perfect scent. Lately they'd been really messed up, their smell experts combining and recombining oils, extracts, and blends around the clock. Her parents were hurting, irritable, jittery, and gone much of the time. Today was the first day she'd seen her mother in the garden since . . . since she couldn't remember when. The gardener had been let go, and the weeds had been celebrating ever since.

Beth got up for a minute to grab a diet cola from the fridge. She offered her mother one but she declined.

There was something else they couldn't hide. The competition, the insecurity, the constant struggle to survive in an industry that ate its young — all of it had conspired to make her an only child. No time or energy for more kids. *I probably made it in just under the wire. What I wouldn't give for a sister or brother to hang out with. It's no fun to fight the kid-parent battle alone. And if they do find the fragrance that wins the prize, I'm only going to end up fighting it for my parents' attention. Been there, done that.*

Out of the blue, the phone call. *Dad vanishes into the night. Every day since, Mom makes references to the great importance of this trip. "This trip Daddy needs our prayers." "This trip is the big payoff." And behind it? A darker truth. Find success on this trip or we go under.*

They didn't think she knew, but she knew plenty. She didn't dare wear something of Chanel's or Ralph Lauren's. Good thing they knew nothing of the tiny vial of Blaise by Bill Blass that she carried in her purse just for Andre. She always washed it off before leaving the salon. *Thankfully, Mom has stopped going with me to get my hair done.*

And yet, dutifully, her dresser drawers were stuffed with Azure products, what she privately disdained as her mom's "thirty-one flavors." She hated hurting her parents' feelings — especially her dad's — and some of the scents were nice.

She took a deep pull of the cola. On top of everything else, she had lost the expensive silk pullover they'd bought for her birthday. Probably earlier at Nutley's when she tried on the tight purple top she knew her parents would hate. *What if the next person in the dressing room stole it?* Her mother didn't want her wearing the pullover except on special occasions. *I can't risk phoning the store without Mom finding out.*

"Beth? What planet are we on?" Beth jumped and saw a bemused expression on her mother's face.

She hopped up to check the freezer for a low-cal microwave dinner for them both. Beth was pretty sure the last sentence had contained the words "can't afford." "Sorry, Mom, but I kept the receipts. If you want me to return the stuff I bought, I'll do that tomorrow."

"Oh, Beth." Hurt and defeat filled the void between them. "Just for now, until the new launch is out; then you'll never want for anything again, I promise."

Beth popped the dinner into the microwave, set the time, and returned to her seat, avoiding her mother's gaze.

"That's okay, Mom. No problem. And I'm

sorry about the call-in today. I shouldn't have fooled around with all the stress going on lately. Forgiven?"

Her mother smiled and pecked her on the cheek. "Forgiven."

Beth hesitated, then said, "You were great on TV today, Mom. You had that Barb Silverman on the ropes. I only caught the last part of the interview, but when you stuck up for Azure after she pounced on you, I was like, 'Go, Mom!' I'm glad you're giving the scent your name. Is that woman in the hospital going to be okay?"

Her mother patted her arm. "She'll be fine. We still don't have all the facts, but we will, don't you worry."

They sat in silence until the microwave dinged. Beth went to retrieve the dinners.

"And you, my dear daughter, for being such a trooper these last few crazy months, shall have one of the first vials of Cassandra ever made." Her mother stood. "Now to bed with me. I'm too tired to eat and I need to be up early, so you can give my dinner to Gretch. Finish your homework, please, and lights out by eleven. And if the phone rings, unless it's Daddy's signal, let it go to voice mail." Before Beth could frown she added, "You just spent three hours with Andre the Magnificent. I'm sure he must have other business to attend to. Tonight we make sure no reporters breach the moat around Castle Dixon, agreed?"

Beth fumed. "That's your department, Mom. I just want to have a normal boyfriend that's not under constant watch. You and I aren't going to be roommates at college, you know. I'm going to date who I'm going to date, and I'll come in when I want to come in, if I come in at all!"

"I thought you wanted to attend cosmetology school so you and Andre could have his and her salons. Sorry, that was petty. All I'm saying, Beth, is that for now and the rest of your high school career, your top priorities are good grades and well-rounded extracurricular activities. No one's ever listed their boyfriend's name on their college application."

Beth tossed her hair in annoyance but left the rest unsaid. She gave her mother a quick kiss on the cheek, grabbed her dinner, and started for the stairs to her room.

"What was that?"

At the sound of her mother's voice, she halted midstep and looked back into the dining room. Her mother was staring at the window.

"What was what?"

"That sound. Somebody outside the

house. I'm sure I heard something."

"Mom, get real. Gretch would let us know if anyone was around. You're just spooked 'cause Dad's not here. Don't get paranoid."

Her mother started to walk to the window, then hesitated. "I'm not paranoid. I can't hear it now, but I thought sure —"

"Maybe it's one of your wounded dahlias calling for backup. No more cop shows for you, young lady!"

"Very funny. I'm going to check the locks."

"Whatever." Beth bounded up the stairs two at a time. She went to her room, set the dinner on the edge of the desk to cool, turned on the bedside radio to the FM jazz station Andre listened to, and flopped on the bed, glad to be away from her mother's jitters. *Why does two years to freedom feel like an eternity?*

She waited and hoped. Her father's special code was three rings, hang up, followed immediately by a redial. Anticipating the call should help keep her mind occupied, that and a five-page paper due on the boring French Revolution for Mr. Raymond. He was still her favorite teacher, but only because he also coached tennis.

Cassie's mind raced. Beth would be fine. Just the normal mother-daughter growing pains. She returned Gretchen to her run.

Upstairs she drew a bath, tossed in two teal-colored beads of Hidden Springs, and sank beneath the suds. Not wishing to fall asleep in the tub, she ignored the massage jets for one night.

She inhaled deeply the sweet scent of buttermint.

The affable Ruggers had agreed to mount a search if Nick did not make contact within four days of their parting. The jungle doc had also promised to relay the contents of any emergency transmission to Cassie day or night, no matter the difference in time zones. It had been four days, eight hours since Ruggers had phoned to say, "The parrot has taken wing," their code for "Nick has begun the search." She told herself it was too soon to panic, that she should allow sufficient time for international communication — and miscommunication — from a primitive location.

Restless, Cassie soaked only fifteen minutes before rising from the water and toweling off. She would wash her hair in the morning. She slipped into her cotton pajamas, turned down the bedcovers, and sprinkled the bedsheets with the as yet unmarketed Block & Tackle talc. Then she pulled out the blue denim shirt he'd worn just a few hours before his departure, and buried her face in it. Nothing triggered memory like aroma, and her heightened sense of smell detected the nuances of perspiration and man-musk that were so uniquely his.

Nick Dixon enjoyed driving his Ford pickup into the forest and cutting fallen cedar for the fireplace. She loved doing his laundry immediately after he finished stacking the wood under shelter. Cassie would hold his shirt against her face and breathe deeply of hard work and tree resin. Once she'd toyed with a perfume blend called Chainsaw, for guys too busy to get out in the woods. He'd teased her and threatened to counter with a blend of motor oil and bus fumes called Inner City Exhausted, a unisex fragrance for working guys or gals feeling the strain.

She couldn't remember the last time they'd felt carefree enough to be that playful.

She snuggled deep into the sheets and wrapped both arms around his pillow. Pheromones were funny things — odors and subliminal scents that strongly influenced how humans and animals lived their lives, from finding mates to recognizing offspring.

Royce the Nose lived in fear of losing his

sense of smell and along with it the zest for life. Anosmics, it was well known, suffered a high rate of suicide.

Well, Cassie thought, *aren't I just Suzy Sunshine?* She tossed about in the king-size bed, which only emphasized Nick's absence. She got up, turned on the light, tried to read.

Why didn't she just meet Brenda's terms and be done with it? The Dixons could move to Tuscany like they'd always fantasized. They'd open a bakery, eat pasta till they popped, and marry Beth off to a dark-eyed Italian boy who would give them a bevy of chubby grandbabies. She wouldn't mind growing large in Italy, where plus-sized women were treated like royalty.

Never! Never would she sell to Brenda; never would she give that woman the satisfaction. Cassie would not be frightened off by a leech, be it worm or of the human variety. She dozed off and dreamed of a grandbaby under each arm.

A sound outside the window startled her awake.

Gretchen growled from her dog run. A warning bark. A car engine gunned. Headlights played across the blinds. A squeal of brakes sliced through the night.

A snarl. A gunshot. A dog's yelp.

Cassie jumped out of bed. Ran to the window.

Another gunshot.

She dropped to the floor. The blinds blew in, peppering her with shattered glass. A man's voice yelled. But she couldn't make out the words.

The front door crashed open. "Beth! Beth!" someone called.

A scream. A car engine gunned again, followed by a screech of tires.

Beth!

Cassie stumbled up from the floor, glass cutting her feet. *Beth!*

Footsteps pounded up the stairs. "Mom! Mom!"

Cassie ran for the door just as it burst inward.

Andre stared at her, wild-eyed, framed in the light from the hall. T-shirt smeared bloody. Diagonal gash to the forehead dripping blood. In his fist Beth's blood-soaked silk pullover.

Cassie shrieked and charged.

CHAPTER 10

Cassie flew at him, fists flying, feet kicking. He stood his ground. Granite. Immovable.

Protect Beth. Nothing else mattered. Wildly she pounded and flailed, fighting the bloody invader. She clawed at his face and was going for his eyes when someone jumped on her back and tried to pull her off.

"No, Mother, no!" Beth's sobs tore into Cassie like shrapnel. "Stop it! Andre saved us. Let go, Mother, I'm fine! But Andre's hurt, he's hurt!"

Cassie felt the fight go out of her. She released her hold, Beth let go, and both swayed on wobbly legs. The gash across Andre's forehead was deep, and now she was smeared with his blood. Pale, his face covered with blood, he pressed Beth's pullover to the wound and leaned back against the doorjamb. Beth rushed to his side and took over the compress from his shaking hand.

"I . . . I . . . ," Cassie stammered, then stopped. The gory scene knotted her stomach and made her eyes swim. Confused, she thought she might faint. "Saved us? From what?"

"The guy, there was this guy," Beth sobbed. "He . . . he had a gun. He was trying to . . . to . . . I don't know what. He shot Gretchen! Then Andre drives up. Surprises him. Tries to catch the guy. He grabs him and the guy hits him with the gun, then tries . . . tries to run him down with . . . with his car. I ran downstairs . . . heard him calling my name . . . found Andre bleeding on the front stoop. An ambulance. We need an ambulance!"

She ran to Andre, who slid down the doorjamb, staring in shock. Her voice was almost a whisper. "Andre was just trying to return my pullover, Mom."

The house and yard were brightly lit in the garishly festive revolving lights of emergency vehicles. Temporary floodlights exposed the shrubbery and made cold ghosts of the dahlias. Police and medical personnel streamed in and out of the house, while still other officers combed the property for evidence and to make certain it was secure.

Cassie and Beth stood draped in warm

blankets while the gurney with Andre was positioned for loading into the back of the ambulance. Cassie reached out a shaking hand and squeezed the hairdresser's arm. "Thank you," she said, voice cracking. "Thank you for being here, for protecting us."

A somewhat revived Andre smiled weakly. His young face and brown hair, highlighted the color of toasted meringue, were still streaked and matted with blood. "When I get cleaned up, I'd like us to start over."

Cassie patted his shoulder. "I'd like that too."

Beth said nothing but embraced the man on the stretcher and gave a little wave as he was loaded into the ambulance. Andre's curled fingers gave the barest of acknowledgements.

"I'll come see you in a couple hours," Beth called as the ambulance doors closed. "Thank you, I love you."

Beth and Cassie had already discussed riding in the ambulance. She wasn't about to let Beth out of her sight.

"You love him?" Cassie said. Beth said nothing.

The ambulance started slowly up the drive, parting the sea of investigators and onlookers with a series of otherworldly *whoop-whoops* from its siren.

Cassie closed her eyes and breathed the night air. Her heart ached with an odd mix of affection and doubt for her daughter. A sixteen-year-old girl loved clothes and pets and her parents, not men who ran salons named J. Primo. What Cassie *did* know beyond a doubt: if Andre hadn't come when he had, the morning newspapers might have been filled with sketchy details of a double homicide. As it was, she shuddered to think what the headlines would be. Not in the way she had imagined, Azure World had gone page one.

As for the media, she was grateful that at her request the police had cordoned off the journalists and TV camera trucks, along with curious neighbors, and kept them from coming onto the property. For now she had no comment.

They found Gretchen huddled in the far corner of her run, very much alive, licking an ugly graze to match the hairdresser's, only this one had been caused by the business end of a gun and had torn the surface muscle of the dog's left flank. Dr. Grayson, the pet's devoted veterinarian, arrived with his on-call assistant to fetch the patient. It took four men to gingerly lift the sedated 150-pound animal into the back of the clinic van. When it seemed as if Beth might climb in the van with the Great Dane, Dr. Grayson restrained her.

"Truly the Apollo of dogs," Dr. Grayson said, a firm arm around both Cassie and Beth. "You two need your rest. Remember, her ancestors used to hunt wild boar and stags, guard the castle, pull the work carts, and participate in battle. It would take far more than this to bring Gretchen to a halt. She's in the peak of condition and will recover quickly, with a war scar to impress her doggie friends." His kindly face clouded. "It's you two I'm worried about. Your feet are bleeding, and" — he reached out a hand and gently pinched a tiny glass fragment from Cassie's cheek — "you've taken a bit of shrapnel to the head. I really ought to examine you."

She squeezed her friend's hand. "Not to worry, Gray; it's just a sliver or two, really. I'll go in shortly and have a look. You just look after our brave Gretchen. They've scoured the property, and whoever it was is long gone. The lieutenant's done his home-work and has been asking plenty of pointed questions. He says they'll post a guard here for the first forty-eight hours anyway." She prayed Nick would be home by then but knew in her heart that if he was, it would be a miracle.

There was a commotion behind them, and they turned to see Lt. Lloyd Reynolds approach. "Found the weapon," he said. "The perp must have dropped it in the tussle with Roth."

"Roth?" Cassie said.

"Andre Roth, your daughter's boyfriend and savior."

It was the first Cassie had heard the young man's last name, and it annoyed her that it had come from a police investigator. Had Beth even mentioned it?

"Thirty-eight special, fairly common. We'll dust for prints." He glanced at the still-open clinic van. "Say, is that a Great Dane? Handsome creatures. Bighearted. Pity they eat so much and their sight is sharper than their sense of smell, or I'd have 'em in the Canine Unit."

Lt. Reynolds shouted orders, and four investigators hurried off to fulfill them. He turned back to the Dixons. "Hope you've got it in the budget to hire yourself some extra security at the office. Between this, the intruder at Azure, and all the media coverage of the leech incident, I'd be extra cautious. Too much of a coincidence that all this should come at once. Maybe take a little family vacation and leave town altogether until we get this sorted out. I know it's a bad time for you, what with the launch of this new mystery perfume and your husband out of the country and all, but these are crazy times, ma'am. Crazy times."

Cassie nodded and thanked him for his concern. He didn't know that the timing was worse than bad. She was thinking about the ridiculous notion of a vacation when a stone-cold realization numbed her insides. Office break-ins and bottled leeches were one thing; getting shot at, their home violated . . .

She needed to talk to Mark Butterfield. No, she needed to talk to Nicky. *Oh, how I need him!*

From the head of the drive came sharp words, a shouted exchange. A knot of officers jostled down the drive to where Cassie and Beth stood, someone in the middle holding them at bay. Cassie shrank back. Where was crowd control? She would not speak to reporters and was in a mood to inflict a little violence of her own.

"Back off, I'm family! Get your mitts off me, buster, or don't blame me for what happens next!"

That voice. Authoritative. One of a kind. Maple sugar and gravel.

"Let go or I'll sue for police brutality!

Listen, Officer Twerp, I was having tea with the Queen Mum when you were still in nappies. Back off!"

The hurricane of humanity, with its one and only nucleus, stalled in front of Cassie. The jackets with SFPD across the back parted. In front of her was the indignant face of Mags O'Connor.

"Oh, Cass," Mags said, her tone softening. When she held out her arms, Cassie melted into them and sobbed.

Mags was exquisite in an Anne Klein pantsuit with matching ribbon brooch, a vision in jewel-toned citron. Cassie detected the refined aroma of citrus freshness, light floral and spice, and a sensual woody finish. Acqua Di Parma, classic Old World essence.

The woman planted a kiss on Beth's head without letting go of Cassie. After another hug she stepped back to check them over until she was convinced they had not suffered more than minor cuts.

Cassie vouched to the three young officers standing nearby that Mags was as good as one of the family. The police escort melted away to attend to more pressing business.

"I was nuts to see my sister Cass, sweet Beth, and my darling Gretch. Had I known the place was thick with militia, I would have called first."

Beth gave her the condensed version of the evening's events. When she came to the dog's role, Mags peered into the open van and saw an apparently lifeless Gretchen. She looked stricken. "Oh dear heaven, is Gretch gone?" When the vet assured her that the dog would be just fine, Mags relaxed. "Thank goodness. That dear pooch has more sense than a dozen men in blue who think nothing of a mother and daughter standing around the driveway in their night-wear when they could be inside drinking hot tea, away from prying eyes."

Lt. Reynolds gave the okay and Mags shooed Cassie and Beth inside. They stood like small children at the kitchen sink while she scrubbed the blood from their faces and hands. She found them fresh pajamas and tucked them in on the family room couches. Mags, with her own cup of tea, kicked off her shoes, took the glide rocker, and tucked her legs beneath her.

"Before you two get some much-needed sleep while Aunt Mags keeps vigil, I want to clear up the *Times* mess."

Cassie sat up against the arm of the couch and blew the steam from her cup. "Maggie, there'll be time enough tomorrow for that."

"Not if I croak before dawn! I'm on borrowed time, you know, and I'll be slapped sideways if you're going to stand around my casket thinking, 'Here lies Mags the Tongue O'Connor. Only death could shut her trap for good!' "

"I'd be lying if I said I wasn't shocked at what was quoted. And getting blindsided with it by Barb Silverman on live television was, in its way, more disturbing than the leech announcement."

Mags grimaced. "I was horrified to see how badly I was misquoted. Shows me that if they can't get me liquored up to say something outrageous, they think they can just make it up. The actual interview was much longer than the part they printed, and the part they printed is way out of context."

The mantel clock shifted its hands and sounded a single chime to denote the hour. Beth's even breathing indicated that the night's draining occurrences had caught up with her.

"The *Times* reporter, a real earth mother type, had caught wind of your new perfume — Cassandra, honey, that's genius, I'm so proud, it was all over the news tonight, that lavish box — and she wanted to know my professional opinion of your chances. I went on at length about how innovative and tenacious you were, that you had survived far longer than the industry norm on the strength of that innovation. But, I said, the Azure World of old, the one known for its trendy, fruit-flavored scents, the one that has for years successfully serviced the harried housewife with kids and soccer and PTA, was about to pass. My exact words were, 'The Azure World that was has run its course. That housewife has rediscovered the gorgeous woman within. When the sun goes down, she goes out. The great American middle class is in a place where they deserve and can afford better. Nick and Cassandra Dixon are in a place where they can deliver what America deserves. You watch.' "

She paused, sipped her tea, and huffed into the cup. "The little twit. She, or some go-getter editor, chopped my comments to make it sound as if America had abandoned Azure World. I never meant for it to be an obituary, Cass, honest." Her friend's last words were said with such a note of sadness that Cassie got up from the couch and wrapped her arms around Mags' shoulders from behind.

"Thank you, sweetie, for sticking up for us. I'm sorry I ever doubted you." Cassie paused before reclaiming her seat on the couch, thinking about the other worries that lay heavy on her heart, especially after tonight. It was too much to keep to herself. She needed to tell Mags.

"I'm thinking of selling our principle interest, Mags. The constant struggle has worn us down. Beth and Nick need more of me than I can give with this company and its struggles on our backs. Nick has always said it's my call. He'd be happier running pack trips into the wilderness, and it makes sense to get out while our equity's still worth something. Nick's silence has to mean he didn't capture the scent." She leaned forward. "And now the aroma wars are starting to get very personal. When that bullet crashed through the window tonight, all I could think of was Beth lying wounded, her life pouring out of her. If I don't back off now and give them what they want, murder could be next."

"Who's 'they'?"

"Brenda Gelasse, for one. I wouldn't put any of this past her."

"It's an act, Cass, has to be. With her, *M* is for minx, not murder. She cultivates the iron woman image so her female customer base feels empowered. You can't dump and run when so much of you is already invested in Azure. Hang on for another year — I can help — then see how things look. At least let Nick weigh in before calling it quits."

Cassie reached over and patted her friend's veined hands. "Dear Maggie. And what if in that year the place is torched or Beth is kidnapped? I couldn't forgive myself. Nick is all about the hunt. If the big one gets away, he loses his appetite. In the long run he'd be relieved if I said it's time for a new start. Brenda has made us a discount offer, enough to get us a new start anyway. We should take it. The way things are going, this time next week our stock in Azure might not be worth the paper it's printed on."

Mags slipped out of the chair and slid down beside her friend. "Oh, Cass," she whispered. "All you've worked for, all you've achieved . . . I'm so sorry . . ."

Cassie felt dead inside. Defeat, yes, but at least they would live to start again. Fr. Byron would be glad to hear it. "I know Brenda's got to be mixed up in this somehow. She has lusted after Azure, Nicky, Royce, all of it too long not to be behind these lies and dirty tricks. Now you can add assault. I thought I could beat her, but she's out of my league. I quit."

Mags was strangely silent. Something in the increased tension of the dear old arms around her told Cassie Mags was holding on to something of her own.

She hesitated, then blurted, "I want you to come with me, Mags, please. After tonight I'm a little short of courage. I . . . I just want a witness to what is said and done. You know Brenda. Where she's concerned, there's safety in numbers. First thing Wednesday morning?"

Mags released her and slumped back into the chair. She didn't say anything at first. "I can't, Cass. I won't. Take it from Maggie, I'm a liability. She'll discount the offer still more if I'm there. I've just always had that affect on the woman. Trust me, you'll be better off."

Alarmed at the undercurrent she sensed, Cassie turned, held the glider still with both hands, and forced the older woman to look at her. "What, Mags, what's wrong? What aren't you saying?"

Mags set her mouth in a tight line. "I am saying it. I will not be humiliated by that woman. We have a nasty chemical reaction to one another. However little time I've got on this earth, I choose not to spend a minute of it with Brenda Gelasse!"

"I'm with you there." Most people reacted harshly to the woman. And Mags O'Connor had more reason than most. Brenda had spoken ill of the "grand dame" of perfume and mocked her dotage in public. Brenda saw Mags as old school, a throwback to another era when the powerful had their way whatever the cost. She once mused in print that Mags may have been born out of time, one who perhaps in another life had been of the guild of personal perfume-makers, some of whom retired to their private dispensaries to concoct beautiful fragrances or lethal poisons, depending on the need. When Cassie had urged her to sue for slander, had even put her in touch with the Dixons' attorney, nothing had come of it. Mags never followed through.

And now Cassie saw the pain her request had caused. She relented. "I can't blame you. If I thought I could phone the sale in, I would. It'll be like trying to reason with the Devil. Maybe I should get Fr. Byron to do an exorcism of the meeting site beforehand."

Mags seemed profoundly unhappy. "That's the Catholics," she said.

Cassie took the next day, Tuesday, to review her decision.

"You know your limits," Mark Butterfield told her.

"It will keep you from hopping out of the fiscal frying pan into the fires of insolvency," agreed the three members of Azure's legal counsel.

She talked to the dahlias, a rapidly recovering Gretchen, and God. The first two were exceedingly noncommittal, and God was apparently in no mood to speak from the clouds.

She decided against confiding in Beth or Fr. B. Beth was infatuated with the heroic and bloodied Andre, while the priest would take her for a stiff philosophical run that would likely lead right back to the starting line.

Not even Nicky, without the scent, could have helped that much. She knew what he would say: "I trust you, Cass. I want you to be happy."

What she needed was the plainspoken, rational facts, and those she could list on her own. "I'm exhausted. I'm scared. I'm not having any fun. I'm letting stubbornness rule my head and my heart. The only reason I've not cut and run before now is pride and the desire to rub some very snotty fashion noses in my success. We could have been a huge success, but a huge failure is no way to finish. Selling our shares is better than nothing."

By nine that evening she stood again among the dahlias, waiting. "For what? An alien spacecraft to land and pointy headed little green men to step out and assure me

I'm doing the right thing? I know that already. But will Nick think me a coward? Surely not with Beth in danger. I have to protect her at all cost."

A heavy mist spangled the flowers and drifted past the yard lights like spray from a waterfall. Cassie felt drained. Beaten. Done. Though she was alone, she said bitterly, "You win, Brenda. I accept your offer!"

Cassie and Mark watched the floor numbers all but spin as the elegant oak and gilt express elevator soared toward the sixty-fifth floor of the Gateway Tower.

Cassie swallowed. She felt desert-dry in her spirit. *What am I doing here?*

At the fiftieth floor Mark said, "You sure you're ready for this?"

"No, but do I have a choice?"

Floor fifty-five came and went.

"William Shakespeare wrote, 'There's small choice in rotten apples.' "

"Mark, don't talk."

At floor sixty-five the elevator came to a queasy stop. "Please stay in the waiting area," Cassie told him. "I want to face this on my own. Plus my cell phone is set to ring you with one press, should I require backup."

The open floor with its breathtaking views

of San Francisco and the Bay Area was hushed with high-level efficiency. The large office to the left had a sweeping view of the Golden Gate and the ocean beyond.

"May I help you?" The long-haired receptionist squeezed the question in between phone calls on a headset.

Cassie handed over a card. "Ms. Gelasse is expecting me." The receptionist's evaluating glance said, *So this is the one.*

Cassie smoothed the pale-blue silk suit by Ann Taylor and breathed deep the Sicily parfum she wore. It was by Dolce & Gabanna and, clean and businesslike, said she was no longer obligated to wear scents by Azure.

The door to the office with the ocean view swung open, and Cassie entered.

Brenda wore a Ralph Lauren skirt and jacket, a study in understated gray and maroon. She was impossibly statuesque, like a Paris runway model. The silver pendant was Cartier, the shoes Louis Vuitton, but the shocker was the scent. One could reasonably expect a day version of Night Tremors, her signature aroma. Instead it was Chypre, created in 1917 by Francois Coty. An accord of oakmoss, labdanum, patchouli, and bergamot, it was itself one of the perfume types in the French classification. It could be difficult to find.

Of course. What better scent with which to seal the deal? Night Tremors says craving, desire, passion. Brenda is past that with Azure. Chypre says conquest, triumph, victory.

"Just to satisfy my curiosity," Gelasse said, purring the words like a well-tuned Masarati, "why the change of heart?"

To her credit, Brenda did not take a position in the room whereby she could loom over her acquisition. She sat opposite Cassie, elegant legs crossed, immaculately manicured fingers laced just above one knee, the pristine burgundy shoes clearly never having left the building.

"We've both seen the *Chronicle* this morning," Cassie said, unwilling to play cat and mouse with her host. "The night before last, my home was invaded and shots were fired, leaving my daughter's friend injured, our dog wounded, and our lives in jeopardy. On the heels of the recent break-in and the bogus lawsuits filed against us, I would say the opposition's intentions are clear. We are such an alluring acquisition that someone" — she paused to let that sink in — "is willing to go to any length to secure a purchase."

"Why not simply go into hiding, or at least

send your daughter to a safe place until the police complete their investigation and those responsible are sent away? I have contacts that could help with that. It is done all the time."

Cassie's stomach clenched. *What kind of charade is this woman playing? I know she's guilty; I just can't prove it.*

"It's no way to live. As I'm unable to negotiate a deal posthumously, I think it wise to take you up on your offer and transfer our shares on this side of the grave."

The words had their dramatic effect. Her adversary's eyes narrowed, creating disturbing shadows in their sockets. Instantly Brenda the tolerant became Brenda the deal maker. "I'm sorry for your gathering misfortunes and relieved no persons were harmed. But what of your pretty promises about 'the very breath of beauty'? Record a failure with this invisible aroma of yours, and that one brassy stunt on *Midday* likely sets the company back a million in ill will. You've placed Azure on rocky footing. What of the new scent, the one your husband went off chasing? Where is it? For that matter, where is he?"

Cassie almost reached into her suit pocket and pressed the button on her cell.

Instead she summoned every ounce of

self-control she possessed. "Rest assured Nicholas is attending to business matters. Granted, for you my signature scent is at this moment a calculated risk. You will be banking on a name, premier packaging, and a carefully considered marketing plan. Worst-case scenario, a woman of your resources, with Laughton deBrieze in her corner, could fill that box with a dozen different serviceable fragrances and carve a decent niche for any one of them. At seventeen million, despite a spongy market position, we both know the Azure stock is a good buy."

Suddenly sick and weary of the whole affair, Cassie gave a defeated, dismissive wave of a hand. "I'm ready for the transfer," she said. "Are you?"

Brenda wanted Azure. She would run it into the ground and eventually sell off the formulation equipment and, once the publicity died down, put the corporate headquarters and lab facilities on the block. *Play it right, and I can easily realize three times my offer.*

But the money was secondary and mostly paid for the inconvenience of making a scandal go away. More than anything, what she relished was ransacking the creative talent at Azure. *That constipated little Blankenship will at last be mine.* And some of the formulators and marketing staff were tops in the trade. Mark Butterfield was a delicious dish in his own right, all cool jazz and clean good looks. Wouldn't he look fine on her keychain?

Nothing, though, compared with her re-acquisition of Nick Dixon. They'd had a chemistry once and she wanted it back. That he'd gone all self-righteous on her after what they'd shared galled most of all. He'd taken the lure she'd dangled then, and she was just as confident that, down and defeated, he'd rise to it again — given the right conditions.

She buzzed the front desk. "Kandace, could you ask Mr. Winetraub to please join us?" To Cassie she said, "Very well, Mrs. Dixon. I won't prolong the suspense. Though I doubt anyone else would offer you half as much for a terminal business, I'll not take advantage. Your family has suffered a sufficient scare, and you need to put the matter behind you. Seventeen million it is, which is over market value but includes the remainder of all employee contracts and the ongoing services of Mr. Dixon until one year from today."

Cassie almost rose from her chair, but

Brenda stopped her with an upraised hand. "I merely wish his professional services to aid in the transition. There is no deal without his expertise. He will of course be well remunerated for his trouble. Well remunerated." Her smile was as suggestive as it was triumphant.

A small, thin man in tweed and a toupee entered the room with a slim black briefcase. Introductions were made, and Cassie felt her stomach take a second drop. *God, what am I supposed to do? I can't risk Beth's safety, but I hate this! We came so close . . .* She wished she could have spoken to Nicky before committing to the transfer of stock and a year of his servitude, or at least scheduled a session with Fr. Byron before making so drastic a move. Everything they had worked and sacrificed for . . .

For the love of God, a mad gunman fired at the house!

She would never forgive herself if Beth were harmed in any way. Thankfully, Mags had agreed to stay at the house for now, but what could she really do against someone intent on murder? No, Nick would want her to take swift action. She had called a press conference for one thirty that afternoon. The transfer must be made public immediately so any further evil would be called off.

"Mrs. Dixon? We are ready for the transfer." The lawyer withdrew a thick sheaf of documents from the briefcase and arranged them on a small conference table in an alcove of the office next to Cassie.

Cassie read the principle terms and felt sick. She shifted uncomfortably in the chair. However early that morning Brenda had had the papers drawn up, she had included the stipulation about Azure employees and Nicholas on retainer. She had been so hatefully smug, knowing she had Cassie right where she wanted her, that she had written it in stone.

She could not look at Brenda, not at the dissolution of her dream. The woman just sat there at her immense, and immensely empty, desktop, sixty-five stories above it all, and waited. Cassie turned away, removed a gold pen from its desk holder, and to the carefully manicured lawyer said without emotion, "Where do I sign?"

The insanely cheery ring of Cassie's cell phone startled them all. For reasons she could not later recall, Cassie did look at Brenda then. There was a scowl on the carefully preserved face at the sudden interruption, but something else as well. Hesitation? Foreboding?

Fear.

Cassie had debated whether or not to leave her ringer on but felt better knowing Mark could call in should anything threatening happen beyond the office door. Calculated paranoia. Gunshots in the night did that to a person.

She dropped the pen and pressed talk. "Yes, Mark?"

"I knew better than to trust that media guy." The rich, playful voice she had been longing to hear resonated in her ear. "You free for lunch?"

"Nicky!" She squeezed the phone as if it were his strong, lean hand. Her cheeks warmed at the thought.

At the name, Brenda, a woman not known to gasp, gasped. Cassie enjoyed the sound immensely.

"Don't talk, just listen," he said, as if she could get out any more words. "Baby, I am sitting here with the second most beautiful girl in the world. Oddly enough, her name is also Cassandra. And though she is the world's number one tease, I'm guessing her flirtations will only plant on you the biggest smile that has ever graced your darling face. We did it, baby. We got the prize. And I tell you, Ruggers didn't say the half of it. This sweet thing is the most unbelievable scent on Mother Earth. We're rich, baby. Rich beyond our wildest imaginings! What do you say we talk about it over an early lunch at the Black Swan, say eleven thirty?"

Cassie had daydreamed she might break into song or dance or both at this news. Instead she forced her voice to remain even. "I think that's an excellent suggestion, Mr. Dixon. Allow me to tidy up some business with Brenda Gelasse, and I'll be along directly."

"Did you say Bren—"

"That's right, dear. Won't take but a few minutes."

"I hope not, Cass. The waiters are giving me, my shorts, and my backpack strange looks. Let's just say I don't look or smell as fresh as the proverbial daisies. Much longer and they may call the vagrancy squad. I don't know what business you have with that woman, but this is our moment and I can't wait to share it with you!"

"On my way, sir. Give your, uh, companion my regards."

She started to press the off button when Nicky said, "Honey, you were magnificent on the news networks. Ruggers showed me

190

part of the segment with Barbie Silverman. The box. Your cool. That awful business with the leech. Are you okay?"

Because of the week's stress, she had refused to watch any of the news coverage. He must not have heard about the shooting, which occurred in the wee hours. That would keep for later. "Fine, now that I know you are. I'll be along. Nick?"

His breathing was music to her ears. "Yes, Cass?"

"Ginger dust."

He paused, and she knew he was savoring their secret code for *I love you and always will.* "Ginger dust," he said. "You're beautiful."

"So are you," she said and closed the phone. She turned to the two people staring at her, mouths agape, and stood to leave. "Upon further reflection, I have decided not to do the transfer. Thank you both for your consideration; my apologies for the inconvenience. Will you excuse me? I'm due in the office."

Cassie rushed from the room. The lawyer, thrown off balance by her abrupt departure, half fell into the seat newly vacated. Just before closing the office door, she noted with giddy satisfaction that the mouths of both the buyer and her legal counsel re-

191

mained fixed in the open and locked position.

CHAPTER 11

Cassandra, the very breath of beauty, was set to roll out in the California test market.

"Nicholas, I work the formulation under duress," the Nose fussed. They sat on a park bench and watched the Azure geese. "Do you wish to be known for a synthetic copy of the real McCoy, a counterfeit fragrance derived from gases and computer printouts? Where is the crushed essence of the flower?"

Nick said nothing, just smiled and listened.

Royce sat straighter, made eye contact, and had time for but brief conversation. "Historic," he repeated often. "I am overseer of an historic formulation!"

He sent one hundred blood red roses to Joy Spretnak at her desk and signed it, "Your other nose." She told a close friend who told an assistant chemist who told Royce that when the flowers arrived, she had to request the afternoon off and make an appointment with her endocrinologist.

Nick learned that SFPD ballistics matched the slug dug from the Dixon ceiling to the weapon found in the Dixon shrubbery. Within ten days the police told him they had apprehended the gunman whose finger-prints were all over the .38 special.

"He's a small-time hood wanted in a string of robberies in Nob Hill," said Lt. Reynolds on the phone. "The shooter's not talking. Won't say why he fired a shot through your bedroom window. Maybe he had the wrong house; maybe he was high on something."

Most important to Nick, Cassie took considerable comfort in the capture. And when he insisted she and Beth carry mace and that they install a home alarm system with twenty-four-hour monitoring, he met no objections.

Nor was that the end of the good news. "Block & Tackle for men made a promising debut," he reported to Cassie. "It felt like a talented opening act for the main attrac-tion. Is it me, or does the air we breathe smell a little sweeter these days?"

Cassie was right back in the thick of it. The rush of activity around the Cassandra launch allowed little thought for other matters.

At strategy sessions with senior management, she kept tabs on the latest developments.

"Presales?"

"Great to off the charts," said Mark Butterfield, checking a clipboard. "The strategic-placement team is experiencing nothing but success. We've got sample sniffs out to the movers and shakers in all the major markets. The First Lady is interested; so is Buckingham Palace."

"Status of the cruet?"

"We're racing the clock, and the design is stunning. We've got the drawing of the *celerides* that Nick made from memory."

"Concept?"

"A sweeping, pale-pink, almost gossamer glass reproduction of the seductive orchid stem. It culminates in a single crystal teardrop signifying the jewel of morning dew he recalls so clearly from the day he first laid eyes on it. We've got the Pochet luxury perfume glassworks in Paris working night and day to reproduce these works of art."

"Per-unit cost?"

"High, but more than offset by the visual presentation. You can't trap the essence of essences in anything less than a high-end vessel. It comes in just over budget for a premier scent, more than made up in the first price increase scheduled to take effect six months post-launch."

"Security?"

"Per your directive, we've instituted three round-the-clock bottling shifts under maximum secrecy and top-clearance protocols."

"Media?"

Mark Butterfield, hair tousled and tie askew, looked every inch like he'd recently enjoyed a satisfying roll in quality-grade clover. "You've been declared royalty," he said. "The Nicholas and Cassandra of fashion cosmetics! Your last-minute reprieve from certain destruction made you the media darlings. Leno's people are on the horn every couple of hours. Letterman says you owe him, and took to the streets of the Big Apple and reenacted Nick's flight from the wild boars and menacing tribesmen who threatened him with death, et cetera, et cetera. You can't buy that kind of exposure! Oprah's doing a whole show around pheromones, for which we're the sole sponsors, and plans another a year from now with a studio audience made up exclusively of moms and all their newborns who are named for you two. Apparently, there are a lot."

Cassie beamed. *Amazing what one orchid can do!* Nor were she and Nick the only ones given the star treatment. Beth, who was transferred to a private school for added safety, called home the first day to ask, "Okay if I give interviews to five reporters who want to know what it's like to be a child of destiny?" She had been asked to auto-graph everything from student backpacks to students' backs.

Cassie did one interview that landed Gret-chen on the cover of *American Canine.* She was even glad Andre hadn't missed out. The media coverage brought in so much new business, he was forced to hire a receptionist, two additional stylists, and a fashion consultant. And he was starting to grow on her. She invited him home to dinner, but it was so riddled with interrup-tions by TV producers, Azure personnel, and well-wishers that Nick finally gave Beth fifty dollars and told her to find a nice anonymous dinner for two. "We'll try again for dinner at home when the storm dies down."

Nick and Cassie supervised the test launch, she from San Francisco, he from L.A. A hundred glassine tubes of Cassandra were given away at each of several major malls, with gorgeous models in flowing pale-pink gowns strolling the concourses, spritzing at random, and having their photos taken with shoppers, their kids, and the out-of-town relatives.

"This is Mark in midtown Manhattan," said an upbeat voice on Cassie's cell. "The animated billboards are flashing Cassandra to the masses. We've got a Broadway exclusive in the *Lion King* programs and are this close to a Cassandra night, when the performers cavorting on the African savannah will daub the wrists of female audience members with scent. I can see the headlines now: 'Lions Beguile with Orchid's Wiles.' All this buzz is fantastic!"

"You're telling me," Cassie shouted above the mall chaos. "Azure stock is up another fourteen percent!"

Back in San Francisco, Mark fielded calls from Hollywood. The most sought-after director in film proposed one of the most lucrative product-placement deals ever devised: "Sole billing in my next two pictures, including a blockbuster with an ensemble cast of household names. Two of my A-list actresses offer to work for free in exchange for exclusive name association."

Mark felt the power. "I'm sorry, but Cassandra parfum has but one name and one identity. We cannot confuse the message. I'm sure you understand."

The results from the test markets were uncommonly positive. Mark heard "show-stopping!" "unparalleled!" and "fragrance revolution!" If the profusion of exclamation points wasn't proof enough, the *Chronicle* hailed its hometown darlings with a flattering profile headlined "The Scent of Success."

The tabloids were the source of even greater hyperbole. Unable to get the exclusive it sought, the *National Weekly* improvised: "Cassandra Cures Impotence and Sciatica."

Mark scorned Barb Silverman's *Midday*. The woman nonetheless camped out at the Azure corporate office, despite repeated assurances that Cassie Dixon would make good on her promise to return and shower the audience with gifts of Cassandra once the test was an unqualified success. Silverman stewed on air, and publicity begat publicity.

"Brace yourself," Nick said to Cassie with a laugh. "My dear, your Azure stock just rose another twenty-three percent yesterday and is headed for eighteen today. Can you stand another historic high?" They strolled arm-in-arm across the sloped back lawn and watched the San Francisco Bay shimmer in the distance.

"Oh, Nick, that's wonderful! I'm so happy for those few investors — especially our employees — who hung with us and kept their stock through the war years. Tell me more good news!"

"Gladly. Word of mouth is gaining speed. They're clamoring for Cassandra in some of the most remote regions on earth. Major metro preorders have gone through the roof, with Harrod's in London requesting ten thousand units in a single order. We've gotten outlandish offers for advance bottles. So many people have stormed the front office demanding product that as of this morning we are now a lockdown facility with entry by voice- and fingerprint-recognition only. Joy has been a real trooper."

He sat her on the lawn and kissed her.

"Nick, I'm so happy!"

"Me too, babe. Azure's hitting on all cylinders, with very little need to expend marketing dollars. Now it's your turn."

"Mark tells me we've been able to settle the leech case out of court, and the zinc class action suit was tossed for lack of evidence. Remember a day not so long ago when we couldn't get the trash collector to return our calls? Nowadays even our garbage smells sweet to somebody."

Nick roared. "I love you. You really know how to romance a guy."

"Credo in unum Deum, Patrem omnipotentem, et in unum Dominum, Jesum Christum (I believe in one God, the Father almighty, and in one Lord, Jesus Christ) . . ." Fr. Byron paused in the recitation of the Creed, fervently crossed himself, and picked up his cordless phone. After pressing in the number, he listened to the rings.

Cassie's cell phone went to voice mail again, and he wondered what he could say that was any different from the last two messages.

How many politicians does it take to change a lightbulb? Two. One to change it, and another one to change it back again. Or is that priests? I forget. No, he didn't feel in much of a joking mood.

He decided on a more direct approach, but not without some wit. "The dying request of a poor, old, and forgotten priest is to speak to you one last time. Fr. B's the name and sermonizing is my game. Please call." He felt no guilt over the content of the message. After all, everyone was dying, and technically every request was a dying request.

"Obfuscation," he said. "The older you get, the more obfuscatory you become." He didn't care if it wasn't a word and returned the phone to its stand.

Not that he anticipated the Dixons building an altar or sacrificing a bullock in gratitude for their remarkable turnaround.

Fr. Chris grunted. Fr. B glanced at the thermostat. With two of them in his tiny kitchen, the atmosphere suddenly felt as hot and itchy as a cleric's collar.

"But where is their loyalty?" Noncommittal though his fellow priest usually was, Fr. B needed someone to hear what he was feeling. "How much fame can one family take? Is there not just as much opportunity to stumble when you are adored as when you are reviled?"

Fr. Chris turned on *Wheel of Fortune,* their nightly viewing ritual, but said nothing.

Fr. B turned off the burner on the stove and poured the pan of boiling water over two plastic bowls of instant cinnamon-apple oatmeal. A little low-fat milk, a light sprinkle of artificial sweetener, two whole wheat rolls lightly spread, and dinner was served. The other priest accepted the orange bowl and yelled, "Spin again, you ninny!"

Fr. B returned silent thanks. After the amen, he said, "Where are the Dixons getting their spiritual nourishment? The mother of triplets, Mr. Shave Cream, even Lydia the Jewish catechist continue to make weekly Eucharist, but who has seen the Dixons anywhere but in the papers or on TV? Have you?"

Fr. Chris shook his head. "Buy a vowel! Buy a vowel!"

In front of Fr. B on the little Formica table that was both breakfast nook and desk, a large newspaper photo of the handsome couple gave the impression they were smiling at him. "Look at them radiating such joy. Accomplishment. Contentment. They look positively redeemed." He frowned. "God, they can't do this without you. At least when they were against the wall, they started to ask the right questions. What should I do?"

"Buy another vowel!" Fr. Chris said around a generous mouthful of oatmeal. "Look, Byron, even though I'm off duty, I'll give you my two cents. Trust God; trust the process. You can't force them to be rational at a time like this. You just be sure you're there when they need you. And trust me, they will need you."

Fr. Chris turned back to the oatmeal and the TV. "Solve the puzzle!" he shouted. "Solve the puzzle!"

Mags O'Connor stretched what she called her ancient limbs in preparation for beginning trapeze and kept one eye riveted to the TV monitor. An extreme animal show was reporting a bizarre incident of a palomino thoroughbred that had earlier that week practically chewed the face off its rider. Despite the warning that due to graphic content viewer discretion was advised, Mags watched the news footage of the emergency call to the ranch outside San Francisco in horrified fascination.

"Nine-one-one, what is your emergency, please?"

The actual recorded call continued with, "My wife's been attacked by her horse." The caller was breathless with panic. "She's bleeding from the head and face something awful. Send help, please!" His agonized sobs made Mags' stomach clench.

"Did the horse buck her off? Did she land headfirst?" asked the call center dispatcher with maddening calm.

"No! She — my wife — was riding in the paddock when the horse just started bucking and whinnying, all wild-eyed. It all of a sudden stopped, turned its head back . . . grabbed her arm in its teeth, yanked her to the ground. Oh hurry, please God, she's dying!" The accompanying wail of anguish made Maggie wince.

"Sir, sir, I need you to remain calm, please. An ambulance is on the way. Is the horse sick or injured?"

A gasp of exasperation and the distraught man replied, "My wife's injured, I told you! He got her on the ground and just started chewing on her face —"

"Excuse me, sir, did you say the horse bit her face —"

"Tore it, lady. Her scalp . . . hanging by a shred . . . had to shoot the beast to get it to stop. Oh, God, tell 'em get here quick!"

A loud crack from an adjoining room made Mags jump. Four more sharp cracks followed. The bullwhip workshop at the San Francisco School of Circus Arts was underway. Five more cracks and a shouted reproof from the instructor. Beginners class. Eventually they would learn that true control allowed them to crack their whips with hardly any sound. On the bench outside the room, Mags fingered a tear in her ratty dance slippers. *Maybe Cass and I should give the whips a whirl.*

"I know what you're thinking, Magsie," Cassie taunted. "I see that yearning in your eye." She was late, but lithe in blue practice tights and snug sleeveless top tied at the waist. The attire accented a figure that graced a growing number of billboards and television spots in the run-up to the national rollout of Cassandra parfum. Positively luminous since Nick came home and changed the equation of their lives, his wife sparkled with health and renewed purpose.

"See that sign?" Cassie pointed to the large letters beside the entrance to what she flippantly called "the whippery." They read, "Warning! Bullwhips can cut flesh, break bones, put out an eye, or slice off an ear. Treat them with respect!" She passed Mags and made straight for the warm-up tramp. "This is me treating them with respect," she called back.

Mags left the bench and followed. "Right. So let's haul our bottoms four stories into the air where it's safe. Have you seen that bitty bar we're supposed to swing on up there?"

It was crowded for a Thursday evening, and while they waited their turns on the trampoline, Cassie gave her friend a hug and teased, "Why the long face? Eventually you get to be caught by hunky young men in tights. Have you seen their muscles?"

All Mags saw was sixteen-year-olds in peach fuzz. "Sorry, dearie, but when you've been romanced by Mr. Lauren, everything else looks like a boy band." She shuddered. "While I was waiting for you, a TV news report came on about a woman who was . . . *mauled* by her horse. Terrible bites and lacerations. She nearly died. It was so unnatural, I can't shake it."

"How odd," Cassie said. "That's not characteristic of horses at all. I've heard of the animals throwing riders, kicking and stomping them, but not tearing at them. Must have been diseased. Talk about weird, did you hear about the cat in El Cajon?"

Mags moved up a spot. "No, what cat?"

"Just an ordinary tabby that went from a gentle chase-the-toy-mouse-around-the-house feline one minute to a raging tiger the next. The owner said it *hunted* her down, yowling and spitting like a banshee. The poor woman hunched on the floor behind the sofa while the puss clawed her clothes, her back and legs, to ribbons. The neighbor found her babbling incoherently and had to beat the cat off her. They put it to sleep. It was in yesterday's *Chronicle.*"

"Rabies," Mags said. "How else do you explain it? I worry about Gretchen, her kennel so close to the woods like that. A rabid raccoon or opossum could infect her while she sleeps!"

Cassie shook her head. "It's well fenced, but let's change the subject, shall we? How's that new project of yours coming?"

"Pretty well, for an old lady's indulgence." In truth she was staging a mini comeback of her own. While staying with the Dixons, babysitting Gretchen, and cooking some meals for the family, she had begun a quiet revolution in independent cosmetics. Choice Brand beautifiers were made of nutritious fresh fruit, vegetables, flowers, and herbs. Organic avocado butter, cocoa cream, ground almonds, lavender extract, and lemon oil were a few of the delicious ingredients that went into Choice bath bars, Choice lotions, and Choice facial balms. She rented a corner of a lab at Azure and shared a part-time Azure intern from San Francisco State. In a couple months Choice Brand products would sell in small beauty boutiques from Monterey to Beverly Hills. Internet preorders were promising.

"That's wonderful," said Cassie. "God knows there's enough success to go around these days, and Nick and I want to see your boat rise right along with ours. You believed in us and stuck by us through fat times and lean."

"And you've been there for me," Mags said. "Always."

"Faster friends do not exist!" Cassie and Mags gave each other a thumbs-up.

"And loving every minute of it," Mags said, the pure joy of a new start lending her a youthful zeal. She had dropped a few pounds since joining the Dixon household and thought her appearance quite smart in the salmon-colored Donna Rico leotard and matching nail polish she wore to the gym.

A pair of female scarf-jugglers took up their station parallel to the trampoline line. Mags watched in delight as the yellow and green fabrics danced through the air, now floating like parachutes, now descending like brilliant jellyfish. The girls were skilled, alternately snatching and launching the scarves with practiced ease. In a gym awash in testosterone and estrogen, their silent, graceful theatrics were lovely to watch.

"What's the best part? Of being in business, I mean," Cassie said.

Mags didn't hesitate. "Being back in the game. I was with Estée at the creation of Youth Dew. I remember the thrill of the GIs bringing home all those knockout scents from France. We knew we were sitting on a gold mine. We made lotion fashionable, and that fragrance became the most memorable of the fifties. It still outsells the competition for half what it cost fifty years ago. Sexiest scent ever — till Cassandra!"

Cassie smiled and smoothed her friend's hair. "Why, Mags? Why do women go gaga over a creamy dab of this and a sensuous mist of that? It's not like it holds the key to world peace."

Mags' eyes sparkled. "Don't be too sure. Perfumes were thought to appease the Egyptian gods. The wealthy ancient Greeks were buried with a bottle of their favorite scent. The Romans sanctioned druidic ceremonial perfumes, and how do you think the sacred virgins got so sacred? One shudders to think how much more tyrannical kings and kingdoms would have been down through history had it not been for the gentling properties of scent. An early French perfume of the industrial age was called Parfum de la Guillotine. I rest my case."

Cassie laughed. "Is there anything you don't know when it comes to the trade?"

"Oh, honey, I've forgotten more than today's bad boys and girls of industry were ever taught. But you're no slouch in this department. You forget, but I was in the audience at the Fashion Institute of New

York when you gave that lecture you called 'The Aroma of Christ.' From Paul the Apostle's second letter to the Corinthians, I believe it was. Nothing short of brilliant how you demonstrated the link between Paul's startling analogy and the Church's priestly use of rose garlands and censers of incense in imitation of the supposed fragrance surrounding followers of Jesus. What did Paul say? To those perishing without faith in Christ, it is the smell of death; to those who trust in Christ, it is the fragrance of life."

Maggie chuckled. "Oh yes, honey. Those heathens in Fashions 101 were more than a little curious about where you were headed with that one!"

Cassie remembered the occasion well. Fr. Byron had urged her to worship God by including him in the natural course of her work. Church on Sunday was where the worshipping and talking about God happened. The rest of the week was business, family, and a rare bit of leisure. But the strange notion of incorporating the Christian tradition into the day-to-day intrigued Cassie. Was it even possible in the high-powered world of beauty?

Fr. Byron gave her a push in that direction by delivering a sermon on 2 Corinthians 2:15. He defined *inspiration* as "to breathe in, to infuse with feeling." The Christian life is the inspired life, he said, and people ought to be able to detect a Christian's "aroma." To those the Holy Spirit was working on, the fragrance was sweet, appealing, a whiff of heaven. To those resisting the Holy Spirit, the fragrance was about as appealing as the stench of the Sumatran corpse flower. The plant, a relative of the skunk cabbage, used its putridity to attract and devour dung beetles and carrion beetles.

The more Cassie researched the topic, the more excited she became. Rose oil in the early church acted as a mild sedative and antidepressant. Entire congregations emerged from worship services with nervous tension soothed, heartbeat slowed, blood pressure lowered, and concentration increased.

The resins in incense contained alcohols called phystosterols, which, biochemically, were remarkably similar to human hormones, especially those found in the armpits, on the breath, and in the urine. It was suggested that when the wise men brought gifts of frankincense and myrrh to the Christ child, they were recognizing his humble start and willingness to stoop so low as to become human.

Who but a classroom full of tomorrow's fashion designers wanted to know that much about what went into the understanding of fine fragrance? And curious they were. The question-and-answer period following her presentation went past the allotted time, and she still received the occasional email from a student or two who were present at the lecture.

"Earth to Cassie. Up you go!" Mags motioned that it was her turn on the trampoline. The stocky male spotters offered her a hand up the steps, but Cass motioned for Mags to go in her place. Maggie gave her a curious look, shrugged, and teased the spotters. "Watch the goods, boys; they're fragile!"

Cassie stepped out of line, went to her locker, and took the cell phone from her bag. She wanted — needed — to talk with Fr. Byron, tell him how sorry she was to not have returned his calls, how sincere she was about getting back in church just as soon as the perfume was launched and things calmed down.

She saw that she had a message from Nick, and punched his number first. He picked up on the first ring.

"I do hope you're sitting down," he said.

She sank onto a nearby bench, heart quickening. "I just got off the phone with Benjamin Lynch, the vice president of the North American Fragrance Guild. He says that the Cassandra sample we sent is sensational, and this from a man whose only comment after Armstrong stepped on the moon was, 'Nice shot.' Lynch called Cassandra the must-have fragrance of the modern era! We've got to get Marketing on that sound bite.

"And now, my darling, brace yourself. Lynch says the Guild decided in emergency closed session to present us with the Grand Crystal Decanter at this year's gala! And what's more, for the first time in the Guild's sixty-year history, the Crystal Decanter Awards Gala will be moved from the Big Apple here to San Francisco! Can you believe it?"

The news was staggering. The NAFG catered to no one. It was the stuffiest, tightest, most elite club on the planet. It made and broke whomever it wanted, whenever it wanted. Never had it given Azure World so much as a nod of recognition. In fact, an insider in the industry reported that the Dixons had been sneered at by the Guild board, and the fashion column in the *Times* had referred to "reliable sources at the

Guild" openly speculating that "the blood-line of fashion" wanted a good cleansing of its gene pool, weakened as it was by "poor performers" like Azure World. That had very nearly driven Cassie to quit the business and still stung to this day.

And now they had voted to present her and Nick with the top prize — the Grand Crystal Decanter for Outstanding Achievement in the Fragrance Arts. Moving the venue for the awards ceremony was beyond stupefying. New York and Paris were the holy cities of the fashion world. Every significant blessing in that realm was bestowed in one or the other.

"I can die now," she said.

"Not before we buy you the finest 'you really like me' gown ever stitched."

"I shall never again catch my breath in this century."

They both laughed. Just when it couldn't get any better, it got better.

"My dear Nicholas," she said, looking about her at people vaulting, leaping, flying, balancing, juggling, flipping, and whipping. It was all so surreal. Was circus life, or life a circus? "I do believe I have never loved you more."

"Sweetheart, you'd better get used to it. On October twentieth, first we go to the ball, then we move into the castle."

They met at Trattoria Pallottino near Santa Croce in Tuscany. It was the eighties, Reagan was in the White House, and if the "me generation" had it, they flaunted it.

She was solo, irritated with her parents, backpacking Europe, and having a light lunch of cheese and salami. At the adjoining table, a lean and sunburned man tore into a platter of the local delicacy, stuffed rabbit. So singular was his enthusiasm that Cassie quite forgot the article she was reading and used the magazine as a vantage point from behind which to spy on the young American.

She found out later that he had early caught on to her none-too-subtle observations and for her benefit had embellished his dinner with little sighs of contentment and much licking of the fingers. Nearing the finish line, but without looking at her, he said in a loud and pleasant voice, "I can eat dessert standing on my head. Want to see?"

Her embarrassment was soothed at his table over a shared goblet of tiramisu resplendent with mascarpone cream.

"You're traveling alone?" Every swipe of his spoon at the lingering traces of cream was a scold to her reckless daring. She liked the unruliness of his dark-brown hair.

"Why do you ask?" Her sudden caution was homage to her mother's dire warnings about two-legged wolves prowling through Europe.

"Because I am prepared to be your companion and guide — strictly platonic, you understand. This is my third swing around Italy."

"What's the attraction?" She couldn't believe the transparency of the question. She even rolled her tongue around her spoon with far more emphasis than required.

"Let me show you."

They spent a glorious afternoon at the Piazza Santa Croce, drinking in Gothic architecture and historic works of art. "The basilica was begun in 1294 but not consecrated until 1443," Nick said. "Imagine a church building program taking a hundred and forty-nine years in the US!"

There was music in the way he said it — said anything — and Cassie clung to every word.

They stepped reverently over the tombstones that formed the floor the entire length of the nave. They marveled at the trussed timber ceiling and the splendid marble pulpit. But for Cassie, the greatest sight of all was the way the light from the magnificent fourteenth-century stained glass windows turned Nick's head and shoulders to gold.

Outside in the sunshine, they walked the piazza arm in arm. In the center of the great expanse, he stopped, turned, and took her hands. "I realize we only met a few hours ago when my chin was shiny with rabbit grease, but I would very much like to kiss you."

He waited, eyes sparking sunlight, blinding her with the joy of a huge smile.

"You're in luck, then, because I very much want to be kissed by you."

It wasn't hungry and excessive, like the kisses popularized by the movies, but sweetly earnest.

Pigeons cooed and strutted about their feet. Across the piazza a crowd of schoolchildren erupted in laughter. "Do you believe in traveling over the Atlantic to find love?"

She did but said, "Love?"

"Yup. Love. Amore. Life partners and all that."

"That's quite a long way from platonic."

"Only about three hours in the company of the most fascinating woman I've ever met."

"You don't get out much, then."

"Guess how glad I am I got out this time?"

Cassie never knew the human heart was capable of that many beats per minute. Try as she might, she could not hear the howling of a single wolf.

He was the perfect friend and gentleman the remaining six days. He stayed at separate hostels, called for her each day at the agreed hour, and bought her a little silver sugar basin etched with two swans, necks entwined.

On the day they parted for home, she to San Francisco, he to Manhattan, he gave her a code word for their rapidly blossoming love. "*Dolceforte* says it all. It's Italian for 'sweet-strong.' It has an earthy intensity that speaks of the many passions of the Tuscan life — sensual, traditional, robust, and powerful. Ours is a sweet-strong love without end."

They wrote, they called, they waited for her to finish her master's degree in business administration at San Francisco State University, and for him to complete the fashion marketing track at New York's Fashion Institute of Technology. He surprised her on graduate hooding day at SFSU with a ring and a double portion of the huge smile he had first unleashed in

Tuscany.

"Marry me," he said after carrying her, gown and all, to a stone bench where they could have their privacy. "Birth my babies."

"On one condition." She loved the laughter in his eyes. "I want a dim sum reception in Chinatown."

"On two conditions." He blew on her neck, giving her the shivers she liked from him. "One, some of the dim sum has rabbit meat filling. Two, our wedding cake is tiramisu."

"Done!"

Then they kissed, a hungry, excessive kiss, just like in the movies.

When Maggie walked up to her, Cassie was lying flat on the bench, daydreaming like a teenager in love.

"What gives?" Mags demanded, out of breath and shiny with perspiration from her time on the tramp. "I look around for my trapeze partner, and you're back here staring at the ceiling, looking as if you've had a visitation from Elvis."

Cassie sat up, straightened her legs, and stretched until fingers touched toes. "Magsie, girl, what did I ever do to deserve all this?"

"What? Hanging out with an old woman

in a gym pungent with smelly socks and mentholated rub?"

"Oh, Mags, what would I do without you?"

Mags gave her an affectionate squeeze. "You, my dear, are the daughter I lost long ago."

Cassie held her at arm's length, puzzled. "You've never mentioned having a daughter. What —"

"Shush." Mags held a finger to her lips and looked regretful for having spoken. "Water under the bridge. Besides, young lady, either you have news I need to hear or you just swallowed a very plump canary. Take me for ice cream; I'm feeling faint."

Cassie laughed. She wouldn't be any good on the trapeze anyway, bursting as she was with the contents of Nick's call. They could make up the session tomorrow. She threw a companionable arm around Mags and they made for the exit.

The foggy night air felt good after the heated gym. Cassie again thought of the cell phone. And Fr. Byron. And the Rocky Road ice cream sundae with double hot fudge that would celebrate the end of the best day ever!

CHAPTER 12

The phone rang. Royce checked caller ID. He knew the number.

The woman is relentless.

Not that she didn't have redeeming qualities. Her season tickets to the American Conservatory Theater were so up close and personal for the Three Tenors that it took him most of the following week to recover from the euphoria.

"Roy-ce." Whenever she drew out his name with a whispered hiss, he knew its tone was meant to entrap. "How's my favorite nose?" She said *nose* with that same hissing snake emphasis.

"Occupied."

"Ah, yes, the launch. Beauty consigned to a glass bottle. Exciting times."

"So they are. The schedule is tight, so if you will excuse me, this is not a good time."

Silence. No one used it with the skill she practiced. Nor did one hang up on season tickets to the ACT.

"Is there something I can do for you?" He thought he heard a cat yowl in the background and wondered if she had twisted its tail.

"Ye-ss." Another syllable doubled. "You can accept twice your current salary, a luxury Lexus of your choosing, and pocket those generous stock options in the deBrieze empire which you so quickly dismissed the last time I offered." Her delivery was pouty, but underlying it was a tone of pure steel.

Despite himself, Royce caught his breath. She had upped the offer. As pretty a bribe as ever uttered. But the interest passed. In its place, cold dislike.

"*Les Misérables* opens tonight," the voice continued. "Exclusive backstage passes to meet and dine with the principal actors after the show. Join me?"

Royce braced himself. "I have other plans, thank you. At any rate, this is not the time for . . . distractions, such as you propose. I am happy and have the rare opportunity to formulate a truly singular fragrance. One does not cross the street during rush hour."

The harsh laugh on the phone was a sour prophecy. For all his loyalty, it implied, he would be buried as deeply in defeat as the Dixons. "Suit yourself, little man. You are aging and your nasal qualities are already diminishing. What then? Are you really prepared to live out your days puttering in the garden? Combing fading memory for the way things used to smell? I'm your ticket to the fragrance patriarchy. The offer expires in twenty-four hours."

"The offer can expire in twenty-four seconds. My answer is no."

He half-expected a string of expletives but none came. Only silence followed by another feline yowl and a click.

He almost wished she had given him a verbal blistering.

The small office near the laboratory felt suddenly claustrophobic. He leaned back in the chair and rubbed the bridge of his nose. He would have enjoyed *Les Misérables* — except for the company he would have had to keep.

He believed he was as proud of his composition as Handel had been of *Messiah.* It was the culminating beauty that he had invested a lifetime in capturing. Most "noses" died never having orchestrated a landmark scent. He was about to be listed with the true greats of fragrance, men like Jacques Guerlain, Ernest Beaux, and Jean-Louis Sieuzac. He would have to brush up on his French.

For all his professional carping about the "fakery" that had entered the perfume industry, Royce had had to adapt with the times. Synthetic substitutes became necessary when the natural essences were too difficult to obtain due to civil upheaval, climatic challenges, natural disasters, and environmental restrictions. Even without the embellishments now titillating TV talk shows coast to coast, Nicholas' harrowing story of escape proved just how serendipitous it was that anything close to the aroma of the *celerides* would ever reach the masses.

Royce had isolated the 26 central odor molecules from the 257 molecules contained in the *celerides* fragrance. While the degree of selectivity would lose some of the subtleties that made the distinctive smell, only the most developed nose would detect the difference. And it was an established fact that once the umbilicus attaching a flower to its parent plant was cut, the flower's fragrance immediately began to fade. Some of the classic fragrances of all time were actually lesser cousins of the full-strength flora from which they had sprung.

It was really the headspace technology that allowed the flower's essence to be captured and restored in the laboratory. If not an identical twin, Cassandra came achingly close to the orchid original. Once the Nose had established the molecular identity of the orchid from the gas-trapped aroma contained in the bell jar, he recombined that identity with subtle tones of violet and lily, a touch of orange zest, and a small flair of fresh, woody aromatics redolent of rain forest and stream.

Ironically, violet and lily were among a handful of popular florals known as "the perfumer's despair" for the difficulty of extracting their perfume by the old, pre-headspace methods.

He was especially proud of the underlying hints, the contribution of his genius and experience, which brought "finish" to the scent. He could detect a whiff of pebble, a whisper of snow water, the heat of bird feathers. All those slight insinuations were now an integral part of Cassandra, the worker bees that served to "lift" the fragrance and give it "memory."

He was grateful that the choice of instruments in the symphony of scent had risen by two thousand additional smells since he first entered his specialty as an apprentice in the House of Chanel. That meant an enormous range of combinations, many of which had yet to be written.

And those which allowed him to finish the

Cassandra symphony were now consigned to his brain and the company safe. No two lab specialists had access to the same piece of the formula. To avoid the risk of being abducted and held for ransom, the Dixons did not want to know the whole story and were quick to say that in media interviews.

Royce was the one person most vulnerable to kidnapping. He knew with calm certainty that were he snatched, they would never pry the secret formulation out of him. The Dixons had attempted to place him under guard at a secret location, which he refused in no uncertain terms.

He had reluctantly agreed to their request that the written formula be included in his will. In the event of his death or disappearance, the Dixons — and after them, their daughter — were the sole beneficiaries.

Others took precautions as they saw fit. For added security, all Cassandra production employees were searched upon entering and leaving the facility. All Azure employees security-cleared for formulation and packaging were required to wear specialized "gas masks" to prevent them from sniffing the fragrance and selling a professional analysis to the highest bidder.

Once or twice in his tenure at Azure, Blankenship had thought about going on the market as a free agent or starting over with a perfumery of his own. The Dixons had seen to it that he was heavily bonded against that sort of thing. But he saw how hard they worked, how much sweat equity they had in the company, and he felt a certain loyalty. The three times he had requested a higher salary and benefits package, they had granted it, no questions asked. He knew his last request, as strained as recent Azure finances were, had been difficult for them. Yet they met his terms and surprised him with a week's cruise to the Mexican Riviera for faithful service. *You don't walk out on people like that.*

Certainly not for the likes of Brenda Gelasse. The woman was shameless. The bribery served only to cement his dislike. He didn't appreciate her killer instincts or the vulgar way she hawked Night Tremors. The scent itself was adequate, though overstated at several levels.

In contrast, his darling Cassandra was destined to become a world classic in the tradition of the most popular and most sustained fragrances of all time, such as Arpege and Tresor. So distinct was its character and meaning. Its elemental appeal had shocked him with pleasure when first he breathed it in. He inhaled three seconds, sealed the fragrance for fifteen seconds, then inhaled three seconds more. And smiled.

He only hoped that if he ever required oxygen, it would be saturated with Cassandra.

"Best to close down for the evening, don't you agree?" Joy Spretnak looked into Royce's sparse office before heading out to her car. The devoted perfumer glanced up from a sheaf of calculations, covering them with one hand from habit.

Joy secretly hoped he would ask her to coffee. If only she were a mite less plump, a tad less middle-aged by, say, five years, he would rise to the bait.

"Ah, yes, Miss Spretnak, it is becoming quite late. What has kept you here this long?" It wasn't like him to make idle chatter. She wished he'd call her Joy but took his words as encouragement.

"Some spreadsheets needed doing. They've been piling up, what with the flood of incoming calls these days." She paused and swallowed. "The roses you sent, they're lovely. Thank you."

He fumbled around, not making eye contact. She patted her hair into place. He straightened an already straight tie, the dark-blue striped one, her favorite. She wished the conversation had gotten off to a more scintillating start.

"Keep them three days, not more," he said. "They've quite lost their robustness after that."

She nodded, unsure where to go from there. His was a response quite lacking in robustness. "I guess the principle bottling will go full bore beginning tomorrow," she said, aware she wasn't telling him anything he didn't already know. Did she dare call him Royce?

"So I understand." He reached a pencil into the electric sharpener before aligning it with two others already sharp-tipped and arranged parallel to the gray desk blotter.

The silence between them became more pronounced once the sharpener's whirring ceased.

They spoke simultaneously.

"I — ," she began.

"Would — ," he began.

They stopped and both drew deep breaths.

"Should — ," she said.

"There's — ," he said.

They stopped. The sound of a forklift moving palettes could be heard through the door into the warehouse. The cruets had arrived from Paris and were being positioned for the bottling machines. The public launch was just a week away.

"I hear each cruet is an exact replica of a glassblown original." She hoped this might be news of which he was less aware.

"Yes, so I understand."

Her disillusionment was temporary. He said, "Would you care to see one?"

Joy felt a trill of delight and nodded. In all the clamor and energy of the past few weeks, the Dixons had found little time to address the troops. A receptionist had to make her own discoveries.

He pulled open a top drawer of the desk and removed an object wrapped in soft white cloth. He removed the cloth with deliberate care and held out an exquisitely thin half moon of milky glass the hue of blush-pink champagne. It was perhaps five inches tall and a half inch in circumference. The silky stem rested on a pedestal fashioned to mimic the soft serrated petals of a single orchid. A clear crystal droplet at the tip of the glass curve flashed spires of light from the desk lamp. A tiny stopper of the same milky pink glass allowed access to the cruet's contents.

Breathtaking.

"Oh, Royce!" Joy gasped, forgetting herself. "It's magnificent."

He sniffed. "A spectacular receptacle for a

spectacular aroma. Fitting."

He started to say something more, stopped, gave her a quick glance, then stared at the wall as if deep in thought. He held the cruet reverently, as he might the Holy Grail.

"Ah, yes, fitting." She hesitated to say more. The conversation, if it could be called that, was experiencing more starts and stops than Bay Area transit. "Well, good night, then. You should head home soon. We'll all need plenty of stamina as the gala draws near."

"I should think." He appeared disoriented, turned toward her, and in the process brushed a pencil onto the floor.

To her astonishment, he left the pencil where it came to rest beneath the desk. "Joy, uh, Miss Spret— I mean, Miss Joy . . . I apologize. I'm not good at this. There's a late diner open on Geary."

"Yes, the Pinecrest," she said, helping where she could. "I'm familiar with it. They do a juicy half-pound charbroiled burger." She felt her cheeks go pink. "I haven't eaten since breakfast. You?"

He gave a fleeting smile. "Half an English muffin, unbuttered" — he checked his watch — "some twelve hours ago. That and your excellent hot springwater during the day, always so prompt, always so . . . hot. How long have I been the beneficiary of your kindness in that regard?"

Joy willed herself to remain steady. "Oh my, since before Eve first broke a nail." He seemed confused. "A favorite saying of my mother's," she hastened to add. "You know, Eve, of Adam and Eve." He looked perplexed. "It's just a colorful way of saying I've enjoyed working with you for some time."

He seemed to get it and relaxed. The fleeting smile sallied forth once more. "The Pinecrest it is, although I'm limited to a garden salad, no dressing. You won't be put off by my nose plugs, will you? Restaurant smells can scramble the vomeronasal receptors. Let's take my car. After, I will bring you back to yours."

"Splendid," Joy said, awed at what for the Nose had practically been a speech. "The raccoons will be annoyed, but they can wait."

His eyebrows arched. "Raccoons?"

"My house backs up to a ravine, and a family of coons come greet me when they see the headlights in the drive. Cutest things but very demanding. I keep a bag of doggie treats in the car, and they line up, biggest to littlest, to wait for a handout. Extortion, really, but a small price to let a little woods into one's life."

He studied her a moment, then said, "If anyone could talk to the animals, you could." She took it as a compliment and felt strangely warmed by the idea.

He retrieved a coat from the rack next to the photocopy machine, and she glanced down to verify that the pencil still lay beneath the desk. It did.

He returned to the desk and rewrapped the cruet in its soft cloth swatch. "For you," he said, extending the gift. "Totally at odds with company policy, and under present circumstances probably illegal. Still, if anyone at Azure deserves the first flask, it is you."

She hung back, not trusting she had heard correctly. This was a monumental overture. Nor did she know if, under present circumstances, she should accept.

"I know what a curiosity people say that I am." The skin of the high forehead puckered, and it was almost as if she could read the pain there. "Eccentric. Acerbic. Prickly. None of that, however true, prevented your kindness toward me. Ever."

Joy Spretnak knew then she would take a primed land mine from this man should he offer it. She smiled and reached for the gift, her fingers brushing the backs of his, where sparse tufts of hair marked the distance between knuckles.

The forehead smoothed, the pain ran back inside, and he seemed almost youthful, as if relieved of a burden. "All I ask," he said, an odd huskiness to the words, "is that you not open the cruet until after you arrive home this evening, nor wear the scent to work until after the launch next weekend, when the Dixons are honored at the fragrance gala. Come tomorrow, I will see the enchantment in your countenance and know that the two of you" — his eyes shifted to the gift now held in both their hands — "have met."

If it wasn't poetry, she thought it came quite close.

The parking lot held all the charm of a cemetery at midnight, barren of most cars but not their apparitions. A soupy mist cloaked the asphalt beneath eerie halos cast by faux gas lamps. What lent a hint of ornate historical authenticity by day, by mist-shrouded night cast a sinister glow.

Were she in her right mind, Joy knew, she would have done the sensible thing and called for security to escort them from the building to Royce's vehicle. Instead she was alone with the Nose, walking arm in arm with him and inhaling the pure fairy dust of his attentions. With her other hand she stroked the cloth wrapping of the first official bottle of Cassandra, illicitly tucked inside a coat pocket. This was one dream from which she hoped never to awaken.

They descended the employee entrance stairs and started a slow stroll across the blacktop to where Royce's '92 Chrysler LeBaron was parked next to Joy's '98 Chevy Cavalier.

Joy tightened her grip on the perfumer's arm. "Lovely night for an abduction," she said, giggling. Thinking he might tense and lecture her against joking about such matters, she was surprised when he did not answer but drew her closer and slowed the pace.

She felt reckless. "Why, Mr. Blankenship, I do believe you did that on purpose. How did you get to be so fascinating?"

He stopped as a foghorn sounded in the distance. Their breath made little wreaths of condensation about their heads. He glanced to the side, at the modest Chrysler with its dents and its patchy paintwork. Still he said nothing.

"What's wrong?" she said, afraid of some transgression.

"Wrong?" he said, imbuing the word with heightened emotion. "Nothing has ever been more right. No one has ever found me fascinating. Oh, the gossip columnists imply as much, but the fascination they speak of is akin to the curiosity generated by a carnival freak show. I am the Elephant Man of fragrance; you are my Madge Kendal, star of the British stage."

To her astonishment, he bowed low, then swept an arm toward the Chrysler. "Your chariot, Lady Kendal. The doors stick but it has heat and intermittent defrost. I have never understood America's love affair with the automobile, but this one, I assure you, knows its way to the Pinecrest Diner."

He could have had the pick of any car at any dealership in the country, she knew, and yet the fussy man's clunker charmed her.

"Then it is a very useful motorcar at that," she said, faking a British accent. "And you, kind sir, are fascinating *and* gallant!" *And playful,* she thought. *My stars!*

A distant car backfired and they both jumped. The Nose attempted to recover his dignity and did the most unexpected thing of the young evening. He laughed. It was a pleasant, satisfying chuckle that trailed off on a merry note at the higher end of the scale.

"Everything okay there, folks?" called a voice out of the shadows, followed by the stark beam of a flashlight.

"Fine indeed, Marcus," the Nose called back. "With you and your colleagues on patrol, we haven't a worry."

"Kind of you," the security guard replied, "but you can't be too careful after hours. You and Ms. Spretnak have yourselves a safe evening."

"That we will, Marcus. That we will."

The fog piled higher, making their faces indistinct in the spare lamplight.

They arrived at the driver's side door of the Chrysler, but there he stopped again. "In order for m'lady to gain entry to said chariot, the driver must first gain entry and unlock m'lady's door, which the key no longer agrees to open from the outside." He was babbling. She smiled.

He slid the key into the driver's side lock, jiggled it from side to side, and was rewarded with a promising click. "You must not think we are home free," he cautioned. "Now comes the coaxing." He pulled up the door handle with both hands, threw his back into it, and yanked backward, each tug accompanied by what could only be described as a grunt — a fastidious "hunth," but a grunt nonetheless. Joy was delighted and strangely comforted that the particular Mr. Blankenship was not above grunting.

After a third thirty-second bout of jiggling, yanking, and grunting in combination, Joy laid a light hand on the man's arm. Blankenship ceased all activity, his intense, determined gaze diverted by the feminine hand.

Joy took hold of the door handle. "I have experience with all manner of things that stick, including but not limited to toilets, kitchen drawers, venetian blinds, and jar lids. Allow me?"

He stood close behind, undoubtedly prepared to jump back into the fray should she find herself in trouble.

She yanked. The door flew open, catching Royce square in the nose. He sat down hard on the pavement with an audible plop, cupped his nose in both hands, and slumped forward with a moan.

Joy crouched beside him, staring in horror. She had clobbered the great Nose right smack in his million-dollar instrument. "Oh, Royce, I'm so sorry! What can I do? Is it broken? Can I see? Let me help, please!"

His answer was muffled but sounded like, "Pine Uhn Uhn."

"Forget the diner," she cried. "You need help. Marcus! Marcus, are you still out there?" She was certain she had shattered her friend's chief sensory receptor and forever ended his career, just as he was entering prime time.

She heard the sound of shoes thudding on pavement. "Ms. Spretnak, I can't see you! Where are you?"

She stood. "Here, here next to the Chrysler. Hurry!"

Another moan, another "Pine Uhn Uhn!"

She knelt and pulled his head to her bosom. "My poor Royce! What are you saying?"

He lowered his hands, and she shrieked at the sight of blood seeping from the most sensitive nose on the planet.

"Nine, one, one," he managed weakly. "Nine, one, one!"

She hardly sensed Marcus beside her or heard the radio squawk and the urgent relay of vital information. Joy reached into her pocket, pulled the cloth from around the flask of Cassandra, wadded it into a compress, and applied it to Royce's nose.

Joy spent the next seven minutes holding Royce close, gently rocking him; then the fire department and the paramedics filled the parking lot, sirens screaming, lights ablaze, and night turned to day.

The Chevy Cavalier almost drove itself home in the predawn hour. A steady rain began to fall. Behind the wheel, a weary, frazzled Joy Spretnak turned the wipers on and fought back the tears that threatened any minute to spill over. Again.

How could she have endangered someone so valuable to the company? In a *Parade* magazine interview, Royce had likened a perfumer to a great musical composer passionately combining notes to make a rhapsody. So highly developed were Royce's olfactory senses, he could analyze a mixture containing a hundred or more scents and precisely tell how much of each had been used to strike fragrance harmony.

How could she have so thoroughly botched the most beautiful and promising night of her life?

The scene played again and again in her mind. Medics stuffing the famous nose with cotton wadding. Mr. Blankenship shouting angry protests, demanding to be seen by his personal physician, a nasopharynx specialist, *before* they did a thing. She trying to convince the skeptical men in white that he did require extra delicate care and that just as they would not twist the neck of a person with a spinal cord injury, they should not violate the nostrils of an injured perfumer. Royce being loaded onto a gurney, protesting all the way inside the ambulance and raging still as the doors closed. She rousing the Dixon household, their dubious acceptance of her story, them agreeing to meet the ambulance at the hospital.

Her decision not to go to Mercy General was not that difficult to make. The magic of the night had vanished in a very mashed nose, and when she tried to hold Royce's hand, he had pulled away. The Dixons seemed distant and angry and were probably wondering what she was doing at the office so late. They must think she planned the whole thing or at least schemed to get him alone for whatever nefarious reasons.

No one would ever credit the Nose with initiating an intimate stroll across the parking lot. Probably not even the Nose himself, once he came to his senses.

It was a horrible, embarrassing mess, one everyone could have done without in the last days before the launch. That thought was quickly followed by another even more depressing. Every newshound worth his salt monitored emergency calls on a police scanner. *Barbie Silverman is probably at Mercy*

The one spot of comfort in the midst of disaster were the raccoons, whose eyes burned brightly in the headlights as she headed slowly up the drive of the dark house. She stopped the car short of the carport, tripping the motion sensor and flooding the cement pad with light. There was the burly dad, the dainty mom, and the three coon kids — she'd named them Mr. Sam, Miss Sue, Sister Sal, and the twins Sid and Sadie. She had no idea if she had the gender right on the young ones, but felt the names fit their personalities to a T.

They faithfully waddled into position by the woodpile at the rear of the carport and waited for her to gather her things, scolding her with growls and chatter for staying out so late. Their beautiful ringed markings, clever expressions, and busy hands never ceased to earn her pleasure. She supposed she shouldn't encourage their freeloading ways, but a bag of doggie goodies every now and then was a small price to pay for their company.

She pulled her keys from the ignition and dropped them into her coat pocket, feeling the flask of Cassandra through the fabric. Sitting there in the car, she thought, *Why not?* The Nose had said to wait until she arrived home and to just not wear it to work.

She snapped on the overhead light and took out the bottle. Joy caught her breath again at the exquisite workmanship that had gone into the cruet. The pink stem felt cool and creamy-smooth in her hand, the tiny teardrop practically aglow with an inner fire. It was an instant collector's item that, once emptied, would be next to impossible to throw away.

A thirst to know seized her. She hurriedly removed the cap, and instantly the car filled with the most sensuous and provocative aroma she had ever breathed. It rose and wafted about her face, caressing and drifting along the nasal passages. It bore the perfection of a succulent ripe peach on an idle summer's day, the intense sweet innocence of warm baby skin, the passionate crescendo of orchid blooms, the insistent musk of young lovers flush with desire.

It brought to her cheeks a flaming heat she hadn't experienced since she was a novice stenographer fresh out of school. She at once felt more alive than she had in years, and she felt an irrational sense of indiscretion that was not altogether unpleasant.

Cassandra was a phenomenon.

Joy's heartbeat quickened, and she felt a mad urge to rush from the car and dance with the animals. She dabbed scent on her wrists and behind her ears before she replaced the stopper, returned the bottle to her pocket, and grabbed a handful of crunchy treats from the bag she kept on the passenger seat.

The receptionist stepped from the car, closing the door behind her. "Okay, kids," she called to her masked friends. "Come and —"

The hiker adjusted the headlamp and stopped. *There it is again. Dogs or something snarling. Somebody's yelling! Dog attack?*

He hurried on in the dark, following the suburban trail that dissected the south slope of Pigeon Creek Ravine. He glanced up at the lights that illuminated the carport attached to the old frame two-story bordering the ravine. It was isolated from the next closest house by a field and a stand of alders.

Shadows in the carport, one large and hunched over. Other smaller, rounder shadows leapt against the large shadow, some falling back, others hanging on, attached to the bulk of a growing silhouette.

A scream. The hopeless, keening cry of the badly wounded.

Heart racing, the hiker extracted a hatchet from the pack on his back.

The trail bypassed the house. He angled up the slope, fought the brush, chopped at the tangle of Oregon grape.

Another scream. Choking. *A woman.* He willed his legs to run, fell, slid, stabbed at the hillside with the hatchet. On the night breeze, the smell of blood and perfume and animal stink.

He panted, gasped, lunged up the slope. At the crest he staggered back. A woman, curled into a bloodied ball, lay on the floor of the carport, covered in snarling raccoons. She cried and whimpered, lurched to her feet, grabbed for the door of a car at the carport's entrance.

With little strength she slapped at the furred fury, bare arms dangling shreds of blouse, flesh raked raw. Bright blood ran in rivulets down white limbs. Her hair was matted with it. The three largest raccoons assaulted her, the two smaller ravished a shredded, red-stained coat on the ground.

He waded into the melee, boots kicking, hatchet and pack swinging. The coons yelped and slashed at him with savage teeth, flying at him from every direction. He stood straddling the woman, dropped the pack, and swung the hatchet backhanded. Two solid blows cracked skulls. The coons yowled and fell away. The hiker dropped the hatchet and wrenched open the back door of the car. He grabbed the woman around the middle with his other hand and arm. With a grunt he threw her facedown onto the car seat.

His back was turned for only a second. Heavy bodies hurled against his legs. Claws and teeth tore the pant legs. Hot needles stabbed his calf muscles. He swore. The raccoons twisted and shook.

Searing pain. With a roar he reared back and slammed the door shut.

The bull raccoon bit him in the thigh and held on. Its eyes stared, vacant as a shark's. Its growls were as frenzied as a rottweiler's.

He clubbed it away with his fist, tried not to focus on the streams of blood turning his pants dark.

His hand closed on a garden hoe leaning against the rear entrance to the house. He used it first as a battering ram, then as a scythe. The blade sliced through the air and connected with flesh. A slashing blow left one coon still, and the others shrank back.

The hiker threw the hoe like a javelin, yanked open the driver's side door of the car, jumped in, and slammed the door behind him. Heavy bodies crashed against the doors and windows. Gnashing teeth clicked against the glass and left smears of pink saliva. After a minute they abandoned the car and fell on the coat and purse lying nearby.

Against the muffled sounds of frenzied fighting and tearing, the hiker heard the woman's moans. A bloodied hand fumbled in a pocket and produced a cell phone. He fought to steady the shaking that made punching numbers difficult.

"Nine-one-one. What is your emergency?"

"Animal attack! Berserk raccoons! A woman here nearly comatose and bleeding profusely — you've got to hurry!" He thought he would wait to mention the intense smell of perfume permeating the inside of the car and filling the inside of his head with the strangest longings . . .

The authorities arrived and managed to shoot and kill two more raccoons before the rest of them disappeared into the ravine.

"Call in the tracking dogs to get those others," Lt. Lloyd Reynolds of SFPD ordered his men. "I want these dead ones autopsied. Put a rush on it!"

He watched the EMTs treat the deepest lacerations before gently bundling an incoherent middle-aged woman and the Good Samaritan who saved her into an ambulance for the ride to Mercy General.

"If that don't beat all," he told the assistant investigator. "She came close to bleeding out, and I'll bet she has acute shock trauma. It's a toss-up whether she came closer to dying of her wounds or sheer fright. That hiker deserves a medal and maybe some skin grafts. But can you believe that smell?"

"Lieutenant? Stuff got scattered, but there's ID in the purse, including a security badge for Azure World. It's got her photo, a Joy Spretnak. We found this in the pocket of the woman's coat." The rubber-gloved officer held out broken shards of a perfume bottle. The alluring aroma that saturated the car, the carport, and the surrounding area had come from that bottle. "You ever know of any other life-and-death struggle that smelled so good?"

"Unbelievable." The lieutenant felt odd. Unsettled yet somehow stirred. "There's something else. Notice how deathly still everything is around the scene? The attack is the work of wild animals, yet there are no animals, wild or otherwise, around now. Isn't this part of the city's green belt usually teeming with critters? Where have they gone, and who — or what — called the evacuation?"

He was met with a shrug, but he noted

that the eyes of his men shifted nervously around the scene. They all felt the eerie silence, yet there was a provocative presence of something inexplicable.

And what in the Sam Hill is the connection between the shooting at the Dixon place a few weeks back and this weird business? Azure World was the common denominator, making headlines for a rare new scent about to debut, and he would bet his retirement that the busted perfume bottle in that coat had held a sample of it. In his experience, there were few if any real coincidences. Certainly none the size of this whopper. *Connect those dots, Lloyd baby, and you could make Detective of the Year.*

"Interview the neighbors. I want to know everything they saw or heard or know about this lady. I'll talk to the people at Azure. Ben, I want you to go to the hospital, and as soon as that Spretnak woman finds her marbles, I want you to learn every move she made this evening . . ."

A bright-eyed, clean-shaven detective in what appeared to be a new leather coat emerged from the house. "Lieutenant, we listened to the answering machine. Not much on it. One message from a dry cleaner's about two pantsuits and a skirt left over thirty days. Another just past midnight from someone identifying himself as Rice or maybe Ross, can't be sure. Sounds like he was pinching his nose shut when he talked. Funny message. Wanted her to know that right up until he took the edge of the car door in the face, he had been having one wonderful time, and could she please come visit. He has the most amazing news. Ends the message with the precise visiting hours and detailed instructions on how to find his room at Mercy General. I may not be his idea of a dream visit, but I'm pretty good around sick people. I'll check it out."

"You do that. I'll have a chat with the good folks at Azure World." And the lieutenant would practice his delivery for the next squad room debrief, when he would tell his colleagues he'd been assigned a case that really stank.

CHAPTER 13

The phone on the other end of the line rang four times before switching to voice mail.

"Cassandra, Fr. Byron here. Your delightful face is everywhere. The news from the market test has even the priests at St. John's yammering. Speculation at Eucharist is almost unholy, the way everyone is buzzing about 'the very breath of beauty.' Lydia thinks it will help her catch a man, as she puts it, but the very thought caused such a severe case of the church giggles that she had to be excused from Communion and catechism both. *Kyrie eleison!* We need to talk about this explosion in your life. Call me."

Talk? Who talked to their priest anymore? Therapists, hairdressers, bartenders, pets — that's who took confession these days. Fr. Byron fumed. Divine forgiveness was no longer sought, because judgment was never passed. Guilt was as outdated as a derby hat.

"Cassie, Fr. B again. So, you can grant interviews to everyone and their poodle, but you can't check in with your pastor? How many perfumers does it take to — never mind. *Crede Deo.* Trust God. How's Beth? Bye."

Marginalize the church. Render it irrelevant. Like letter writing, who anymore engaged in soul searching?

He banged out the number a third time and chewed another two Tums.

"Hello and thank you for calling. The Dixons are unavailable except through Azure World. Please contact 1-555-555-1313, extension 65, and we will see that your call is returned by an Azure World representative. Should this be an emergency, please wait for the beep, then press zero for the operator."

Fr. Byron's bellyache intensified. He did not wish to go through an intermediary, so for a moment he toyed with the thought of being an emergency. *No, I will not play games.* He opted to leave yet another message in the hope they would screen the ones left at their home number despite the recorded brush-off.

"Cass? *Spes tutissima coelis.* The safest

hope is in heaven."

Cassie almost called Fr. B twice. But between tracking the results of the market test, doing interviews and photo shoots, overseeing the design and execution of new print and electronic media ad buys while Mark attended to the bedridden, and combing the most exclusive shops for the perfect gown for the coronation, she barely had time to eat.

"It's ludicrous!" Cassie complained to Nick at a rare late-night ice cream binge on a couch in the family room. Between them was a quart of sugar-free Chocolate Chunk Madness. "It's all you and Mark can do to hold back the mounting tide of licensing proposals before Cassandra's official roll-out."

"What none of the pitchmen understand is that Cassandra is no common fragrance. It's Old World luxury in a fast-food nation. America is just going to have to realize that Cassandra is one of a kind and treat it as the rare find that it is."

Nick carved out a round lump of Madness and fed it to Cassie.

Cassie rolled the creamy cold over her tongue and swallowed. "The tag price should send one of the loudest signals: $225 per ounce. The 1.7 fluid ounce cruet will retail for $382.50. That should help supply keep pace with demand."

Nick stared at the ingredients on the ice cream label. "How do they make this sugar-free? It's delicious!" Nonetheless, he waved away the next spoonful Cassie served up. "Can't. Gotta stay focused. Our early indicators are that Cassandra eau de parfum is intoxicating beyond earlier estimates. The Queen of England has ordered a cruet for every female employed or in residence at Buckingham Palace. The Miss Universe Pageant ordered one for every contestant. One of the wealthiest women on the planet requested — and was denied — enough Cassandra to fill her private bathing spa."

"Whoa, whoa! If that's the wealthiest woman I think you mean, she's worth more than some countries. How about we at least fill her birdbath?"

Nick laughed. "Don't worry. We'll keep her number handy. Remember, we are sponsoring her next network giveaway show, but it will take a while to get inventory up, so for now we can't overextend."

Cassie hugged him just as he was aiming for her mouth. She took a chocolate smear from chin to ear. Dabbing it away with a napkin, Nick said, "Did you ever think we'd be concerned about overextending anything but our credit?"

Cassie grinned, gloriously happy. "Twenty years, darling! We let the Liz Claibornes and Paul Sebastians hire outside fragrance formulators, but we kept control. We beat them, Nick; we beat them at their own game!"

He turned serious. "And now we need to once and for all put Brenda behind us. Can we?"

"I want to."

"Then let's do it. Out of spite, she has tried to embarrass us and get you to doubt me. But she's just the smallest of footnotes now. The Nicky and Brenda stories will no longer circulate. I've talked with a couple of journalists I know, and their media want to curry favor with us, and if it means squelching the rumors, they are only too happy to ignore her. Brenda is passé. I'm telling you, Cass, we suddenly have a great deal of currency in this town and beyond." He studied her. "I know a fresh Brenda story. Want to hear it?"

She wished they could talk about something or someone — anyone — else. But he was so pleased with himself, she couldn't bear to tell him no. "Sure, let's hear it."

"Well, you know how she rarely meets

suppliers outside the office. There aren't many who have what she wants, and seldom does anything they present make it into her polished glass-and-chrome showcases. So what does she do? She forces them to take the elevator to the sixty-fifth floor of the Gateway Tower so she can ignore them in style."

He paused. "Go on," Cassie said. "You're dying to tell."

"So the other day she's standing at her floor-to-ceiling windows watching the international shipping lane and probably thinking about the good stuff from Ceylon and Sri Lanka, when this diamond importer from Antwerp who hand mixes his own cologne and hopes to gain a deBrieze endorsement comes in and throws his fine scent around and does everything within his power to impress. But the longer he hangs around, the more her indifference reduces him to a stammering fool. She shows him the door, tells him his aromas are too European, but says she will buy a five-thousand-dollar diamond collar for her cat! Mr. Antwerp flees the six hundred fifty feet to the street.

"Because everything he planned has been turned upside down, he rushes across the street to the Pearl Diver Lounge, owned, naturally, by Brenda, and gets into a private high-stakes card game. He loses badly — his business, in fact — until all he has left is Brenda's check for the cat collar. Based on his personal line of credit, he bets the farm, using the check and her good name as collateral, and wins it all. He promptly goes back to the Gateway and leases the entire ground floor for his first diamond outlet — and perfume boutique — in America. Not only did Brenda not get rid of him, he's now one of the building's most influential tenants, and every time she enters or exits, his success without her help stares her in the face. Isn't that rich?"

Cassie smiled. "I might do a little shopping of my own at Mr. Antwerp's diamond emporium. I've settled on my dress for the gala. It's a pale-pink satin evening gown by Luisa Beccaria. Mags' style consultants urged something sophisticated yet understated. 'It should become your frame, not your fortress, dear.' " She exaggerated her voice to sound pompous. " 'You're looking for elegant, not pretentious, something that envelops, not imprisons. Avoid either showy embellishments or the torn butterfly look. Keep the sexuality on a short leash. If in doubt, edit, edit, edit.' "

Nick hooted. Cassie went on. "The Beccaria, they said, is a beguiling statement of fairy tale come true. All I know is that it makes me feel more beautiful, more desirable, than I've felt in a very long time. I can't wait for you to see me in it!"

"If it makes you happy, sweetheart, that's what matters." The love in his eyes completed her joy.

"Oh, Mags, the launch is coming at us like a stampeding bull," Cassie said, hanging up the phone in the kitchen. Mags sat at the dining room table surrounded by press clippings. Cassie had been perusing them with her, but her heart wasn't in it. The strain was becoming too much. She had borrowed Beth's Miata to run errands and to make a series of meetings at the office. She and Beth had agreed to rendezvous at the mall. But Beth had not showed and could not be reached.

"A step at a time, dear girl," said Mags, admiring a full-page photo spread in the *Chicago Tribune.* "You are surrounded with competent people. Stop worrying and delegate. Delegation is what saved this girlish figure." She got up and strutted to the kitchen, hands on saucy hips.

"Thank goodness you and Gretchen are a pair, and thank you for looking after this place. If you didn't live here these days, who would?"

"You and that fine man of yours just make sure you finish each day back here," Mags said with a wag of an index finger.

"Sorry we've had to forego trapeze for a while. We'll get back up there, I promise." The phone rang and Cassie snatched it to her ear. "Beth? Oh, Beth, thank goodness. I've been frantic! Where are you?"

"Mom, I've been waiting this whole time at the Art Galleria in Westfield Centre, like we agreed."

Cassie gulped. "Westfield? I was in Union Square at the Funky Easel. Oh, honey, I'm sorry. Did you have your cell with you?"

Beth was slow to answer. "I loaned it to Andre. Now, before you freak out, he's negotiating for another shop, Mom, and didn't want those calls coming into J. Primo's. You know how his employees gossip."

"And the man can buy another shop but can't afford a cell of his own? We bought you that phone for the express purpose of being able to contact each other anytime. What on earth were you thinking?"

"What were *you* thinking, Mom?" Cassie could hear the tears in her daughter's voice. "I told you I worked out a package price with the manager of the Galleria. We haven't bought anything at the Funky Easel since you got me those bathtub paints when I was, like, five."

Cassie wanted to say, "You weren't *like* five; you *were* five" but held her tongue. She remembered like it was yesterday: Beth smearing her eyelids red, her face bright green, her chest and arms navy blue, and her tummy yellow, then grinning for the camera. "Okay, all right, I'm sorry. We'll talk more about this when you get home. Right now I have an important meeting at Azure. We'll have to try again on the weekend. Can I send a cab for you?"

"No, Mom, I have cheer practice back at school. You were supposed to drop me there." The growing frustration in her voice stabbed Cassie to the quick. "Can't Daddy come get me?"

"Daddy's with Mark doing color corrections on the Cassandra typography. It's critical we get it right." She could have slapped herself. Weren't Beth's needs critical?

"Then I'll just have Andre pick me up again. You go to your meeting and I'll grab a burger somewhere. Don't worry about it. Andre's used to it."

That hurt. Cassie shot a glance at Mags, who was basting a chicken. Her friend nodded. "I can put the oven on timer and go pick her up."

"Hear that, honey? Maggie will come down and get you."

"No, Mom, that's fine. Andre's closer and Mags is making dinner. Not all of us forget what's supposed to happen."

Cassie let the dig go. "Did he get the fan belt replaced on his car? That thing whines like a wounded animal, and it's bound to snap any day now."

"It's fine, Mother! I'm fine, Andre's car is fine, this whole messed-up day is fine. I've got to get off now; the store manager wants the phone back."

For some reason Cassie didn't want to let Beth go. "Right, sweetie. I'm really sorry for wrecking our plans. You and me, we okay?"

"Yeah, okay. Bye."

Cassie hung up the phone and leaned both hands on the counter. *Children, the only beings capable of filling your heart one second and dropping it from the freeway overpass the next.*

"Everything good?" Mags slapped the chicken before covering it in tinfoil.

"Just fabulous. You don't need to get Beth after all. Andre comes through again."

She watched the two people on the screen

in her living room — happy, healthy, flowing, she gorgeous, he handsome — and wondered again who they were. The woman looked like her, the man like Nick. They were called Nicholas and Cassandra and were CEOs of a company named Azure World. Strangely, though, they were different in a way she could not name.

And she was afraid.

"You two look scrumptious." Mags was sitting on the opposite end of the couch, wearing her TV glasses.

"The preliminary response has been beyond belief," Nick told the entertainment reporter at the Metrofashion Show that afternoon at the Disney Concert Hall in L.A. Behind them, people cheered and pressed in close to share the camera frame with the instantly famous. "We are pleased to bring to the world a fragrance so beguiling, it defies explanation. Who can explain how it captures the senses, the chemical reaction it sets in motion?"

Cassie rubbed her temples. He had followed the agreed script perfectly, touting the mythical, enlarging on the perfume's mystique with every word. If the glittering perfumers were sore pressed to explain, who were mere mortals to resist its allure? They didn't need to understand. They were only asked to buy.

"Women were created in similar fashion," the prerecorded Cassie said, further embroidering the legend.

Mags clapped and cheered. "Honey, you're on message!"

Cassie shushed her and looked back to the TV images.

"Sensual. Captivating. We're a beautiful force of our own. It is an honor to put woman and scent together. Cassandra reveals the enchantress in every female!" Nick was all teeth, and she smiled at him with just the right mix of warm and tart.

The crowd roared and the Dixons waved.

On the couch, Cassie bit her lip. "I hope we're not setting people up for shattered dreams, Mags."

"Of course you are, but that's how the game is played. You're responsible to make the best perfume you can, not for the irresponsible ways people behave under the influence of that fragrance. Perfume cannot make people kind and caring, but it can mask their brutishness. Some of civilization's most loathsome overseers have been among its best-smelling."

Cassie's head throbbed.

Mags switched the TV off and regarded her appraisingly. "I thought you put that worry to rest long ago, kid. God gave Cassandra to you and to Nick and to Beth. It's your namesake and your future. Now you live it up and don't think twice about it."

Cassie squeezed Maggie's hand and went in search of the ibuprofen.

Later that evening, the Dixons went to the hospital to visit Royce. They left the parking garage and had not yet reached the automatic doors leading to the inpatient surgery wing when Cassie's cell phone rang. She snapped open the phone and motioned for Nick to stop.

"Cass? Mark here. I've some bad news. Joy Spretnak is in intensive care at Mercy General." Mark explained the horrible attack at Joy's home.

"Joy's been badly injured," Cassie told Nick.

"What?" Nick said, his expression alarmed. "What hap—"

Cassie held up her hand. To Mark she said, "Do they know what would cause that kind of freak behavior? Were the raccoons rabid?"

Nick's eyes showed questioning concern. "Wild animal attack," Cassie said to him as he pushed the elevator button. "Her condition is guarded. Yes, Mark?"

"I was just saying that I will do everything to keep this out of the media. You put Royce's accident together with Joy's, and you've got a press circus. The last thing you need is something weird to distract people from the focus on Cassandra. I've got Joy's station covered with a temp. Also ordered a giant get-well floral arrangement from the management team, and a separate planter from you and Nick. Begonias, one of her favorites. You let me know the status on Royce. Don't mean to sound callous, but all things considered, the sick will keep while the well need all the help and concentration they can get."

"Bless you."

Mark hung up, and Cassie filled Nick in on the details as they passed through the entrance doors and hurried toward the elevators. "What's with the animals in this state? It's like some crazy virus in the air or something."

"Good question. It's creepy what's going on. Poor Joy, such a sweet lady. She's the voice of Azure corporate."

Cassie felt again the stab of apprehension she experienced when watching their performance on TV. "Let's do all we can for her. She's as much a part of our team and the launch as anyone." She watched the floor indicator change from P to L to 2. The car slowed to a halt. They stepped out and headed for Room 207. In its own way, Royce's accident was even more serious. How could he ensure quality control over production with a nose covered in gauze and adhesive tape? What was it Mark said? *"The last thing you need is something weird . . ."* She prayed Royce's sense of smell had not been compromised.

Cassie was shocked to see The Nose sitting cross-legged on the bed, smiling despite the bandaged bulb stuck to his face, and swiftly writing on a clipboard, his gown exposing two knobby knees. She stared at him. Was that a happy sparkle in his black-and-blue eyes? His greeting was positively debonair.

"Nicholas! Cassandra! So good of you to come. I have capital news. Sit. Sit!"

They sat. "My specialist feared the worst, but no sooner had he started rooting about in my nasopharynx than he discovered the most remarkable thing. Will you hazard a guess what in the world he found?"

Before either of the Dixons could answer, Royce said, "Of course you can't guess. Let me enlighten you!"

Cassie was stunned. The Nose, crippled

though his God-sent nasal organ appeared to be, was actually *enjoying* himself. And he sounded as if he were able to breathe just fine.

He gave a gleeful clap. "The good doctor shone a light up my left nozzle, and what did he see but a polyp the size of a pea! For some time I have feared — without wanting to worry you — that I was losing some of my powers of smell, when in fact a benign blockage had the audacity to park in my beak. The odor molecules were beginning to back up against this fleshy dam; many were prevented from entering at all. A single clear nostril is all but useless to me, as you know. One requires stereo olfactory for accuracy. Thankfully, I have such prodigious receptors, it did not prevent me from birthing my darling Cassandra! But a polyp up there is an affront to my profession.

"Glad to say, the devil is now removed and on display in the drawer in my tray table should you wish to view it. Best news? I can again breathe fully free and am able to identify seventy-seven distinct smells thus far in this room alone." He rapped the clipboard with the pen. "I can name them if you like."

Nick said swiftly, "This is such great news, although I'm troubled we weren't informed of the time of your surgery."

Royce waved a dismissive hand. "Tut. Butterfield took care of it; that's what you pay
him for. He saw me into surgery and was
here when I emerged. Forty minutes, in and
out. But I am most anxious for word of Miss
Spretnak."

He appeared momentarily nonplussed by
the emotion with which he had spoken her
name, then quickly recovered. "I mean that
I can imagine she feels awful about the accident, and I want to allay her fears. She's
not returned my call."

A Dr. Fleming was paged over the hall
intercom. A pill cart collided with an IV
stand just outside the door, and while loud
apologies were exchanged, Cassie gave her
husband a meaningful look. Nick cleared
his throat. "Well, Royce, about Joy. I'm
sorry to say that after she left you that night,
she was herself injured."

Cassie thought Blankenship was going to
fly off the bed and beat Nick with his
clipboard. "What! How? It was that
wretched car of hers, wasn't it? I didn't
think it was safe. H – how bad is it?"

Cassie laid a hand on his arm. "She will
recover, I know she will. It wasn't a car accident. She was bitten by some raccoons at
her property. They scratched her up pretty

269

badly." She deliberately avoided the worst of it.

Royce looked faint. "She is the best thing that's —" He seemed to recognize where the sentence was headed, thought better of it, forced himself calm, and started again. "Don't you see? She did me a favor. I was so intent on the launch that I don't know when I would have made time for a checkup. As you know, I'm not fond of them probing my nose."

Indeed he was not. Cassie was willing to bet it had taken at least two burly orderlies and one husky nurse to hold the Nose still enough to capture the polyp. The mental picture made her wince.

Royce seemed so sad. "I left messages on her home phone and at the office to call here, in order that I might alleviate her concern myself." He paused. "May I see her? I know I can help her recover." He appeared flustered at how that might sound. "I hasten to add that I have requested to be released in the morning and will soon be at my station. No one signs off on Cassandra for delivery without my approval."

Cassie nudged Nick, who sent her a warning with his eyes. She understood. Royce was in love, and his Joy was two floors up in the same hospital, unconscious and unresponsive. Cassie sighed. "We'll check on her and let you know when she can have visitors."

"Good," Royce said, sagging only a little. "I want to show her my list of smells and compare them with hers." He was disconcerted. "Her room's, I mean."

Nick tried to hide a grin. Cassie blushed and was grateful when food service swept in with a fish sandwich, Jell-O with cottage cheese, and a sharply dressed young man right behind in suit and overcoat.

"Royce Blankenship?" He shook hands with the patient. "I'm Detective Ryan Philips of the San Francisco Police Department. Sorry to trouble you as you're visiting and all, but I do need to ask a few questions about an acquaintance of yours." He glanced at the Dixons. "Perhaps you folks wouldn't mind waiting in the hall?"

Cassie did mind, but she said, "We'll be right outside the room, Royce, if you need us." Was it her imagination, or had he gotten smaller at the prospect of having to answer undoubtedly personal questions from a stranger?

CHAPTER 14

They paid a brief visit to Joy's room on the fourth floor. Cassie buried her nose in the red, yellow, and purple flowers Mark sent. They formed a sharp contrast to medicine's stark utility.

It hurt to look at the bed where Joy lay. She was barely recognizable. And what was familiar was covered in angry red welts and bandaged lacerations. The few words they spoke did not rouse her, and Cassie soon suggested they leave.

In the car, still disturbed by Joy's injuries, Cassie saw that she had another message from Fr. Byron. Though he did not identify himself, there was no mistaking his rich, patrician lilt. "Did you build an altar?"

"Now, what does that mean?" Cassie asked, holding the phone to Nick's ear so he could hear.

"Priests," said Nick, "are notoriously possessive. He probably thinks you're being stolen away and that next week he'll hear you're worshipping over at St. Whatever's in the next county."

Cassie regarded the backs of her hands in the glow of a passing streetlight. "More likely, it's that we haven't worshipped anywhere in a long time." She sighed. "It's all happening so fast."

Nick kept one hand on the wheel and gently rubbed the back of her neck with the other. She felt some of the tension subside. "Write him a fat check for the roof repair fund, and he'll lay off. He's bucking for dean of the cathedral, and the more denari he can show for himself, the more votes at ballot time. It's all percentages."

"What is?" She sounded snappish but she didn't care. Upset over Royce and Joy, the last thing Cassie needed was one of Nick's cynical commentaries about the church.

"Church governance. Priestly succession. Hail Byron, full of grace and aspirations to a higher chair. With clerics, it's all about promotion in this life to guarantee plusher surroundings in the next."

"Fr. Byron's not like that and you know it. He really cares. He worries about us. I think he's afraid we'll get run over by the glitz and glamour."

Nick whistled through his teeth. "They

can blind me with all the bright lights in Vegas, baby, and I won't complain. And the good Reverend Wills is one to talk. Look at those fancy brocade vests he wears. The cost of one of those would feed a homeless person for a month of Sundays. He can stop worrying about us. We hold tickets on the success express!"

Cassie suppressed her annoyance and smiled at the goofy face he made as he tried to tease her out of negative thinking. Lately he'd grown fond of saying, "When you've outrun screaming savages and killer bees and wild hogs, you come to appreciate an IRS audit so much more!"

He still bore the lingering bug bites and sunburn of the jungle. Wore them like badges of courage. Still, she wondered how he could not be more troubled by the recent accidents.

They stopped for a red light. "Cass, honey, why so glum?" he said, brushing her cheek, smoothing her hair. He studied her a moment, then added, as if reading her thoughts, "I'm sorry for Royce and Joy. Rotten luck. But let's don't deny ourselves. Those industry jerks who once wouldn't give us the benefit of the doubt now freshen our drinks and plump our pillows. I say let them. Nicholas and Cassandra are gonna live forever!"

She tried to share his optimism. The accidents were just that, surely. She should read nothing more into them. Instead she should count her blessings. Beth's future had been assured. And Azure had been handed a stay of execution.

The Brenda episode had come and gone, a weak moment late in the pregnancy when Cassie's body had ballooned and Nick's maturity had deflated. She remembered that awful moment when the stark truth stared them down and would have pushed them to jump from the highest bridge had it not been for her parents and Fr. Byron. And a grace greater than sin.

Brenda had not taken Nick's departure with good grace. She sought ways to embarrass him and cause Cassie to doubt. Foolish things that, though never signed, bore the unmistakable mark of Brenda's wrath. A napkin with lipstick stains arriving through the mail. An exotic dancer showing up unexpectedly at the unveiling of Trapeze for Men. A quarter-page display ad appearing in the *Chronicle,* congratulating Nick on both his fortieth birthday and his lithe physique.

Nick had been reluctant to bring Fr. Byron in, but Cassie needed the priest's firm guidance and his healing humor.

"How many priests does it take to change a lightbulb?" he asked at their first counseling session.

Nick fumed but Cassie played the game. "I don't know, Fr. B, how many does it take to change a lightbulb?"

"Change?" The priest was incredulous. "Blasphemy!"

Cassie felt it was a good start to facing change in their marriage. They settled the issue and emerged stronger than before. She had married Nick forever, including "in sickness and in health." The Brenda affair had been a brief sickness, and that was the end of it. Nick adored Cassie, as she did him.

The rest of their lives blurred: the struggle to build and keep the business; Beth's metamorphosis into a teenager; the inevitable drifting apart of two lovers who, now defined by their profession, neglected that which first drew them together. Then along came Cassandra, the impossible dream. How strong was this elixir?

Stronger, she prayed, than their ability to blow it. She was not so smug as to think a marriage didn't take constant work and refreshing. First on her agenda after the launch was to arrange a Jamaican cruise for the family. And church. It was certain they needed to get back into the habit.

"Maybe we will," she conceded to Nick. "Live forever, I mean." They neared the steep climb to their home off Portolo Drive. Despite the expense, he had insisted they live in the Twin Peaks area with its spectacular views. Now, at last, they could afford to burn the mortgage. Build a mansion. Nick's extravagance had been a self-fulfilling prophecy.

"At least the Dixons will survive long enough to snatch the Grand Crystal Decanter from the paws of the jackals of doubt and put it on display in its rightful place," she said. "Nothing too ostentatious, you understand. Maybe on a nice little bed of crushed blue velvet that just happens to revolve in a glass-enclosed case atop a stainless steel obelisk studded with jewels and lit by a beam of purest light that never goes out."

"Very modest, my dear," said Nick with a straight face. "And the tricky Dixons should survive long enough for Mrs. D to rub Barbie Silverman's face right in her sanctimonious cue cards."

He saw her stiffen and said, "Sorry, babe. Poor choice of words." He pulled her close and gave the required reassurances. "We're fine. No more bad news for us. It's been more than six weeks since the intruder. I say we hire a night watchman and tell the SFPD we no longer need them to be on alert."

Cassie said nothing but snuggled up against him. After a few moments' silence he said, "Hmm. 'Jackals of doubt.' I like that. Mind if I use it in my acceptance speech?"

She managed a smile and kissed his cheek. "Now, now. Must we stoop to their level?"

They were almost to the driveway when Cassie punched a number on her cell phone. Nick arched his eyebrows and said in a low, seductive voice, "What's this? Alerting Beth to call off the ferocious Great Dane so you and I might save ourselves for activities of a more, how shall I say, intimate nature?"

She gave his arm a playful slap. "How shall I say, it's no in any language, buster!"

Nick grinned. "And just when are we going to perform our own personal field test on this scent of yours?"

Cassie batted her eyes. "Don't you worry, eager one. But know that I'll not take Cassandra out for a test drive until the night of the gala. It's too personal, and I want a day that we'll remember forever. Play your cards right, mister, and I might use a double dose.

Right now, however" — she put his hand back on the steering wheel — "I'm returning the call I should have answered long ago. Aren't you dying to know exactly what that message from our dear priest meant?"

In an unused storeroom in a dim corner of the basement at San Francisco City Hall, cleaning crew shift manager Patricia George adjusted the volume on the Walkman until the earphones poured forth with a more balanced Vivaldi's *Four Seasons,* Concerto no. 1.

Satisfied, she moved some wooden crates aside in the ongoing search for old library records kept in an antique desk filled with pigeonholes and drawers said to have secret compartments. At least that was the sudden recollection of old lady Brampton, a librarian so ancient that she was checking out books at the time of the Frisco Quake.

Some city councilwoman had got it in her craw to track down the old rolltop she claimed was stored at city hall, one of its drawers containing a shopping list for printing supplies rumored to have been compiled by Ben Franklin hisself. Supposedly, the cabinet, in the cylinder or tambour style, had been Po' Richard's and worth a mint at auction. How it got out to the West Coast was anybody's guess.

Patty liked the forgotten storeroom under the beautifully restored hall of immense size and classical architecture. Stacks of canvas-covered whatnot lined the walls, hidden and unremembered. The room held a certain dangerous charm. Joe DiMaggio and Marilyn Monroe had gotten married in elegance upstairs, but an assassin had been in this room. Came in right through that window over there and bypassed building security. Slipped upstairs and murdered the mayor and one of the municipal supervisors. Patty had been two days on the job.

Twenty-seven years later she was management, free to roam the building at will. Patty had volunteered to search for the phantom desk. No gussified councilwoman was about to muck about in a den of dust and infamy when she had a veteran custodian on the city payroll.

Patty was in no hurry. Years ago she might have lit herself a cigarette and turned it into a proper break, but now with smoke detectors, heat sensors, fire codes, and what all, she didn't dare. And so she role-played.

She was an African Scarlett O'Hara in yards of blue silk and Irish lace. From the pocket of her jeans she fished up the tiny glass vial of that new fragrance she'd scored at the mall south of Oakland when she'd gone to visit her cousin Carmen. A test, they said, only a test.

While Vivaldi played and she danced the tarantella, she dabbed the contents of the vial on her wrists and behind her ears for the first time. Immediately a smell sweetly blissful and beguiling took possession of the room, becoming air rather than replacing it. Gone was the odor of dank, musty abandonment. In its place was an enticement to passion more intense than any she had ever felt.

The room tilted and a light-headedness forced her to sit. She felt the heat rise, tore the headphones away, and fumbled open the collar buttons of her denim shirt. What in the world?

She prayed. Mama said when the world spins out of kilter, you pray. The faster it spins, the harder you pray. The tangle of feelings pricking her now sure enough qualified. Had they all escaped from that little bitty glass vial?

Why hadn't she seen it before? There, amid the discards of another era, hulked a separate item wrapped in canvas. Right shape, approximate size. She'd bet her mother's pension it was a rolltop. Without hesitation the shift manager forced her way to the back of the crowded space, unmindful of those pieces that blocked the path. Table legs protested, chair backs collided, a coat tree fell over.

She stopped. She thought she'd heard something else, something higher pitched than the scrapings and bangings of solidly made wooden furniture. She turned the Walkman off to silence the music.

Nothing but the distant hum of heating and ventilation. And the sound of her own breathing.

There. She waited. *What is that? Nothing. I'm so fuzzed from the perfume, I'm hearing things. Must use less.*

She forced herself to continue. The moist wall and damp floor beneath the object warranted a maintenance request. She made a mental note. Queer how all she could smell, though, was a sweet cloud of orchids.

Grabbing the near edge of the cloth covering the object, she gave it a yank.

The cloth slid off easily. Patty gaped. Despite dim lighting, the flowing lines of the venerable rolltop revealed themselves in soft amber contours, small ornate drawers, and a serpentine lid of horizontal laths connected by lengths of stiff fabric.

Two knobs of wood snugged into the base of the tambour. Patty grasped them firmly with her fingers and pulled upward. Finely made, the roll glided along the slides as if in daily use.

A single rat leapt at her, followed by a thick pelting of rat bodies. They struck her in the face and hands. Entangled in her hair. Bit her flesh. She stumbled, fell backward over a low table, and cracked her skull against a tall bookcase. Stunned, she screamed, flailed with her fists, beat back the tough, sinewy forms and needle-sharp teeth that raked and made her bleed.

Her dying thoughts were of how loud rats were, their attack on her ears wild with rage, and how unlike diseased things they smelled.

They — in fact, everything in the dusty old room — were sweet with flowers.

On his side, Koki the killer whale swam slow, lazy circles in the show pool at San Diego's Sea Spectacular. The three-ton teenager was close to breeding age and full of restless energy.

Bri Lasworth, Koki's leggy trainer, trotted onto the concrete apron in snazzy blue, skintight wetsuit, flush from a stolen afternoon with her fiancé. She knew she would cut it close for the four o'clock performance, but it had been worth it. Brad adored her new scent, the sensational test sample of

283

Cassandra they were giving away at the mall. It was the most intoxicating thing either of them had ever experienced.

Sea Spectacular regulations discouraged entering the performance pool wearing strong perfumes or deodorants. Whales were sensitive mammals with a heightened sense of olfactory awareness. But there was an allure about Cassandra that made it difficult to shake. Crazy as it sounded, it was like it insisted on remaining.

If anything, the scent was stronger now, and she concluded it was heat-activated. And there were subtle changes with the passage of time: one moment the fragrance was ripe and insistent, an hour later shy and flirtatious. She was almost out and could not wait to return the survey sheet and receive another vial for her trouble. Hers was going to be a rave review. Within an hour of first applying Cassandra, she had placed a preorder with a one-hundred-dollar deposit.

"Huh, Koki boy, that's a love." Typically she'd arrive early at the pool and spend some warm-up time with the whale. But because of her tardiness, it was five minutes to showtime and the stands were nearly full.

Three thousand visitors waited to be entertained. The arena buzzed with conversation and shouts of excitement.

She slid into the water and Koki sidled up for a scratch. Bri ran her hands over the smoothness of the whale's hide. She knew how much he enjoyed the human contact.

Koki blew a geyser of water out his blowhole. A little girl squealed. "The whale snorted!" Her happy family and those nearby laughed. Koki was one of the smartest orcas Bri had ever encountered in five years with the show.

She gave an arm signal and some herring to the whale, and he went "gulling." He dove down, slowed his momentum, and spit the herring high into the air to simulate jumping fish. Timing was everything and Koki's was spot-on. A passing seagull screeched and flew at the silvery prey. The bird caught the fish and Koki caught the bird. It disappeared inside the great mouth to a chorus of surprised aahs.

Before the commotion got too big, another wave of the arm and Koki spit the bird into the air. The soggy gull flopped twice on the surface of the pool before making an erratic escape into the air. Out of deference to animal rights groups, gulling was a stunt the management officially discouraged. But it was a guaranteed crowd pleaser, and Bri was in a spunky mood.

She felt a hard bump. "Hey, Koke, not so rough. Be a love, be a love!" She signaled the other two trainers to wave their whales into the opening formation. Nothing turned on the crowd like a bevy of behemoths doing synchronized leaps.

The announcer launched into the welcome spiel, cued the music, and the crowd hushed. Those in the front rows, including a den of Cub Scouts, adjusted their rain gear in squirming anticipation.

Bri climbed onto Koki's back and gripped his body with her knees and elbows for the deep dive.

On the upward thrust, trainer and whale burst from the pool high into the air, in perfect alignment with the two other whales and their trainers.

Without warning she felt Koki twist left, throwing her off balance and off his back.

She landed hard, the impact with the water driving the wind from her lungs. To her horror, a giant shadow blocked the sun. Hastily Bri dove under the instant before Koki's body slammed down with an enormous splash.

Pushed deep by the force of the whale's descent, Bri panicked. She had not had time to fill her lungs with sufficient air before the massive body fell. With astonishing speed

Koki vanished from sight, and she realized a trainer's worst fear. She had seen the same signs in younger, untrained whales. For whatever reason, her whale had gone rogue.

He wants to kill me!

Koki came about, gaining speed for another attack.

Bri choked on water, broke the surface, sputtered, gasped for breath. She half-heard someone yell, then a cacophony of screams.

Again the immense shadow blocked the sun, but Bri was quicker this time. She was well underwater, with a good lungful of air, when the whale crashed down.

Bri surfaced. Out of the corner of an eye she saw the other trainers run along the concrete apron, shout, blow their whistles, kneel to slap the water and divert the killer whale's attention. Koki circled for a third time, his adolescent hormones swollen with aggression.

She was tired but mustered all her strength and swam in the direction of the advancing whale. He would not anticipate her so soon. So while he was still in the water, she would leap onto his back, then dismount off the opposite side onto the safety of the splash ramp before he had a chance to breech again.

It never happened. Bri felt a searing pain.

Her thigh was on fire. The whale had her in his teeth. The next instant, the sky rushed toward her, followed by the sick sensation of falling backward into emptiness.

She called Brad's name before all went black.

CHAPTER 15

"How goes the aerial training?" asked Fr. Byron as Cassie showed him into the living room. He had been waiting at the end of the driveway when she and Mags arrived home. "I assured your security patrol that the clerical collar is not a disguise. It helps that I recognized one of the officers and reminded him that his second son had received infant baptism from one Fr. Byron G. Wills. But tell me, have you been caught yet — you know, on the trapeze?"

"Are you kidding, Father?" Cassie said. "I'm working up the nerve to try a simple knee-hang from a moving swing. Have you any idea how much courage is required to dangle from that skinny little bar, lift your knees up between your arms, hook your legs over the swing, let go with your hands, arch your back, and look to the catcher?"

Fr. Byron grinned and gratefully accepted a cup of coffee from Mags. "I hear male flyers are warned never to flirt with the catcher's wife."

They laughed and Mags said, "I'd like to get Pierre Cardin on a swing. We could live for a week off the change in that man's pockets."

More laughter and Cassie began to relax. After the initial irritation at being ambushed by her clergyman, she realized she had brought it upon herself. Never ignore the family cleric, especially one as persistent as Fr. B.

After further small talk, Mags broached the weird string of California animal attacks making the news.

"What's happening, Father? Is it the tides? Global warming? El Niño?" Mags was serious. "It gives me the willies."

Cassie motioned the priest to sit. She knew that her friend had been uneasy ever since the report of the deranged horse. Every day seemed to bring an ever more disturbing rash of incidents involving whales, rats — and this morning there was a story out of Yosemite National Park about a *pack* of bears storming Muir Campground and critically mauling a soccer mom from Modesto in front of her two small children.

Joy lay in a coma still. For half of every day, Royce Blankenship did not leave her bedside. For the other half, he worked late into the night, refusing to exit the office until too fatigued to think.

"What have you heard, Father B?" Cassie asked. "Why would animals behave so peculiarly? And why only California animals mostly in San Francisco and L.A.?"

Fr. Byron stared into the steam from the coffee cup in his hand. He swallowed without first taking a drink. "It certainly is a disturbing phenomenon, I agree. That poor woman killed by rats in the basement of city hall was a sister to my parishioner Yolanda Bates. Yolanda, bless her soul, remains inconsolable. I pray to God these things cease, but as to their origin?" He shook his head slowly. "Even the experts are at a loss. They can't always connect the victims and their attackers. They've pretty much ruled out rabies and other viral causes. None of the quarantined animals have tested positive for disease. I'm stumped."

Cassie shuddered. "It's like an episode of *The Twilight Zone*."

The three sat in silence.

"Sorry," Mags said at last. "I didn't mean to bring us down." She got up, went to the kitchen, and returned with a plate of molasses cookies to help brighten the proceedings.

A clatter from the garage and Nick joined the party, sitting beside his wife. He had changed into faded green running shorts and a T-shirt with the Azure World logo, a stylized globe the color of an unclouded sky, framed by an equally blue *A* and *W*. He exuded fitness and vibrancy.

"Jog with me, Fr. B?" Nick said, sitting forward on the couch as if about to spring into action. "It'd do wonders for your homily. Might even tighten your matins." He was obviously pleased with the wicked banter.

Fr. Wills did not bite but instead sipped the hot coffee. "Thank you, Nicholas, no. I'm addressing a gathering of the Recovered Alcoholic Clergy Association in two weeks. Tonight is one of the few I have to prepare, and I hear you jog till the bars close. But before you and your wife go out on that stage tomorrow night and accept your accolades, I felt it wise that we talk."

Nick jumped to his feet. "Then I'll leave you to it. Cass, I plan a double circuit tonight, so don't forget to set the security alarm if I'm not back."

Cassie nodded, wishing Nick would give Fr. B the courtesy of a hearing. It worried her that her husband was all action and little introspection. Though lately she had been no better.

The priest stood and laid a firm hand on Nick's shoulder. "There's something I need to say to you both. Please, it won't take long."

Nick sank to the couch beneath the weight of the ecclesiastical hand and Fr. B joined him. The expression on Nick's face was anything but eager. Mags took one look and scurried to the kitchen.

Cassie smiled hesitantly. "I hope you can join us at our table tomorrow night, Father B. No excuses. I've been awful at returning phone calls, and I thought this might give us a few minutes to reconnect. Besides, this is our golden hour, and I want you to be there."

Fr. Byron avoided her eyes. "I did receive the invitation. Many thanks to you both, but I lead evensong and, with Fr. Krell down with gout, it would not be a good time for me to miss. If I do the accelerated version, I can catch some of the ceremony, the best of it, on television after. Plus the entertainment news shows will be nattering about it for days."

The words were right but spoken with only halfhearted enthusiasm. "What, Father?" Cassie insisted. "What are you leaving unsaid?"

His usually expressive hands were still,

folded over a slight mound of belly beneath the brocade vest. "The collect for Saturdays is, 'O God, the source of eternal light: Shed forth thine unending day upon us who watch for thee, that our lips may praise thee, our lives may bless thee, and our worship on the morrow may give thee glory; through Jesus Christ our Lord. Amen.' "

The priest let that sink in, then said, "I haven't seen either of you or dear Beth for a very long time. We haven't talked. You haven't attended services." He paused thoughtfully. "Do you watch for him, Cassie? Do you, Nick? Are your lips filled with praise? That's what I meant by my last phone message. In the typhoon of publicity and public adoration, have you, blessed now beyond all measure, thought to build an altar of thanks to the Lord? I don't mean a literal stone upon stone, but one of the heart." His lilting voice softened. "Have you thought about requesting a service of dedication and gratitude to the One who has given you the desires of your hearts?"

Cassie felt the sting of tears. Everything had happened so quickly, the last weeks racing past in a blur.

"Look, Father, I mean no disrespect," said Nick, "but you sit protected behind cathedral walls from which it is pretty safe to lob

294

the occasional cheap shot. We've both been working eighty-hour weeks to get Cassandra on the market, to pay our creditors, to reward our loyal employees, to pay our stakeholders a decent dividend, to give Beth a good education, and to finally give ourselves a break so we can at last enjoy some of the fruit of our labors. And we did it, mind you, by finding and formulating the most fascinating fragrance on God's green earth and making it available to everyone. And where was God all this time that we were the laughingstock of industry wags? Thanks to Cass, you'll get your tithe, Father, but could you at least wait the customary thirty days for payment?"

Cassie gasped. "Nicholas! That was uncalled for. Fr. Byron only wants the best for us. How could you be so rude?"

"I won't be accused of ingratitude," said Nick, back on his feet, set jaw daring anyone to intervene. He turned on the priest, his words an angry rush. "How dare you rate my church attendance, and where do you get off accusing us of being in it for the applause? Excuse me while I go commune with nature. At least the moon doesn't judge." Without giving Fr. Byron a chance to respond, Nick stormed out the front door with a slam.

Cassie's expression was forlorn. "You were pretty blunt," she said.

Fr. B sighed. "I get that way sometimes. Forgive me, Cass, and make my amends to Nick. It's just that behind every great symphony there is a composer; behind every flowing dance, a choreographer; behind every magnificent scent, a Creator. You said it yourself once: 'The senses are a doorway to God. If we are made in his image and meant to love and enjoy him forever, then it is in part the senses that enable us to experience him more fully.' I've always thought that was such a beautiful expression."

"I said that?" Cassie stared at the cookie in her hand before parking it on the rim of her saucer.

Fr. Byron smiled kindly. "Yes, you did. All I ask is that you not seek your identity in Cassandra the fragrance, but in Christ the Rose."

"How do I do that, Father? Everyone wants a piece of me, and honestly, I'm enjoying the clamor. You've always been one to point out how we ought to take joy when in rhythm with the life God gives. Well, brother, I'm happy to say that for the first time in my life, I've got rhythm!"

Mags retreated to the dining room to watch

Beth do her homework.

After five minutes of being stared at, Beth said around her wad of gum, "What!"

"It's not often I get to see a teenager at home on a Friday night doing schoolwork. Have I entered another dimension?"

Beth shrugged. "I'd been spending a lot of time with Andre lately. Then my parents got a call from the vice principal. I figured I'd better do some catching up."

Mags nodded and gave her an old-as-I-am-I-understand look. "Carry on, then; don't mind me."

"Mags, why do people get so upset over perfume?"

Mags thought it over. "Renee Gaudette, the fashion designer, used to say that perfume is a haunting memory more reliable than the rest. Of all the senses, the sense of smell is the most powerfully linked to subconscious thought and memory. Am I making any sense?"

"Sure. I went to camp one year and took that old green shag pillow for comfort. Gretchen liked it too, and her smell was all over it. I wasn't homesick until I smelled that pillow. I spent half an hour on the phone with Gretch. Mom never lets me forget that one." Beth started to go back to her homework, then hesitated and looked up again at

Mags. "So how come you and your daughter are strange?"

"If you mean *es*-tranged," — Mags stifled a laugh — "it's because we're two strong-willed and independent women who found themselves on opposite sides of the fragrance wars. I believe in Old World sophistication with a pinch or two of restraint. My daughter thinks interesting and chic are found in the most outrageous promotions and outlandish claims."

"Can't you agree to disagree?"

"Not that I want to keep talking about this, but I'll tell you one more thing. To her I'm a dinosaur. Outdated and always shooting my mouth off. The more I tried to advise and console, the more she pushed me away. So I stopped trying and sort of adopted you and your parents as my family. Now, don't you have a date with a handsome hypotenuse?"

Beth grinned and opened her geography text. "More like a report on hunky Honduras. How did you and Mom meet?"

"Oh, now I like that story. It was right after another good friend of hers died, and we were both at a trade show in Brazil. Cass was missing her friend, and I was feeling like there'd been a kind of death in my family too. We just hit it off. I think she liked my spark at a time when she'd lost hers. I convinced her to partner with processing plants in Asia. Japanese women on average spend about fifty percent more on beauty products than women in America and Europe — put that in your social studies report sometime. That partnership helped Azure stabilize."

"Wow, that's great. Mom never talks about this stuff. Did you ever meet a geisha?"

Mags showed her surprise. "No, no geishas, but I do admire the Japanese sensibility. Don't tell your mother I told you this, but the traditional Nippon women never perfume their skin directly. If they did, it might compromise their purity or advertise a woman of easy morals. Their method is to stitch fragrant wood shavings into the hem of their kimonos. Though perfume can damage fine clothing, pearls, mink, and silk, I *love* the idea of scented clothing as a sign of one's virtue."

"Huh, pretty cool. How's this?" Beth placed closed fists against her forehead, eyes squeezed shut, as if in deep thought. "A name is coming to me . . . yes . . . yes . . . I give you Fragrant Fashions by Maggie O!"

Mags made a face but was secretly pleased. "Laugh it up, dearie, but you may have just named the next wave of sensible wearables. Don't worry, I'll share the credit."

Beth played with the gum in her mouth. "That sculpture you gave her must really have sealed the friendship."

Mags looked pleased. "Ah, the Salvador Dali perfume bottle from the house of Baccarat."

"It's so pretty. Must be worth a mint."

"Yes, but a one-of-a-kind cut crystal decanter in yellow and gold by Dali is a tribute, not a commodity. Anyone who can love me despite my flaws is that special."

Beth started to ask another question, but Mags held up her hand. "It's getting late. I'll leave you to Honduras and get myself to bed. Good night."

Beneath the covers of her bed in the guest room, Mags thought about her daughter, their estrangement, and the hollow place that would always be in her heart. She had long wanted to tell Cassie how precious the mother-daughter relationship was, also how fleeting, and how tragic when it was too late to save it.

After the gala, she decided. Then she would warn Cassie with straight talk like only she could deliver. Poor girl. First from the priest. Then from Mags.

But not until Cass and Nick had their date with destiny. The gala would be their coronation. As for Mags, she wasn't going near that glitter dome of excess. She would instead curl up with Gretchen in front of the TV with a big bowl of buttered popcorn. They would woof and holler for the home team like hockey fans at the playoffs.

Better make that two bowls. Gretch could really stow away the popcorn.

A shadow crossed in front of the side bay window, accompanied by heavy breathing. Cassie awoke from the couch with a start. She threw off the afghan and jerked upright, confused in slumber. Had she set the alarm?

"Beth?" By the light of the lamp Cassie had left burning after Fr. B's departure, Nick bent over her, sweaty and breathy from running. He kissed her and she protested. "Phew! You smell like the bottom of a gym bag."

Nick flopped to the floor and leaned back against the couch, hair flipping droplets of sweat. "Now there's a scent promotion that needs work," he joked. "Just so's ya know, watchman, I told the rental cops to call it a night. No, you did not set the alarm, but I see you sent the parson packing."

Cassie squinted at the clock. It read 2:35.

"I think parsons fizzle past midnight. Sorry about the alarm. I was dead to the world. Where'd you go?"

Nick's breathing slowed. "First I stopped by the laundry room and screamed my remaining aggression into the wash machine. Those big front loaders can really take a substantial pile of belligerent buildup. Then I circled Mt. Davidson, took a turn around Glen Canyon Park, outraced Mrs. Parker's Pomeranian, and returned to drip on you."

He threw a hand up and playfully Cassie nuzzled it. "My, my. We were having a nasty bout of preacher pique, weren't we? Fr. B didn't stay long after you left."

Nick sighed. "I was unfit company. Forgive me? The good reverend must — it's in his contract — but you may choose a different door." He craned his head back, looking vulnerable and chastened. He must have flogged himself the whole route.

She didn't care how sweaty he was. At that moment he needed to be kissed, and she obliged. "One more of those," she said, "and all is forgiven."

Nick pulled her, giggling and protesting, into his moist clutches. "The fuzzy slippers are a nice touch," he murmured, nibbling her neck and ear. "But I'm betting if you mix a dab of Cassandra with that little back-less number tomorrow night, it'll take the vice squad to sort us out!"

She laughed as he buzzed her under the chin. Then he drew her close, and she no longer cared about the perspiration and the soggy clothes. In fact, she marveled at how agreeable he suddenly smelled.

A man watched from the shadows of the privacy hedge a few driveways up the street, a borrowed mutt on a leash. A handful of kibble and the little female mixed breed had gone along without a whimper. The man didn't remember which house he filched the mutt from, but it would be up to her to go home when her services were no longer required.

For now, he was just an ordinary insom-niac with a big mortgage, walking a dog with a small bladder.

He'd stayed back and watched the place for three hours. He needed time to think and sort through the options. If anyone thought that was a long time to be airing a dog, they didn't ask, and if they had, he had his spiel ready. *"She's incontinent, poor thing, but I've not the heart to put her down. I mean, look at her."* Whereupon closer scrutiny would earn a hangdog expression from Miss

Mongrel. Natural actor, that one.

He noted the arrival of the clergyman, the return of Cassandra Dixon, the departure of the clergyman, the departure of Nicholas Dixon, the return of Nicholas Dixon, and the departure of the security guards. Other than a couple of halfhearted woofs from the Great Dane, a yowler of a catfight, and a couple of late-model, oversized cars passing on the street, he and Fifi had had the neighborhood to themselves.

And now, judging from the shadows dancing against lamplight, the Dixons were having a cozy little reunion.

He'd considered poisoning the Dane, just for the fear factor. And a week before, he'd come close to snatching away old Mags, out for her morning constitutional in sea green designer walking togs. For that matter, he'd toyed with plugging the security guys on principle. Didn't SFPD think he was a sufficient threat to warrant ongoing taxpayer-funded law enforcement? Blame that two-bit thug he'd hired to do a little damage. Shots had been fired with zero to show for it except a whole lot of unwanted investigation. You got what you paid for these days, and he'd bought a double helping of incompetence.

Maybe he should poison the guest list at

the Crystal Decanter Awards Gala. Or start a fire in the hotel. Or detonate the Dixon limo en route.

Too imprecise, the collateral damage unacceptable. And far too impersonal. No, the best way to bring down the house of Dixon and make Nicky pay was to march into the Fairmont San Francisco tomorrow night and gun Cassie down on live TV. That way, he could look Mrs. D in the eye at the moment her lights went out, and Mr. D in the eye at the instant he understood the full consequences of messing with Brenda Gelasse.

Fifi stirred restlessly in his arms. He set her down, fed her the last of the kibble, and unsnapped the leash. The dog wandered off, casting uncertain backward glances at the man in the shrubbery.

"Yeah, mutt. Get lost," the man said. "And next time you'd do well to keep better company."

CHAPTER 16

At 10:47 on the morning of the gala, the phone startled Cassie awake.

Her hair appointment with the most in-demand stylist west of the Mississippi on the most important day of her life was in exactly forty-three minutes. Miss it, and she would have to wear a wig. No, she would have to wear someone else's head entirely.

"Nick. Nick! We've overslept, my hair appointment is now, and you smell like the 49ers locker room after a tough loss. Get the phone!"

Nick moaned from beneath the glass-topped coffee table and groped above him for the source of the jangling. He found it, lost it, and regained it on the fourth ring. He mumbled something that sounded like, "The Nixon resonance," then listened intently.

After a couple minutes he told the caller to hold on and waved the phone in the air.

"It's your daughter," he said. "She left early to help set up for the grade school carnival. She doesn't know why we resembled a pile of dirty laundry in the middle of the living room floor but she has a pretty good idea and it's disgusting. Now she's at Andre's — he helped her with the setup — and plans to stay there until tonight when no, she is not joining us for the gala but fulfilling her promise to Mrs. Gaylor next door from seventy months ago that she would babysit Max and Martine so the Gaylors could go celebrate their tenth wedding anniversary. If we had been listening, we would remember that she told us eleven-something times that this was coming but oh no we had to go and schedule the gala at the same time and no the Gaylors do not want to join us at the hotel because they really want to be alone for the first time in a million years and how could we forget? And why you had to go and make a hair date with that pretentious Molaire or Feraire or whateverthe-heckhisname is beyond her when Andre is standing by perfectly willing to give you the most incredible style since Queen Nefertiti's. My head's killing me. Where's the ibuprofen? It wasn't in the medicine cabinet last time I looked."

Cassie's own head was doing the Watusi,

and her neck felt as if she'd slept on rocks. She took the phone and heard the now-familiar sounds of a hair salon in the background. "Beth, I want you to come home and get ready for the gala. This is the most important night of our lives, and you can't not be a part of it!"

"That's a double negative, Mom, and you told me the most important night of your lives was the night I was born. As if it matters these days. In two months have we spoken two sentences? I promised the Gaylors I'd be there for them, and . . . and . . ."

Cassie heard the catch in her daughter's voice. "What, Beth? What is it?"

Beth paused, then hurried on. "It's just I thought you would have invited me to go dress shopping with you and maybe given me a test sample of Cassandra. I wouldn't have anything to wear now, but it doesn't matter. I've committed to the Gaylors and can watch the gala on their TV. Sorry, Mom, but you just haven't been around to talk with. I'd really love it if you'd come here to J. Primo's and get your hair done."

"My hair!" Cassie shrieked. "Beth, I feel awful about the dress. But I've decided Cassandra's an adult fragrance; it's not appropriate for a young teenager. I know I'm going back on my word. And you're right, I haven't been there for you. This is going to change. But right now I've got to get off the phone. An event this important — well, Beth, I just think it best that I see Geno Figare. It's an international broadcast and I've got to look . . . you know, international. I'll make this up to you, I will, once the madness has died down. I love you, honey, believe me, but your dad and I have been scratching and clawing for this day, and I'm afraid it consumed us more than we want to admit. Please understand."

"Yeah, Mom. I get it. You guys knock 'em out. Andre says to wish you luck. Bye."

"Beth!" But she was gone before Cassie could say, "The night you were born *was* the most important of our lives." Beth didn't get it. The sad hurt in her voice said that loud and plain. Still, Cassie didn't have the time to call her back. Not now.

"Our baby girl standing us up?" Nick asked, wiggling out from beneath the coffee table.

Cassie fought back the tears. "We haven't been there for her, Nick. I planned for this night with little or no thought for Beth. She's hurt and has every reason to be."

Nick stood and worked the kinks out of his shoulders. "She's a strong girl, just like her mom. You know kids — she'll get over it. You and I need to get ready for our close-ups, Miss Lamour." He leaned over her and leered. "Is the bed head look this year's emerging trend?"

With another shriek, Cassie ran for the bathroom, yelling on the way. "Nick, call Geno. The number's on the corkboard. Beg him to hold my slot. Did you pick up your tux? Has anyone fed Gretch this year? Have you seen my speech?" The rest was swallowed by the hiss of the shower.

Nick flopped on the couch and stretched, luxuriating in the memories of last night. And that was without benefit of so much as a single drop of Cassandra.

What on earth will tonight bring?

The television in the hospital room was tuned to a twenty-four-hour news station. The anchor spoke somberly about the previous day's extraordinary incident at the San Diego Zoo, in which a garden-spade-wielding chimpanzee attacked a female keeper and nearly decapitated her. Horrified onlookers reported that the chimp "had murder in its eyes" as it held the spade like a weapon and pursued the screaming woman about the primate enclosure.

One odd side note to an already bizarre

event was reported by the paramedics who rushed the injured keeper to the emergency trauma center. The cut and battered woman, they said, carried "the most beautiful aroma about her." Investigators were said to be closing in on the cause of the rash of animal attacks in the Golden State.

Joy ignored the broadcast, gazing instead at Royce Blankenship. He sat at her bedside, head bowed, eyes closed, lips moving ever so slightly. He appeared to be praying and she felt an enormous peace. The weariness she wore upon awakening, as if arriving in Room 607 after a long and arduous journey, drained away.

Royce loved her.

So frail was her touch on his elbow that for a full two minutes he did not appear to realize she was awake. Joy savored those minutes. Just the two of them.

A nurse came, checked the IV drip, made a quick adjustment, and was gone. Royce stirred and turned to look at her.

His eyes said he might want to kiss her, to tell her the depth of his loss when he thought she might not return. He held her hand to his cheek, and then he smiled. "Of all the many thousand smells I know, I can smell only one at the moment, the warmth of your hand." Inexplicably, it was the hand that had fed the raccoons and was one of the only expanses of skin on her body that did not bear the scars.

His lips brushed the back of her hand, and the fingers that had not moved in many days gently caressed the stubble of his upper lip. For her, and her only, he had not shaved. She knew somehow it was the way of grieving, the way of loving, for a man of discipline.

"You are my Joy," he said, voice tight with emotion. "I won't lose you again." And without hesitation, "Please marry me?"

Her sensible brain said it was too soon. Not that she came from a long line of patient people. Her navy father waited just six weeks to pop the question, and her mother's philosophy was, "Seize the sailor." When did this tidy, reserved professional turn into such a man of impulse? Why was she so glad he did, so glad he'd asked the question?

She studied the fine, lean features, the close-set, nut brown eyes. The hair trimmed military-precise. The ears too large, the chin too thin, the brows forming two C-clamps of deadly seriousness. And, of course, the nose. The Nose. That amazing pathway to all things aromatic. She had tempered the fierceness in him, damped the fire that was far from out. He wanted her middle-aged plumpness, saw past the bandages and the coming cosmetic surgery into the chambers of her heart.

Joy wet her cracked lips before speaking. "Royce Blankenship, I will marry you on one condition. You must buy a new car."

They held each other for a good long time before the mirth at last subsided. And for a little longer after that.

He had checked over the .38 revolver, knowing it was clean, operational, and reliable. No plan of his would go awry due to faulty equipment.

And if Brenda's .38, the one he insisted on keeping at her place, should happen to be the weapon used in carrying out the Crystal Gala Assassination Plot, then so be it. She had not played fair, cuckolding him for that flower-sniffing pretty boy from Azure.

He was Brenda's husband, divorce or no divorce. He had more testosterone in a single earlobe than Nicholas Dixon had in his entire miserable body. Brenda always did like the newest bauble. She saw Dixon lose interest for a moment in his swollen pregnant wife, and bam, just like one of those Amazonian tree frogs snatching a beetle off a branch with a flick of its tongue, Brenda had him in her arms. She never behaved the same again. *It's Nick this, Nick that, "if you were half the man Nicky is . . ." Well, Nicky boy, you decided to take my wife away from me, and now I'm going to take your wife away from you. I'd lost interest until your mug started showing up everywhere, reminding me of the revulsion I still have for you. Let's call it unfinished business.*

And Brenda, sweetheart, you don't change out a husband like a spent lightbulb. Not this one, you don't. Stormy we were, but not without magic. You happen to be the most maddening woman ever to don a pair of pantyhose, but you have fire and you have money. When I'm done with Nicky's missus, I'm coming for you and old man deBrieze, and we're going to jet on down to Argentina and see if we can't get ourselves lost on one of those mega cattle ranches they've got there. Then we start a new life on your millions, and deBrieze goes away.

He had spun the cylinder on the revolver and listened to the satisfying clicks. That baby would spit death clean as a viper strike. The evening would be spoiled for all the pretty ones and all the good-smelling ones. But it was all business, baby. All business.

CHAPTER 17

Faye Guterman, lead investigator for the Crime Prevention Analysis Lab, or C-PAL, at California State University, San Bernardino, eyed the tall stack of reports crowding her desk. They'd started as a trickle but soon formed a gush.

Tall, willowy, red-haired, and tanned the color of caramel, Faye was the glamour girl of lab research. The interview process with a male supervisor had been swift, and it was "job filled" before the ink dried on her application. Fortunately, she had a plentitude of scientific qualifications to meet and exceed any number of physical assets.

"You'll find the causes of crime in public parks or the likelihood of suffering a car prowl by parking at the Delgado Cineplex," her employer had said on day one, "but whenever a rash of associated adverse events threatens the public good, look out. The local police will handle the easy cases; the difficult ones they'll dump on you. Goes with the job." The truth of that assessment was hard to tell from the job description, unless it was under "other duties as assigned."

Brittany Edmunds, a lab assistant and the report dumper, added to the stack. "Don't look at me," the stout woman said. "A little expertise in animal behavior, and wham, the strange and unusual flow your way. What was it you said the other night on TV?"

Faye looked sheepish. "That I've encountered every aberration in the human animal, so why not delve into nature's other oddities?"

"Bingo! You get the press, and C-PAL gets the grants. You look good on the tube, sugar. All fire and command, flowing copper-red hair, like you was the new Kate Hepburn or something. I love those funky little awards you're always handing out."

"The Sawdust for Brains Honors."

"That's them. America's salute to the dumbest human interactions with the animal kingdom. This year's winner was something. Dad takes his family to the national park for a photo op with nature. Smears marshmallow cream on his kid and snaps away while a black bear licks the kid's face like a lollypop. We got to get that man out of the gene pool!"

Faye gave the barest of smiles. She thought of her controversial paper comparing psychiatric disorders in humans and animals, which had brought her to the attention of the chief of staff at C-PAL. Her views were decidedly unorthodox. "It's that ongoing conundrum posed by the similarities in the neurological/behavioral continuum in the canine and the human male. You study the dominance aggression and cognitive dysfunction in dogs, and one day you will have a clearer understanding of the forces compelling the common street thug — or thoughtless dad with a camera."

"Don't I know it? My shiftless cousin Cletis broke out of his kennel, and it will take Animal Control and a tranquilizer gun to put him back." Brittany paused, and a huge grin broke like morning across the broad face. "Listen to us, the Thelma and Louise of political incorrectness!"

"Hey, I just follow the facts wherever they lead." The latest facts were leading Faye into strange waters. "Listen to this recent rash of human-animal encounters:

"Six orca trainer incidents — stomach rammings, pool draggings, and arm, leg, and head bitings. By the grace of God no deaths, but a total of one hundred thirty-eight stitches, a set of ruptured kidneys, a lacerated liver, a fractured pelvis, two near drownings, and a lot of frightened people.

"Twenty-one canine incidents — not just the typical pit bull or rottweiler bitings, but Aunt Matilda's cocker spaniels, Welsh corgis, and retrievers gone wild, plus a pinky finger lost to a crazed Chihuahua in Point Loma. Sadly, two children have also lost their lives, three others are in critical condition, two mothers will require years of reconstructive facial surgery, and all but two of the dogs had to be put down."

Faye shook her head. The several reports of the growing number of strange occurrences across the state were especially disturbing when seen together. "In an entire year, the average number of dog-bite deaths nationwide is seventeen. Four in a single state in three weeks is alarming.

"That's not all, Brit. The list details attacks on humans by seven head of cattle, nineteen working horses, and three prized thoroughbreds. Rats have grown unusually aggressive in six reported cases, including the highly publicized city hall death. No less than thirty domestic feline incidents. From hamsters in Hayward to ferrets in Fresno, in the past month the California animal world has gone haywire. And because of the state's mostly mild spring climate, the attacks are almost as likely to be from wildlife. Two big cat attacks and two mountain lion maulings in Trabuco Canyon. The citations also name bear, raccoon, primates, a zoo elephant, and perhaps strangest of all, a coyote that jumped a rancher in broad daylight and mangled the woman's ear so badly that it had to be amputated. How is it possible? Nonrabid coyotes are highly wary of human encounters and go out of their way to avoid them."

"So what's the answer?"

"I wish I knew. I began by looking for commonalities, patterns. The attacks happened across the spectrum of age and socioeconomic groupings, and have a wide distribution geographically, with higher concentrations in the counties around Los Angeles and San Francisco. That makes sense. Higher density populations result in higher frequency of both the presenting phenomena and those willing to report them."

Brittany smacked her hands together. "Happens every August when my extended family gets together for barbecue."

Faye ignored the levity. "Time of day and day of the week were within statistically acceptable norms for randomness, with predictably more events on weekends, when more children are at play and more people of all ages engage in outside activities.

"The techies gave me a grid showing kind of attack, location, victim names, results, and other vital details. I studied the focused printout of facts-at-a-glance until three significant indicators emerged.

"First, all the primary victims are female. Second, their attackers are all mammalian, although a couple of the more rural reports mention the eerie absence as well of natural audibles, or vocalizations, from other animals common to the area, such as birds or frogs. Third — and this is most intriguing — in all cases a notation is made concerning the presence at the attack site, and on the victim, of a distinctive and appealing odor. In many instances, the report filer struggles to express how potent, beguiling, even tempting the smell is. That allure is personally upsetting to witnesses and emergency responders alike, who consider it sensuous and inappropriate to the scene. As one sheriff's officer report eloquently expresses, 'It was in sharp and unsettling contrast to the violence of the attacks.' "

She pointed to a plastic evidence bag beside the stack of reports. "This is from a feline incident in Anaheim that was so vicious, the animal had to be euthanized at the scene. Animal Control reported that a mature tabby cat had 'risen like a spitting, snarling monster' and attacked an adult granddaughter visiting her widowed grandmother in an assisted-care facility. The cat raked the victim repeatedly, nearly tearing an eye from its socket. The screaming granddaughter had the presence of mind to run into the hall, where a custodian clubbed the beloved pet with a length of pipe, breaking several of the cat's bones in the process. The animal was too deranged and badly injured to be saved. A lethal dose of drugs ended its suffering. The traumatized grandmother required sedation."

Brittany sat heavily on the corner of Faye's desk, no more smiles. She gripped its edges and appeared light-headed.

From the bag, Faye extracted a beige silk blouse soaked black with blood and torn in several places. "I'm used to similar specimens rank with the aromas of struggle and carnage. Often the vapors that rush from those bags bear the stench of death and decay."

Brittany swayed slightly.

"But not this time. Smell that?" The room filled with a divine aroma wafting from the gory blouse.

Faye had never smelled anything so lovely, so engaging. She had to fight the urge to bury her face and nose in the stained cloth. Three days before, she had determined what it was, and the blouse only confirmed it. It had to be the new perfume creating all the buzz. Cassandra. What were they calling it? The very breath of beauty.

The stout woman straightened and sniffed the air with what Faye could only interpret as enthusiasm.

"I verified that in sixty-four of the incidents, the victims had received a sample vial of that new scent Cassandra that's been in the news. They got it at a mall giveaway and applied it to their skin within two hours preceding attack.

"The unfortunate granddaughter must have been among the few to obtain one of the test vials recently distributed free of charge to gauge public reaction." Faye shook her head. "There would be a reaction, all right, and I've got to find the root cause." She bunched the blouse in both hands and brought it close to her nose.

Then she abruptly flung the blouse away, knocking the work stool over in her haste to put distance between her and the evidence.

She grabbed Brittany's arm and towed the reluctant woman outside the building. Faye bent over an empty bicycle rack and gulped air until her heart stopped racing. Brittany half-fell to one knee on the grass and shook her head as if bewildered by what she was doing outdoors.

Faye fought for calm. "Here, I'll help you up. Go back to your office, Brit. Thanks for the reports." The woman tottered off once her legs again agreed to work in tandem.

Faye pinched the inside of her elbow, and things came into sharper focus. She knew in her professional heart of hearts that there was something in the profoundly sweet perfume on that blouse back in the lab. Something inexplicably deadly.

Something evil.

Faye held her breath, returned the blouse to the evidence bag, and zipped it closed. She secured the papers on her desk and turned the floor fan on high to push the lingering scent out the door to dissipate in the hallway beyond.

I need an informed opinion. Brit's just an assistant; I need another researcher, someone more clinically objective. She grabbed the phone and punched in a four-digit extension.

"Hello. You've reached J. Wyatt's voice mail. Leave your name, number, and a short message, and I'll get back to you. Believe me when I say, it's worth the wait."

Faye rolled her eyes and changed lab coats. She placed the one with the lingering scent into the laundry drum, assuring herself that the lid was tightly fastened.

The activity helped her to focus, to filter out the chaff and concentrate on the main thing. In humans, behavioral disorders were among the most complex and incapacitating of all pathological conditions. What most people did not know was that the same was true of canine and feline behavioral disorders. They accounted for the relinquishment and death of more pet animals each year than infectious, neoplastic, and metabolic disease combined.

The conditions that could cause anxiety in animals to the degree seen in the recent attacks had her stumped. The animals went ballistic, then catatonic, and frequently nothing could be done short of killing them. It was similar to the crazed aggression of an animal about to be consumed by fire. But there were no indicators of any such abnormal circumstances. In fact, the reports were filled with bewildered comments on just how ordinary the days of the attacks had been. In the total absence of fire or comparable triggers, the deranged actions of the attacking animals were positively irrational.

Unless the fragrance was somehow responsible for the atypical behavior in mammals with the exception of humans? Unable to shake the feeling of lost control that had made her flee the building, she wondered if the fragrance didn't also have a strange hold on the people who wore it.

A funny feeling was not going to hold up in court. Faye needed to corroborate the feeling with facts. She had read that retail sales of the perfume would begin on Monday. So little time. She punched up J. W.'s extension again and this time got an answering, "Howdy, Faye. Just about to call you back."

"You free to bounce ideas? Ten minutes, tops?"

"Sure."

"Good. My office."

"Ok, Figgy, what's up?"

Faye made a face at J. W.'s silly nickname for her, but with him there was no going back. The short, rotund coworker had purchased one of her mastiffs and named her Cruella. It didn't take much for him to sing the entire song from *101 Dalmatians.* Silly as it was, every time he warbled the words, she smelled warm puppies. It put her in a better frame of mind.

"What do you make of these animal attacks that have been in the news?" she began.

He peered at her through thick lenses, which he seemed to have found at the bottom of a barrel of cast-off eyeglasses. "Rabies?"

"Ruled out. None of the biters display the classic symptoms — no increased salivation, no affected motor function, no paralysis. None of the animals have tested positive."

"Seizures?"

"Do whales seize?"

He shrugged. "Any presenting confirmations for seizures?"

"None."

"Provocations?"

"None."

"Startled response?"

"None reported."

"Number of cases?"

She checked the grid and made a quick calculation. "Close to one hundred and fifty reported cases in three weeks." Only a fraction of animal aggressions were ever reported. Given the severity of the attacks, most of these probably would have been, even without the media hype. But still a percentage may have remained under the radar, for whatever reasons people had for preferring to keep their private lives private.

J. W. whistled through the gap in his front teeth. "That's a bunch. Fatalities?"

Again Faye consulted the grid. "Seven. Plus three survivors in critical, five in serious, seven in guarded. Dozens in posttraumatic distress."

"Commonalities?"

"Victims all women, attackers all mammalian, presence of an outside stimulus."

"Which is?"

"In many if not all of the cases, victims are scented with a powerful, sweet-smelling perfume. Many report having applied the perfume immediately preceding attack. I suspect in every case we will find that the stimulus is Cassandra, that new orchid fragrance sensation set to go retail on Monday. The number of reported attacks spikes on weekends, corresponding with the cycle of free samples distributed in malls and other public places. People try it on, arrive home from a day's shopping, Fido greets, Fido goes berserk."

J. W. sat on an adjoining stool and spun slowly counterclockwise. "Theories?"

She took a deep breath and let it out. "I've narrowed it to olfactory hallucinations, maybe in combination with or the causation of additional visual and auditory hallucinations, producing sudden and/or severe psychic manifestations of an extremely unpleasant degree."

"Doggie LSD?"

"Looks that way."

J. W. took a minute to revolve, deep in thought. Faye knew better than to interrupt. Jake had solved more than one mystery on the stool's sixteenth revolution or higher.

But after only thirteen revolutions he stopped and said, "Disposition of the attackers?"

"A large percentage had to be destroyed, but in the larger animals, most notably killer whales, there have been no repeats of aggression by the same animals. I suspect that it is simply the absence of the olfactory stimulus."

"Meaning?"

"I'm not sure." She was reluctant to say what was at the back of her mind. Pleasant odors, the oils of certain plants, herbs, and flowers, had been shown to improve life physically, emotionally, mentally, and spiritually. They made people feel better about themselves and others and encouraged positive attitudes, creativity, and innovative problem-solving. She'd seen the studies touting certain fragrances as useful therapy for reducing stress during medical procedures — both for the patient and the surgeon. She had friends who swore by lavender as an aid to relaxation and sound sleep. And hadn't the scent of lemon been proven to help clerical workers make fewer computer keyboarding errors?

It would be wonderful if one day aromas replaced prescription drugs in people's medicine cabinets. But if she voiced what she was thinking, she could set those developments back a century or more.

J. W. gave her a piercing look. "I don't need to tell you, Fig, that the olfaction of mammals is way superior to mankind's. But mutant nasal passages aren't unheard of either. More than one dog with dysosmia has eaten tainted fish and died. My cousin's basset has parosmia and smells imaginary aromas. I could put gravel in its dish, and it would chow down because it smells beef-flavored nuggets. Whatever this perfume is doing to these animals isn't humane. We've got to tell the authorities."

He hadn't smelled what was in that evidence bag. It was exquisite and captivating and unlike anything she had ever smelled before. Injury and harm made pleasant. She had held bloody rags contradicted by the ethereal smell of heavenly places.

What was she thinking? Quite simply, that it masked the odor of violence and of the grave. That it redeemed death. That it was the scent of eternity.

Only for a fleeting second, far back and fading fast, came the memory of how, with just one whiff, she had nearly lost control of all that was good and godly.

She glanced uneasily at the laundry drum. It remained securely fastened.

"Many animals use pheromones to establish dominant-recessive structures within a population, say a pack of dogs," she said. "Why not an aberration of the system, leading to inappropriate pecking orders and unprovoked attack on the dominant species — us?"

J. W. spun once. "I'm listening."

Faye tapped the eraser end of a pencil against her teeth. She appreciated open ears. "We know that the discriminatory power of the olfactory system is immense. Even a slight change in the structure of an odorant can alter its perceived odor, as in the razor-thin delineator between an orange and a sweaty armpit."

"Why, Miss Guterman, how you do flirt!"

She ignored him. "Change the concentration of an odorant or even slightly alter its molecular structure, and you change its sensory receptor code. Change the receptor code, and you change the neural mechanism responsible for the perception of citrus and perspiration."

"Mama warned me about girls like you."

She made a face and his lit up. Theirs was a strange dance but it worked. "Stay with me, Professor Wyatt. We're near a break-through."

"Carry on."

"Somehow the chemical stimuli in Cassandra misdirect the emotional reaction and 'trick' mammals other than the human variety — and even that's not a clear given — into pathologically aggressive and vicious response. Nature has a number of these frauds up her sleeve — the voracious Venus flytrap, several mate-eating spiders, and all manner of camouflage, from insects that resemble sticks to fish that mimic their undersea surroundings. This is the first one I've experienced that, misapplied, invites harm."

J. W. frowned. "You're telling me that in its natural environment, the Cassandra orchid's pheromones send out a warning to animals to steer clear, as a kind of super defense mechanism."

Faye nodded and picked up the line of

reasoning. "But when that scent is duplicated and taken into a foreign environment with no warning and no preconditioning to avoid it, the fauna panic and attack, no questions asked."

J. W. rose from the stool and began to pace the room, hands clasped behind his back. "Why the overkill? Why so severe a reaction?"

Faye stared at the laundry drum. "Perhaps it's like fish or snakes being endowed with venom far more potent than required for normal daily routine. Lavish excess is all around us. Why do many men remain fertile long after their spouses' childbearing years? Why is the gestation period for a mouse just twenty-eight days? Does the world exponentially require that many more rodents?"

Her colleague shrugged. "It'll take the Man Upstairs to answer that one. All I know is, you've got to tell someone. That perfume cannot roll out on Monday. If it does, there will be carnage."

The criminologist flipped the pencil down. She walked over to the laundry drum, hesitated, lifted the lid, then quickly closed it again. That fast, the smell of heaven draped the room.

Her associate's eyes grew big. He gave a short, soft whistle. "*That's it?* Incredible!"

Faye Guterman's shoulders dropped and a sudden weariness possessed her. She gripped the edges of the drum and shut her eyes.

Her clinical training forced her to focus. She experienced a strange sense of abandon, the willingness to commit improprieties with her round associate. Faye hoped the urge wasn't mutual.

"How hard do you think it will be to locate the state's attorney general on a weekend?"

J. W. gave her an oddly frank stare and laid a pudgy hand on her sleeve. "Locating him's going to be fun, but not half as much as *convincing* him. You okay, Fig?"

She snatched back her arm and felt the earlier panic return and fought it down. " 'Cruella DeVille,' " she said. "Just a few bars."

CHAPTER 18

US Drug Enforcement Agent Greg Heidler strode toward the elevators in the east wing of Mercy General Hospital. His partner, Ladd, a German shepherd narcotics detection canine, trotted in harness at his side and a little ahead.

Drug traffickers smuggled contraband into the country by ever more ingenious means and had moles and couriers in the most unlikely places. Like Mercy General. Orthopedic surgeon Enrique Juarez, from Guatemala, was seeing an unusual number of immigrant patients. A tipster said that the new leg cast of one Roberto Esteban, applied by the good doctor, was actually nine parts packaged high-grade marijuana and one part plaster. Discharge the patient, discharge five kilos of illegal substance onto the streets of San Francisco.

As busts went, Heidler knew, it was small potatoes, but always there existed the chance of following the leads higher up to the exploiters of the poor and vulnerable.

Hospital security would meet Heidler and Ladd outside Room 209.

Heidler cast a quick glance at Ladd. The canine had a nose that contained twenty to forty times more receptor cells than his handler's. Heidler was proud. With the right training, Ladd had learned to sniff out the tiniest quantities of drugs under often-adverse conditions.

Ladd's nails tapped against the tiles, and the dog and handler drew admiring glances and smiles from staff and visitors alike. Heidler liked to watch him move. When Ladd was on the job, he wore his mission in eyes bright and muscled body flowing with focused determination.

In the elevator, the agent pressed the button for the second floor and told a curious little boy that Ladd was one of six brothers and sisters. "But he's the only one in the service of his country," he said, pride in every word. "The only one."

In Room 207 Royce Blankenship combed Joy Spretnak's hair and kissed her forehead. She had emerged from the coma and, joy of joys, had been moved to his old room to convalesce.

To her hospital gown he pinned a corsage of four double orchids in pale-blue and yellow with throats of red-gold. Like magic, he produced a beautiful yellow rosebud from thin air and tucked it carefully into place over her right ear.

A thermos of virgin strawberry daiquiris appeared next. And two glasses. "A toast to a very special night," Royce said after pouring the drinks. "You are my betrothed and the Dixons are royalty." He motioned to the Weather Channel on the TV bolted to the ceiling, where an overly cheery woman meteorologist was discussing the local weather. "Mild and dry," he said. "There will be no rain on the Dixon parade."

They clicked glasses and Royce said, "Why must they turn every one of these awards ceremonies into an exercise in excess?" He waved a dismissive hand. "We could have thrown a street fair in the Azure parking lot and put Poochie Cunningham in a dunk tank. Don't you think Bridgette Sigafoos would have been first in line, my love?"

She rewarded him with a wan smile. Thus encouraged, he continued. "On Thursday I overheard those two discussing ballroom dance lessons. Bridgette insisted she was pretty good at the famous Latin dance the

Casanova. The more Poochie attempted to convince her it was the bossa nova, the more she dug in her heels. She ended the argument by saying, 'For someone so ill-informed, you should stick to the Carlton.' When asked what dance that was, she replied, 'You know, the one those flapper girls made famous.' "

Joy's laughter pleased him. Whatever was in her IV was working. "The corsage isn't too much, do you think?"

A little more laughter through yet-swollen lips. "Look at that weather girl, all stylish and pretty," she said with a dry rasp. "Now look at me. Backless smock. Hospital-issue booties. No makeup. No jewelry. A corsage is a blessing."

He gazed at her, thinking how much he adored her. She shook her head.

"Stop," she said, flustered. "I haven't gotten you a thing."

He stroked her arm. "Not true. I'm the proud owner of a new heart, and by Tuesday noon I will own a new Chrysler. Were it not for you . . ." He left the sentence unfinished. It was her uncommon kindness and grace, flowing from an inner spring, that had touched his soul. Yet that same kindness and grace had also threatened her demise. *What had made those filthy raccoons turn on a friend?* The world was unhinged.

It made him sad that she yet was unable to talk about that troubled night when his life had found meaning and hers had nearly ended. *Time,* he told himself. *Time.*

He reached behind him into a bag, and when next his hand appeared, it held an exquisite bottle of Cassandra.

Joy caught her breath. Royce took her dazed expression for a sign of pleased surprise and pulled the stopper. The sensuous elixir fanned across the room and entrapped everything in it. "I wanted to replace the one lost in the attack. In fact, I will see to it that you are never without Cassandra. Why wait, my love? Wear this now in celebration of new beginnings for us and for the king and queen of fragrance!" He thrust the cruet toward the ceiling in homage to the Dixons, splashing scent onto the bed, the floor, and his beloved.

The bouquet intensified, insistent, to seize the room in a mad dance between attraction and violation.

It began as a low moan, quickly rising to a wail. Joy's fists beat against the bed, and she thrashed side to side as if dodging unseen attackers. He stared at her face, a twisted agony, eyes darting wildly in their sockets. The wail became a keening, and alarm bells sounded in the hall.

Royce backed away, horrified at his own thoughtlessness, flinching with Joy's every tortured jerk. He beat his forehead with bony knuckles. *How could I be so stupid? Of course the very sight and smell of Cassandra would conjure the assault, replay every awful thing she has endured.*

The room shifted. Royce Blankenship's legs verged on collapse. Everything went out of focus.

Why won't she stop crying?

There was no shaking the ghastly realization that like Dr. Frankenstein, he may have unleashed something over which there was no control.

Slender, unseen rivers of aroma escaped the room to invade the hall. The perfumer sank to the floor.

The ultimate burning question followed him down. Who among mere mortals held the power to force Cassandra back into its bottle?

Agent Heidler later tried to recall which came first, the sound of the hospital alarm code or the beguiling smell that threatened his resistance.

In whatever order, the smell was the adversary, which he knew instinctively. It

339

wanted to take him out, erode his defenses to dust, neutralize all he had sworn to uphold. Like the rogue cop ensnared in his own prostitution sting, he was tempted to taste the forbidden fruit, betray the sacred trust. In an instant he came that close.

That smell is a deceiver.

But Ladd's altered behavior threw ice water on his human partner. One minute they were striding in step on their way to a reckoning with Roberto Esteban and the false-faced Dr. Juarez, and the next Ladd was creeping forward on all fours, emitting a menacing growl, teeth bared in preattack mode. The canine had not been trained to attack.

"Halt!"

For the first time in his life Ladd ignored the command. With a ferocious snarl the dog hurtled forward. Caught off balance, his partner stumbled, and the leash went flying from his hand. A nurse screamed, and people in the hall either dropped and covered their heads or fled in the opposite direction. They might have saved their energy. The shepherd had but one destination in mind.

Room 207.

In a split second, as if awakened from a fog, the drug agent assessed the situation.

He could read his animal's every twitch and with sinking heart made the professional decision. Assuming the stance, legs firmly planted, knees slightly bent, he gripped the service revolver firmly in both hands and took aim. "Get down!" he commanded, and anyone in the hall still standing within a hundred feet of his voice dropped like bags of cement.

Ladd rocketed through the doorway of 207 and with a half-howl, half-bellow of primitive rage launched himself at the thrashing woman in the bed.

Royce heard the snarl and stood, resolutely facing the doorway.

In a millisecond his primary sense took the lead. With all the ease and unconscious thought of an experienced trucker down-shifting a semi, he parsed the odors in that room.

Others would testify that Cassandra over-powered the rest and was all they could smell. But Blankenship wasn't like others. He smelled the toxic spill of his own fear. He smelled the deadly radiation of panic emanating from the wounded woman he loved. And God help them, he smelled the sulfur of their demise.

Death hurtled through the door, propelled

by canine rage. A tan and black blur, it launched at the bed and met the muzzle-cracking resistance of a metal bedpan. Swollen large by devotion, Royce wielded the pan with deadly accuracy. The dog twisted sideways and missed the bed at the instant the gunshot sounded.

There was a single, anguished yelp of surprise, dead weight shattering delicate machinery, a sickening thud, and then a sudden, stunned silence.

Silence that was at last broken by the sobs of Agent Heidler.

CHAPTER 19

Cassie drew a deep breath and smiled for the cameras. At her side Nick waved to the crowd and blew kisses to familiar dignitaries of the aroma world.

She felt a thrill of excitement. The North American Fragrance Guild threw the biggest, glitziest party the City by the Bay had seen in a long while. In the tradition of the glamour years of Hollywood, searchlights lit up the night sky over the elegant Fairmont Hotel, Mason Street was cordoned off, and a one-hundred-foot red carpet kept all the expensive footwear dry and cushioned. According to the papers, not since delegates from forty nations met in the hotel's historic Garden Room to draft the charter for the United Nations had there been this much excitement and self-importance.

At every turn in the Fairmont, the Dixons met with applause, cheers, and glitter. They walked a red carpet into the Grand Ballroom, which resembled a wing from the golden palace of Louis XIV. Mirrors and chandeliers, bone china and weighted cutlery, crystal goblets and fine linen by the skein, brass candelabras and velvet-coated waitstaff struck the proper tone of pomp and polish while head chefs, house managers, and maitre d's warred with camera crews, lighting specialists, and sound technicians for the room to maneuver and treat the world to one of the year's most lavish assemblies.

The Dixons were told that in the great kitchen, Master Chef Dom Frederick Condolora orchestrated dinner for a guest list of eight hundred that included the presidents and first ladies of five countries; the US vice president and his wife; the mayor of San Francisco; the governor of California; six state legislators and as many federal; four state and two national Supreme Court justices; a dozen leading men and ladies of cinema; eighteen household names in fashion and cosmetic design; fragrance moguls from Faberge, Max Factor, Revlon, Elizabeth Arden, Estée Lauder, and Lanvin; industry reporters from ten magazines and newspapers; and the chief buyers for Bloomingdale's, Bergdorf Goodman, Lord and Taylor, Marshall Fields, Neiman-Marcus, and a dozen lesser retail corporations. De-Brieze was there, but in the form of a token vice president.

"Table for one," quipped Nick in Cassie's ear, nodding in the direction of the unfamiliar deBrieze executive. "I'm glad it's not you-know-who!"

Cassie felt regally stunning in the Luisa Beccaria original. She shimmered in the lustrous light and graciously acknowledged the many appraising and appreciative looks she received from men and women alike. Her coiffure had been worth the wrathful tongue-lashing from an indignant Figare, the man who had had his fingers in the hair of royalty and cover models on five continents. By the time he added up all the surcharges, what he called "inconvenience taxes" for her tardiness and for not treating him with proper respect, the swirling layers of burnished hair and sapphire sparkles had set her back in the low four figures. All for a single night's froufrou. But what a night!

And Nick's adoring glances were worth every cent. He beamed like a young suitor to whom the homecoming queen said yes she would love to go with him to the dance. Besides, Cassandra would be in the stores on Monday, and she could afford to put finicky Figare on retainer.

"Great Scott!" exclaimed Nick, taking in the spectacle of silver, crystal, and flame. "This is no time to get one's cummerbund in a bind. New York might worry it'll ever get the Crystal Decanter Awards Gala back!"

They were seated at an immaculately laid table just below the lectern. Their tablemates were the mayor, the governor of California and his wife, and representing the North American Fragrance Guild, President Perry Montague, Vice President Benjamin Lynch, and their wives.

Cassie watched the arrival of a hot appetizer consisting of roasted quail filled with brioche and foie gras on napa cabbage with truffle sauce. Her expert sense of smell announced the cream of artichoke soup dusted in toasted hazelnuts and dark rye croutons before it appeared. "Yesterday at this time, I was having cream of tomato and grilled cheese," Nick joked.

They soon made way for a salad of Sonoma greens with pears and gorgonzola sprinkled in champagne vinaigrette.

Mayor Grant Hodgson nodded earnestly. "My kind of dinner party! There is nothing too good for the people who put us on the map. Anything we can do at city hall to make Azure comfortable, you say the word.

We haven't had this much positive attention since Tony Bennett left his heart here!"

With precision clockwork, no sooner were the salads at an end than the main dish floated into place, a trilogy of beef tenderloin, Chilean sea bass, and grilled prawns in shiitake sauce with Israeli couscous.

Governor Mitch von Bruegger, a large mustachioed man vigorously working a mouthful of sea bass, added his praise. "I quite agree with the mayor. If you folks can corner this state a nice slice of the global personal care market, there are some sweet tax incentives in it for you. And should you, Nick, or you, Cassie, for that matter, ever get an itch in your political aspirations, I've got people who'd scratch it for you like you wouldn't believe."

Cassie stopped her fork midway with its sliver of tenderloin and blushed. There was an expectant hush at the table until the governor realized how coarse his words had sounded, and laughed in a way that was half-hearty cover-up, half apology. It was a sound with which the taxpayers of California were quite familiar.

Relieved laughter erupted from the others. "Men!" said Jillian von Bruegger, a large, powdered woman in robin's egg blue, who rolled her eyes in disapproval. "Subtle as whoopee cushions. But really, Cassandra, we could use a woman of your moxie in the capitol."

Cassie was flattered but not in the least tempted. "Thank you all, but I know my limitations. Our daughter has campaigned for a home-cooked meal now and then, but that's about the extent of our politicking."

They laughed appreciatively. Nick blew her a kiss and said, "With regrets to such fine company, a fragrance legend does not mix in the affairs of mortals. Her tasks are those of a goddess."

Had Cassie's mouth been full, she would have choked. Still, she took a generous swallow of water to be on the safe side. "You'll have to excuse Mr. Dixon," she said to the rest. "He suffers the lingering effects of the jungle madness."

Easy laughter ringed the table and greeted the coconut caramel cake in fresh lychee, chocolate, and mango sauce. Cassie wondered if it was proper etiquette to ask a master chef for the recipe.

He watched the comings and goings at the Fairmont. A convention of peacocks soon to crown their king and queen. Pity to poison the program, but hey, that's what hotel contingency plans were for.

Bribe a member of the waitstaff who happens to be a cousin twice removed. He takes the gun inside three days before they erect metal detectors the morning of the gala and places the weapon on a ledge on the underside of the stainless steel prep table inside the southwest entrance to the main kitchen. At exactly 7:45 p.m. he wraps the gun in a linen napkin and slips it into a pocket of his white waiter's jacket.

Sometime in the next fifteen minutes dear cousin springs the huge surprise planned just for the guests of honor.

While he wanted the pleasure of wreaking havoc in Nick Dixon's life for himself, he knew that mayhem was not an exact science. That's what distant relatives were for. The helpful waiter was prepared with sufficient prepayment to take matters into his own hands. To save your own neck sometimes required letting others have all the fun.

He checked his watch. Six twenty-nine. He'd drop by Brenda's penthouse, pay his respects, and establish an alibi. She was a witch but they'd had something, however brief. Tonight he'd take the time to remind her of just how much she'd thrown away.

Besides, he was dying to know. Had she even noticed the gun was missing?

Beth Dixon popped through the privacy hedge separating the Dixon brick trilevel from the Gaylors' brick colonial. She'd finally gotten the energetic Gaylor twins, toddlers Max and Martine, to sleep and realized she had forgotten her chemistry textbook at home. It contained the homework she'd started at school. It was a mystery why she had to commit the covalent tables to memory when she knew she would never ever use them again in her entire life.

But Mr. Kenshaw did not look kindly upon slackers, especially females like Beth who obviously were in class only to fulfill the state's science requirement and flirt with their male lab partners.

Since Andre, though, there had been a lot less random flirtation. Beth now flirted with a purpose, saving it for her hero at J. Primo's. While it was the only chemistry she really cared about, boring boron and Mr. Kenshaw would not be denied.

"Mags? You in?" The security system was disarmed, and the television was blaring one of those entertainment programs prehyping the gala at the Fairmont. Beth had it on over at the Gaylors' too.

"Maggie?" She could hear Gretchen whining in the laundry room down the hall from Mags' room and suspected she had shut the Dane in — unattended, the dog was a chewer — while running to the market for snacks. Beth knew they were low on the essentials, but who had had the time to restock? The family friend loved her popcorn, and Gretch had picked up the habit.

The snacks at the Gaylor home were more varied and heavier on the chocolate. Beth saved her candy cravings for babysitting.

Mags should have reset the alarm. Much as she liked her, Beth thought she was overly dramatic and had too much of Cassie's ear and too much run of the place. Just once, though, Beth would have liked to be invited along on trapeze night.

She ran upstairs, found her chem text, ran down, and detoured to the laundry room and freed the excited Dane. "Oh, baby Gretchy not like solitary confinement? Poor Gretchy, poor baby!" The Dane stood tall on hind legs, plopped giant paws over Beth's shoulders, and with the slap of a meaty tongue gave her a good wash.

"Ugh, Gretch, that breath! Have you been into Mom's fertilizer again?" She giggled and fought the dog down. "Enough, young lady! I have to get right back to the twins."

Beth dashed into the adjoining bathroom to wash off the dog slobber, Gretchen at her heels. She stopped and stared at a message smeared on the mirror in red lipstick: "To my fragrant Mags. Thanks for catching me! Love, Cass."

There was a crude drawing of a stick figure hanging upside down from a trapeze and crying for help. A squiggly arrow pointed playfully down to the counter and a beautifully distinct box of Cassandra parfum. A flash of anger and jealousy swept over Beth, and she almost threw the box in the toilet.

She shut the door. "So, Gretch, what do you think? Do I drain the bottle, throw it out, and leave the empty box, or what?" Gretchen sat patiently by, mouth wide, tongue lolling, pink and black gums and bone white teeth bared as if she got the joke.

Beth took a deep breath and removed the graceful work of art from its box. "Wow! Not bad." She held the bottle up to the mirror. "Mother, Mother. Remember me? It takes a village to catch you." A terrible hurt lodged in her stomach. Just once, couldn't her mother have shared a private moment of triumph with her before rushing off to an adoring public?

A mature fragrance for a mature woman.

Beth knew what that meant. A woman applied "the very breath of beauty" to lure a man, and Cassie did not want her daughter luring anyone — especially Andre — for another fifty years. Even though she could have washed it off after a few minutes, and only mother and daughter would have been the wiser. A token of future happiness, a secret held between sisters. *Why not, Mother? Why not?*

She cradled the decanter in her hand and decided she would do it. She would release the contents of Pandora's box and test friendships all around. But what really mattered here? If God made the orchid that gave rise to Cassandra, why should the woman for whom it was named prevent her only child from knowing its heavenly odor?

Gretchen woofed and shifted her front feet nervously. She watched every move of Beth's hands. "You want to know too, don't you, girl? How about just us girls see what's in here, just us girls share the secret?" She grasped the stopper and pulled.

The side door opened, and Mags called, "Gretchy girl, here I come, ready or not!"

Beth jammed the stopper back into the bottle, but not before the barest whiff of Cassandra escaped. She had stuffed the decanter back in the box and returned the box to the counter when a low, ominous growl sounded from behind.

Like hearing a rattlesnake's warning for the first time, Beth instinctively knew that the gentle Dane was no more. Every nerve ending at full scream, Beth slowly turned and saw something she'd never seen. The dog had flattened her ears, risen stiff-legged on all fours, and taken a teeth-bared stance of imminent attack. "No, Gretch —"

The doorknob turned, the door flew open, and Mags stuck her head in. As if slapped awake, Gretchen stood down with a look of bewildered uncertainty. "Oh, Beth, goodness! I'm sorry! I saw the laundry door open and this door shut, and I thought —"

A tearful Beth grabbed her textbook and bolted from the bathroom.

Mags trailed after, pleading with her to come back, to stay and talk.

Beth slammed out the front door and was halfway up the steps of the house next door before three thoughts fully registered.

Gretchen would have killed her.

Beth wanted the scent more than anything in life.

Andre's match had been met.

He arrived at the Gateway Tower at 6:46 p.m. The night-duty guard placed a call to the penthouse, and after a long pause Brenda Gelasse agreed to see the visitor. He was given a special elevator pass key and went up.

The TV was tuned to an entertainment show about the party at the Fairmont. Brenda mixed him a martini while Molinard the snooty cat shot him laser bursts of contempt from its green eyes.

"You came why, John?" Brenda asked, reclining on the couch, exquisitely long and languid in black silk lounging pajamas.

He studied her. How like the cat she was. Impudent. Scornful. Haughty. Unattainable, which made her all the more desirable.

"I thought you might be feeling out of sorts, what with the Dixons getting all the applause."

"And you're here to cheer me up?" Her sneer left no doubt that such a notion was preposterous.

"If you'd let me, I could put a smile on your face that would cheer you well into the new year."

Even he knew that sounded cheesy, but he didn't care. She was doing it again. Driving him crazy with her aloof act. She was as lonely as he was. Why pretend?

He sipped the martini, made just as he liked it. He'd done the right thing. It was too risky for him to go anywhere near the gala. Let Cousin Richie take the fall. Yeah, it meant giving up the pleasure of plugging Nicky's little lady himself, but no way would he be able to escape the Fairmont once the deed was done. He wanted the cattle ranch and the millions and the freedom to do anything and go anywhere he wanted. Let baby Richie do the honors and reap the consequences. The dumb grunt would get a real education in Folsom. But Brenda didn't need to know. "There will be an unexpected twist at the festivities tonight," he said, "and I've put it there."

"You?" Few could do as much damage to the second-person pronoun as Brenda Gelasse.

He wanted to rub her face in it. "Look behind the sliding door at the head of your bed. It ain't there."

She showed no emotion, cold to the end.

"Go on, look. It ain't there."

Like Molinard, she moved not a whisker. "Let's say I believe you. What significance should I attach to its absence?"

The room was hot. He removed the jacket and cummerbund, undid the bow tie, and removed the top two stays of his shirt, talking all the while. "Ask yourself, 'If it's not here, could it be there?' " He pointed the martini glass at the TV reporter standing in front of the floodlit hotel. " 'And if it's there, what function might it perform before the evening draws to a close?' Keep your eyes on Cassie Dixon when she exits the stage."

That got to her. She visibly winced and sat up. She set her glass on the side table and stood. "It's too warm in here, John. Take your drink out to the veranda. I'll just freshen up and be with you in a moment."

If sharks could smile. He followed her suggestion. He liked the veranda. They used to take their lovemaking out there under the stars until the fighting and the hitting and business got all mixed up with pleasure.

Maybe he'd show her for old time's sake what could have been. Right here. Right now. Why not? Anything could happen after the gun went off. Better to take what was his and to take it now.

Brenda hated that John Lexington was here, that he'd probably helped himself to her gun, and that he still held something over her. She really thought she was through with him, but with his dark complexion and solid build, he did do justice to a tux, and she was feeling less than desirable these days.

She knew what it was. Nick had slipped

her grasp, found the mother lode, and didn't need her. She was another day older and was losing her touch. What chance had she for love now?

She reached for the test vial of Cassandra. She'd made sure to attain one, a purely clerical interest to be sure. One eye on the competition and all that. Despite the wildly positive reviews, probably because of them, she had been unable to touch it to her skin before now. To do so would have been an admission she had lost. To Azure World. To Cassie the soccer mom. To Nick Dixon the playboy who had come to his senses and asked forgiveness from his wife for an affair with a she-devil.

She would anoint John's head with it instead. Admit defeat. Be his conquest. Shut up and let nature take its course. There were no alternatives. She had made a name for herself and a reputation no decent man could overcome. She'd settle for an indecent one.

The Dixons, and whatever measure of decency they possessed, had won.

She ran a comb through her hair. Freshened lipstick. Muted the TV and turned on a soft jazz CD. Took several deep breaths and walked out on the veranda. Molinard followed as far as the sliding doors, sniffed the brininess of the night breeze, then went to sit beneath the chaise.

Her ex-husband came up behind her and slid his arms around her waist. He nuzzled her neck and she felt the old stirrings. They stared out at the diamonds of city lights and began to sway to the rhythm of Harry Connick Jr.

"Why, John? Why couldn't we make it work?"

"Because we forced it. We tried to take you and me and make an us, and neither was ready for that. You didn't want me calling the shots, and I didn't want to be Mr. Brenda Gelasse."

She sighed and turned to face him. "That's the most honesty out of you since we first met."

He kissed her hard and held her close. Her defenses melted. She felt a rush of emotion and looked up, shocked to see regret clearly etched in his moonlit face. She played with the hair on his chest before he again kissed her, long and with surprising tenderness.

Behind his back she took the little glassine vial of Cassandra, unstopped it, and sprinkled it over John's head and down the back of his shirt, splashing a few drops on herself in the process. Instantly they were entwined in tendrils of aroma rich and intoxicating. Their kisses became more urgent, awareness of their surroundings less distinct.

John lifted Brenda and carried her to the chaise lounge.

With a deranged yowl, Molinard leapt from beneath the chaise and sank its claws into the man's back. Brenda stumbled aside, disoriented by the scene. Horror snapped her from the trance. Molinard, the hissing hellcat, clawed her ex-husband's back and neck to bloody shreds. Green eyes stared unseeing, teeth flashed, long, crimson slashes opened across the man's scalp, and blood spattered onto the veranda floor.

John yelled and smashed blindly into two enormous clay planters. They fell over with a crash and a clatter of broken shards. He careened on, reeling and slapping at the howling banshee that held his torn head in its sharp, unyielding grip. The black tornado whirled and slashed its victim with supernatural ferocity.

Brenda shook off the terror and ran inside the apartment for something to swing at the cat. Her hands closed on an ornamental rolling pin from the kitchen, and wielding it like a battle-ax, she raced out onto the veranda.

In the melee, she smashed the rolling pin

against the small of John's back. With a moan he abruptly changed directions away from her and lurched pell-mell toward the railing. Blind and unheeding, he grabbed the cat in a stranglehold, and together they pitched over the side of the Gateway Tower in a six-hundred-fifty-foot free fall. The scream turned her insides to water.

Brenda, in numb shock, sank to the veranda floor amid the broken planters and blood-spattered mess. The scene on the muted TV had shifted to the interior of the Fairmont Hotel. A sweeping shot of the Grand Ballroom showed elegant people in their finery. From somewhere way at the back of her stunned psyche a persistent thought formed. *Go there! Hurry!*

But curiously, in the air was a lingering scent of Cassandra that she very much wanted to breathe. The thought that all trace of it would soon be gone brought her to tears. She felt the floor until she found the tiny vial from which had spilled sweet death. Brenda held it to her nose, and hot tears spilled down her cheeks.

Sirens sounded in the distance. Their approaching wails brought her to her feet. They were coming for John, and she was glad he would not have to lie long in the street alone.

CHAPTER 20

Shouts. Flashing emergency lights. The throaty bleat of arriving fire trucks. Confusion. People running, caught in the floodlights of the Gateway Tower, shouting about the gruesome discovery. Screaming about the unidentified body sprawled on the pavement.

Imitating the stealth of the cat she so recently lost, Brenda skirted the noise and chaos. She wanted to avoid questions, make the main thoroughfare, and hail a cab for the Fairmont. There was no time for police procedure, and she most certainly did not want to catch the minutest glimpse of John's shattered body at the unsecured scene.

"Ms. Gelasse!" The rich, familiar baritone rang across the garden mall outside the building. Brenda froze. "A word, please."

In heels, she walked stiffly over to the six-foot-four chief of building security, Landry Moss. The crisp uniform accentuated an imposing presence, and a shiny badge glinted in the night lights. He had the biggest hands she'd ever seen.

"I – I heard the police and fire department so close. What's happened, Landry?"

"Beg pardon, ma'am, but it looks like a jumper. Terrible thing. Strange thing. Your side of the building is a crime scene, so you won't want to linger. Judging from the spatter —"

She winced.

"Apologies, ma'am. Judging from the condition of the body, it will be some time before they identify the guy. The deceased is wearing part of a tux, so I'd say he was having a good time somewhere up there this evening, except he'd been clawed something awful. Maybe too much to drink, thought he could walk the rail of one of the verandas. Seen it before. Me, I gave up the hooch years ago when I started seeing pink elephants —"

"Excuse me, Landry," Brenda said. "I'm late for a fashion gathering this evening. How do you suggest I best get to the street to catch a taxi?"

The security man straightened to his full importance. "The awards ceremony at the Fairmont? Almost pulled that detail myself. I figured you for the top of the guest list.

Am I right?"

She nodded, keeping what she was certain must be telltale eyes on the pavement at her feet. Her stomach rolled at the thought of John and Molinard and their moment of impact.

He seemed to take her averted eyes for modesty. "Not to worry, Ms. Gelasse. There is no sense in the police bothering a classy lady like yourself with the details of such a sorry end. Any questions they would ask of you can be asked later. And may I say, you are looking right fine this evening. I'll escort you over to the street and call that cab myself."

"Thank you, Landry. You are one of a dying breed." Her stomach rolled again at the choice of words.

"Not at all, ma'am. I need to get me away from the scene for a moment. Strangest thing I ever smelled."

Brenda jerked involuntarily. "Smelled?"

"Why, yes ma'am. Weirdest thing. Here's this poor guy, with the claws of a dead cat still imbedded in his flesh, flattened all over the paving stones — please forgive my frankness — but the place where they fell smells like the gardens of God, all sweet like. Messes with your head."

"Yes, I'm sure it does."

The security man appeared lost in thought.

"Landry?" Brenda said insistently. "A taxi?"

He led her to the opposite side of the building, where the street was not yet sealed off, and with two fingers and a piercing blast whistled a cab to the curb. He took her arm and helped her inside. "Fairmont Hotel," he barked at the cabbie. Before shutting her door, Landry gave her an intensely curious look. "Forget this business, ma'am, and just have yourself a wonderful evening." Still he did not close the door. Suede brown eyes bore into hers. "And if I may say so, Ms. Gelasse, you do smell exquisite."

Before he could say more, Brenda gave him a sickly smile and yanked the door closed.

The cab pulled into traffic and, with the help of two officers with orange flashlights, began to maneuver around a gleaming crimson fire truck. On impulse, Brenda turned and stared out the back window.

The security chief stood at the curb staring after the departing taxi, big hand still gripping an imaginary handle.

Wearing her TV glasses, Mags O'Connor settled into the recliner in the living room with a large bowl of hot popped corn, a six-pack of chilled diet root beer, and the remote. She felt badly about Beth, knew there was jealousy there, but chalked it up to adolescent hormones and general angst. She could testify all about the clash of wills that could make a home a battlefield. The last few weeks had strained them all. The last thing she wanted to do was come between this mother and daughter.

"Gretch, old girl, it's a good thing Maggie's in the house, because if I was there at the Fairmont, I'd be shooting my mouth off every five seconds." An answering thump-thump told her the Dane was in complete agreement, which earned her a handful of popcorn on her Mickey Mouse beach towel beside the recliner. It disappeared in two or three sweeps of the tongue.

"Can't help it, Gretch. I used to be a force to be dealt with back in the day. I don't put out to pasture willingly." Thump-thump. More popcorn. Mags knew the dog was working a regular Pavlovian scam, and that she herself was the test subject providing the conditioned response. Mags didn't care. Two of the most deserving people in the world were about to take highest honors, and Monday Cassandra hit the stores. Stand back and marvel.

"Bet there's more expensive perfume wafting through that room right now than you could name." Thump-thump. Popcorn. "The ones who want to earn points with certain perfumers are wearing theirs; the ones who want it made clear they cannot be owned are wearing a private formulation. Watch and learn."

The Dane watched the hand sprinkle popcorn on the towel. Another swipe of the tongue. Popcorn gone.

She turned her attention to the TV just as North American Fragrance Guild President Perry Montague began speaking in front of a floor-to-ceiling red velvet curtain. "Tonight we honor those who this year went above and beyond to improve, strengthen, and raise the visibility of fragrance in the public consciousness. Many, many things vie for our time and attention, but it is the basic appeal to our senses that undergird them all.

"By far the most romantic, the most ethereal, the most otherworldly of those senses is the sense of smell." To a collective gasp, the curtain dramatically parted to reveal a lush garden of delights — huge bouquets of glorious roses, lilies, orchids, and tulips tier upon tier in a dazzling array of colors; flowering trees; cascading waterfalls and meandering streams; melodic birdcalls; and attractive Polynesian and Asian women dressed in the most beautiful leis, sarongs, and saris of seemingly every color and hue. An announcer voiced over the scene by pointing out not only the details of the set but the fact that one hundred aromatherapy nozzles were at that moment misting the air of the Grand Ballroom with a pleasing mixed bouquet of floral scents.

"Looks like Bollywood," said Mags archly. "Wonder what extreme excess costs these days." Thump-thump. Swipe.

"Good smell is the essence of human existence," the Guild president continued. "With more than half a million separate odors in the world, the future of aroma is open to interpretation and exploitation. In the home of the future, not only will the walls speak and change scenes, but every room will present a smellscape." On a giant screen behind, images began to illustrate the address. "Perhaps Junior will want a bedroom that today smells like grape jelly and tomorrow like cherry soda. On Tuesday Sister programs a day of carnations; on Wednesday she's feeling playful and dials in the essence of chocolate syrup. Mom's having houseguests for the weekend and for the spare room programs a mountain cabin combo of cedar and pine. Dad's a leather man for the garage but wants the workshop smelling like that Alaska fishing stream where he caught the fifty-pound king."

Montague added a few more verbal strokes to his glimpse of the future before the curtain closed. "And now, esteemed ladies and gentlemen, we honor the winners of this year's highest awards in all aspects of fragrance formulation, packaging, market branding, new launches, and revival of established brands. Here from the smash Broadway hit *Power Play* is the exceptional cast to present the Tony Award–winning song that captures this evening so beautifully. Welcome them, please, as they perform William Jackson's 'The Sweet Smell of Fortune'!"

The live orchestra began the familiar fanfare for the hit song, and five men and five women in expensive business suits whirled from the wings, dancing and tunefully declaring, "Whatever you do, smell good doing it."

Mags munched and hummed along, answering Gretchen's periodic woofs with more popcorn.

"What a show, ol' girl," Mags said, producing a frantic thumping. "There's Cass, see?"

She leaned over and pointed to the tight camera shot of the dog's gorgeous mistress. Nick came next, then a prolonged shot of them both looking dazzlingly handsome and happier than Mags could ever remember.

Gretchen ignored the screen but watched Mags with intense interest. The Dane whined, licked a giant doggie snout, and received a buttered and salted reward.

Nick checked his watch and leaned closer to Cassie's ear to be heard over the brass horns and the rousing chorus filled with the melodic success mantra of "Smell sensational to sell sensational." He winked. "Should the buildup go on much longer, this silly grin will become a permanent part of my anatomy."

Cassie patted his arm and slid the last oval of mango-and-chocolate-accented lychee fruit discreetly between blush rose lips. "I think I like it. Better than a permanent frown."

Nick's countenance softened. "Tomorrow's papers, my love, will be filled with nothing but the exquisite enchantress who held the room and an audience of millions by the sheer force of her comeliness."

His wife raised an eyebrow. "No more bubbly. Your vocabulary is straight out of the Middle Ages. Hush now."

Nick hushed, but not before casting the governor a knowing look. The old lecher had been surveying Cassie every chance he got, and Mrs. von Bruegger looked ready to kill.

The smile returned bigger and sillier than ever. Nick relished the thought that he was going home with both the Crystal Decanter and the woman of the hour.

"You can always tell," the cast members sang, "fortune by its smell." The orchestra swept into the crescendo of the song's finale. The male dancers each flashed a wad of bills under the females' noses, then went down on one knee and sat their partners on the other. "Take a whiff. Get my drift? The scent of money, honey, that's . . . the . . . smell" — drumroll, clash of cymbals, blare of horns — "of . . . suc . . . cess!" The girls swooned, and the guys flung their arms wide, releasing a blizzard of greenbacks.

Nick applauded with extra enthusiasm. It was their fortune being sung. Those were their greenbacks. The Dixon estate was about to change forever.

Seven fifty p.m. In white coat, black shirt, and white bow tie, Cousin Richard was plenty antsy. He couldn't loiter by the kitchen door without a tongue-lashing from Chef Condolora. Worse, he never saw himself as a trigger man, but his darkly imposing relative had been quite clear on that score.

"You be in place and make sure Cassandra Dixon never leaves that stage alive. Once she has the Crystal Decanter in her hands and the Dixons have given their acceptance remarks, the paparazzi will go nuts. That's when you send her your greetings, understand? Don't you fail me, Richie, or my people will hunt you down and leave your Maria and the baby a little damaged. Got it?"

Richie got it. Big John had promised a generous ten grand for the job, and even if Richie went to prison, which he surely would, his girl and baby son would be set. He'd have better luck turning water into wine than getting ten Gs waiting tables. He knew opportunity when it made a banging noise.

He took a deep breath and felt in his pocket for the hard metal wrapped in linen. Shooting the Dixon woman was the lesser of two evils. Bad for him but good for his family. And in California, with a "my life was threatened; what could I do?" defense and good behavior, he might even get out before his arteries permanently hardened.

There were tables to be cleared before the awards and speeches. Richie grabbed a tray and headed for the ballroom.

Brenda paid the cabbie and gathered the hem of the Missoni gown in vintage gold. Concentrating, she walked the red carpet to the Fairmont. She knew what she had to do. John always had a Plan B. When the two of them hadn't worked out, he went straight into the arms of another woman he'd probably kept on retainer. Oh, John had an alternate plan, all right. Knowing eventually he would die by the sword, he was ever hatching one last plot to destroy. Even in death, as unexpected as it had come, his will would be done. He'd paid someone to use that gun by proxy, and Brenda could not bear to think of living the rest of her life knowing she could have stopped it.

The shaking was starting to subside. She could do this. Had to do this.

Yes, she was jealous of Cassie Dixon. Yes, she resented Nick Dixon's rejection. Yes, she thought little of Azure's accomplishments over the past twenty years. And yes, she had taken perverse delight in the reversal of fortunes that should have made Azure World her acquisition. If put on the witness stand and made to swear on a Bible, she would have to say that she wanted to buy out the Dixons only to close Azure down and convince that pompous Royce Blankenship to cut his losses and come work for deBrieze.

And what of Mags? The sodden old mare knew better but had persisted in ingratiating herself with the Dixons. Encouraged them in their impossible dreams. Joined the circus school with Cassie like some Ringling Brothers clown. It was undignified the way the two of them attempted trapeze and, according to her sources, giggled over it like goofy sisters. Mags had to be pushing seventy by now. It was like the Dixons had adopted her when what the woman needed was to face up to —

Brenda made her way to the elegant hotel doors flanked by red-coated sentries who smiled at her approach. Closing the doors at Azure would have been a service to the fragrance world. It certainly did not need a woman out of her element dumping treacly little aromas on the market. Oceans Ahoy? Lemon Twisted? And what in the name of all that was sane was the male scent Brace Me? It was strictly pipe and slippers. Men needed to be aroused, not declawed. She half expected Azure's next release to be Out to Pasture.

But Cassandra! Now, there was a scent. Out there on that veranda, Brenda had wanted nothing less than to crawl inside that tiny vial and pull the beguiling aroma tight around her thin shoulders. Never had she smelled anything like it. Floral and earthy and, God help her, at once primitive and sophisticated. Cassandra hijacked the scent receptors, scrambled the mind, took the emotions hostage, and tore aside the inhibitions. It was at once holy and dangerous. It was Sin — not sinful, for that implied only partial transgression, but Sin itself, committed by a heart unwilling to settle for anything less than dark surrender.

The trembling returned. Though muted in intensity, the memory of Cassandra remained terrifyingly strong. It was in her in a way she could not express. "What are you?" she whispered to the unseen presence. "I've got to see Cassie Dixon, tell her what she's unleashed." She thought how foolish that sounded, that she had lost her identity in a perfume. Who would believe her? She wasn't sure she believed it herself. As engulfed and lost as she had felt, she had also felt intense pleasure. Was it stronger than the dread?

Another shiver passed through her.

The doors parted. The sentries doffed their felt hats. Brenda took little notice. She needed to hurry. The police would put it all together soon, but not before a second tragedy struck.

Laughton deBrieze would call his considerable connections and untangle her from any legal snags resulting from tonight's events. Would that he had equal access to that which calmed the soul.

For that she had Fr. Byron. A pang of regret gnawed at her. *I have so far to go.* But without that priest . . . now, *there* was a man with considerable connections.

No more thoughts of John. Not now.

Brenda made straight for the ballroom.

CHAPTER 21

"*Benedicat vos omnipotens Deus, Pater, et Filius, et Spiritu Sanctus. Amen.* (May God Almighty, the Father, Son, and Holy Spirit, bless you. Amen.)"

Fr. Byron lifted his hands from the television and shook a small handful of Tums from the bottle. He had a bad feeling about this night. He didn't know about praying over inanimate objects, but if this was as close as he could come to being at the Fairmont, then he was pretty sure the loving God would honor his supplication.

At evensong he'd been jumpy as a heroin addict. Fr. Krell, gout and all, would not have botched the collect for Saturdays. "Grant us that as we sing your glory at the close of this day, our joy may abound in the morning as we celebrate the Maschal Pistory . . ." *The what? The Paschal Mystery, you dunderhead — the Paschal Mystery!* Agnus Dei, *the Pachal Lamb, the redeeming*

377

sacrifice, the only fit substitute able to ransom me from eternal death. By the grace of God, I shall not be judged by my twisted tongue, but covered by the atoning blood of Jesus the Lamb of God. Gratiae, *my Savior. Thanks.*

At last the awards were about to be presented. He turned the sound up louder than necessary to drown out the faint chattering of the bats that had been gathering in the belfry of St. John's for the past week. There were always a few in residence, and he was usually grateful for their devout dive-bombing ways that kept the bugs of summer and fall in check. The fascinating creatures were the only mammals that could truly fly, and he'd heard that each could eat half its body weight in insects every day.

But this was different. Thousands of bats had massed by now, and like water from a fire hose, a dense stream of them gushed from the bell tower every night to invade the city before returning to the tower with the dawn. Parishioners were becoming reluctant to attend evening services — tonight's attendance had been considerably down — and there was talk of raiding the church coffers to hire an exterminator. What else could be done? The church's chief benefactor had gotten a bat entangled in her coif and broken a heel, and very nearly an ankle, in the dark rush of wings.

His uneasiness hadn't been helped by the breaking news earlier of the incident at Wolf Glen, north of the city. The TV announcer said that four wolves kept at the popular wildlife sanctuary had turned on their female keeper. She had stopped by for "bed check" before rushing off to her sister's wedding. The wolves had to be tranquilized. Why had the keeper entered at all, dressed as she was in lavender bridesmaid dress and slender silver heels, hair glamorously up-swept? Her colleagues surmised their kind-hearted friend had just left her home on the property, saw a need — one of the new wolf pups in distress, perhaps — and went to correct the problem.

Fr. B flipped over to the all-news channel just to see if there were any more particulars. The keeper had managed to trip the alarm that sounded in the main office. The two on-duty biologists rushed to the enclosure and darted the insane animals to stop the vicious attack. They entered the enclosure and were physically ill. The bloodied keeper lay on her back in wide-eyed shock, staring at the sky, as if unable to comprehend her gentle charges turning on her like that.

"*Miserere nobis* (Have mercy on us)," the priest prayed.

He turned the channel to the gala. NAFG President Perry Montague quieted the crowd at the Fairmont, then said, "Who among us would not wish to stop the hands of time, to defy the aging process, to tell Mother Nature, 'Thanks for everything, but we'll take it from here'?" A wave of contained laughter rippled through the ballroom as the camera panned the crowd to capture the beautiful people nudging one another and nodding in agreement.

"And so we live in an age of two thousand antiwrinkle products that, alone, tally nearly four billion dollars in sales per annum. And I must say, looking at you, that the attar of apricots seems to be working." More laughter, more panning to capture the rich and famous touching their faces and — Fr. Byron sniffed — trying to look younger than when they had arrived.

Montague beamed at the reaction. "But all the cucumber juice, grape seed extract, and oil of hyacinth on earth are powerless to smooth the creases of the human heart, until what I call 'the miracle moment.' That is the moment when divine providence and man's ingenuity meet in a cream or a fragrance so beguiling that it reaches deep into the psyche, penetrating even to the human soul."

Fr. Byron flinched. *Leave the theology out of it, President Montague. It's still just a bit of this and a pinch of that combined with ninety percent alcohol.* He poured himself a cup of peppermint tea and sat with it on a straight-backed chair. Where would the world be without the spin doctors?

"Just as flowers in their natural adornment are meant to attract, so with our bodies. It is our privilege as master blenders and formulators to work with personal chemistry — body heat, if you will — to perfect the human aroma. It is our alchemy to turn up the heat, to make things, how shall I say" — here bushy eyebrows arched suggestively — "more interesting."

Fr. B stirred the tea with more than his usual vehemence. "Saints alive, that whole room is overheated, you blowhard. What they — no, what we all — could use is a little ice in our undergarments." He stopped himself, surprised by so earthy an outburst. This was why he watched very little television.

Montague settled the crowd at last. "Tonight we honor those select few individuals who in the past year took the industry in unexpected directions. By a mix of devotion to the art, uncommon sensitivity to detail, entrepreneurial drive, and at times sheer tenacity, they took this thing we do to another plane. And so we gather here in this magical setting to lift them up. To them we say thank you.

"This evening, our first two Silver Roses, so magnificently created by the great glass artist Chihuly, are for Best in Advertising and Best in Packaging. Here to help me make the presentation is the star of stage and screen . . ."

Out glided the famous starlet in a gold lamé dress that the cleric was certain had to have been spray-painted on her willowy frame. Behind the presenters the curtain parted, and a giant screen brightened with the now-famous thirty-second spot for Azure's new perfume. It was Fr. Byron's first time to see it, and he was a little shaken by the seductive female mouth filling the entire frame and exhaling wispy streams of gorgeous pink. The voice-over, equally seductive, kept repeating two words: "Beauty is." In the last ten seconds, an equally seductive male mouth and neck entered the frame, drawn by the insistent pink wisps, and the two mouths joined in a passionate kiss. All faded into that famous pink and gold box, the answer to the repetitive phrase: "Cassandra, the very breath of beauty."

"Oh my," said Fr. Byron, gulping his tea. "Oh my."

A door opened to the ballroom, and Brenda Gelasse heard the swell of applause and saw the chandeliers brighten.

"The Silver Roses go to Azure World, to Vice President for Marketing and Media Relations Mark Butterfield and Director of Product Packaging Safi Voronin, and their teams of promotional savants!"

"Your name, ma'am?" the tall, tanned man in charge of the guest list asked.

Without hesitation Brenda replied, "Sheila Drummond, Drummond Cosmetics." She did business with the Drummonds and knew that their vacation in the Alps had been extended by an early blizzard.

The young man was possessed of a military bearing and athletic build. Brenda guessed Marine Corps. From the looks of the high and tight haircut, probably a recent discharge. Or, with all the government dignitaries in attendance, perhaps Special Detail. He ran a finger down the list and stopped at Drummond. "Will Mr. Drummond be joining us this evening?"

Brenda felt momentary regret. "Ted, my husband, was taken ill at the last minute. The lipstick magnate is flat on his back. Flu, we think. I am here to uphold the family honor. I know I am quite late, but Teddy was projectile vomiting and that was the least of it. He's got the worst case of —"

The handsome young man held up a sympathetic hand. "That's fine, Mrs. Drummond; you needn't explain. I'm afraid, though, that dinner has already been served, but I'm sure we could find you something from the kitchen."

Brenda leaned slightly forward. She could see by the quiver of his nostrils he was tracking the Cassandra. There was an involuntary widening of the eyes, a perceptible acceleration of breathing, a softening of features. He was disarmed without having been touched.

"I wouldn't think of it. Waitstaff are among the world's least appreciated and most overworked, wouldn't you say? They don't need me to add to their misery. No, my girlish figure doesn't agree with the glazes and sauces they trot out at these things."

The young man leaned closer and nodded. "Attend a lot of them, do you?"

Brenda met him halfway. "You have no idea. Teddy drags me to all of them and they bore me stiff. I mean, how many canapés can one person eat?" He moistened his lips, eyes half-closed. "But duty calls," Brenda said, the words brusque. He was left standing at an awkward angle as she stepped over to the metal detector. "May I?"

The young man jerked upright as if in response to the snap of a hypnotist's fingers. "Certainly, ma'am, please."

She stepped through the frame and received a perfunctory wanding. No alarms sounded.

"Thank you, ma'am. We can't be too careful in this day and age. I will call someone to escort you to your seat."

"Oh no, don't bother. I require a quick trip to the powder room first. Just show me on the seating chart where I need to go, and I'll find my own way. Remember, I do know my way around these things."

He nodded. They shared an intimate understanding of "these things."

Brenda, familiar with the layout of the Fairmont, bypassed the ladies' room and made straight for the ballroom.

She slid inside as Mark Butterfield concluded his acceptance speech. ". . . the collaborative effort of so many . . . Thank you to all the Guild for this grand honor."

Brenda couldn't stop to think about what she was doing. The hopelessness of it. Whether she should convince security to detain her suspect. There wasn't time to convince bureaucracy. She scanned the room. John talked of a distant cousin who worked at the Fairmont. Rocky something? No, not Rocky, more like Ricky or Richie — that was it, Richie. Worked his way up from dishwasher to food preparer to waiter. To hear John talk about it, Richie was only a couple heartbeats away from hotel manager.

If he was distant, he might not bear a lot of family resemblance. *Think, Gelasse, think.*

"Esteemed members of the Guild and members of the fragrance profession, invited guests, and television viewers," Safi began in her formal way, "you have paid us so large an honor, and we do not receive your approval lightly. You have our gratitude and our pledge to uphold the highest ideals of our profession in the never-ending search for beauty. Thank you very much."

Brenda surveyed the tables and tried not to think of John's broken body lying lifeless in the street. He was a menacing jerk at worst. At best . . . a horrifying image of a twisted corpse and a face crushed beyond recognition squeezed past her defenses. Nobody deserved those few seconds it took to go from the sixty-fifth balcony to sea level. Maybe they could have had some kind of life. Now her life would consist of instant replays of his plunge and that unearthly scream of pure, irreversible terror. Something as awful was about to play out, and John's unannounced visit was all the warning she would receive. It was time to act.

She would deal with the police later.

She waved at several diners who recognized her, but refused their overtures to join them. She watched the few waiters allowed, now that the tables were cleared, to enter the room to refill coffee cups and water glasses. More than one of the white-coated males making the rounds was swarthy and might be related to John. Given his excesses, they probably were.

Montague was back at the dais. "Our next Silver Rose is for Most Creative Use of Mixed Media." This one went to Oscar de La Renta for Volupte, an established scent of floral bouquet. The lights went down, and tribute was paid on-screen for the clever use of TV ad buys and "random acts of flowers," in which giant bouquets were delivered arbitrarily to office workers. The recipients' shocked reactions had been filmed to great effect.

Brenda pressed back into an alcove, between the wall and a coffee cart. Maybe she should be looking for the Nose. Convince dear Richie to shoot him instead for all the times he refused Brenda's offers to treat him as he deserved. *Stubborn loyalist.* And where was Mags? Probably in the wine cellar trading war stories with the steward. *"The year I drank Italy dry . . ."* Brenda forced herself to focus on the reason she was there at all. This was no time to aggravate old wounds.

She waited through the interminably long acceptance speech for the lights to rise. When they did, along with the applause, she spotted the floor captain instructing two waiters and headed her way.

"Brenda!" hissed someone at her elbow. A soft-gloved hand steered her to a halt. It was Angelina Croix, plump heiress to a sizeable portion of the Dichter-Lowe intercontinental fragrance dynasty. She was forever hounding deBrieze to load up on every product DL carried, a considerable inventory, much of which was too understated for Brenda's tastes.

"Not just now, Angie dear," Brenda purred, taking back her arm. "I want to be seated by the stage steps when the Crystal Decanter is awarded."

Angelina raised a questioning eyebrow. "Really? Isn't there bad blood between you and Cassie Dixon?"

Brenda leaned in, wrapped Angie and her

seven tablemates in a sweet zephyr of Cassandra, and gave a chummy laugh. "When Mrs. Dixon trips, I've been asked to catch the Crystal Decanter before it puts out someone's eye."

She left them laughing, the men clearly befuddled by pheromone overload.

The leggy starlet now onstage pressed on. "The Silver Rose for Most Improved Sales of an Established Brand goes to Givenchy for Eau de Givenchy! Accepting for Givenchy is Director of Sales . . ."

When Brenda arrived at the floor captain's station, the woman had a radio handset pressed to her ear. She gave orders, then quickly terminated the call. "How may I help you?" she said in a concerned tone. "Is everything all right?"

"Lovely," Brenda said. "The dessert was a subtle mouth-pleaser."

The captain beamed. "I will let Chef know. And the service?"

"Stellar. I'm here from out of town and understand that one of your waitstaff is the son of a dear friend. Could you point him out for me? His name is Richie."

The captain beamed a little less. "Richie Marin. Yes, Richie. A bit distracted, a lot going on. I suppose the same could be said for all young people today. There he is, right there near the stage. If you go around to the right, you won't get caught up in the TV cameras."

Brenda slipped the woman a twenty-dollar bill and a look of sympathy. "I hear you. It's not enough you have to serve a room big as a football field. No, they make you babysit a bunch of media brats as well. What are they thinking?"

The captain leaned close. "You have no idea. Still, it's quite an affair!"

"Most affairs are," said Brenda, zeroing in on Richie. There was a black-sheep family resemblance. Her stomach fluttered. She wished she had at least let the broad-backed security guard find her a breadstick.

She was a third of the way to the target when Perry Montague spoke again. "And now, ladies and gentlemen, the evening's piece de resistance. It is time to award the Crystal Decanter for Outstanding Achievement in the Fragrance Arts. With the World Series of baseball now settled" — some groaned, some cheered — "we are here to acknowledge that two among us have hit the ball out of the park."

The emcee peered down from the dais, and that's when Brenda spotted the Dixon table and its boatload of dignitaries. She had to admit that Cassie was striking, the reigning queen of fragrance, all smiles and sparkle. Gone was the soccer mom persona, the strawberry fizz. In their place were beauty and elegance. But it was Nick at Cassie's side that made Brenda's knees weaken. How had she allowed someone that robust and good-looking to walk away? Perhaps the things people said behind her back were true, and she was a shrew. How else to explain an uncanny ability to repel the most important people in her life?

"Permit me a brief history lesson," Montague continued, eliciting a groan from the assembly. "No, hear me out. This will help frame for us and our TV viewers why this achievement above all others is as momentous as it is."

As he droned on about the use of scents in the tenth century BC, Brenda observed Richie methodically moving into position closer to the stage. At the moment, he was serving the Dixon table. His proximity to the bright and happy couple made Brenda anxious. Anxiety turned to alarm a few moments later when he walked to a serving cart, glanced furtively about, then slipped a hand into the right coat pocket and felt for something.

With racing heart, she knew what that something was.

"It was Queen Cleopatra, of course, who used the powers of perfume to seduce her many lovers and was probably the first to invent pomades from bear grease. Ever versatile, perfume was used both to appease the gods and to embalm the dead." Montague went on and on, covering 350 BC and the Greeks, followed by the Romans, who allowed it for ceremonial use.

He paused and looked directly into the camera. "With the spread of Christianity, perfume use declined. With the rise of Islam, it thrived. By the twelfth century, the international perfume trade was established and has never looked back. I think I saw Brenda Gelasse a moment ago, chief buyer for the deBrieze chain. We owe you a debt, Brenda, and the perfume world thanks you for your advocacy."

Pure drivel. I'm only as good as the unit volume I push out the doors.

Applause erupted. Brenda saw Richie Marin visibly jerk at the mention of her name and look wildly about. She turned her back and quickly slid into an empty seat with a table of surprised product packagers.

"But this year," Montague rolled on, "history has been made again by the discovery of one of earth's rarest flowers, with a fragrance so rich and arresting that its three-week market test has resulted in the single largest preorder in the annals of perfume. More than ten million units have presold, forcing parent company Azure World to subcontract bottling and packaging operations to half a dozen vendors on four continents.

"Oh, we say that a particular scent is alluring, inviting, irresistible, and have been saying it for decades about several of our products. But now comes an aroma that literally and legally heightens human awareness and enhances human olfactory receptors in heretofore unknown intensity. The Guild board has declared it the must-have fragrance of the modern era, and we stand by that assessment.

"And as good as this new scent is, the story of Azure World is as good. Ladies and gentlemen, I give you Nicholas and Cassandra, whom we honor this evening with the Grand Crystal Decanter for keeping the dream alive and never giving up their quest for the finest scent in all of creation!"

"The most dangerous scent," amended Brenda under her breath, "and the most deadly."

The orchestra played regally while the Dixons made their way to the microphone amid a standing ovation led by the mayor and the governor and cries of "Bravo!" from every quarter of the room.

Brenda covered another third of the distance between her and Richie the waiter. What had John said? "Keep your eyes on Cassie Dixon *when she exits the stage.*"

She joined a table of journalists, most from the trades, including the suave Claire Benoit from *Paris Review* and the acidic little gnome from *Drug and Cosmetic Weekly.* She sat next to a writer for the *San Francisco Chronicle.*

"What's your take on Cassandra?" he said into her ear.

"A beguiling scent that wears a mask," she replied.

"What's that supposed to mean?"

"It means write nothing until you have *all* the facts."

For the third time that night she leaned closer.

He sat stunned, face flushed with both a new understanding and a new bewilderment.

The scent had persistence. It was now innocently playful, a moment later carnally urgent. One minute soft as a sigh, the next subtle as neon. It kept Brenda off balance, glad to be seated. Her face heated, heart fluttered, the sensory confusion diving deep into her being. Never had she been as incapable of defining a scent. She could not walk its perimeter, was incapable of parsing its essential elements. She felt disabled, and no word existed for her crippling condition.

Nick spoke first, or tried. The uproar would not die. He waved and smiled broadly and held high the exquisite Crystal Decanter, a cut glass flagon that flashed bolts of refracted light. Still they clapped, cheered, and shouted their approval. Brenda drained the wineglass belonging to the flustered *Chronicle* reporter. Savagely she pinched her cheeks. Clarity slowly returned. She knew that none had missed the significance of this night. When the Guild moved the gala to the opposite coast for the first time and their president admitted the organization's pigheadedness to an international audience, for them it was as if the earth had moved.

When everyone finally resumed their seats, Nick said, "Ahh, that's okay!"

Another roar of applause. Another, briefer, standing ovation.

"My folks taught me, as I'm sure many of yours taught you, that nothing worth having comes easy." He turned and smiled at the woman by his side. "A marriage, to last, takes hard work. And Beth" — he blew a kiss to the camera — "parenting is a tough job, and who of us is really equipped to do it as well as we'd like? This award is for you too, dear Beth.

"Sticking to a plan and believing in it year in and year out is not easy. Especially when so many negative voices, what Cass calls the jackals of doubt, tear away at your resolve. When your own peers think you're not up to the challenge or dismiss the thing of your own making, it wears you down. More than once we seriously considered quitting and opening a bait store and gift shop at the seashore. There just aren't enough of those." He got the laugh he was after.

"But no, we gutted it out and stuck to the plan. We never lost the house or the car, but we did lose a lot of sleep, and there weren't many vacations together. Many's the time Cassie was left to wonder where and how I was. And my most recent battle with wild things and hostile forces is well documented. For that I would thank the press, who finally got it right." He pointed playfully to the journalists, spotted Brenda, then fumbled and seemed to lose his place.

Nervous, Nicky? I won't bite.

Richie worked his way down the center row of tables, his movements hurried, his countenance decidedly cloudy. It wouldn't take a lot for someone to wear a whole pot of Colombia's finest.

What she wanted was to look at Nick, take in every detail of how he moved and spoke, get close enough to him to allow him to drink in the scent reacting with her body, but Brenda instead watched the waiter.

Nicholas took a deep breath and continued. "Cassie says we owe a big thanks to God for creating so majestic a flower as the orchid that has surrendered the world's most voluptuous fragrance. I thank heaven for creating so rare a creature as my Cass, for making her stubborn enough to never give up, and for giving her the instincts to believe that with enough time and providence, our search would be rewarded."

He turned to his wife. "It feels like our wedding day," he said, voice low as if she were the only one in the room. She smiled back, her love clearly a sparkling gift. "Now, as then, it's all giddy and wonderful and terrifying," Nick said. "I know I've not always been there for you, but this is your night and here I am. You loved me, even when I gave you cause to doubt. Forgive me, Cass, for ever being less than you needed me to be. This Crystal Award is our completion, but it is your tribute, your shining moment. I too stand in awe of you."

The ovation soared into a tumultuous wave of adulation. Just as it began to recede, the couple kissed, and the second wave rose higher than the first. It was at that moment that Brenda Gelasse recognized true devotion and the unadorned, tragic truth. She had been for him an impulse, a weak moment, a fling, nothing more. Cassie Elaine Dixon — all Midwestern pie and potpourri — was this man's one true love. There would be no reclaiming Nick, because he had simply never been hers to begin with.

Brenda felt empty, yet strangely indebted to Cassie Dixon. What other tragedies might she have prevented by remaining loyal to the man who had betrayed her? If anything existed that could divide them now, Brenda would place her money on Cassandra. Would they heed her warning? Coming from her, would they ever believe that their precious perfume was the Devil's potion?

The best she could do — the best thing for all of them — was to stop Richie before he carried out John's revenge . . . and shattered all their lives.

As the uproar subsided, Cassie stepped to the microphone, the Crystal Decanter hoisted overhead.

Richie stopped midpour.

Brenda tensed.

Richie set the coffee pot in the center of the table he was serving, freeing his hands. He edged closer to the stage.

Heart hammering, Brenda wondered if her dangerous plan would work.

CHAPTER 22

Maggie awoke with a start. Gretchen had belly-crawled to the TV screen and stretched out, woofing excitedly at the image of Nick and Cassie at the dais.

The popcorn bowl had been licked clean.

Maggie saw that Cassie was about to speak and figured by the decibels of the applause that she had just enough time to visit the powder room before Cassie got into the heart of her speech.

"Gretchen, stay!" Mags commanded. The dog gave her a "more popcorn" look and obeyed.

Mags flipped on the bathroom light and saw the message that had not registered earlier during the strange scene with Beth and Gretchen. The lipstick scrawl on the mirror, the hastily reassembled Cassandra box on its side on the counter, the memory of Beth's pale face. Now she knew why the girl had been so upset.

She was genuinely sorry for Beth and the whole craziness that had hijacked their lives. Mags knew what a wall of separation felt like, and she certainly disliked causing any division between Beth and her mother. But right now she also had to admit that the stronger feeling was a burning curiosity about the contents of that box.

"Cassie girl," she whispered, "what a nice thing to do for your old adopted mom." Mags wouldn't ask for a bottle, Cass knew that. Couldn't ask; not professional. She had fired off her yap enough to know bad form when she saw it. So this premarket gift of the scent was doubly meaningful coming on the night of Cass Dixon's triumph.

Hastily, for Gretchen was woofing for her return, Mags slid the elegant decanter from its box, pulled the stopper, and released the fragrance.

The seductive essence of the world's rarest orchid surged from the bottle and swaddled her in redolence so evocative, so suggestive, her knees nearly gave way beneath her.

The euphoria ebbed, and in its place a sweeping wave of intense heat radiated outward from the core of her. It was as if her image in the mirror possessed an aurora of such color and glow as she had not experienced even as a young woman. Though the physical signs of age remained, the sense of age faded. Mags put out a hand to steady herself.

Was this perfume or hallucinogen?

In her travels from Andalusia to Zanzibar in a career that spanned five decades, never had she inhaled a scent so frank, so revealing. It carried its own agenda in defiance of all convention. It allowed itself to be placed in a bottle but beyond that kept its own untamed counsel.

Torn between emotional restraint and abandon, Mags forgot why she had come to the bathroom, and didn't care. It was several seconds before she recognized that the rapid breathing in the room was her own. Something else. Gretch no longer made a sound. Odd.

Quickly she dashed Cassandra on her wrists and behind her ears, then twisted the doorknob and stepped into the hall.

Ears flat, teeth bared, long limbs stiff as chair legs, the Great Dane was there, staring at her, *through* her, a rumble of menace building in its throat. Fear stabbed her. Mags knew that stare. It was the same look she'd seen in Gretchen's eyes the moment she barged in on Beth. Was there something about Cassandra —

On television Cassie said, "Thank you, members of the Guild, esteemed guests, friends, and foes — for without our foes, how would we know our friends?"

Maggie rushed past the dog. *Show no fear; call her bluff.* Mags felt an invincibility she hadn't experienced since high school, when friends dared her to drive from one end of the block to the other blindfolded.

"There are thank-yous that must be delivered here at the outset," Cassie continued. "One is to the Azure team — Skip, Forrest, Siggy, Mark, Safi, Royce, Joy, Lyle, everyone in the office, everyone in production, every one of our suppliers and retailers. You're amazing, talented, special people. Yes, there will be a Christmas bonus this year!

"The second thank-you goes to all of you out there in the wide world who have remained faithful customers and who have created the buzz around Cassandra." She intently looked into the camera. "To you we say, 'You will not be disappointed!' "

Mags made it as far as the recliner before she heard the deranged snarl from behind, the heavy lope of paws on carpet, then nothing more in that suspended second of time from leap to contact.

The thickly muscled weight of the dog propelled Mags forward with all the resistance of a rag doll. Her glasses flew from her head. Slammed face-first into the back of the recliner, she heard a lamp and a vase of dahlias smash against the coffee table while Cassie delivered her verbal honors.

Dizzy, nauseated, she reached back to slap at Gretchen's muzzle and teeth. Her palm came away red with a warm stickiness and the metallic smell of copper mingled with the scent destined for greatness. Black unconsciousness bore her down.

She tried to rise again.

But she couldn't.

Just before the snapping savagery stole her senses completely, she screamed her daughter's name.

Beth couldn't concentrate on any chemistry other than that which existed between her and Andre. Plus she shouldn't have treated Mags so hatefully. It wasn't Mags' fault that she and her mom had lately grown distant. Not really. Everybody wanted to succeed, and sometimes that meant sacrifice. Mags was caught in the middle.

Plus — and this was a mighty big plus — Beth could not stop thinking about that gorgeous bottle of Cassandra. She still tingled with the memory of the scent.

But why had Gretchy reacted that way?

She was fine until the perfume leaked. It was a total Jekyll-and-Hyde thing — what was that biological term? Oh yeah. Metamorphosis, "a striking change in appearance or character." It was freaky.

She saw her mother on TV and stopped to listen. "My next two thank-yous go to the two most important people in my life. To my daughter, Beth, who could not be here because of a looming chemistry final. You are our sparkling diamond, and I want the Crystal Decanter to sit on your dresser, where it will remind you what your patience and long-suffering and good nature have achieved. We're not just gaining market share, Button; you're getting your parents back! Thank you, sweetheart, for never giving up on us!"

Her mother was so beautiful, like Cinderella at the ball. This time, though, the royal coach would not turn back into a pumpkin. *Will they really allow me to display the Crystal Decanter in my room?*

She made a face. Her mother had called her a sparkling diamond and Button in practically the same breath — on national TV. She couldn't go back to school, ever. And if Andre said a word, she would hairspray him to the wall.

Sparkling diamond had a nice sound,

though. Things would be better now. They would. Lately she had seen her parents begin to mellow a little.

Beth checked in on the sleeping Max and Martine. Babysitting money meant gas money, which meant more of Andre. Recently, though, it felt more like her chasing him than him pursuing her. Maybe it was time for a break. Fr. B had urged her to join a mercy mission to Haiti for spring vacation, and she was seriously considering it, especially after she heard that the ratio of guys to girls was two to one.

She'd do it. She'd go back over to the house, apologize to Maggie, bribe her with chocolate for a decent dab of Cassandra. Her friend Elise at school had sneaked some from a test vial her mother had snagged at the mall; then she had turned all moody and distant like she knew something no one else did. It was weird. It also made Beth all the more curious to try it herself.

On TV her mother continued. "To my Nicholas I say, 'What an incredible man!' His courage and strength rank with the explorers of the New World because he too risked life and limb, launched into the unknown, and claimed the prize for queen and country." She squeezed his arm and lowered her voice. "You and Beth are God's good gifts, and now that we have won our freedom" — she held the crystal trophy high and laughed — "we will put our house in order."

"Go, Mom!" Beth said.

"Last but not least, I must thank a woman who has been a mother to me, especially since the death of my parents in the past year. No one knows more about the art of perfume, or where more of the skeletons in this business are buried, than my dear friend Mags O'Connor. Unbeknownst to many of you, you have drawn your legacy from the 'old guard,' of which Maggie is the matriarch. She fought for our industry, nourished it, and cultivated the genius in the Estée Lauders and Max Factors of the world so that fragrance did not remain the exclusive domain of the rich and famous but reached out to every man, woman, and child.

"There's no quit in Margaret O'Connor, and when I needed a knowledgeable confidante, she came alongside. Thanks, Mags, for saying to me I don't know how often, 'It's only a matter of time.' God bless you for being so right!"

Eyes bright with tears, her mother concluded, "It has been a long and at times lonesome journey, but to the Guild and to all of you, I say don't let your dreams die.

Allow your God-given resilience to carry the day. May Cassandra bring you much joy, much love, and the most promising of possibilities. Again, thank you!"

It was over. Beth was proud her parents had done such a great job. The orchestra struck up a reprise of "The Sweet Smell of Fortune," and to another standing ovation her mother took her father's arm and started to descend the stage.

Beth grabbed some dark chocolate candy morsels, Maggie's favorite, hopped down the front steps, squeezed through the hedge, and ran for the front door of her home. She was behaving in a very grown-up fashion, Beth decided. *Won't Mags be surprised at my peace offering?*

Brenda had no time to think. The Dixons exited the stage near another press table.

Richie Marin made straight for them, right hand planted inside his coat pocket. He pulled the gun out and raised it to eye level.

It was now or never.

She kicked off her heels, gathered her gown midthigh, and rushed toward him.

At precisely the same time, Cassie Dixon stepped onto the main floor a little ahead of her husband. She headed straight for the grim-faced server.

Brenda sprinted between the tables of startled guests. Her knee collided with a table leg. She went down. Up again, she ignored the pain. Elbows flying, she sent two servers crashing to the floor.

She watched a handheld camera operator, trying to get a shot of Cassie and Nick, collide with Richie. Cameraman and camera lurched sideways but didn't go down.

Richie hesitated.

Brenda leapt at his back. Hooked his armpits and sank her nails into his shoulders. His balance faltered, and she pulled him down on top of her. They crashed onto the press table. It collapsed with a thud.

"He's got a gun!" she shouted from beneath him. "A gun!"

Six media veterans joined the fray.

A panicked Richie and the *Chronicle* reporter played keep-away with the revolver. *Drugs and Cosmetics Weekly* twisted him into a headlock. *Paris Review* tried to knee him.

The gun waved skyward and fired twice. Two bullets hit the ceiling. Shrieks and screams came from all directions. Finery flew as guests dove for cover.

Governor von Bruegger loomed like an iceberg through the fog. He grabbed the wrist of Richie's gun hand and squeezed it dry of blood. The revolver fired again, this time hitting the floor captain. With a moan she pitched forward. The weapon clattered to the floor. *Paris Review* kicked it out of the assailant's reach.

Brenda extricated herself from the pile and saw with relief that the Dixons, encased in security personnel, were being hurried from the building.

As a stranger offered his coat to hide the tear in her dress, Brenda cast a rueful eye at Cassie and smiled. A little less together than she had been moments before, Cassie held the Crystal Decanter in what even the most gracious would call a death grip.

Cassie breathed the cold night air and fought for calm.

Two federal law enforcement agents and a visibly distraught Mark Butterfield met Nick and Cassie at the hotel's rear loading dock.

"Are you two all right?" Mark was green around the gills. When they nodded, he said, "Some guy went nuts up front with a gun, so they played it safe and hustled you out."

Cassie's hands flew to her face. "I heard shots! Was anyone hurt?"

"The floor captain was hit in the arm. Nothing life-threatening and the only casualty, thank God. World's full of wackos.

They went to commercial, so I doubt the television audience knew the difference."

"But why?" Nick insisted. "Who was he after?"

"Don't know. He had a roomful of likely targets. The police are interrogating him now."

Cassie felt ill. Did this have anything to do with the shooting at their home? "Please send someone to the house, Mark. Beth's babysitting next door and Mags is alone with Gretchen. Is there a phone?"

Mark laid a hand on her arm. "Done, Cass. Try to relax. I'll let you know as soon as I hear back from the police. Now, I'm afraid, these two gentlemen need to speak with you. They're federal agents, and they say there's a problem with the perfume. Agent Piersal and Agent Saganen."

"Nicholas and Cassandra Dixon." Piersal, who looked slightly older than his partner, stepped forward and presented a document dense with fine print. "This is a cease and desist order issued by the Food and Drug Administration. We are hereby authorized to seize and embargo all stock of a cosmetic perfume manufactured by Azure World to be sold under the brand name Cassandra. Further laboratory analysis is required to determine the degree of consumer safety in the application and use of the product."

Cassie started to speak.

Mark cut her off. "Don't say anything, either of you. Let's let full legal counsel handle —"

Cassie took two deep breaths. Mark's expression went way beyond the annoyance of tabloid make-believe and perfume bottle tampering.

Nick, now visibly pale, said, "What is it, Mark? Give it to us straight-out."

Mark ran a shaky hand through his hair. "You know those strange reports we keep hearing in the news about animals attacking humans? Some crazy scientist for the Crime Prevention Analysis Lab at CSU studied the incidents and believes there is a high prob- ability —" He stopped, his expression troubled. "This scientist thinks that the incidents are linked and that in all likeli- hood each victim wore Cassandra at the time of attack and that the scent caused the aberrant animal behavior. We'll clear it up. It's just someone's idea of weird science."

Cassie felt a mounting horror. "What are you saying, Mark?"

Agent Piersal looked as if he suffered indigestion, and the sour expression made Cassie weak in the knees. *God, no.* First that mad end to her speech, and now her dream fragrance was the alleged cause of these bizarre attacks?

"There have been deaths," the agent said, softening nothing. "Many of the survivors are in desperate condition. We cannot permit distribution and sale of this product until such time as more thorough testing has been done."

Nick whirled on their VP. "What is this, Mark? Tell me we did due diligence. Tell me that we tested Cassandra on animals."

Cassie didn't like Nick's tone or the implications of his words.

Mark's pallor intensified. He spoke to the officers, then motioned the Dixons to a more private corner of the loading dock. "Animal testing?" he said, a strangled quality to his voice. "Who are we kidding? There wasn't time, Nick. The pressure was on to roll out the ad campaign, fast-track the production, go for the media buzz. The Food, Drug, and Cosmetic Act doesn't require animal testing for cosmetic safety. Plus you know the animal rights people get on us if we do too much of that stuff."

Nick was shaking. "Too much? How much is too much worth, Mark? One life? Six? How many?"

"Nick," said Cassie, "Mark's on our side."

Mark's chin jutted defensively. "That was

your call, Nick. Yours and Cassie's. We test for sun protection, shelf life, and hypoallergens. We guard against combustibility, skin irritation, and potential lung damage. We wage war on fungal infections and biodegradability. And we don't go near mercury compounds, vinyl chloride, chlorofluorocarbon propellants, or hexachlorophene. We have been controlled, regulated, and administered to death, so forgive me if when they cut us a tiny bit of slack, we don't invite more scrutiny, more expense, and more delay. Nothing's been proven here, so let's stay calm."

Cassie was anything but calm. *People dead? Others near death? What is going on?*

Nick buried his face in his hands. When at last he looked up again, the pain of incredulity cut deep across his features. "The FDA will have our hides unless somewhere on the front of those high-priced decanters we slapped a fine-print warning that reads, 'The safety of this product has not been determined.' That's our minimum obligation, man!"

His trusted VP could not meet his gaze. "And how would that have played right below 'the very breath of beauty'? I did what you pay me to do absent any specific direction from you. I put it in the positive on every label: 'Cruelty-free, not tested on animals.' That probably plays a little loose with the legalities, but you know animal testing will soon be obsolete. The FDA's developing alternatives. I'm telling you, I think our fannies are covered! Again let me say, the Food, Drug, and Cosmetic Act does not require —"

Cassie had had enough. "Stop it! While you two debate labeling and liability, families grieve for their loved ones. So we roll out a week or two later than planned. You heard the man. Further testing required. Nothing's certain just yet. Find that scientist and let's look at the evidence. This is no time to assume the worst. We go for a second opinion. These things have a way of clearing on their own." Brave words. She wished her insides matched them.

She wanted to be alone with Nick, to sort out the incredible events of the evening in private. "Mark, please track down the people involved in these attacks and offer them our support. Say nothing of theories, but simply express our heartfelt sympathies and promise whatever assistance we can give."

Mark registered shock. "That's more than a hundred households. Besides the logistics, do you think that wise, Cass? It might be seen as either an admission of Azure's liability or an attempt to toot our own horn. If this ends up in the courts, who knows how it might look?"

"I'm not interested in second-guessing appearances. If there's the faintest of chances, God forbid, that we brought misery into these people's lives, no matter how unintended, we must provide what solace we can and do it now, whatever the extent of the problem."

Shaking his head and muttering something about hindsight, Mark left. The federal agents remained, milling about uncomfortably as if waiting for a signal to stand down.

"I don't know, Cass," Nick murmured, face a field of sadness. "It was all good in there. Then once we claimed the prize, it came undone. Have we offended God in some way? Does he take delight in watching us struggle?"

She did not know and her silence said so. "This is where Fr. Byron might say we trust to the Truth," she said at last. The next words were bitter with disappointment. "Seems pretty pat, as answers go, and what are we supposed to do with it if it's the right one? I'd like to see the good Reverend pull a rabbit out of this hat!" Her lower lip quivered and the tears fell. "What did happen in there? People were saying a table server had a gun, but next thing I knew we were smothered by security and I couldn't see a thing."

He shrugged. "I was as blind as you. Some security breach, but don't ask me what." Eyes squeezed shut, he had the look of a man beaten. "This delayed rollout will create such chaos, Cass. Warehouse fees. Supplier penalties. Lost shelf space. Not to speak of idle employees and bad PR. I was hard on Mark but he's right. Some lab rat looking for a name is all this is."

The older fed called over. "The scientist's name is Faye Guterman. You may have seen her on TV."

Nick groaned, letting his shoulders sag. The abject look he gave Cassie filled her with cold fear. He lowered his voice. "I never told you this, because I didn't want to sound too far-out, but in the whole area around the glen in the jungle where the orchid grew, there were no animals. It seemed minor compared with the discovery of the flower. But it felt plenty eerie to go from noisy chaos teeming with chattering monkeys and macaws to a place of such quiet, empty of fauna. Like there was a spell over it. And the hold that little orchid had on me and over the Waronai was hypnotic.

A part of me wanted to curl up with it and never leave. The warriors treated it like a god to be worshipped and appeased."

Something else was bothering him. She could see it crawling through his mind.

"It was my place to order animal testing," he said at last. "I was too busy being interviewed to give it much thought. How could I have been so full of myself and so sloppy? It's inexcusable."

Cassie sighed. "I egged you on. We were living the glamour life, no time for crossing the t's or dotting the i's. Beth fell by the wayside; *we* fell by the wayside."

The federal agents handed Nick the cease and desist order and left. Cassie sat close to him on a low bench in an alcove, out of sight of the banqueters, blankly watching the valets scramble for cars. Gown forgotten, she stretched shoeless on the bench and leaned against Nick, whose undone tie hung from his neck, limp as a wind sock. The Crystal Decanter, a little less spectacular in the glare of garage lighting, tilted against a cigarette ash can at their feet.

Fifteen minutes later Mark found them. He appeared more stricken than when he left.

"It's Mags," Mark said, voice cracking. "She's been attacked by Gretchen. The doctors at Mercy General say she may not pull through."

Instantly alert, Cassie cried, "What? Oh, God! And Beth? What about Beth?"

It was clear Mark was on the verge of collapse. "Beth's with her at Mercy. Beth's injuries are minor. Had she not beat the dog off with a baseball bat, we'd be going right now to identify the body. Gretchen sustained a skull fracture and has been impounded. Rabies is all that's been ruled out."

Bile rose in Cassie's throat and she fought it down. The note on the mirror, the gift of Cassandra — an impulsive favor for a good friend . . .

A sob escaped her throat.

God, don't let my Maggie die!

CHAPTER 23

Fr. Byron wanted a drink more than at any time in three years of sobriety.

He almost called his AA sponsor, Fr. Richards, who had once talked him down from a relapse after twelve years of sobriety.

Back then, it had been one of those dark nights of the soul when he questioned if he was making a difference. A single man in Protestant ministry was a lightning rod of innuendo. He realized one night after the third round at the Alcatraz Bar and Grill that despite all the Latin he contained, he was not going to finesse his way by sounding educated. He joined the team at St. John's "parish of the poor" because there was safety in numbers and a searing honesty inherent in poverty.

His AA sponsor was a severe man, a put-up-or-shut-up type given to sympathy in small doses. He was good, if what one needed was a hair shirt and a firm hand. At twenty, Fr. B had needed just that.

The news that made him at thirty-five visualize the inside of a bar and a frosty mug required a measure of clemency and a light touch. There wasn't time to find an alternate counselor. So alone, hands clasped around a glass tumbler of ice water, he leaned against the bathroom basin in his apartment and kept repeating what he'd been taught and believed so fervently: "We are given a daily reprieve from alcoholism contingent upon the maintenance of our spiritual condition." It was why he had stuck with seminary and become a clergyman. Selfishly, he had done it to save his own life, and along the way he had learned to love his parishioners. It made him a more forgiving priest because he had been forgiven much.

He spoke the AA truth again and again and again until after four tumblers of water, the phone finally rang and his friend the taxi dispatcher informed him that the cab was five minutes from his door.

He felt spared. "Hallowed be thy name."

Despite the lateness of the hour, Mercy General blazed with light and rose from the mean streets in a shaft of brilliance completely alien to its surroundings. Inside the automatic double doors of the trauma center sat, slept, and moaned two dozen persons vacuumed from the streets. Another, disgorged from the back of a battered passenger van onto a gurney, rolled past those waiting, one bloody suit-coat-draped arm raised overhead like a flag of privilege. *Maximis ad minima,* thought Fr. Byron. From the greatest to the least.

Fr. Byron made his way to intensive care on the sixth floor. Somewhere around the fourth floor he surrendered the judgment of his heart and asked the Holy Spirit to make him the clement one, inclined toward mercy. After all, what he had been thinking might as well have been his own indictment: *Behave foolishly and suffer a fool's fate.*

The elevator doors parted, and his nose wrinkled at a smell that if not of death, was of near death. Not so much an identifiable odor, really, as a heightened sense of mortality. He had been in enough hospitals to pick it out. It gave him a forlorn feeling, what his father used to call "the jimjams." Some patients claimed they were ready to meet their Maker, but Fr. B doubted that was true of very many. Most people clung to life and fought against death with their last breath, even those who were about to inherit the kingdom of heaven.

There wasn't much if any fight left in those who checked onto the sixth floor of Mercy General.

The Dixons exited the hospital elevator. Cassie almost collided with a teary yet elegant Brenda Gelasse, who rushed from the room where Mags O'Connor lay swathed in bandages, breathing with the aid of a respirator. Brenda, a white lace hankie clutched to her face, said nothing and hastened for the elevators. Cassie was far too stunned at seeing the woman to form a coherent sentence.

Without thinking, Cassie stormed up to the charge nurse. "What was that woman doing in the room with Ms. O'Connor?"

The nurse took in Cassie's expensive gown, Nick's rumpled tux, and Beth's jean shorts and with the detached air of one who had seen it all, said, "It is hospital policy in such cases to notify the next of kin immediately. Are *you* family?" It was obvious she had serious doubts.

Cassie ignored her. "Whose next of kin —"

"No," Nick said, overriding her half-formed question. "We're not next of kin. Mags — uh, Ms. O'Connor — rooms with us and has been a family friend for years.

423

We consider her family."

This did little to mollify the nurse. "Then, technically, you're not allowed in here without permission from Ms. Gelasse. But since you say Ms. O'Connor lives with you, and you look like nice people whose evening has just been ruined, I'm going to make an exception. Ten minutes and no more."

As they approached the doorway, Cassie noticed Fr. Byron kneeling on the far side of the room, one hand on the bed rail, head bowed in silent prayer. Mags lay between them on her back, covered everywhere in white bandages — some seeping red — except for nose, eyes, and mouth. A plastic hose ran from her mouth to the respirator. The apparatus jerked rhythmically, forcing her chest to rise and fall. *Machine-operated lungs,* thought Cassie. The parts of Mags that were visible had not much more color than the bandages.

For the second time in as many minutes, Cassie felt jarred by circumstances not of her making. The priest gave them a weary nod, but she wanted answers.

"Hello, Fr. B," she said. "How did you hear the news?"

He did not reply immediately but looked to be weighing the options. None appeared to bring him any relief. His answer was quiet and noncommittal. "Brenda asked me to come."

Before she could process what she'd heard, Fr. Byron rubbed his eyes, stood, and turned to look out the window at the glittering lights of the financial center of the West Coast. After a moment he turned to Cassie again. "Mags is Brenda's mother," he said. "Though they all but disowned one another and haven't spoken in years, thank God blood is sometimes thicker even than our thick skulls. I said nothing before as it was obvious there was little love lost between you and Brenda."

Nick was swift with the chair that Cassie, knees of rubber, sank into.

He thought of that day sixteen years ago in the same hospital, only another floor and another chair, when a very pregnant Cassie plopped heavily to a sitting position in the entrance to the ER. "Time," she said between breaths. "Oh baby, it's time!"

She held his hand in a vice grip. *"Get this out of me!"*

That "this" was a child, their child, seemed to have momentarily escaped her. "Easy, honey," he murmured, the way he'd been taught in the birthing class. Calm and reassuring, just like the chief negotiator in a hostage situation. He smoothed her damp brow, the hair limp and plastered together by perspiration into unbecoming strings.

"That's my girl . . . You're doing great . . . You look so pretty in that maternity smock . . ."

She gave him a dangerous, feral grimace. Her body language said, *You moron. I look like a hippo on steroids. Quit that stupid cooing and deliver me before I scream this hospital to the ground!*

He started to match her puffs of air, but it was for his own benefit. Nick Dixon was terrified. Who said he knew how to be a dad? Who said they had enough money in the bank or had the first clue about raising a human being? They couldn't even keep a bird alive. Their beautiful orange canary — less than a third the age at which such creatures die on average — had expired on their second anniversary and was buried under the mulberry tree. And now they were being promoted to parenting a child?

The rest was a blur until the doctor held up the product of their love and it let out a wail. Washed and swaddled, it turned out to be a girl, and their little Bethany lost no time in hijacking their hearts and their lives. *By the grace of God . . .*

After sixteen years Nick was no closer to

writing the manual on parenting, and there were days when he preferred the uncharted wilderness to tracking the mood swings of the North American female, but oh that sound! That first wail of life. And what compared with being hugged by someone you helped make?

He smoothed the hair on Cassie's bewildered brow. She needed to understand the inexplicable. He hoped she didn't expect him to translate. How badly had he gotten it wrong when he'd gone to Brenda at a time when his wife and his life were most vulnerable?

That she had taken him back and they had stuck it out was a miracle.

By the grace of God . . .

Now, today, how were they ever going to undo the damage, regain the trust, be of use to anyone again, find forgiveness for the tragedy of their own doing?

He felt Cassie's hand warm in his, and Beth's tight grip around his waist, her sweet head pressed against his side.

By the grace of God . . .

They overstayed their welcome by five minutes, but when Mags had not responded and her weary watchers had had all they could stand of the respirator and its robotic rhythm, Fr. B took Cassie's hand and pulled her to her feet. She reached out and touched a tiny patch of Maggie's pale cheek. Cassie felt cold inside, shell-shocked.

"The attending angels are here to look after her. Come to St. John's," he said softly. "We hold a late Saturday service for what I like to call the night crew. They're the people who are invisible by day but come out at night, more comfortable then than they are with the starched Sunday a.m. crowd. You'll find the midnighters a colorful lot, but accepting."

Cassie allowed herself to be led. Nick and Beth followed, Beth silent and clutching both her parents by an arm.

Cassie breathed the faint fragrance of incense. And remembered. She had been away too long.

Two stark white spotlights illuminated a glowing ivory altar, on two sides flanked by kneeling rails. A thin wooden cross, perhaps twenty feet tall, hung suspended above the Communion table. Twelve gothic chandeliers burned dimly in the upper atmosphere of the immense sanctuary, and above them the ceiling rose halfway to heaven, as it had when Cassie knelt there as a little girl.

Around the sides of the great room, dark

wooden walls surrounded row upon row of unpadded pews. In those pews stood, sat, and knelt a large gathering of Fr. Byron's "night crew."

A teenaged boy in flip-flops, blue-striped pajama bottoms, a shirt of white thermal underwear, and a spiked Mohawk the color of saffron scooted down to allow the new arrivals a place to sit. The pallid girl next to him, head shaven, wore rings in both nostrils and a plastic crucifix pinned to one ear. Next to her, a boy of about eight lay curled into the corner of the pew, barefoot, knees to chin, gently rocking.

Around them, the young and the grizzled prayed and slept and listened to the sacred silence. Several lounged on the Persian carpeting that covered the steps leading up to the altar.

Had the Dixons wandered into an oddly quiet slumber party? Cassie, still cold as if her blood had ceased to circulate, sensed a borrowed warmth from those collected about her. They waited for something.

It came like warm, fragrant air from a kitchen doorway. Hushed and gentle, the purest male tenor voices, unseen, unaccompanied, bathed the assembly in sacred sound. Cassie was soothed despite her pain. Or because of it.

My poor Maggie. You don't deserve this.

She saw in response to the singers the transformation in the bodies of those around her. Kneeling in contrition, foreheads pressed against the pews ahead of them, or heads thrown back and eyes fixed on the dim recesses above, or eyes shut fast against the knife-edge reality of the street, almost to a person they relaxed. Wary tension fell away. Against all hope, hope seeped in.

Cassie wept for her friend. "Oh, Mags, how could you keep this secret from me all these years?" she whispered. "What a sad burden. What a weak friend I made, so absorbed in my own ambitions, unheeding of the pain you carried. I tried to pull you into my fight and said such nasty things about your only child. Hauled you up on that trapeze when all the time you were flying through life without a net, heartbroken for the very woman I despised. Yet you told me I was the daughter you always wanted. Forgive me, Maggie; I'm here for you, here to listen and to care. Please don't leave me. Please."

The anger returned. *How could Brenda have treated her mother so cruelly? How would my knowing the truth have helped Maggie in the end?*

Poor Maggie. To have a witch for a daughter and be too ashamed to confide the fact even to your closest ally.

She wished they had brought Mags with them. Bodily loaded her, the bed, and that infernal machine she was tethered to into a U-Haul van and wheeled her right up to the altar, where God could just disconnect the hose, restore her lungs, her looks, her life, and repair the whole sorry mess.

Is anything too hard for you? She prayed it to the One aloft, taunting him, daring him. *But of course, being God, you can heal Mags long-distance, can't you? Pop in here to one of your prayer stations, say the magic words, and watch the healing take place back at Mercy General.* Miracles on demand.

Cassie blinked. She was a far cry from the innocent little girl who had once knelt beneath this same dome, chubby hands clasped in fervent belief.

"Thou, O Lord, have mercy upon us." It was Fr. Byron. Having slipped away, he stood before them now in vestments, arms outstretched, head bowed.

"You are the light of the world. A city set on a hill cannot be hid."

Cassie could not detect the faintest flicker of light left in her. The Fairmont had been awash in light earlier that evening, but God

431

had thrown that switch, smashed her world to smithereens, and left her for dead. For having captured death in a bottle, she'd be lucky if she avoided wearing an orange prison suit the rest of her days.

Suddenly everyone around her was up and singing, "I stand, I stand, in awe of you!"

And they were in awe of him. They didn't know, or care, who she was. God they knew. Enrapt by his presence. Enveloped in some mysterious ancient bond that had no beginning and no end. Why was it so much harder to find fault with God when praising God?

She felt a hand slip into hers and beheld Beth's beautiful wet eyes. Cassie stood, thinking she would resist the pull, the emotion, the death-defying absurdity of it all. That was when Beth and Nick both embraced her and half-turned her to the left.

Cassie glanced across the aisle and gasped. Not ten feet away knelt Brenda Gelasse.

It's wrong for that conniving schemer to be in this holy place!

"Glory be to the Father, and to the Son, and to the Holy Spirit . . ."

Staring at Brenda's back, Cassie was struck by the most unexpected thought. Here was the one she blamed for all the troubles at Azure, the break-in, the leech in the bottle, the attempts to steal Royce Blankenship, all the media woes and bad PR, and the near destruction of her marriage. There was just one problem with that list.

Except for the infidelity with Nick and the competitive offers made to the Nose, all the rest was circumstantial. Cassie had not one shred of evidence that Brenda was the cause of any of it. A convenient explanation for the Dixon woes, even logical, but unproven. *So who do I blame it on? The Evil One? Myself?*

"I believe in God the Father Almighty, maker of heaven and earth, and in his Son . . ."

Cassie felt rooted to the spot, until Brenda's shoulders began to quiver. The sight was wholly unexpected.

No, God, I won't do it. I've got nothing to give her. That's when Cassie saw the bottoms of Brenda's expensive shoes. Never before had she seen even the slightest hint of common humanity in the woman, but here, now, in the presence of God, everyone's shoes were the same underneath. Dirty, scuffed, worn — not unlike those who wore them.

I can't.

She was certain she heard in answer to her defiance, *You must.*

Cassie's shoulders fell. She squeezed Nick's hand and slipped from the pew. She crossed the aisle, hesitated, then slid to her knees beside the weeping Brenda. She breathed in the tiniest memory of Cassandra that yet lingered on the toughest buyer in retail, and did not miss the irony. Cassie and Nick had waited until this night when by now they had planned to indulge in the scent meant to save them, to salvage their future. It was to have been their private celebration under the influence of the very breath of beauty.

But now the enemy wore the prize. A prize that was poison in disguise.

Even at reduced strength, the trace of Cassandra entranced, like something from another dimension.

"Give us life everlasting through Christ our Lord . . . Let our cry come unto thee . . ."

She reached out a tentative hand, stopped, swallowed hard, and cautiously touched Brenda's arm. Like an electric shock, a tingling spread up her arm, and she pulled her nemesis close. "Lean on me, Brenda," she whispered. "For once in our sorry relationship, let's swallow our pride and see if between us there might be enough strength to carry on. Can we?" She glanced back for reassurance from Nick and Beth. Beth smiled and Nick gave her the thumbs-up.

Brenda stiffened at the touch and the sound of Cassie's voice. Then she allowed her shoulders to yield, and when she whispered in return, there was resignation in the words. "I . . . I don't know if I can. You're too much like my mother. Pigheaded. Unrealistic. Relentless. And now you've created an unholy brew that messes with the biocircuitry in man and beast. What have we in common?"

"We have Mags in common." Cassie didn't have the fire to answer Brenda's outlandish claim.

Brenda blew her nose. "We are so different, Mother and I," she said, hurt in every word. "But as God is my witness, I never wished this upon her. I guess I was jealous of your friendship with her and too stubborn to have one of my own. She can't die without knowing I love her, and you need to know it was my ex-husband who was out to wreck you and your reputation. He died tonight, the way he lived, taking all the way."

Cassie patted Brenda's shoulder. "Tell Mags. You may not see signs that she hears, but you've got to tell her you love her."

"I tried," Brenda said. "At the hospital I

did try."

Pausing in the liturgy, Fr. Byron regarded the two women, then smiled at his ragtag congregation. "I lift you up as a sweet-smelling offering to the Lord," he said. "By *sola gratia,* grace alone, are we saved. Isn't that the best news you've heard tonight?" There was a general nodding of spiky, shaggy, and shaven heads, and an amen or two. "And those of you who have come from dark places and inky crises, I have more good news. There will be no more night terrors in the New Jerusalem to come. We shall inherit a kingdom where the Lamb of God is the lamp. There will be so much glorious light that the sun and the moon will be redundant. Central lighting, people, in a place where power bills are paid for life!"

"Come on," Cassie said to Brenda. "Let's slip out for a moment."

They rose and left by the side aisle, going around a wall emblazoned with the words "Come unto me" and into a small alcove.

"The authorities believe that Cassandra is behind all the strange animal attacks in the state," Cassie said without preamble. "They have seized all of our stock of the new perfume pending further investigation. It may be what caused the attack on your mom."

"And my ex-husband," Brenda said softly. "I know what that scent is capable of. You've got to destroy every ounce of it."

Before Cassie could ask what she was talking about, Brenda, the old bristle back, rushed on. "I'm sorry for your troubles, I really am. No matter how resentful I was — and I was! — once I caught the scent of Cassandra, I knew you and Nick deserved every accolade and more. I applauded your achievement as vigorously as anyone tonight. But that perfume is a destroyer. It's volatile. Unpredictable. It's almost as if it possesses an intelligence of its own — one with no conscience."

Cassie felt her stomach tighten. She spoke pointedly. "We will fully investigate all claims against Cassandra, no matter how outrageous."

Brenda nodded, fatigue granting an odd tilt to a normally ramrod posture. "I don't expect you to believe me, despite the fact that this evening I saw a man leap to his death to escape the consequences of Cassandra. Nor am I asking to be your friend, Mrs. Dixon. I'm asking you to look after that beautiful daughter and handsome husband of yours and to keep them close. I'm asking you to teach me how to get closer to Mags. She's one tough customer.

If, in the process, we should bury some of our animosity, neither of us can be blamed." If it was a smile that punctuated the last sentence, it was a small one.

Cassie shook her head in amazement. It was surreal to be standing in a church at midnight discussing painfully personal, even unthinkable, matters with the one woman she had been prepared to despise until the day they sang "In the Sweet By and By" at her funeral. "It is fair to say that the fruit did not fall far from that tree," she said.

Brenda dropped the fierce gaze and sighed wearily. "What if we trade maxims? For the time being, perhaps we could subscribe to 'Keep your friends close, but your enemies closer.' "

Cassie studied the calloused negotiator who, even in crisis, exuded a stylish cool. Despite the best effort to suppress it, Cassie permitted herself an awkward grin. "When's the last time you were on a swing?" she asked.

They built an altar of forgiveness and praise that night. Cassie marveled when pockets of conversation erupted all over the sanctuary, with perfect strangers praying for one another in twos and threes. It was announced that such intercession in recent

438

days had resulted in four job proposals, six offers of housing, and a dozen bags of boxed and canned goods supplied from the St. John's pantry. Corporate prayer was made for Mags and the other victims of the animal attacks, and spontaneous thanksgiving erupted as the congregation expressed gratitude that the Dixons had survived the attempts on their lives. The assembly hushed when Brenda told of her husband's scheme to punish the Dixons and the sudden fall to his death. When her role in foiling the plot was revealed, the gathered voices rose on a fresh wave of praise for divine intervention.

"I suspect this is awkward for all of us," Brenda said to Nick, "but my hope is that one day we can get past it."

Nick drew Cassie close. "That remains to be seen," he said.

Cassie gulped. She was not so naive as to think all would be solved this night. It was a beginning, only a beginning, but how could she express that here, now, with everyone striving for "one accord"?

Spiky Mohawk prayed fervently out loud for Gretchen, asking God to "spare that righteous Dane."

Nick used his cell to call Mark Butterfield, who, true to form, was not only awake but strategizing a plan for aiding the people affected by the rash of animal attacks. Nick thanked him for his loyalty and friendship, for monitoring the status of Mags, Joy, and Gretchen — all, even Mags, reassuringly stable at that hour — and apologized for unfairly criticizing his work. Nick took full responsibility for any shortcuts taken to rush Cassandra to market.

Then Brenda asked Fr. Byron for the floor. She was once again composed and assured, as if addressing a board of directors who believed in extreme diversity. "I am by my actions and my relationship to the late John Lexington culpable in what has happened at Azure World. I ask not only for Nick and Cassie's forbearance but also that they keep my mother's dream alive by assuming her business, Choice Brand, until such time as, God willing, she can herself resume the leadership. I am authorized by deBrieze to buy the full line of Choice Brand products for all our stores, and this will require accelerated production facilities which, I believe, the Dixons possess and, due to unforeseen developments, are immediately available for retrofit.

"Now if you will excuse me, I must get back to the hospital. My mother needs me."

Cassie watched her go. The leaden numbness she had barely held at bay since the

Fairmont overwhelmed her. She rushed from the sanctuary into a night braced by chill marine air. She made it as far as a garden bench before she sank to its cold stone surface and allowed herself to weep.

Royce arranged a double bunch of scarlet tulips in a plastic hospital water pitcher. He had spent a small fortune on multiple bouquets and begged, borrowed, and commandeered every possible container along the hallway leading to Room 212 to place them in. An orderly had reclaimed the bedpan filled with red and white carnations, but thus far everything else remained secure.

When Joy awoke from the trauma of the shooting in Room 207, he wanted her to come to consciousness in a floral garden. His stupid act had nearly cost her life a second time, and if he had to lay down a carpet of rose petals before every step she took for the rest of their lives, he would gladly comply.

Anything to erase the awful memory of her terror-stricken face and the sound of wailing from another world.

He brushed her hair, plumped her pillow, wet chafed lips with an ice chip, and hummed the theme music from *Dr. Zhivago.*

He held her hand and when it squeezed back, he felt a thrill unlike any he had ever before experienced. Royce lightly brushed her cheek with the back of his hand, and Joy visibly relaxed. He bent over the bed and kissed her.

Kissed her on the very tip of her nose.

CHAPTER 24

SUSPECT PERFUME SEALED AT UNDISCLOSED LOCATION

Cassie let the morning *Chronicle* drop to the floor and drained the glass of merlot, her second. She cared little for wine, except as an anesthetic.

She bent to tighten the laces on little-used running shoes and felt light-headed. The headlines were like snakes that slithered through the mail slot instead of letters. They'd been showing up for days, cold-blooded serpents that attacked without regard. *People* magazine barely refrained from printing a special section devoted to the fall "of the most promising scent in cosmetics history."

The has-been crown was all hers. All hers and Nick's. Good thing he was off doing damage-control interviews and didn't have to witness today's meltdown. *What's the matter with me? When's the last time I thought straight?*

Next to the lead article was one that galled even more.

DeBrieze Makes Bid to Save Choice Brand

Spokesperson Brenda Gelasse, with the power of attorney she had somehow coerced out of her incapacitated mother, took controlling interest in the booming beauty line her mother had created, and wanted to form a partnership with Mags and the Dixons. How did Brenda always land on her feet and get what she wanted? Not Nick, though. Not Nick.

Nick. He had been humbled by the fall of Azure. Cassie didn't deserve him and she should cut him loose. He'd have sufficient gas left in the tank to marry some kindly, twiggy socialite with gobs of daddy's money with which to finance his poking about in this jungle and that backwater for the rest of his days. The new Dixons could have two-point-five blonde babies that grew up to be world-class surfers with enough photo power to supply celebrity spreads from Miami to Madrid.

Babies. *Beth.* The girl — woman, really — could have been a pop sensation or Mother-blessed-Teresa if the orchid hadn't harbored a monster. Now she was "that Dixon girl."

If.

Cassie emptied the wine bottle into the glass and finished the contents off in one swallow. Draining wine bottles before the breakfast oatmeal. *Not a good sign, Cassie dear.*

The living room swayed as a room does in a mild earthquake. She laughed a joyless laugh and gripped the back of the sofa until the walls once again stood still.

Run, Cassie, run.

In a pair of Nick's gray sweatpants and faded Azure T-shirt, she ran as if demons nipped at her heels, wobbly at first, then with desperation, ran until the pounding of heart and head deadened the cruelty of what had been snatched from them. What she could not outrun, even for a moment, was the terrible vexing irony that bound her and Mags and Brenda together. Brenda's offer to save the day with stepped-up production of Choice Brand beauty products was like nails on a chalkboard. That the woman who had for so long conspired against her should now be her rescuer made Cassie sick to her soul.

She would outrun the awful truth.

Zigging and zagging across streets and

around parked cars, she lurched downhill like some crazed animal caught in rush hour traffic. Car horns blared, joggers shouted warnings, dogs barked, and children scattered in her wake.

She cared little for their alarm. They could take it up with God, who might have the time to listen now that it was painfully obvious he'd gone deaf to Cassandra Dixon.

Pride on every side. Proud mama keep on burning.

Heart about to burst from her chest, Cassie pitched headlong onto the grass at a pocket park. Ignoring the wet lawn and the grass blades tickling her nose, she panted and sobbed and tore at the ground. A mother with two small children smelling the flowers in a tiny nearby rose garden herded them to safety.

Fr. B retreated inside his Latin and the rituals of the faith. He could dress up in vestments, surround himself with stained glass, or sport a goatee if he desired to be someone else. The entire church and two thousand years of history were his sanctuaries. Without holy office or ecclesiastic authority, where did the person in the pew take refuge without confronting the Almighty head-on?

For the life of her, she could not recall

one of Fr. B's jokes. Nor could she, her brain fuzzy with wine, remember the list she had compiled of ways to kill Brenda. Hard as she tried to think, her wandering mind could produce nothing remotely amusing.

Then it occurred to her. That morning's *Chronicle.* When at last she flopped onto her back, it was with a lopsided smile. The federal authorities had rented an empty warehouse, swooped down on Azure and its bottling vendors on four continents, and seized every ounce of Cassandra for quarantine — or so they thought. They did not know that she had kept one bottle back for herself.

The last laugh.

And why not? It had her name on it. It was the embodiment of all she had planned and slaved for. God was not going to deny her one last indulgence in the very breath of beauty.

She ran home without stopping, uphill, knives of pain stabbing at lungs and legs.

Cassie finished her makeup and stared at the woman in the mirror. The transformation, helped along by more merlot, was striking. Freshly showered; hair caught in a tasteful swirl of amber waves; blush, shadow, and lipstick in place, she wore a strapless Pierre Laroze that fell away from neck and shoulders in ripples of velvet black as midnight. The latticework lacing that loosely restrained the bodice allowed for plenty of fleshy peekaboo. The formfitting fabric ended long before Cassie's yet-shapely thighs met her knees. An impulse buy to ease the depression of Azure's dwindling market share, the dress had gone unworn once cooler heads had prevailed.

I am a wife and mother, she remembered thinking when she brought the dress home. In the privacy of her closet, the purchase had morphed into something scandalous. Despite its having what Mags liked to call "a decency jacket" to put over the shoulders, Cassie had consigned it to the back of the closet with a firm, "This is the dress of a high-priced escort on an expense account."

But this evening the dress was only what she deserved.

She slid her feet into a pair of spidery thin black and silver heels and adorned her ears with the tiny diamond teardrop earrings with which Nick had surprised her for their anniversary. She left the matching necklace in the jewelry box, liking the illusion of nakedness conjured by its absence.

She called and ordered a taxi to arrive in twenty minutes.

Cassie seated herself at the dressing table made of dark cherrywood. Box quickly discarded, slender, black-lacquered fingernails caressed the curvaceous neck of the perfume bottle from bottom to top. The stopper parted from the bore of the cruet with a soft pop, and Cassandra enveloped the room.

Cassie gasped involuntarily. A scent so succulent as to defy human language curled and eddied about her body. At first she applied the scent with the stopper, slowly brushing skin and hair with liquid strokes. But frenzy took hold and she frantically splashed face, neck, and limbs with the craving in a bottle.

A terrible, violent need shuddered along her spine, and Cassie cried out. She sucked the air for oxygen, but all the respiratory passages were thick and saturated with the unrelenting fragrance. There was not an easy breath for the taking.

The aroma expanded in the confines of the room, refusing to allow the existence of anything else.

"Stop!" Cassie thought it; what came out was a ragged gurgle. And to whom had she spoken? It was as if something were in the room, a presence, a genie, unseen but enormous.

She struggled to stand, to break free of the presence. She stumbled for the bedroom door, horrified to watch her hand lift the bottle and rapidly douse her head in perfume. A scream died in her throat. She would drown.

A smooth, round object in her hand. Cool against hot palm. *Doorknob. Must turn. Throat closing. Must drink.* Cassie opened her mouth. The bottle of desire rose, tipped.

Before she could drink, her shin slammed into the three-legged stool at the foot of the bed. The muddle of her mind cleared. She bit her lip against the hurt and jammed the stopper back in the bottle. She threw the jacket across bare shoulders and with a vicious twist of the doorknob flung open the bedroom door and careened into the hall. She half fell down the stairs, snatched her handbag off the dining table, jammed the cruet inside, and ran from the house.

The cabbie had no sooner pulled up to the home than Cassie wrenched open the cab door and flung herself inside. She all but spit the destination at the startled driver. "St. John's Cathedral." And because she'd always wanted to, she added, "Step on it!"

She was going to return God's stinking perfume, and the Devil had better not get in her way.

Fingers of evening shade lengthened over the manicured grounds of the imposing cathedral. The spires that pointed to God held back the sun and forced it to go around. Chittering bats called from the belfry, anxious for the coming night.

They had driven with all the windows down. Still, she had not liked the awful longing that shone in the cabbie's eyes as he too was ensnared in the scent that drenched her. She could just hear Mags. *"What do you expect? It's the good stuff. Thirty percent extrait perfume oil in ninety percent high-grade alcohol. You should ease up on the dosage, sweetie."*

The cabbie, in five o'clock shadow and short-sleeved Hawaiian shirt bright with bananas and pineapples, kept glancing in the rearview mirror every five seconds, and the look in those eyes could only be lust. Cassie was grateful for the seat between them.

She ordered him to wait and climbed the steps to the cathedral. At the top she uttered a quick "Thy will be done," drew back an arm, and hurled the elegant cruet with all her might against the heavy ornate wooden doors. The bottle shattered into countless glittering shards, a few of which peppered her face.

Picking glass fragments from her flesh, careful not to smear her makeup, Cassie backed down the steps, mind a roiling cauldron of ambiguities. Her beef was not with Fr. B. Her beef was with the grace-filled, redeeming God of life. How could the maker of heaven and earth craft a flower that was both gloriously beautiful and stupefyingly toxic? Why tie her fate to that flower? Why lead her on for years only to use her dreams against her? What was the Latin for "big divine laughingstock"?

Never in twenty years of highs and lows had Cassie felt so defeated.

"You kind of doing a Martin Luther back there?" the taxi driver inquired when she climbed back into the cab. "You know, nailing your beefs to the church door and all like that?" He held out a clean handkerchief. After a moment's hesitation she took it and dabbed at her bloodied forehead and cheek. He turned the rearview mirror so she could inspect the damage.

Cassie watched him warily, but seeing that the threat level in his eyes had dropped from lust to longing, she answered, "That particular door belonged to the Catholics, but yes, something like that."

"Me, I'm a lapsed Baptist m'self. Nothing like a good protest now and then." He smiled sympathetically. His was a wide, friendly face, eyes alight with a merry outlook. "You're that perfume lady what got shafted by your own sword, am I right?" He must have read the defeat on her face, and quickly added, "Mukta told me about the time he picked you up from the TV studio. Said you was a little deranged but nice and a big tipper. Just so you know, I don't want no tip this trip. Fact is, the whole thing's on me, you maybe being out of a job and all. Keep the snot rag too, come to think of it. Now, lady, I ain't no high-class perfume expert, pardon the expression, but I'm thinking that whatever flavor you're wearing right now has hit written all over it. Hope it's one of yours."

Cassie stared out the window and said nothing.

With a sigh of disappointment, the cabbie asked, "Where to now, lady?"

Cassie blew her nose. "The zoo," she said. "I want you to take me to the zoo."

The San Francisco Zoo was northern California's largest zoological park. An oasis that beckoned her as a young girl, the zoo had exerted its pull over Cassie ever since. She loved the lemur park with its incredible leaping primates, and the African Savanna exhibit replete with giraffe, zebra, ostrich, and big cat habitat.

It was where she loved to bring Beth whenever Nick would go off on one of his scent-finding missions. They felt closer to him when gazing at animals from Madagascar or the Brazilian rain forest, or wherever on the planet he happened to be at the moment.

"Will Daddy bring me a lee-moo?" five-year-old Beth would ask. Cassie would distract her daughter by explaining how much care lemurs required, including feeding and cleanup. When Beth had impishly inquired about "lee-moo poo," both mother and daughter had giggled at the sound of it. To this day one of them only had to say the words if the other was taking life too seriously. It saddened Cassie to think of how long it had been since the last time they'd giggled together.

With barely an hour to closing, Cassie bought a bag of popcorn and made straight for the big cat habitat, where male and female lions roamed in a natural setting that brought them closer to the public than ever before.

Fighting the fear and nausea that churned inside, she all but ran to the fence in front of the big cat enclosure and steadied herself by holding the low rail between her and the fence. Her scanty late-evening wear drew stares. She forced herself to eat a little popcorn to show she was, despite appearances, just another lion lover out for a gawk.

Between the eight-foot fence and the lions was a concrete pit ten feet deep and fifteen feet across, forming a man-made cliff at the boundary of the lions' domain.

Cassie felt woozy, disoriented, callous. Or was it careless? The twin effects of the wine and the Cassandra yanked her between languid bon ami and coarse impropriety.

A baby protested with wails of fatigue. A couple ten feet away with their backs to the enclosure fed each other the remains of two hot dogs. In a nearby pen, a peacock wandered in front of the patrons, stopped, and fanned its shocking blue feathers for a crowd of appreciative shutterbugs.

I should fan something for the crowd. The thought made her giggle.

Across the divide, a lioness roared and cuffed her cubs into line. A hoary male with an impressive mane huffed repeatedly, as if in the act of dislodging a kingly hairball.

Cassie exhaled. Alternating waves of silliness and impudence washed over her. One certainty was paramount. The horror of feeling unable to breathe was fresh in her mind. She kicked off the heels and set her handbag and the popcorn on the ground. She vaulted the handrail, grasped the fence with both hands, and raised up on tiptoe. There was a tightening in her bare calves. A strong breeze from behind whipped at the dress where it could ill afford to be whipped. The mane on the old lion blew forward over its face, like that of an ancient rock singer in need of a clip.

The beast turned, sniffed the air, and opened its fang-filled maw to emit a thunderous roar. The other cats rose, tested the wind, and as if of one mind crept forward to the edge of the cliff. Even the new mother abandoned her cubs and trotted to join the pride there.

Proud pride. Proud mama. Pride goeth before a pretty perfume. Cassie grinned like a gargoyle.

The lions paced the rim of their enclosure, sometimes stopping to stretch front legs and paws down over the ledge, as if gauging the drop and testing the concrete's grip with their claws.

Suddenly the separation between creatures and spectators felt chillingly inadequate.

Her heart raced. The urge was strong within her to climb the fence, drop into the pit, and scale the cliff opposite. What then the headlines? Not of defeat nor of derision but of collective guilt. *"City Mourns Promising Perfumer." "Critics Honor Creator of Suspect Perfume after Deadly Mauling."* Poetic. Just. A fitting end for the sorrow Cassie had caused.

The lions eyed the pit and the fence beyond. Their roars grew more insistent, their agitation plain. The visitors, even those viewing other habitats, took notice. Heads turned. Fingers pointed. A young child shrieked in fear.

She climbed the fence and teetered near the top. She waited for the world to stop spinning. *I must go over with dignity.*

"Hey, lady, we done here?"

Startled, Cassie turned. The talkative cabbie stood a few yards behind, hands in pockets, Hawaiian shirt exploding with tropical fruit. She shook her head. "Did I ask you to wait?" And then she knew she hadn't. "Bartenders and cab drivers," she said without feeling. "There's no fooling them."

He smiled. "Add librarians, barbers, and

fifth-grade teachers named Mrs. Pritchard, and I think you've got yourself a list."

He joined her at the fence, looked up, then averted his eyes. "Come on down, lady. Aren't you cold in that outfit?"

"It's warmer than it looks," she said, sounding braver than she felt. " 'Sides, I like it up here. The lions are nicer without bars in the way." She put one foot on the crossbar, braced herself, and tried to swing her other leg over. The alpha lion watched and paced. The other cats, sensing his agitation, circled at his back. Their roars intensified.

"No, lady, please, this is not a good day for this. I gotta couple more fares before my day's done, but first I need you down here, on the ground, by me." He reached up and took her foot.

She considered the hand with the hairy knuckles gripping her ankle. "Do we look as ridiculous as I think we do?"

"Yeah, we do, and speaking of looks, I been seeing the warm ones you get from the guys out here." He stared hard at one middle-aged ogler in safari shorts, straw hat, and sandals. "Hey, buddy!" the taxi driver shouted. "You got a problem, or should maybe I create you one?" The man hurried off, pink-faced.

Cassie cringed. When it was apparent that her champion was about to verbally accost a soldier in camouflage uniform, she kicked loose of his hand. "Okay, point taken. I'll go quietly, if you will."

The cabbie grinned. He picked up the handbag and the sack of popcorn while she made an ungainly descent. Holding out the bag, he said, "Mind if I have some corn?"

She took the handbag and shook her head. "Help yourself."

He licked up some popcorn and stuck out his hand. "I'm Lenny. Lenny Feletti. After you left the cab, I'm thinking I'm a little too attracted to you. You're not safe out here . . . like that. Thought maybe I could see you back to your nice family and that nice home of yours. No charge."

She eyed him suspiciously. "An Italian Baptist?"

He shrugged. "Told you, I'm lapsed. Membership under review."

"Lapsed from the Italians, or lapsed from the Baptists?" She retrieved her heels, trying to match his optimism.

The cabbie shrugged, stuffed his mouth with a handful of popcorn, and hurried Cassie away from the big cat habitat.

The effects of the perfume and wine were

wearing off, though the scent still lingered. But even so, Cassie was sorry to see Lenny Feletti drive off. He had waited until she was inside the front door. She stood with one foot on the porch and the other inside the entry until the red of the cab's taillights vanished out of the drive.

"Cass? My God, Cass, where have you been?"

If Nick was surprised by her choice of evening dress or the appearance of her face, he said nothing. Instead he wrapped her in strong arms, kissed her neck, and waited until she wished to speak. He smelled good. The last of the Block & Tackle.

She knew she smelled fantastic and could tell from the way his nostrils flared and his eyes widened that he was receiving the signals. Desire and alarm shadowed his face and left him confused.

"I've been at the zoo," she said, not caring to elaborate. "I had to get away."

"You're cut. Hold still." She did and he removed a splinter of glass from her scalp.

"Don't ask for details, Nick. I'm fresh out of explanations." He kissed her neck. She pulled back.

He kissed her again. "I could take an educated guess at why you smell of Cassandra and our bedroom reeks of it. The room is unlivable until we get it fumigated, the furniture reupholstered, our clothes and bed linens cleaned. I just shut the door until we can deal with it. But right now, I want you —"

She slipped from his grasp. "You don't want me," she said. "Face it, Nick. You want my namesake, and but for the grace of God, you might not care who was wearing it."

He looked sad but did not contradict her. "Are you okay, Cass?"

She didn't know what to say. She'd thrown a bottle of disappointment in God's face and gone to the lions to do something unspeakable. Had she been lured there by some dark force or the unrequited longing for something more, a yearning that was so central to her DNA?

Cassie's exhaustion was bone deep. She needed to sleep, but to sleep meant more time alone in her own head, and it was plain where that had gotten her. "I-I'll shower it off before bed."

"You take that couch and I'll take this one and we'll see what tomorrow brings," Nick said. "Honey, we'll get past this. You're — I'm — we're all grieving for the loss. Beth's spending the night with her friend Mindy Lowery from school. I figure she needs her peers to help process all this."

Cassie nodded, unable to express an opinion either way. Everything in her life moved at half speed these days. She wanted to sleep and not have to think.

She awoke to moonglow slanting through the dining room windows. Her head ached. Nick's even breathing and inert, blanketed form told her that he had at last given in to sleep. When she had finally nodded off sometime after midnight, her head was in his lap and he was stroking her hair.

Cassie listened to the silence of the house, the home they had shared for thousands of nights. Without Beth and Mags and Gretchen, it felt empty and forlorn. Not unlike the life that was being stripped from her one dream, one loved one, at a time. She understood why at times like this, some people's thoughts turned to the Golden Gate Bridge and a watery demise more than two hundred feet beneath. San Francisco drew its share of dreamers and very practically provided them with the means for a swift and dramatic exit should the dream die. Every couple of weeks on average, someone made use of it.

She felt guilty for thinking the macabre thoughts. Were she still alive, Cassie's mother would prescribe work as the cure to depression. Polish the silver. Paint the trim. Scrub the tub. Banish the blues.

Disbud the dahlias.

Disbudding was the process of removing the side buds to encourage bigger flowers to grow from the tip buds. Cassie had neglected the flowers for weeks and needed to get out there, gather in what blooms were fit for the house, and do the disbudding. Ancient as the Aztecs, dahlias gave pleasure when pleasure was in short supply.

She moved quietly so as not to disturb her husband. In white sweatshirt, mint green pajama bottoms, and a worn pair of moccasins, Cassie slipped out the side door armed with gloves, a sharp knife, a plastic bucket of warm water, and a burning desire to put something right. She was not troubled in the least to do the gardening at half past three a.m. The best time to cut dahlias for bouquets was in the evening or early morning, when the air was cool and the stems coursed with moisture.

Beneath the yard lights, she examined a sea of white, yellow, red, and maroon blossoms sturdy and alert in the chill of the predawn air. They were showy and decorative, some measuring as much as ten inches across. Their geometric beauty filled her with order and calm. Their minimal fragrance allowed her nose to remain clear for the important work of fragrance distinction. At least it had.

Upon closer inspection, the stems and flowers were ratty from neglect. Cassie felt an unreasonable irritation at the disorder of discolored leaves, rogue shoots, and arrested blooms ruined by her inability to keep up with the disbudding. They were as worn down and diminished by her quest for the holy grail of scent as she was.

Suddenly it was as if the dahlias mocked her. As if her greed and defeat grew outside her door as surely as inside her heart. Their sad, dilapidated appearance advertised her weakness, shouted her failed priorities. They were her accusers.

The knife slashed downward, decapitating a giant reddish orange bloom that landed on her moccasin. Savagely she kicked it away and swung the knife in a slicing arc that severed a half dozen blooms at once. For the first time in days, Cassie felt a tingle of genuine satisfaction.

She kicked the bucket of water and received soaked feet in return. Another round-house kick and the now-empty bucket rattled and bumped across the driveway, coming to rest against Gretchen's empty dog run.

Breathing hard, intent on mass destruction, Cassie wielded the knife indiscriminately. Blossoms flew, stalks fell, and what wasn't knifed in two was trampled beneath.

With little grunting cries, she took the knife in both hands like a samurai and attacked the dahlia beds with a rising sense of achievement. With every hacking blow, she shed a little of the thick, tarry pitch of grief and hate that had disabled her spirit as surely as an oil slick incapacitated a seabird.

"Take that, Brenda!" she yelled at a large pink bloom that had gone brown at the edges, and sent it flying into the night. She knew she would feel vindicated by the action. What she did not expect was the sense of closure that came with it. She would no longer need the "hit list" with Gelasse's name at the top.

Two strong arms came out of the darkness and encircled her upper body, but a last surge of resentment gave her strength. She broke free, whirled, and missed cutting Nick with the knife by the slimmest of margins.

"Whoa, Cass!" He was barefoot but had pulled on a pair of jeans and a windbreaker. He took in the destruction of the garden and the sight of his wild-haired, knife-wielding wife braced for attack in sweatshirt and pj's. The look on his face was equal parts shock and sorrow. "For the love of heaven, what is this?"

Cassie's answer was to turn and, with another satisfying sweep of her arm, put another dying dahlia out of its misery. "That's the past, Nicky — Brenda, Azure, Cassandra, selfishness, covetousness, pride — all of it. Maybe it was idolatry, but that's it. It's gone, all gone."

The look on her husband's face went from anxiety to a loving anxiety, tinged with a healthy respect for the butcher knife still in carving position. "Please drop the knife, Cass."

She took in her surroundings, then studied the weapon. It was as if for the first time she saw the results of the morning's work. She looked back at Nick, and the old fire was there. "Maybe I'm not done."

He waited. Minutes passed before she let the knife fall to the ground, then went to her knees and began to gather all the severed blooms into a pile.

Nick dropped to his knees beside her, grabbed her arms above the wrists, and held her still. "Cass," he said, his voice low and gentle, "you'll always be my ginger dust. Let it go, babe, let it go. There's nothing more we can do."

Tears in her eyes, Cassie said, "You're wrong, Nick. There has to be something to take the ache away. Help me build an altar."

He studied her and the gathering of torn and wilted dahlia blooms. The dying embers of stubborn resistance flickered in his eyes for a moment, then were gone. Silently they collected the rest of the scattered blooms and added them to the heap.

Cass took his hand and faced into the faint light of the new dawn breaking over the Twin Peaks above San Francisco Bay.

"I don't know if I'm done swearing," Nick said, voice breaking. "I don't know if I'm done shaking my fist at God. I don't know what to do with Azure's ashes."

They held each other until one could find the words. "We've built an altar, Lord," Cassie said. "It may not be regulation, but here it is and here we are."

Then they were still.

CHAPTER 25

Cassie stroked burnished hair the color of buckskin and marveled at the sheen of it. She laid the brush aside and trailed a fingertip along the bridge of Beth's nose.

"I'm alive, Mom, really."

They sat together on the lawn opposite Gretchen's deserted dog run. Beth laid her head in her mother's lap. Cassie leaned back against a pink flowering dogwood.

In the weeks since that awful night when, as Nick put it, "God took an ax to all our presuppositions," Cassie took every opportunity to draw her daughter close.

"I know, Button, I know. Just let a grateful mother check once in a while, okay?"

Beth did not protest the endearment. All the Dixons were staying within easy reach — physically and verbally. Nick said it best. "How closely must we skirt disaster before we stop leaving memos and actually see the person standing right in front of us?" He spent a few hours each day overseeing the stepped-up production of Choice Brand beautifiers but always came home early for dinner, a movie, or long walks in the park, just the three of them. Four, if you counted Andre, but Beth was seeing less of him these days, deciding to apply herself more to her studies so she did not end up "with bubble-gum for brains."

They rejoiced in Maggie's slow but steady progress. She was now in physical rehab, with a series of plastic surgeries beyond that. Cassie, though, predicted swift improvement now that Brenda was her mother's personal rehab coach. Mags had moved into Brenda's penthouse apartment, and it was apparent that rebuilding the long-dormant relationship was as medically beneficial as learning to walk again. "She gives bloodthirsty pirates a good name," grumbled Mags, but it was apparent from the twinkle in her eye that she thrived on the attention. And she should talk. For her part, Brenda cooked their favorite Thai food and forbade her mother from going any-where near a microphone or reporter's note-pad. They took up painting shorebirds from memory, their easels once again side by side.

Gretchen's skull fracture healed nicely. The family canine seemed normal in all respects, with no lingering memories of that fated night. For now, however, the dog remained in a kennel at Dr. Grayson's. It would take longer for Beth to regain trust in the Dane, but progress was being made. The nightmares were less frequent. As for Mags, she insisted Gretchen be restored to the family. "You wouldn't hold it against Cousin Willie if someone slipped him a bad batch of mushrooms and he burned down the barn," she said.

In three weeks Joy and Royce would become Mr. and Mrs. Blankenship. Nick agreed to be best man and Cassie maid of honor. Joy was out of the hospital, recuperating nicely, the Nose her constant companion. They would honeymoon in France to tour all the famous perfumeries for him, all the classic cheese makers for her. In the meantime he managed the Choice Brand operation for the Dixons and helped Brenda purge deBrieze stores of all but the best scents. Although Night Tremors was allowed to remain, its advertising budget was slashed in half. Brenda said not a word.

Joy's remaining raccoon neighbors were trapped and shipped to a remote forest far from town, where she hoped the kits were able to find other raccoons with which to cleave. Despite the relocation, she put the house and its painful memories on the market and was already rescuing from bachelor neglect the home she would share with Royce.

After massive media warnings to return all remaining samples of Cassandra, the bizarre attack incidents involving a variety of animals across the Golden State had fallen to zero. The investigation into the true nature of the impounded perfume was ongoing and fed the newsmagazines and talk shows. The tabloids sharpened their knives over what they dubbed "the deposed king and queen of fragrance," but when the Dixons used the Crystal Decanter prize money to establish a foundation for the attack victims and trust funds for the children of those who had so tragically died, the raking of muck subsided. Fr. Byron, with the blessing of his fellow clergy at St. John's Cathedral, agreed to administer the fund. Laughton deBrieze contributed one hundred thousand dollars to the cause.

Mark Butterfield, who likened the case to the Tylenol poisoning of 1982, began adoption proceedings for a brother and sister, five and four years old respectively, who lost their single mother in a dog attack. There was no one else in their extended family who could take them, and he had seen the impoverished circumstances in which the kids lived. Mark brushed off the admiration of others, saying that it was strictly a selfish ploy to get his girlfriend to commit. But Cassie saw the tears of a paternal love whenever he talked about the children who would one day be his.

Cassie surveyed the dahlia garden, now brown and battle-beaten by her dark night of the soul. The soil where Nick and she had knelt and waited for God bore still the slight depressions of their desperate vigil. It was only then, hours after the battle had been so spectacularly lost, that they had finally surrendered.

The hacked blooms crunched beneath her feet.

She thought of Barb Silverman and making good on her promise before a vast television audience swollen by the Cassandra scandal.

Instead of providing free Cassandra to the studio audience, she gave the host an on-air facial and provided everyone with a double dose of Choice Brand beautifiers. Thanks to a national news feed, that afternoon sales of animal-tested Choice Brand products at all deBrieze stores experienced a sharp rise. There had only been a single call-in threat from a group calling itself FAR — For Animal Rights — but there had been no criminal trespass, and bottling plant security had been stepped up. Understandably, Cassie did not receive the apology owed her by Silverman from the first appearance, but a new respect for Cassie's resilience was evident from a gentler line of questions.

"How many catechists does it take to change a lightbulb?" Fr. Byron asked when she showed up for the first of the weekly classes in the Christian faith.

Cassie shook her head. "I don't know. How many does it take?"

"Just one. The rest stand around saying, 'Why? Why? Why did the light go out?'"

He hugged her; she sobbed on his shoulder. "Let it out, Cassie. You're broken, and that's when the Lord's grace runs richest. Where's Nick?"

Cassie sniffled into the royal blue brocade vest. "He said to tell you to count him in the next round if you agree to be his permanent running partner. I c – can't come home without a yes."

Fr. B laughed. "You tell that swindler that I agree in principle but will seek medical approval. And if I don't hear what I want to hear, I reserve the right to a second opinion.

If God had meant for priests to run, approved vestments would include a pair of jogging shoes."

Cassie asked all of the former employees to stay and gave those who did a loyalty bonus and a five percent raise. The Azure World name had been erased, but the acceptance of Choice Brand products was on the rise.

The only trusted member of the team they lost was sales manager Forrest Cunningham.

"I wish you all well, but I don't have the vinegar necessary to starting over," Poochie said when he gave his notice. "Early retirement's the way to go. Let the young Turks in sales take the CB line and run with it."

Two weeks later he was charged with using his top-security clearance to set up the botched robbery of corporate secrets and with placing the leech in the bottle of Swirl.

He actually seemed relieved. At Cassie's office desk, shoulders slumped, he awaited arrest. "When the tampering incident failed to bring down deBrieze as well, John Lexington went ballistic and threatened to kill me. I've been living on the edge of a heart attack. That Lexington was a real artist — nobody could paint pictures of the horrible ways there are to die like he could."

All the same, he confessed most regret that his longtime verbal sparring partner, Bridgett Sigafoos in product development, was on antidepressants over the news of his moral collapse. "He's a regular Eggs Benedict," she told Cassie as they watched the authorities take him away in cuffs.

Cassie noted Poochie's hangdog expression and utter silence. *For once, he has neither the heart nor the guts to correct her.*

Once Poochie was gone from the building, Mark Butterfield said, "The public is ready to forgive and move on." He once more invoked the Tylenol poisoning comparison. "There have been a few cries of corporate negligence, but swift action by the Dixons on behalf of the stricken families cooled most of those."

"Culpability?" said Nick. Cassie was glad the question had been asked.

"The courts ruled that due diligence was performed in compliance with the law. A couple of enterprising politicians are introducing legislation that will make animal testing mandatory on products manufactured for cosmetic consumption. The animal rights people promise unspecified reprisals. Listen, you two, I'm sorry for the way things turned out."

"No need to be," said Cassie. "We had

our moment in the sun. Now it's Faye Guterman's turn." She picked up the newspaper with a photo of Guterman on the cover and read aloud, " 'Hailed for the discerning analysis that brought the bizarre attacks to an end, Guterman has accepted a six-figure advance for her book *The Case of the Killer Perfume* to be published next fall by Random House.' "

For Cassie, the capper to the day came in a phone call from Perry Montague of the Guild. "Cass, what a miserable turn of events. Please accept my profound regrets."

"Thanks, Perry. It hurts, no way around it, but there's good with the bad. Walls have come down and people have reconciled. I'm just so sad for those who suffered in the attacks. No one can give them their lives back. No one. Hopefully, the foundation can at least provide the families with some renewed hope."

Montague personally donated fifty thousand dollars to the fund.

On the sixty-fifth floor, Brenda received Lt. Lloyd Reynolds with her usual cool.

"My ex-husband was an underworld regular, however suspicious you think the circumstances under which he died. What's really strange is how long he survived, given

476

the company he kept."

She wasn't in the least surprised when, true to her prediction, Laughton deBrieze parlayed with the chief of police. Whatever was said at that private meeting aboard a police cruiser in the middle of San Francisco Bay, her credibility was restored overnight and her ex-husband's death ruled a tragic accident.

Cassie shifted against the dogwood, and Beth smiled up at her. "Fr. B called while you were at school," she said. "You remember my telling you about Lydia's catechism classes and the growing interest she had in the Protestant guy with the Barbasol on his neck? Well, it turns out that as soon as Lydia completed catechism, she wanted to join the church, worship Yeshua as Messiah, and propose marriage to shaving cream man! They will be the first wedding at St. John's since the bats vacated the belfry. Lydia becomes Mrs. James Fields on the last day of Passover. I'm serving at the reception. Want to volunteer?"

"Can Andre come?"

Cassie couldn't hide the fact that the request was unexpected.

"I know, we're not the item we once were. But Andre's been asking questions about life and an afterlife ever since he took his lumps from the intruder. I think it's time for him to see how a church family operates. Please?"

"Of course," Cassie replied. "We'll put him on beverages. Fr. B wanted me to be sure to tell you he's come up with a title for his new cathedral newsletter. He's calling it *The Sheepskin: News for Ewes, Rams, and Lambs.* I'm supposed to ask you what you think." She grinned.

Beth groaned. "Tell him he's as funny as stale fruitcake."

They were silent a time while clouds piled high like mashed potatoes slowly passed overhead.

"Mom?"

"Hmm?"

"You told me once you wished that we — you and I — could be like Jeanne Lanvin and her daughter. You never told me what you meant by that."

"Ah." That was all Cassie said for several minutes. To her credit, Beth waited without comment.

"Well, you remember me telling you that the Lanvin name is highly regarded among perfumers? But Madame Jeanne Lanvin, the oldest of eleven children, first made her name as one of Europe's premier fashion

478

designers. She made beautifully feminine dresses for her only child, Marguerite, and when demand for her clothing grew, Madame Lanvin opened a couture house selling mother-daughter garments.

"So close was the bond between mom and daughter that a famous illustrator captured it in the logo for the House of Lanvin — a little girl at her mother's knee, both in lavish ball gowns. When the daughter became the talented opera singer Comtesse de Polignac, she always turned out in her famous mother's beautiful gowns. Because they loved each other so much, they were able to set the standard in youthful mother-daughter fashion for Edwardian England."

Cassie went silent again, and when Beth asked her what was wrong, she looked away. "I wanted that closeness for us. Not for you to think I'm a terrible person, leaving you to your own devices, putting people at risk, causing a lot of pain and suffering because of my pride. I've asked God and your father to forgive me, but will you?"

Beth got up on her knees and wrapped slender, tan arms around Cassie's neck. They sat head to head in silence for a few minutes before Beth said, "You and I are okay. We both lost interest for a time. It happens. But you didn't knowingly hurt those people. Who knew such a deadly aroma existed in so beautiful a flower?"

Cassie clung to her daughter's words, a verbal lifeline in a wave-tossed sea of guilt. She knew what she really needed was to forgive herself.

Beth wore a worried frown. "Sorry, Mom. Guess I haven't been a whole lot of encouragement the last year. I used to like it when I was one of the first to get a new Azure scent. And I liked the attention from the other girls, who thought it would be cool to have a mom who made perfume. It was cool, but I guess I had some fantasy going about inventing perfume right along with you. Then other interests came in, then I hit sixteen, thought I was too cool, and resented that you were targeting an older crowd. What did my opinion matter?"

Cassie held Beth close, rubbing her back like she used to when she was little. "Your opinion means everything to me."

"Then is it okay for me to become a UN peacekeeper?"

Cassie gulped. "Get a good liberal arts education and call me in the morning," she said, trying to make light of a terrifying prospect. "For all the peace those keepers keep, they do get shot at a fair amount."

Beth laughed. "Just testing you, Mom. You

kind of passed okay. At least there wasn't an out-and-out no in there anywhere."

"Of course not," Cassie said. "Are you thinking of some kind of outreach work?"

"I think so. No offense, but most of the people in our circle spend an inordinate amount of time trying to get ahead. When is it time to give back?"

Cassie smiled at her daughter's altruism and the rapid growing up she'd done in just a few short weeks. What was it Emily Dickinson said? *"The truth must dazzle gradually or every man be blind."*

"Who are you, oh wise one?" Cassie said aloud. "I thought you were leaning toward hairstyling — or at least a certain hairstylist. And since when do you use *inordinate* in a sentence?"

Beth stared into the distance. "Hair is just there to keep skin cancer at bay. And Andre uses *inordinate* a lot. He thinks most women use an inordinate amount of hairspray. I want to do something meaningful, something that counts. Like midwifery. Well-baby care. Bush clinic. Jungle surgery."

"Whoa there, Dr. Livingston. You're not so good with needles, remember. And the last time you had to cut up a chicken for dinner, I thought you'd pass out."

"I was dehydrated from tennis, Mother. A

481

little Gatorade and I was fine."

They made a face at each other and burst out laughing. "I wish we had recorded that little exchange," said Cassie. "All I'm saying is, liberal arts before medical school. You want to be a person of broad interests."

Beth sighed and rolled her eyes in the way of all daughters when their mothers are being especially parental. Cassie didn't blame her. "How are you at heights?"

"Serious?"

"Serious. Thursday night. If I don't get back there soon, they'll revoke my leotard. Think you can do it?"

Beth lifted her nose high in the air. "If someone *your* age can do it, how hard can it be?"

Cassie pulled her sassy-tongued offspring into a bear hug and buried her nose in the clean, youthful scalp. "Mmmm. You smell good."

"I'm not wearing anything," Beth said. "It's just me."

"I know." Cassie tightened her grip on her daughter. "I know."

CHAPTER 26

The Waronai chieftain lay in the little clearing near the stream that had given life through three wives, nine children, a dozen tribal wars, and enough days for his body to shrivel and rebel. It wasn't the accumulated hatchet scars, spear thrusts, and burnt flesh that had finished his days. It was the ancestors calling him home. In the days since the theft of the sacred flower stink, it was as if every one of his dead had slipped inside his body, he supposed by entering through his nose or mouth while he slept, or perhaps through some other orifice while he bathed naked in the stream.

All he knew with certainty was that this was the day of his leaving. He had forbidden either tribesmen or kinsmen to fetch the husk he would leave behind. He wanted flesh and bones to decay into the same earth in which the roots of the sacred flower grew. In the next season, when the flower birthed again, it would draw him up from the ground into itself, and they would be one in a way not even he and his wives had achieved.

He peered through slitted eyes at the plant by which he slept. It was a faded apparition of its once-fertile, succulent glory. He had sent the warriors back to the village, but he had remained until the flower stopped itself and died. The death was swift and the bloom soon turned brown and ugly. He watched its fall to the earth, there despite its royalty to collapse inward, turn to crisp, and then to dust.

And still he remained, consuming the last of the rancid pig meat. Before the next moon came and went, he vomited violently again and again until he had to look to see that his stomach had not fallen out. The vomit stink that defiled the small bowl between two fallen trees was nothing like the sweet breath the flower had exhaled during its twelve suns and twelve moons. That breath had escaped the earth's soft lips; this stink leaked from the earth's rumbling bowels.

Lingering memories of the flower's insistent pleasure continued to assail the chieftain day and night. But even its powerful magic could not stir what was beyond stirring. He ate and drank little and did not return to the head of his family or the governance of his village. He became weak and delirious, assaulted by the fearsome, misshapen creatures of darkness without his having chewed a single betel nut.

He faded in and out of the world. Day and night ceased to take turns ruling his life and became one gray mass. Someone ignored his edict and brought small parcels of food and water while he slept and left them inches from his face. Sometimes he drank a little and took a bite or two; the rest he left for the jungle creatures that worked far too hard for their meager nourishment.

Gradually life above, beside, and beyond the clearing returned. It always did following the death of the flower. He heard the chirrups and caws, the screeches and scratches of life all around him. He also perceived the chuckles and coughs, the snorts and hoofbeats of monsters, sent to test his dying will. They stamped and cavorted about his body, and occasionally one would take a nip from a bare arm or toe. *Devils feeding. Scavengers! Cowards nibble a man gone. Take me whole!*

What of the albino? He did not wish his last thought to be one of frustration, yet no one brought news of any villages falling into ruin. Was he, a chief, to be denied the satisfaction of knowing that the white one paid for his transgression? *That is the way of revenge. It cannot be rushed.* Death, however, had a way of speeding up once the ancestors determined the manner. All other sounds faded now, but for the gurgle and rush of the stream. It intensified and filled his head with roaring.

He wished for just one of his ancestors to meet him halfway and offer a hand across.

None came.

He listened to the thud of his heart slow, stutter, stop. The old warrior tried to rise but couldn't, caught his breath without knowing from where the next would come.

None came.

CHAPTER 27

Fr. Byron lifted knobby knees higher, hoping the cramps at the backs of his legs would subside. They didn't.

Jogging effortlessly at his side, Nicholas Dixon asked, "So how about it, Reverend? What do you say to a man when the dream has died?"

Fr. B veered to the right and flopped onto the park grass in the shade of a giant maple. He massaged protesting thighs and thought about interceding for a Good Humor ice cream truck. He peered up at Nick running in place. "You tell him to acknowledge that while the dream has died, not a single thing has been lost. The man who has God lacks nothing."

Nick stopped running, planted hands on hips, and began a series of deep squats. "That's the . . . book answer," he said, grunting in midsentence. "What's your . . . gut say?"

Attempting to ignore the fire that had now spread from thighs to calves, Fr. B flopped onto his back, locked fingers cushioning his head against the hard ground. "It says what C. S. Lewis heard his gut say: 'This tension fuels my faith.' "

His running companion sank onto the grass. "I wasn't sure clergy had guts that talked, but if they did, I always imagined them saying something like, 'Shut up and don't ask so many questions.' " Nick's smile was rueful.

Fr. B considered that for a moment. "We're no different than anyone else. Some of us ignore the still, small voice whether it speaks to us from the belly button or from somewhere inside the cranium. Ordination guarantees neither insight nor compliance. Have you talked to God about it?"

Nick groaned. "These days, prayer feels like I'm talking to myself. I know that when the chips are down, you're supposed to cry out to the Almighty. But every time I do, I hear the echo of my own voice. Crazy?"

The leg spasms appeared to subside. With lumbering effort, Fr. B got to his feet. He walked in tight circles and shook his arms to stay loose. "Not crazy, and more common than you might think. The cause is simple. Think of it in terms of a man who ignores his wife. He pays attention to his golf, his career path, his investments, but little or none to the one he promised to cherish to the end. For the longest time they don't talk; there's no time, what with the golf and the career and the portfolio. When at last he senses a wall there, it has thickened to such a degree that it appears nearly impenetrable. He speaks but all he gets is bounce-back. Next comes the isolation, followed by feelings of abandonment, followed by stony rejection, when all the time the wall is of the man's own making."

Inverted, the small of his back braced against his hands, Nick began pedaling an imaginary bicycle. "So it all comes back to my spiritual neglect?"

"As it does for all of us, Nicholas. God is not indifferent." Fr. B thrust forward in a slow stretch. "Most of us lack the humility to return on bended knee" — he flinched at the sudden creaking of joints — "and miss the fact that it wasn't God who moved, it wasn't he who built the wall."

Brow furrowed, Nick said, "I'm afflicted by my faith, Father. Even before everything collapsed. My faith jabs me, stabs me, throttles and interrupts my thoughts and my plans. Cass is closer to a breakthrough than I am. I feel like my membership in

God's realm has lapsed and there's no renewing."

Fr. B shook his head. "There were seven *me*'s and *my*'s in that statement. Nick, it's not your membership that's lapsed. What has lapsed is your passion."

Nick wiped an arm across a forehead as wet with frustration as with perspiration. "Perfume *is* my passion; can't you see that? Can't God?"

"Perfume is your god."

Visibly staggered by this blunt verbal blow, Nick said nothing. He studied his running mate a moment. Fr. Byron waited. Not every day did a man see a dripping wet priest in lime green Bermuda shorts and a T-shirt declaring him to be a "Holy Terror." Yet the clergyman kept his countenance as solemn as if he were in full vestments administering the Lord's Supper.

"Now you're losing me," said Nick at last, sullen and defensive. He twisted his torso alternately clockwise and counterclockwise to stay limber.

Fr. B winced, though unsure why. Maybe because Nick was so reluctant to see God's handwriting on the wall. "When you have God, Nicholas, you have everything. But if you start the day scheming how you and your desires can impact the world instead of seeking God's direction, the thing you desire quickly becomes an idol."

Nick stopped moving and watched a man sail a Frisbee into the jaws of a leaping golden retriever. "We built that altar you kept talking about," he said finally. He told the priest about the early-morning gardening session and his wife's meltdown that ultimately resulted in a hallowed pile of torn dahlia blooms. "Pretty unconventional, I guess, but it brought us comfort, maybe even a kind of closure. When there was nothing more to say, we just held each other and waited. No big thunder and lightning display, no burning bush. Just a whole lot of headless dahlia plants and a hunger to know what had happened to us. Maybe that night was the beginning of a new direction of some kind. Maybe it was God's way of gaining our attention, a second chance that might have been lost had we had the success we wanted. I don't know and it's maddening."

Fr. Byron was deep in thought. "Perhaps God yet has a higher purpose for your knowledge of the sense of smell. I have heard that certain aromas could help improve the appetites of the elderly. Or as one freak theory goes, future wars may end a great deal sooner by the use of odorant weaponry that pacifies the enemy and renders the battlefield benign. Peace by fragrance."

For a time they were silent. Before long the evening breeze blew chill off San Francisco Bay. Nick visibly shivered and Fr. B patted him on the shoulder. "I smell the beginning of wisdom," he said. "What do you say we put an end to this torture and continue our probe into the unknown over waffles at that breakfast joint at the bottom of the hill? My treat. I find that exercise heightens the senses and leads to a ferocious appetite."

Nick laughed, loud and long. "You're on, preacher man. I've always said that if you served bacon and eggs at the cathedral Sunday mornings, it would be standing room only!"

"Ready to fly?"

Well rested, properly stretched, hands thoroughly rosined, and nothing to eat but a single celery stick in the past four hours, Cassie nodded. She wanted trapeze. She wanted to soar above the floor and feel the stuff of life whoosh through her veins. Flying trapeze was the stiff bottle brush that scrubbed away anxiety, indecision, and the scummy buildup of disappointment. She had a lot of scum.

"Ready!"

Ruggedly handsome Blair was training today, and his unquenchable attitude gave her confidence.

"Up you go."

Today she would execute her first knee-hang, progress that constituted but half a victory because Mags was not there to share it. Still, Cassie had promised to visit later that day and fill in her friend on every dizzying detail.

She waved to Beth on the minitramp. Judging by her dreamy expression, Beth had also discovered Blair. Her daughter responded with a distracted flutter of fingers.

Amused, Cassie tightened the leather grips she wore to help soft hands avoid rips. Just in case, she kept a tin of Badger Balm in her gym bag. The balm was a blend of beeswax, olive oil, and birch essence ideal for quick healing.

In white tee and gray tights, she climbed the ladder to the beginner's bar. All about her, flyers at different levels of competency engaged in a variety of aerial maneuvers. The gymnasium echoed with commands and the occasional cry of anguish as someone plummeted to the net after a missed try. The thrum of the rigging, the crack of bullwhips, and the comic patter of jugglers passing pins gave the illusion of a three-ring circus.

Cassie looked down to the benches in the waiting area. They were empty except for one gangly kid sulking in the corner. He must have succumbed to every boy's dream and cracked his whip inappropriately. "Uncontrolled and unscripted" use of a whip had doomed more than one budding Zorro to the time-out bench.

The front doors opened and in she walked, lithe as a bowstring, skin gardenia white against designer black leotard and sweatpants. She glanced up and offered the slightest of nods. Cassie was glad Brenda had been exonerated by the police in the death of her ex-husband. Richie Marin had confessed to the entire plot to aid his cousin in murdering Cassie. The charge was kicked down to attempted manslaughter because, as the police well knew, few said no to John Lexington and lived.

Cassie excused herself to Blair, descended the ladder, met Brenda halfway across the floor, and took her by the hand. "How's your mom?"

Brenda grimaced. "Stubborn. Demanding. Opinionated." She caught herself. "Better."

"I'd say a lot better," Cassie said, and they shared a knowing smirk that quickly faded. Both understood, though it remained unsaid, that Mags' aerial career had come to an abrupt end.

"As for us," she continued, "I can't say as we'll ever get to the place where we dare to catch one another in the air. That takes more trust than we may be prepared to build." Cassie felt a surge of concern for the woman. It surprised her how much her words rang with regret. "For now, I'd like to spot you on the trampoline, help you gain a sense of being lighter than air."

Brenda regarded their clasped hands, as if that were as strange a sight as the incredibly young twin brother and sister in clown makeup who fearlessly swung by their knees high overhead. "I am told that eventually my 'air awareness' will enable me to flip, fall, and sail through space with the greatest of ease," she said. "That's a great deal of grace for just eighty dollars a month."

Cassie smiled and let go of Brenda's hand. "That's why they call it amazing."

Brenda studied her a long moment, appearing to consider all the possible ambiguities in Cassie's statement.

Cassie nodded toward the trampoline.

Brenda paused, drew a last deep breath, and took a determined step forward.

ABOUT THE AUTHOR

Clint Kelly is a communications specialist for Seattle Pacific University and the author of novels for both children and adults. As a journalist and freelance writer, Clint has written on a wide variety of topics from dinosaurs to child rearing. Clint lives with his family in the Seattle area.